No Kiss Goodbye

By

Janelle Harris

Edited by Jenny Sims @ editing4indies

Cover by Najla Quamber @ Najlaquamberdesigns.com

Table of contents

For Dad

Thank you for teaching me to be a bookworm.
Example is powerful xx

Prologue

The nightmare fell so suddenly upon us that I don't remember exactly when or how it began. I don't remember seeing the lights change or pressing my foot on the accelerator. I don't remember if the baby was awake and wriggling or if she had lulled herself back to sleep. I don't remember the nursery rhyme Bobby hummed to himself as he munched on a mouthful of mushy Milky Bar. But I do remember the fear, the burning horror that stuck to my mind like superglue. It was, in reality, a split second, but for me, it played out in terrifying slow motion.

My own petrified screams drowned out the high-pitched squeals of my brakes, fighting to grind my car to a halt. The thud was so sudden that my mind struggled to catch up with the rapid images that flashed before my eyes. The pressure of my heart pulsating viciously against my chest was almost painful.

My car was spinning, that much I knew, but I had no idea in what direction. I was moving at a speed my car had never seen. The normal events of the busy street were interrupted as passers-by held their breaths in disbelief. Trees, street lamps, and traffic lights blended into an array of muddled colours as they rushed closer to the windscreen. It was like a scene from a Hollywood action movie, but the crash dummies were real people. They were just babies. And I couldn't help them.

Painful pressure forced my eyes shut; the outside world was now blank. The flip of my car as the driver's side wheel mounted the curb was, I'm sure, a breathtaking crescendo to the scattered spectators powerless to help. The seat belt banished the air from my lungs as it fought to save my life. My body, restrained in the driver's seat, thrashed from side to side like a rag doll between an angry dog's jaws. For a moment, I imagined myself outside the car. Just a casual shopper stumbling upon a horrific crash and hoping nobody would be hurt; all the while suspecting survival was impossible.

Suddenly, there was a ferocious bang on the passenger side of the car, and I couldn't hear crying anymore. And then, just as quickly as it had begun, it was over. A few seconds had left a mark that would last forever. Nothing would ever be the same again. Everything was still and terrifyingly silent, as my mind lay trapped inside my limp body. Maybe people were rushing to help, or maybe no one came. I don't know. All I do know is at that moment I stopped fighting for my life. At that moment, I stopped being me.

Chapter One

Well, Heaven really sucks...and stinks. The smell is very unique; an unpleasant combination of overcooked mashed potatoes and an antibacterial cleaner of some sort. I always thought Heaven would be white and fluffy with harpists in oversized white robes dotted on every second cloud. I was expecting clichéd classical music and radiant, bright light, but this place is pitch black. Maybe there is an Earth-to-Heaven time zone difference, and I've arrived at the pearly gates in the middle of the night Central Heaven Time.

Maybe I'm in Hell, but again, I'm sure I'd see a little more action than just complete darkness. A bit of chanting around a fire-filled crater or some searing, red flames would help convince me. Maybe the devil has misplaced his trident and everyone is busy looking for it. And once they find it, the hellish antics will begin.

A few minutes later, when I'm still on the edge of existence with just my thoughts for company, I'm decidedly confused. I can't believe I wasted all those childhood years afraid of ghosts, and now that I finally need a floating apparition, I can't find one.

I decide if I'm not in Heaven or Hell, then maybe I'm playing a waiting game in limbo. Perhaps God and the devil are in a massive boardroom thrashing out a huge superior-being argument over who gets my soul for all eternity. They will probably call me in at any minute now, and it will be the ultimate interview. I really should have paid more attention the

9

last time the head of human resources gave my department that life-coaching pep talk.

Just as I'm completely losing my patience, it hits me. *Oh crap, crap, and crap.* What if I'm in the morgue? I've heard of that kind of thing; you see it on those weird reality shows on the telly, don't you? Where they think you're dead, but you're not, and you wake up all freaked out with a load of dead people beside you. So far, I am definitely freaking out. I just have to figure out the waking up part. I'd roll my eyes if I could. I've just jumped from the bliss of Heaven to the isolation of the morgue all in the same thought process. Maybe I'm losing my mind.

And that was it...my best explanation so far. I'm obviously in a psychiatric hospital, and they've heavily sedated me to prevent self-harming. No wonder I can't move; my straight jacket is on too tight.

Oh c'mon, Laura. Get a grip. Great, just great. I've started talking to myself. Do they still say that's one of the first signs of madness? And now I'm asking myself questions. *What the hell?* I'm slipping further into my own crazy, little bubble. I would slap myself if I could figure out how to move my arm. Okay, I really have to stop thinking like this. Because if I'm not already in an institution, then it's definitely where I'll end up.

The strengthening smell of detergent interrupts me from the very profound analysis of my current location. It's such a familiar smell, but I just can't put my finger on it. I become irritatingly aware of the presence of people all around me. People who are pushing and pulling my body in all directions, but they are rudely ignoring me. I'm so angry with myself. I just want to stay conscious long enough to decipher what the fuck is happening. Finally, I recognise the smell. If I'm in the hospital, then at least I'm still alive. And then the most awful reality shakes me. *The kids? What about the kids?*

The accident flashes in my memory as the smell of burning rubber still stings my nose. Where are the babies? My heart is aching with fear. The last thing I remember is the numbing silence where the children's screams should have been. I can't stand it. I have to get out of here.

I know almost everyone says they don't like hospitals. After all, they smell distinctively clinical, they are full of terrifying torture-like instruments, and they are a forceful reminder of our own mortality. But I don't know anyone who hates them quite as much as I do. I can barely breathe; my own thoughts are torturing me. I. Have. To. Get. Out.

My legs and arms still refuse to move. Every part of me is completely limp. I can feel the self-pity engulf me, and the hysteria that follows is so overwhelming it actually hurts. And I scream. I just let it all out. I can't live like this, as just a mind trapped inside this lifeless body. I'll go mad; I already am. I need to be normal. I have to look after my kids. I *know* I have kids to look after because I'm not prepared to think about the alternative – not for a second.

I have to calm down. If I keep screaming like a banshee tangled in a hairdryer, then I'm going to scare the other patients. But if I'm screaming so loudly, then why can't I hear anything? I'm either deaf or no sound is coming out. I lie very still for a few moments. The room is now eerily silent except for the occasional beeping of a monitor of some sort. *Where did everyone go? Who cares.* At least I know I can still hear. Now I just have to face the realisations that not only can I not move, but I also can't speak. I'm a cabbage. *A fucking cabbage.* This is not fair.

I must have drifted back to sleep because it felt like hours had passed before I finally hear voices again. This time I recognise the voice. It's deep and almost a whisper. It's Mark. His sentences are broken, and I can't make out what he's saying, but it's wonderful just to hear his voice. I know he's crying, and I wish so hard that I could reach out to him and tell him it will all be okay. But I'd probably just be lying to both of us. The longer I go without moving, the worse the prognosis. My obsession with Saturday morning reruns of *ER* has taught me that much.

I soon realise Mark isn't talking to me. He's discussing my condition with a doctor. They seem to edge a little closer to me, and I strain to gather jumbled bits and pieces from their conversation. Mark's voice is becoming very jumpy and agitated, and it's not like him. *Maybe he found out something awful about my condition.*

'I'm very sorry, Mark, but your wife has lost the baby.'

My heart literally stops. *Nooooo,* I scream again without sound or movement. *Not Katie. Please not my beautiful little girl?* I plead with God to exchange my life for hers.

'Oh Christ no,' Mark says. 'Is there something you can do? Anything? Please?'

'I'm so very sorry, Mr. Kavanagh. Was the baby planned?'

'No. Not really. It's complicated.' Mark sighs heavily.

'Unfortunately, the pregnancy did cause complications, and despite our best efforts, we struggled to control the bleeding.'

'And…' Mark's voice is a little above a soft whisper now.

The doctor doesn't reply, and there is a moment of silence. Maybe he shakes his head or makes some sort of other gesture, I don't know. But if it's possible to hear anguish, then that's definitely what I hear.

'Laura will be so devastated,' Mark says, suddenly shattering the silence. 'She won't be able to cope with this on top of everything else.'

Pregnant? I feel such a poignant sense of loss for something I never really had in the first place. I can sense the pain in Mark's voice. I'm so damn selfish for putting him through this.

And then the tightness in my chest loosens, and I am aware of my chest rising and falling as I breathe. They are talking about an early pregnancy; they are not talking about baby Katie. Of course, the news hurts, but there's also the guilt. Guilt that I'm so relieved. Relieved it's not Katie. *It's not my little girl.*

'It is possible your wife is suffering from depression. It's not uncommon. Is there anything in her home life that may be causing her stress?'

I resent the doctor's condescending tone. He has no right to make assumptions about me or about my life. He doesn't know me. Or Mark. I concentrate, but I don't hear Mark respond.

'We have liaised with the Gardaí at the scene, and it is being suggested that your wife took off at a high speed while the traffic lights were still red,' the doctor says, before clearing his throat with a dry, uncomfortable cough.

I shudder with the shock of his accusation. *He wasn't suggesting I crashed intentionally, was he?* I wonder if the monitor will show my blood pressure soar.

'Was Laura very concerned about the pregnancy or birth?'

13

What is this guy's problem? *Mark, don't let him poke holes in our relationship. Stand up to him,* I plead internally. I beg my hands to move. I want so desperately to touch my husband. To give him a sign that I'm here. I'm still here; my stupid body has trapped me inside and it refuses to cooperate. But Mark remains silent. He's close enough for me to sense the heat from his body, but he's still so far. Too far. I can feel the empty distance between us. *This must be killing him.*

The distance grows. And grows. Mark is gone, and I have no way to ask him to come back. My heart is breaking, and I have no way to make it stop.

Days pass, maybe even weeks. I'm finding it hard to keep track of time. It's difficult to differentiate between day and night. Deep sleep washes over me in fitful waves, never allowing me to fully wake. I suspect night time is when Mark leaves the vigil he keeps by my bedside and goes home to hopefully get some sleep and check on things back at our house. I'm alone with nothing but my overtired thoughts for another twelve hours. I look forward to his return; when he will whisper happy memories and hopes for the future to me all day again, just waiting for me to respond.

'Bye, princess. I have a surprise for you tomorrow,' Mark whispers, while leaning over to kiss me.

For a second, I think I can feel his lips on my forehead, but the giddy bubbles of excitement in my tummy make it hard to concentrate. *A surprise?* Maybe he is going to bring the kids to see me. *God, I miss them so much.*

Jesus, Mark, a moment like this and you have to fart. *Ah, yuck!* You were eating in the canteen again, weren't you? Only hospital food can do that to a system. Where are you going?

Don't you dare walk off and leave me with that smell. *Mark?*
Mark?

Chapter Two

When Mark suggests we get off the bus a stop early and walk the rest of the way to his house, I eagerly agree. I've a suspicion that he'll try to kiss me along the way. Well, I'm hopeful at least. However, had I known that the last stop was about thirty million miles from his house, I would have taken a rain check.

Blistering feet and still no romantic kiss later, I'm starting to get fed up. My hand has reached that irritatingly sticky stage, which can only be truly achieved when you hold hands too tightly with someone for the duration of a painfully awkward conversation. If we don't release our grip soon, then we're fast approaching full-force sweaty palms. Time for the old tried and tested 'something in my eye' routine.

As Mark gazes into my heavily mascara-laden eyes, I chew roughly on my extra minty chewing gum and prepare for the fairy tale kiss all teenagers dream of. I've waited all sixteen years of my life so far for this Cinderella moment, and I know it will be amazing.

~~~

Just as I pucker up, I feel the stinging stab of a needle in my right arm that viciously draws me back to reality. I'm back in the hospital ward and fourteen years have passed since that special kiss. There have been many more amazing kisses since then. Hundreds of happy memories flood my mind—Mark and my wedding day, finding out I was going to be a mother, being a family. My heart pinches. *What if I never wake up? What if fourteen years is all I get and now my time is up? What if Mark and I never get the chance to grow old together, or I never experience the joy of watching my kid grow up?*

I'm startled by the pounding of footsteps rushing past me. I've become so used to everyone tiptoeing around that it's really quite exciting to get some action. It only takes a second before the reality of the situation hits me. The doctors and nurses don't rush around this place to test their jogging stamina; someone is in trouble, and they need immediate attention. I feel sympathy for the patient, of course I do. I haven't turned to complete stone yet, even though some days it's hard not to...but then, I feel relief. Relief that they're not rushing to me. But this place, the loneliness and often near-silence, reminds me that it could be me at any moment. And maybe it wouldn't be such a bad thing if it were. *What kind of person am I becoming?* I manage to make everything about me. I'm self-obsessed and broken. My body is shattered, but my mind is fast becoming equally as damaged.

Morning brings a renewed stillness. The activity of last night is just a memory now. It must be visiting hours because Ava, my best friend, is here. I didn't notice her arrive, but I'm so glad for her company and my mind smiles. Ava could talk for Ireland; I rarely get a word in edgeways. So, the one-sided conversation, as she rambles on, is actually pleasantly familiar.

Ava and I have been friends since we were six. We were in the same class in school growing up, and even though we went to colleges on opposite sides of the country, we've always stayed close. I know her as well as I know myself, and I love her to bits. But sometimes her ability to speak first and think later still shocks me. Like now.

'So the guy in the room next to you kicked the bucket a few hours ago,' Ava announced as if she was reading the news on *National Television*.

A little vomit swirls around in the bottom of my near-empty stomach. The man was a stranger to me, but his death affects me now in a way I don't fully understand. He was someone's son, a husband, perhaps even a father. And now he is gone, leaving a hole in his loved one's hearts where his smile once was. I'm still here, still clinging to life, but I feel that hole. That little cavity I'm burrowing into the hearts of everyone I love.

'Seriously, Laura, this place is depressing as hell. You really need to wake up soon. I mean, I know you like your sleep and all, but don't you think it's time to flutter an eyelid or something. C'mon, hun. Give us a sign you're still in there. I miss you,' Ava says.

If I could roll my eyes and laugh, then I would. Sarcasm is Ava's middle name, and the familiarity of one of her terrible jokes sets me at ease.

I can tell Ava is fidgeting nervously and moving around the room quite a lot. It's a little embarrassing that the situation is making her so uncomfortable. *I wonder if my cheeks are flushed.* I wish she would sit down and relax. Her voice is jumping all over the place and making me dizzy.

'Laura, you've been out of it for ages now. I have the biggest news of my life to tell you, and you're not even listening.'

Ava pulls a chair close to my bedside and leans in. I can feel her breath falling rough and heavy on my pillow. Even with my eyes closed, I know Ava is bouncing on the spot. *God, I really wish she hadn't had garlic for lunch.*

'Okay,' Ava stammers. 'I'm just going to spit it out.'

I wonder what the massive earth-shattering news is now. Maybe Ava snapped a stiletto and will be admitted to the bed next to me suffering from shock or even more seriously perhaps she has lost her Prada purse somewhere in the waiting room. That kind of thing could cause a coronary.

I don't like this version of myself. A good gossip with Ava is usually one of my favourite things but not today. Today it reminds me how life goes on for everyone else while I'm trapped in here.

Ava slurps in a huge gulp of air and blurts out, 'I'm getting married.'

A long pause follows and I wonder when Ava is going to start laughing and tell me that she's joking. I know her hands are twitching at the edge of my bed, and I guess she's spinning a ring on her wedding finger.

'Now, I know what you're going to say. Or at least I know what you would say…you know, if you could and all that…' Another awkward pause follows and then a loud clearing of Ava's throat. 'But Adam loves me. He's completely over his commitment issues. His proposal was so romantic. Much better than Mark's attempt. Blurting out, 'let's get hitched' between mouthfuls of Coke and a bite of double cheeseburger is never the romantic gesture you make it out to be, Laura.'

Ava was right. Mark's first proposal was laughable, and I couldn't take him seriously, even if he was generous enough to offer me a bite of his burger while I thought my answer over. But we were only eighteen at the time, and although it was a bit of a whirlwind, I always knew that I wanted to spend the rest of my life with him. I did have to wait a few years for the big sweep-me-off-my-feet proposal of my dreams. A romantic proposal by candlelight meant I had almost said yes before he'd had a chance to ask the question.

The atmosphere is stagnant as Ava hovers over me. I can't figure out what she is waiting for. Does she think I'm suddenly going to spring to life and congratulate her on a ridiculous decision? I've always kept my opinion of Adam to myself. But Ava can read me like a book, and I know I didn't have to actually *say* anything. Their relationship dramas are more intense than all the episodes of daytime soaps added together.

Ava never seems to grow tired of defending Adam. She loves to tell people they are just like the original Adam and Ava. We all know she means Eve, but no one has ever taken it upon themselves to correct her. We all like our heads attached to our bodies too much. Just as the biblical couple fell in love in the Garden of Eden and had all that trouble with the apple of temptation, Ava and Adam met in Molly Keogh's back garden at the neighbourhood summer barbecue. When the sleeve of Ava's cardigan caught fire, Adam had thrown his pint of cider over Ava without haste or sober judgment in an attempt to quench the blaze. Now maybe Adam never knew, or just momentarily in a fit of blind panic forgot, that alcohol tends to have the opposite of the desired effect when trying to put out a blaze. And so began a not so beautiful relationship. Ava insists that fate brought them together. The rest of us put it down to barbeque lighter fluid and a little stupidity. But one thing is certain, Ava Cassidy and Adam O'Rourke will always be remembered for their trouble in the garden with apples.

Mark's arrival interrupts my trip down memory lane. I'm concentrating hard on trying to smile. I can feel twitches somewhere near my ears, and I'm almost sure they're the same muscles that make my mouth move. I'm determined today will be the day I let him know I can hear him, but I'm distracted by a female voice entering my room.

After a few moments of everyone chatting among themselves, and me becoming incredibly frustrated, Mark finally gets around to an introduction.

'Laura, honey, I told you I had a surprise.'

My heart is racing…*the kids, he's brought the kids.*

'Well…here she is,' Mark announces, maybe pointing at something, I can't tell.

I hold my breath and wait to hear Katie coo.

'Hello, Laura,' the woman's voice chirps.

'Nicole wanted to come see you. Isn't that a nice surprise?' Mark says.

My heart sinks into my ankles. It feels like an eternity since I've seen the kids. They are the only surprise I want. Not Nicole. Not this bitch. How could Mark bring her here? He knows how much I hate her. I've spent half my life bitching about her. *What the fuck was he thinking?* God, I just want to cry. Everyone is silent for a moment, but there is an excited buzz in the room. I just know Mark is smiling. It makes me even angrier.

'Nicky has been amazing helping out all week. I don't know what I'd have done without her. She's been so worried about you.'

'We've all been worried, Mark,' Ava adds dryly.

Ava has my back, just like always. I think I smile, but everyone is too preoccupied to notice.

Mark ignores the remark. 'I suggested Nicky come and see your progress for herself.'

Progress! What progress? I'm only half-alive. And it's Nicky now, is it? When did they progress to nicknames? My head hurts.

I've never trusted Nicole. I don't believe her intentions are anything less than selfish. I'm certain she's less about helping out and more about edging in on my family as soon as I'm out of the picture. She's the same age as me, give or take a few months. She is also slim and glamorous…and conscious. I'm none of the three.

I also can't believe Mark would leave me alone with that woman. *Where has he gone now?* Houdini has nothing on that man lately.

For about forty minutes or so, I tolerate Nicole's ramblings about how she's cleaned the house so it will be nice and tidy when I get home. Did it ever dawn on her that maybe it was messy for a reason? Maybe I like messy. I ignore her speech about getting fifty euros off because she batted her eyelashes at the mechanic when she took the car for a service. I even cope when she praises herself for having my in-laws over for a healthy family meal. If she's trying to hit me when I'm down, then she's doing an excellent job. I got it. By all accounts, she's much better at being me than *me*.

I struggle to find five minutes in the day to grab a shower, but wonderful, amazing, super Nicole managed to have a surplus of time to hand stitch a new tablecloth that I imagine is sitting proudly on my now finely polished dining room table. I could handle all that, really I could. But I finally see red, or more like neon scarlet, when she explains how Mark has enjoyed some homemade soup because he was badly in need of some nourishment. *My arse!* If there's one thing I've learned in all the years Mark and I have been together, it's that the way to his heart is definitely through his stomach. Buy him a burger and chips and he'll be your best friend for life.

My temper pounds in my temples, and I visualise myself leaping forward and wringing Nicole's very thick neck.

Nicole gasps dramatically. 'Laura! Laura, can you hear me? Did you just move? Laura?'

*Oh God…*I moved. I really did. I'm still working. I forget everything that has happened in the previous days, and all I care about now is doing it again.

'Oh my God, this is fantastic. Wait there. Don't move. I mean do move, move as much as you can.' Nicole is hard to understand because she's speaking so fast and moving away from me.

And then there's complete silence. That damn silence that I've grown to hate. And I know I'm alone again.

Noisy footsteps pound the corridor and thoughts of the last time the ward saw this much activity rushes into my head. But this time, the footsteps are rushing towards me.

'Laura, Laura, can you hear me?' Mark asks struggling to catch his breath.

Mark's voice is shallow, and for the first time, he's not making an effort to hide his exhaustion. I want so badly to reach out to him and wrap my arms around him. I want to hold him so close we're just like one person.

'Laura…' He pauses, as if waiting for me to answer. 'I'm holding your hand. Can you feel me, princess?'

Without thinking, my fingers flex and attempt to grip his. There's a piercing squeak from the steel legs of Mark's chair as they are forced backwards along the highly polished tiled floor. My heart pounds. Maybe I've scared him. *Is he in shock?* I hear him shouting in the corridor, but I can't make out what he was saying. My heartbeat is deafening.

'She moved, Doctor. I felt her. Laura held my hand. She's going to be okay, isn't she?'

Chapter Three

Ava paces around the room like a greyhound on steroids. She stops every so often to fidget with some poor defenceless bouquet of flowers perched on the cluttered table beside my bed. I wonder why she's so nervous. It's rubbing off on me. The butterflies in my tummy are rocking out to their own Zumba class.

'How are you feeling?' Ava asks.

'I'm fine,' I snap. 'I was fine when you asked five minutes ago, and I'm still fine now.'

I notice Ava's cheeks flush, and I feel awful. It's not fair to take my wobbly emotions out on her. Ava is watching every word out of her mouth, and it disappointments me that making conversation is this difficult for us. I hope this isn't a sign of things to come. The accident has left its mark on me; it doesn't get to leave a mark on our friendship, too. I have to make sure of that.

'I'm sorry, Laura,' Ava says, hanging her head sadly. 'I'm useless at this kind of thing. I keep thinking of things to say, but then I stop myself because I'm sure you don't want to talk about anything.'

She has a point. I'm not exactly little Miss Chatterbox lately. If I have to listen to one more friend or relative make small talk about the weather or politics, then I'm going to scream.

'We could always bitch about Nicky?' Ava suggests.

I smile.

Ava mirrors my expression and pulls a chair over to sit beside me. 'I love you, you know.'

'I do know. Thanks.'

'You must be the strongest person in the world,' Ava says, as she lovingly knocks her shoulder gently against mine.

'No, I'm not. I'm so not.' I shake my head. 'If I was, then I wouldn't have marshmallow legs and I wouldn't need that fucking wheelchair.'

Ava doesn't move from staring at her shoes and I regret making things even more awkward.

'I will walk again, you know. They say it's just a matter of time. Did I tell you that I'm getting more and more feeling back all the time?'

'Yeah. Yeah, you said that…'

'Oh, well, yeah I am. It still sucks arse at the moment, but by this time next year… I'd say I'll be flying it.'

'Yeah. Of course. I bet you will. And, in the meantime, you can enjoy everyone waiting on you hand and foot. We're all here for you, Laura.'

'Yeah, I know,' I mumble. It's my turn to gaze motionless into space.

Ava sees Mark peer around the door just before I do, and she beams brightly. 'Your knight in shining armour is here,' she says turning to face the door.

'I think I'm the one in shining armour,' I joke, pointing at my very shiny, silver wheelchair that's eerily lurking in the corner.

Mark and Ava look disgusted. It's actually kind of funny.

'Ah c'mon, don't look at me like that. The jokes have got to start sometime.'

Trying to lighten the atmosphere isn't really working. I want them to laugh. I need them to. If we laugh, then maybe they won't see through my crumbling exterior.

'I have to wait for the discharge papers and then we're good to go,' I explain as if the doctor hasn't already told Mark all this. I overheard them talking, so I don't know why I need to say it again. But I'd say the alphabet backwards on repeat if it drowned out the silence. *The damn silence.*

'I can't wait to get you home,' Mark says as he bends down to kiss my forehead softly.

His lips feel warm and comforting against my skin, and I want him to do it again.

'The house has been way too quiet…' He stops himself abruptly mid-sentence and forces a loud, almost tearful, cough. He changes the subject to something trivial, wondering where we would put all the flowers when we got home.

I hate this. I hate all this damn tiptoeing around me; everyone is afraid of saying something that might upset me. Why don't they realise all the pretence is hurting me the most?

Mark leans over the edge of the bed, and I know the routine. I wrap my arms around his neck and smell his yummy, citrus aftershave as he lifts me into his arms. *Damn, I'm self-conscious.* Mark has picked me up plenty of times before. Like the time he carried me up the stairs the night of my cousin's wedding because I was so drunk I wanted to sleep on the bottom step. But this is different. He's never before lifted me because I'm simply incapable of doing it myself.

'Jeez, Laura how many of those hospital desserts did you eat?'

I glare wide-eyed at my husband.

27

'Oh, I see how it is. It's only okay for you to make jokes.' Mark smiles.

I tuck my head under his chin. I felt safe in his strong arms, so I close my eyes and relax.

I've a crick in my neck, and I try to stretch out without elbowing Mark in the face. I'm still wrapped in his arms, but we are both sitting back against the pillows at the head of the bed now and my legs are draped across his knees. I glance out the window; it's dusk. I'd expected to be discharged ages ago. Hours have passed, and I must have fallen asleep. Ava has left and my cheeks flush as I realise I had dozed off and didn't say goodbye.

'I'm so sorry to keep you waiting,' Doctor Hammond says as he comes into the room and takes his usual position of standing at the foot of my bed.

'S'okay.' I shrug.

Realising I'm awake, Mark wriggles out from underneath me and stands up. I've grown quite familiar with Doctor Hammond over my rehabilitation but I know his presence always put Mark on edge.

They are both staring at me. *What are they waiting for?* It's weird and uncomfortable, and I don't like it. I feel like some wild animal being stalked by a predator. *Stop it.*

'What?' I finally snap.

'You fainted again, Laura,' Mark says softly.

'Again?'

'Yes, Laura, you have fainted a lot recently,' Doctor Hammond adds.

My eyes narrow and dart towards my doctor. He has a habit of saying something simply to analyse my reaction. Like he's always testing me. And even though I know it's his job – he's a psychiatrist, after all – it still wrecks my head. After a traumatic experience, counselling is heavily suggested by the hospital. I'm not interested, but I know my going makes Mark feel better. After everything I've put him through, if talking about my feelings for an hour twice a week gives him peace of mind, then it's the least I can do.

'Any more bad dreams this time?' Mark asks. He's so soft spoken it's almost irritating.

'No.' I shrug.

'You were out of it for a while this time.'

'Really?'

'Really.' Mark nods. 'You were saying some stuff about how sorry you were.'

'Sorry for what?'

Mark is speaking to me in the tone he saves for when the kids do something naughty. I wonder if he's talking about the accident. But I've already apologised. Over and over. I suspect the car is a write-off, but I haven't asked. Mark hasn't mentioned the car, either. Maybe he's angry with me for destroying it. But with everything that is going on, why would he care so much about that? The insurance will cover it, and we've been talking about getting a new car for a while anyway. I press my fingers into my eyes, hoping it'll help the headache I feel coming on.

'Doc, maybe if you leave us for a while…' Mark suggests. 'Laura might feel more comfortable speaking to just me about this,' Mark whispers, as if I'm not right there beside him.

I shake my head. 'There is nothing to talk about.'

Mark and the doctor stare at me anxiously. It's really uncomfortable. *What the fuck do they expect me to say?*

'I don't remember any dreams,' I reiterate.

'Any flashbacks of the accident?' Doctor Hammond elaborates.

'No.'

'No, you don't remember? Or, no, you don't want to?' Doctor Hammond asks.

'I. Don't. Remember,' I hiss. I want to slap the doctor across the face – hard! *Is this guy for real?* I understand he's doing his job, but seriously, he needs to work on his bedside manner. I glance at Mark, avoiding eye contact. He seems annoyed, too. His fingers twitch speedily and sweat visibly rests on his palms. I hope it's because he's anxious to get me home and away from this constant reminder of the nightmare that our lives have faced.

Doctor Hammond continues to pry, increasing Mark's distress. And mine. If there was ever a time when I wanted to storm out of a room and slam the door dramatically behind me, then this is it. But, of course, my stupid legs won't budge.

Finally, the doctor concedes to the mounting tension and moves a comfortable distance away from my bed. 'The guards are outside. They're hoping to run through the accident with you, Laura. Do you feel up to that?'

I'm nodding, but Doctor Hammond doesn't notice me. He's looking at Mark, who is shaking his head furiously.

'No. It's too soon,' Mark stutters. 'She's not ready. Jesus, Doc. Give her a break.'

'The guards just want to get a few things straight, Mr. Kavanagh. They need something. Anything.'

'I said it's too soon.'

Mark's eyes are bulging and a very unflattering red appears around his cheeks and nose.

'It's okay.' I stroke Mark's arm. 'I don't mind talking to them.'

'Good girl.' Doctor Hammond smiles as he leaves the room.

I wonder if the exaggerated stomp of Mark's boots against the floor tiles as he storms away is an echo of his pounding heart. He's furious. And I feel it's reasonable. I know Mark just wants to protect me, but without my help, the bastard responsible for the crash is still out there.

Angry voices filter into my room from the hall. Mark rarely swore but a seasoned rapper wouldn't use as many profanities in a number one hit as Mark is throwing at Doctor Hammond. I feel my cheeks redden – mortified. This is so unlike Mark. I decide to hold off on speaking to the guards. Deep down, I'm grateful for Mark's outburst. I can't even think about what happened, so how would I even begin to talk about it?

Chapter Four

Mark tucks my wheelchair beside the passenger door of a blue saloon while he walks around the back of the car and throws my bag into the boot. I look through the back windows searching for the children's car seats. I expect to find Bobby's chocolate stained booster and Katie's little pink carry chair, but the backseat is empty. This car is new and spotless and an extreme contrast to our usual car.

'What do you think of the car?' Mark asks, reappearing.

'It's okay.' I shrug, surprised he's gone ahead and chosen a replacement car without discussing it with me first.

'It's only a lender from the insurance company until the paperwork is finalised on our claim.'

'Oh.' I swallow. 'What paperwork?' The mere hint of any complication resulting from the accident puts me instantly on edge.

'Yeah, the feckin' assessor says we'll be waiting a few weeks. Something about getting someone to look at the car to make sure it's beyond repair. The usual red tape crap.'

I try to smile as hazy images of our mangled car swarm my mind. *I don't want to think about it.*

Mark takes my hand. 'They're probably checking things like brakes and stuff. If they find a fault, then they can claim from the manufacturer rather than having to fork it out themselves. You know how insurance companies are. Any excuse not to cough up; don't look so worried.'

'Faulty brakes?' I pull my hand away. *I hadn't thought of that. What if it wasn't an accident?*

Mark shakes his head, and I know how paranoid I sound. I close my eyes. I need to stop avoiding the blame and just face the fact that I ran the red light and the car approaching from the other way was driving way too fast. It didn't stand a chance of stopping on time.

'It's no big deal. I bet we'll have a cheque by the end of the week. We can start shopping around for a new one in the meantime, yeah?' Mark is smiling, but his eyes are sad.

I have no plans to go out in public anytime soon, but I nod and smile back anyway.

I open the door of the car and accidently smack it on the big, clunky metal wheels of my wheelchair. I slam the door shut again, almost taking my fingers with it. Mark crouches down beside me and his big, round, blue eyes peer into mine.

'I love you,' he says softly and leans forward to kiss my forehead before starting the awkward task of getting me into the car.

A strong hour and a half later, we near home. I know the road like the back of my hand from so many hospital appointments during my pregnancy; the journey usually takes about twenty minutes, even in traffic. But Mark is driving painfully slow. I get the distinct impression he's trying to put me at ease about being back in a moving car. He glances across at me every five seconds, and I know he wants to ask if I'm okay, but he doesn't say a word. I've been so quiet the whole way, and I'm probably freaking him out a little. I just sit and stare out the window, but I'm not actually looking at anything.

I glance back at Mark. His hand is on my knee. *When did he put it there?* I want to ask him to take it away because it's

33

reminding me of my paralysis, but I also want him to keep both hands on the damn wheel. Yet I decide not to say anything.

I close my eyes. I can see the kids' faces, and it makes my heart race. I've never gone so long without seeing them. I can't wait to hold them and kiss them. But I also can't help but worry about how they'll react when they see me; especially when they see me in my chair. I keep imagining all sorts of ridiculous scenarios. Worst case is Bobby running out into the garden screaming that a transformer has eaten Mommy. I admit that's slightly excessive, but Bobby has inherited my overactive imagination, so I'm anticipating some sort of freak-out.

At home, Mark makes it halfway into the hall before he spins around on the spot. His face flushes a rosy red as he races back to the car to open the door for me.

'Oh shit sorry, Laura, I forgot!'

'It's okay.' I giggle. 'I forgot, too. Well, until I opened the door and nearly fell out.'

'Well, if that does happen, try to aim for the grass,' Mark says.

I laugh until I realise he's actually serious. He must have had to force himself to think about strange stuff like that recently.

'Eh, okay,' I reply. 'Or I could just wear a helmet.'

Mark looks appalled at first, but then he starts to laugh. It's a new sounding laugh. One I'm not used to, but one he's often doing lately. He reverts to it every time he says something that he instantly regrets. Mark always speaks his mind. Even if it is to tell me that my jeans really do make my bum look big. But since the accident, he's taken to watching every word that comes out of his mouth. It's not him. It's taking a lot of getting used to, and I don't like it.

Mark lifts me out of the car and throws me over his shoulder a little haphazardly.

'I've always wanted to carry you over the threshold,' he says.

I say nothing. I'd appreciate Mark's romantic gesture more if he didn't have to huff and puff his way up the stairs and then if I didn't hear him finally sigh with relief when he dropped me onto the bed.

I'm disappointed we didn't stop downstairs or go straight to the playroom. Our bedroom looks so different that I almost don't recognise it. My dressing gown, which usually resides in a pile at the foot of the bed, is hanging neatly on a new coat hook on the back of the door. The old, cream rug at the end of the bed that proudly sports some discreet hair dye stains has been replaced with a pretty new one, and some beautiful, fresh red roses sit on the windowsill in place of the regular artificial ones. It's all lovely, but I miss seeing Katie's cot in the corner. Mark has obviously gone to a lot of trouble, so I'll wait until later to ask him to put the cot back. I snort as I suspect it was Mark's mother who wanted to move Katie's cot out of our room; interfering is her middle name.

I lie back against the pillows and try not to cry. The house is painfully quiet and I resign myself to the idea that the kids aren't here. I try to hide my upset from Mark because I know he's struggling to do what's best. If he's sent the kids to his mother's, I know it's because he thinks I need my rest. All I need are the kids. I want to ask about them, but I'll wait for the lump in my throat to go down.

Mark helps me change into one of his old t-shirts and tucks me into bed. He orders me to relax while he goes to make some tea. He must have noticed me gazing around the room because he turns around at the door.

'Are you okay?'

His voice is a whisper, and I almost don't hear him. Mark hangs his head and shuffles his feet awkwardly. 'Ah, Laura, I'm sorry, I didn't mean are you okay…of course, I know you're not. I just mean...' He stops talking and actually scratches his head. 'I don't know what to do here. I keep saying stuff and then realising how stupid it sounds once I've said it out loud.'

'It's not stupid to ask me if I'm okay. What *is* stupid is you thinking that you can't ask me. You can always ask me anything.'

'I just feel so useless. I want everything to go back to how it was before,' Mark mumbles.

'Me, too.'

'I don't know how to help you,' he says, walking back to sit on the bed beside me. 'It makes me feel like shit. Like I'm sucking at this. And then I realise I have no right to feel crap, not compared to you.'

'Yes, you do. And I'm glad you finally told me. It actually makes me feel so much better. You know, knowing that I'm not the only one struggling to cope with all this.'

Mark leans close and kisses me. It's the first proper kiss we've had since the accident. All my tension is set aside, and for a moment, I enjoy the warmth of my husband's lips on mine.

'How will we get through this?' Mark asks, and I moan as he pulls his mouth away from mine. 'Shit. See, that's not a very helpful question. I told you I sucked at this,' he says.

Finally, Mark is saying what's on his mind. I smile. For the first time in weeks, I recognise my husband.

'I don't know all the answers either, Mark.' I roll my shoulders. 'Actually, I don't know any right now.'

'They gave me all this crap at the hospital last week.' Mark points at a small pile of depressing-looking, pastel-coloured pamphlets on the bedside table.

'Did you read them?'

'I tried to. But it's a load of bollocks. They're all about 'expect this, say that.' Made you sound like a bloody washing machine that needed programming.'

'Well, that's it, then. There's not a hope for us. You haven't a clue how to use the washing machine.'

We both laugh. A real proper chuckle, not just something put on to fill the air.

'Do they say anything about how to deal with being pissed off one minute and depressed the next?' I ask when the silence returns.

'Yeah. I think they do, actually.' Mark races around the bed and starts flicking through pages.

'I'm joking. I don't need to read those. And neither do you. We'll figure this out ourselves, okay? No handbook telling us life is shit now, yeah?'

Mark closes the pamphlet and looks at me. His eyes are less sad than usual.

'Do you know what I do want though?' I ask.

'What?'

'A cup of tea that doesn't taste like monkey piss.'

Mark pulls a face. 'How do you know what monkey piss tastes like?'

We laugh again. It was so much easier to laugh in the familiarity of our home than it was in the hospital.

'I think we have some elephant wee downstairs. I'll bring you up a cup of that instead.'

'Perfect. Thanks.'

Mark is downstairs for a long time, and I drift in and out of fitful sleep. He arrives back up with the vile antibiotic that makes my stomach heave and a large glass of ice water. No tea.

'Here,' he says, handing me two little blue tablets. 'These things smell a bit like sweaty feet.'

'They taste like it, too,' I say, gagging before I even put the pills near my mouth.

I throw the medicine into my mouth and slug back a huge volume of water to force them down my throat as fast as possible. 'Ugh, yuck,' I protest and stick out my tongue. 'Were you on the phone downstairs? I thought I heard voices.'

'I was talking to Nicole,' Mark replies.

My face scrunches. 'She's here?'

'Stop that,' Mark says, as he pushes his index finger playfully against my wrinkled up nose. 'She only stopped by to see how you are getting on.'

'Getting on?' I'm developing a habit of repeating most things that Mark says.

'It's no big deal. She mentioned calling over when you got out of hospital, but you must have forgotten.'

I don't remember. But, then again, I forget a lot of things lately. The bang to my head has affected my short-term memory, the doctor said. The doctor had to explain that to me about five times before I finally began to remember that I forget.

I also doubt very much I've agreed to Mark's mother looking after the kids, but I can't remember one way or another, and an argument over who said what is the last thing

38

we need. Much as I hate to admit it, even to myself, I know I'm in no fit state to look after the children right now. And Mark is exhausted just looking after me. I can't ask him to bring the kids home. Not yet.

I can only imagine the number of broken ornaments we will have to replace in my OCD mother-in-law's house. I shudder at the thoughts of her passing out chocolate buttons for breakfast or letting them stay up half the night. I cross my fingers that Mark and I will have settled into a routine within the next day or two and we can bring them home then. I won't be able to go much longer without them. The thoughts of seeing their gorgeous little faces are all that's keeping me going right now. *I really wish my parents were still alive.* I miss their support almost as much as I miss the kids.

'I have a bath nearly ready,' Mark says, peeking his head out of the door of our en suite. 'It'll be good to wash that hospital smell off you.'

The fumble to the bathroom is almost comical, and I really hope we get better at moving about with some practice or Mark will need to see my physiotherapist too for his back. Tears trickle down my cheeks as Mark begins to undress me. It's not his usual loving touch of each breast as it's exposed. It's more like a heartbreaking military operation. He sits on the edge of the bath with me awkwardly across his knee. My head is heavy and aching with the weight of holding itself up. It's very much a balancing act between pulling off my t-shirt and not letting the weight of my dead legs drag us both to the floor.

Finally, when I'm sitting naked on his lap, he wraps his arms around me and holds me close. *Is he going to cry?* I wish he would. Maybe we could cry together.

'I'll get better at this. I promise,' he whispers.

'I wish you didn't have to.'

Getting Mark to actually leave the bathroom is the most difficult task of all. He's watching me like a hawk. Maybe he's afraid I'll slip under the water and not be able to pull myself back up. Or, more disturbingly, perhaps he fears I won't want to. On some level, I understand how he could fear that. Of course, I've thought about how easily I could end all this crap. But I wouldn't, I couldn't.

'Call me if you need anything,' Mark says as he finally leaves to go downstairs.

Chapter Five

The soft bubbles are heavenly as they float against my skin. The smell of eucalyptus is a little overbearing, but compared to the smell of the hospital, it's delightful. I pull the bottle off the windowsill and read the label, just to make sure Mark hasn't accidently emptied in toilet cleaner instead of bubble bath. Romantic gestures like this aren't Mark's thing. He's even gone to the trouble of lighting a few candles and dotting them across the back of the toilet.

When the water begins to cool to the point of being uncomfortably chilly, I decide it's time to call for Mark. I start with a little shout, but he doesn't hear me. A couple more yells go unanswered. Finally, I begin shouting throat-scathingly loud as I become uncontrollably panicked. *What will I do if Mark doesn't hear me?* I'll be stuck. It's a Jacuzzi bath, not a tsunami, but either way, I'm stranded until someone comes to rescue me.

I've worked myself into a complete frenzy with forceful screaming and intermittent tearful crying before Mark comes racing up the stairs, apologising profusely.

Getting dressed is every bit the struggle as undressing was. I'm distressed by my helplessness, and I know my unintentional lack of cooperation is irritating Mark. I'm honestly not trying to be difficult, but my indulgence in self-pity is definitely becoming worse rather than better.

After an exhausting trek downstairs, Mark plonks me uncomfortably into the wheelchair that waits patiently for me after the last step. The metal of the large wheels bangs viciously off the kitchen door as Mark tries several angles to get the bloody thing to push through the frame. We eventually have to give up, and Mark wearily carries me into the kitchen instead.

I catch a glimpse of Mark's laptop on the counter. It's open on a web page about grants for home modification. My heart sinks. *Mark thinks this will be long term. He thinks I'll be stuck like this!* I want to argue, but I can't bring it up now. We have guests. *Bugger!* A combination of embarrassment and resentment hit me as I spot Ava and Nicole sitting at the kitchen table, smiling happily. Nicole scrambles to her feet as we near the kitchen table, and she quickly pulls out the chair beside her for Mark to set me down on. She sits back down and silence falls over everyone.

I stare at the table. It's littered with half-empty cups of coffee and the crumbs of what was obviously a plate of biscuits. I glare at Mark. He had been downstairs entertaining while I was disintegrating in an icy bath. I worry this scene is a taste of the future; a future where I will become more and more absent. Even in my own home.

I attempt to join in the conversation. I nod along and pretend to have a keen interest in what they're saying. But I'm easily distracted. Every time Ava stands up to go to the toilet, I'm jealous as I watch her walk effortlessly across the room. Every time Mark crosses or uncrosses his legs, I'm jealous. When Nicole lightly taps the heel of her shoe against the ground in time to the beat of the song on the radio that plays softly in the background, I'm not just jealous – I'm insanely irritated.

I stare at my watch numerous times. I hope Nicole takes the hint, especially since I've shoved my arm so close to her face that I've almost scratched her nose. But when she's first to pour a refill from the fresh pot of coffee Mark's made, I know she doesn't plan to leave anytime soon.

Ava is filling us all in on her wedding plans, oblivious that neither Mark nor Nicole seem to be listening. They are too busy studying me. Looking me up and down and nodding to each other afterwards. At first, I think I imagine it, and brush it off as just being oversensitive about everything. But when Ava whispers to me about how rude they are being, I'm tempted to confront them about their ignorance. I bite my tongue. Now is not the time.

Nicole continues to bug me with her fake laughter and random batting of her eyelashes. *Christ! Just fuck my husband already and get it over with.* I pull my mind back from those dark places. Nicole natters away to Mark as if they've been best friends for twenty years; behaving more like a part of the family than a nosy neighbour. They exchange jokes and a Cajun chicken recipe. Mark, who hasn't turned on an oven since almost burning down his flat while in college, insists it sounds amazing and he must give it go. *Are they fuckin' kidding me?* He returned the Jamie Oliver cookbook I got him for Christmas last year for a *Game of Thrones* DVD, yet there he is planning to become the next *Master Chef* winner.

I zone in and out of the conversation. My mind drifts back to the accident before I quickly pull it away again and block it out.

'The classes start next Friday, but the deposit has to be paid by tomorrow,' I hear Ava say.

Nicole doesn't reply.

'Don't worry if you're not into dancing - I'm useless. That's why it will be fun,' Ava continues.

'What's this?' I ask, finding myself finally taking an interest in what they were talking about.

'The pole fitness class I was telling you about,' Ava explains to me.

'Oh yeah...I remember. Are you still thinking of going?'

'I really want to, but I don't want to go on my own. Help me convince Nicole to come.' There's giddy excitement in Ava's voice.

I try to hide my disappointment. Ava and I were supposed to go to that class together. I was anxious to find a fun way to lose weight after having Katie, and Ava wanted to get in shape after years of just sitting around the office. We were going to make it a girls' night out and go for a drink or two after the class. Now all that seems as unrealistic as a fairy tale.

'Are you okay, Laura?' Nicole asks suddenly.

I glare at the interfering woman I had grown to hate.

'You were talking to yourself.'

I shake my head to protest, but I notice Ava has left the room. That wasn't the first time Ava has left in the middle of a conversation without saying goodbye. Lately, every time I'm distracted, even for the briefest of moments, Ava disappears.

It's only when the room begins to spin that I realise I'm still shaking my head. Nicole tries to steady me, but I resist her touch, pushing her to the ground accidentally with a strength I didn't know I had.

A little vomit rises in my throat, and my palms begin to sweat. I can see Nicole's lips moving, but I can't hear her voice. I search the kitchen frantically for Mark, but I can't find him because the room is spinning so fast around me. Furniture and walls are just a mess of muddled colours closing in on me. My body begins to tremble furiously, and I struggle to breathe. I blink and my eyes refuse to reopen. I'm alone in the darkness. Again.

I wake lying neatly tucked into bed with a sharp headache. Someone is knocking gently on the bedroom door, but my head hurts so much I feel as if they were hammering against my skull.

Doctor Hammond opens the door and lurks erringly in its frame. He stands silent for what feels like an eternity. I struggle to pull myself into a sitting position. Doctor Hammond's staring is making me uncomfortable, as it always does. I know he wants to discuss what just happened. Tiptoeing around is just going to prolong the discomfort for everyone.

'Hi, Laura,' he finally says, softly.

'Hi.'

'How are you feeling now?' His caring seems fake and rehearsed. Or maybe it's just my mood. I desperately want to be left alone. He's walking towards the bed, and I grab the duvet tight in my fists. He must sense my discomfort because he glances backwards and nods his head slightly. Mark suddenly appears from the shadows on the landing, and I ease my grip on the duvet.

'You okay, honey?' Mark asks. His voice is strange; on edge. Exhausted maybe.

'Not really; I don't remember how I got upstairs.'

'I carried you,' Mark explains.

Well, no wonder he's exhausted. Carrying me around the house all day must really be taking it out of him. My mind wanders to the information I'd seen on Mark's computer. Maybe a grant would cover one of those fancy stair lift things. I wonder if installation would damage the wallpaper. There's no way we could afford one ourselves. I'll download the forms later and we can fill them out when Dr. Doolittle pisses off. I snap back to reality when I feel Mark poking me in the shoulder, pulling me to sit back against the pillows he's propping.

'I know you are struggling to deal with everything that has happened, Laura, so I am going to give you a little medicine to help you sleep,' Doctor Hammond says as he rolls up the sleeve of my t-shirt. I shake my head. But I'm tired. I look at Mark for reassurance. He's nodding supportively.

The needle stings as it pierces my flesh, and I shudder and pull away. Mark's arms wrap tightly around me, and I can't fight against him. I don't want to. I accept the peaceful feeling that follows and allow myself to drift off to sleep.

My sleep is littered with strange disjointed dreams. As if my mind has invited every memory I've ever had to come and have a drunken house party in my skull. I can remember most of the images when I wake up, but they are so messed up that I have no idea what they are about. Maybe it's a good thing. I've been over analysing everything lately. It's pointless to try to do the same with meaningless dreams.

I'm still half asleep as I lay earwigging on the conversation between Mark and Doctor Hammond. They're downstairs, no doubt consuming more of Mark's infamous coffee and discussing everyone's recent favourite topic - me. I'm frustrated that the sound is muffled as it carries through the floorboards.

'I really think Laura needs to come back to the hospital,' Doctor Hammond says.

'No! She wasn't happy there.' I can hear Mark more clearly than the doctor, so I know he's shouting.

'She's not happy here either,' Doctor Hammond replies.

Yes, I am.

'I know. But she will be. She is coming around. She will be back to normal soon.'

'Mark, I know you are not foolish enough to believe there is a quick fix to all this.'

Neither man speaks. It's deathly silent.

'I have to help her,' Mark says at last. 'She's still my wife, for God's sake.'

'I only want to help her, too.'

'Please,' Mark begs. 'I don't want her to go back to the hospital. I will get through to her. She will be fine. Please. I just need more time.'

'Okay,' Doctor Hammond finally agrees. 'We can give it one more week. But we really need to see some improvement in her memory by then.'

What a prick. How dare he lay down the law to Mark.

'I understand. Thank you, thank you,' Mark repeats over and over.

'Don't thank me yet. Another outburst like this and we'll be left with no more options. She'll have to come back with me. You understand why, don't you?'

I don't hear Mark's reply.

'Baby steps, Mark. Baby steps. I know it's hard, but we're just taking it one day at a time. But don't lose hope. She needs all the hope she can get.' Nicole has the last word.

Hearing her voice shakes me. Why is she here? And especially when my medical condition is being discussed. *Fuck off!*

Chapter Six
Mark

I drag my sleeve across my eyes to wipe away the tears as I tuck the soft, pink blanket neatly into the corners of Katie's cot. Katie's room at my parents' house is fit for a princess. The dreary guestroom I remember growing up in has been transformed into an exquisite nursery with every baby gadget imaginable. But my parents didn't stop there. They were so excited about having a granddaughter that they even placed an announcement in the local paper a few days after Laura and I showed them the scan picture. Katie was the first little girl to come into my family in three generations. It was huge.

I stare at the frilly pink bows that tie back the cot bumper. They're pretty and delicate. *Just like Katie.* My chest tightens and I'm hyper aware of my heartbeat, so I have to look away. I toss my head to the ceiling and gaze at the plastic cerise pink chandelier that my mother ordered from some grossly overpriced online baby store. One of the bulbs isn't working, and I think about changing it, but I shrug off the notion. I know I should leave the room; I've been in here almost an hour. But my feet are heavy, as if they're set in cement, and all I want to do is lie down right here on the floor and sleep.

My mind has drifted far away when I feel Nicole's hand lightly on my shoulder. I don't turn around. I try not to react at all as I pull my sleeve over my hand and use the already damp material of my jumper to dry my face. Nicole slips her arms around my chest and rests her head on my shoulder. I soak up her comfort.

'Are you okay? Are you still freaked out about what the doctor said?' Nicole asks in a delicate whisper.

'He said she needs to show some improvement soon or he'll take her back to the hospital. He'll take her back, Nicole.' The words are catching in my throat, and I can feel my palms begin to sweat. 'I can't let that happen. God knows what Laura will tell him if he keeps prying.'

Nicole takes my hands in hers and tucks them against her chest. Her grip is tight as she rocks back and forth.

'You are going to be okay, Mark. I promise.'

I want to tell Nicole not to make promises she can't keep, but I keep my mouth shut.

'And, in the meantime, it's okay to fall apart every now and then. This is hard, shit hard, you know. You don't have to be this super-strong person all the time. No one expects that of you.'

'I am okay,' I lie. 'It's just guilt, I think…yeah, that's it. I feel so fucking guilty. I know when Laura finds out it'll break her heart. I don't want to do that to her. I almost wish she never had to know.'

Nicole looks disappointed in my confession.

'She deserves to know the truth, Mark. Maybe you should just tell her.'

'That's not how this works, and you fucking know it,' I snarl. 'We've talked about this. You agreed this is the best way.'

Nicole closes her eyes. 'Yeah, I know. Sorry. It's just that waiting is hard, you know.'

I roll my shoulders. 'I didn't say it was easy.'

'I never said you did.'

I have to look away. Nicole looks like she's about to cry, and I know it's my fault. She lets go of my hands and steps back.

'I'm sorry,' Nicole whispers.

'Me, too.'

'Look, I hate all this pretence, Mark. I can't lie. But I know you're just trying to protect Laura as much as you can...'

'But that's the problem. I can't protect her from herself. No one can.'

'You don't think she would hurt herself, do you?'

'Yeah. Maybe. Sometimes! Do you think she would?'

'Yeah. Maybe. Sometimes,' Nicole echoes.

I force a painful lump of air down my throat and press my hands against my head. Hard enough to pinch. 'I have to go back.'

'I know.'

'No. I mean now. Right now. I need to get back to the house. Christ, I never should have left her. What the fuck was I thinking?'

Nicole puts her hand on my shoulders. 'It's okay, stop freaking out. Laura's asleep.'

'No. It's not okay. It's so not okay.'

'You need a break, Mark. You can't keep going like this. You're driving yourself into the ground.'

I toss my shoulder away from Nicole's hand. 'I'm fine. Or I will be fine when I get back to the house.'

I race downstairs, fling open the sitting room door, and find my mother watching her favourite soap from the couch. She quickly reaches for the remote control and fiddles with the buttons to try to turn off the blaring television in the corner.

'What is it?' my mother asks, standing up. 'Has something happened?'

'No. Well, not yet anyway, but I have to go home. I should never have left Laura alone.'

My mother sighs, and I see her rigid body relax.

'Mark, you're here less than an hour. Laura will be fine on her own for a little while.'

'You don't know that! God, why did I ever leave her alone? I'm so stupid. What if Laura woke up? God knows what clues she could find lying around the house. She could come to any number of conclusions.' *Shit, shit, shit.* 'I have to go.'

Nicole thunders down the stairs and almost skids on the hall tiles as she comes to a stop just behind me.

'Honey, sit down,' my mother orders as she drapes her arm over my shoulder and tries to steer me towards the couch. 'You're in no fit state to drive. Your father is in the kitchen making some coffee. I'm sure he can stretch it as far as a cup for his only son.'

I'm shaking my head so hard it's blurring my vision.

'Keep an eye on him,' my mother whispers as she passes Nicole.

'Tom, Mark wants a cup of coffee,' my mother shouts towards the kitchen as she leaves the room.

'No, Mom, I don't need coffee. I need to go.' I race after her.

My mother turns around and so much concern and worry are written in the lines of her face that it breaks my heart. And all I can do is offer her a reluctant smile.

'Okay, honey. Okay,' she placates, and for such a slim, agile lady, she suddenly looks heavy and weary.

I rush from room to room, frantically gathering up random bits and pieces. I grab my phone and my coat. Then spin around in circles, searching every room for Mr. Snuggles, the teddy I brought to the hospital for Katie's arrival. And then I remember; the furry, brown bear is lying next to his beautiful, young owner. Mr. Snuggles is keeping baby Katie company.

'Mark, calm down, please. You'll make yourself ill,' Nicole advises. 'I'll gather everything while you start the car.'

'Nonsense!' my mother exclaims quite loudly. 'The only thing you need to take home is yourself. None of this other stuff matters right now. Nicole is right. You need to calm down or you'll be the one who ends up in the hospital, and that certainly will be no good to Laura.'

I come to a stop, standing in the middle of the floor, letting my hands fall limp by my side. The routine that Laura has always been such a stickler for has descended into chaos. I ache for familiarity. I know our lives have changed permanently, but if I could just find a hint of who we used to be, perhaps stability and calmness would follow.

'Yeah you're right, Mom. I'm just going to go…' I say.

'Good,' Patricia confirms with a clap of her hands. 'Now, go on. And drive carefully, for God's sake.'

***

Chapter Seven

Mark pulls back the curtains in our bedroom and the soft, morning sun stings my eyes.

'What time is it?' I ask, wincing as I run my fingers through my knotted hair.

'Time you were up, you lazy sod,' Mark jokes. 'You really need a shower. You stink!'

'Thanks. I love you, too.'

I try to sit up, but the sudden movement of my head tortures me and pain darts around my temples. Mark hands me a glass of ice water from the bedside locker. The ice hasn't started to melt, so I know he got it fresh from the kitchen just moments ago. He must have anticipated my pounding skull.

'God, I'm so hungover,' I admit. 'I must have been completely out of it last night; I can't remember a thing.'

'You really don't remember?' Mark says.

'Nope, not a thing, sorry. Was it a good night? I'm sure it'll all come back to me later.'

'I doubt it,' Mark mumbles as he crouches down at the end of the bed. He doesn't stand back up. I try to lift my head high enough to glance over the edge of the bed to see what he's up to, but every movement sends a stinging shock down my spine.

'You weren't drinking last night,' Mark says.

'Really? I have a hangover from hell that begs to differ.' I massage my temples with my fingertips.

'That would be the sedation medication wearing off. You've been asleep for almost twenty-four hours.'

'Sedation?' I sit upright, making my head feel like it might explode. *Why would I need sedation?* And for a whole day. I don't remember seeing sedation meds on the prescription I got leaving the hospital, but then again, I hadn't paid close attention. Mark looks after all that.

I squint as I look down at Mark, and then the ground. *Why is he picking up little shards of shattered glass off our bedroom floor?* Mark hangs his head as soon as I catch his eye. *He can't even look at me.* And for a brief, horrible moment, my husband feels like a stranger to me. I slip my fingers inside the neck of my t-shirt and pull it away from my skin, but it doesn't relieve the tightening in my throat.

'Laura, come on, think. Do you remember chatting in the kitchen? You were tired and angry. You insisted everyone leave.' Mark pauses while he stands up. He looks at me – finally. 'You insisted *I* leave.'

'Leave? What? Go where? This is your home. Why would I want to kick you out?'

Mark doesn't reply; he watches me, scrutinising me. I don't like it.

Whatever this sedation stuff is, it's killing me. I shut my eyes as my brain feels like it's liquefying and draining out of my ear. I lean over the edge of the bed feeling like I might throw up. Hazy images of me guarding the door holding my favourite crystal photo frame in my hand suddenly pop into my head. I remember screaming loudly. That's probably why my ears are ringing now. Anger and pain surged through my body into my hand. My knuckles whitened as my grasp on the frame grew stronger. I stared and stared at the beautiful picture and then I suddenly threw the frame as hard as I could. I watched it shatter into little pieces on the ground with a haunting feeling of regret.

My hands fly to cover my mouth. *Mark. Oh God.* I had thrown the frame right at him. *Why?* I was vicious - I remember, but I can't fucking remember why. I open my eyes as the images began to scramble again. Mark is sitting on the bed beside me; his arms are wrapped tightly around my shoulders.

'We will get through this,' he whispers as we rock back and forth, together.

'I know, I know,' I say, soaking up his comfort. But I have no idea what the hell it is we're supposed to be getting through, and for the first time, I realise paralysis is not my biggest problem. *Fuck.*

'God, Mark…I'm sorry.' And now I'm the one avoiding eye contact. *This is ridiculous.* 'Did I hurt you?'

'You weren't in control. It's okay.'

'Of course, it's not okay.'

'You're right; it's not okay. It's terrible. We really need to work on your aim. You completely missed.' Mark's laugh is dry and forced, and I know it's a crappy attempt to cover up his tears.

Maybe I should pretend to laugh, too. But how funny is it that I tried to decapitate my husband with some finely polished Waterford Crystal?

'I hear the doorbell,' I say abruptly, and I can see Mark is as grateful for the interruption as I am.

Mark kisses my forehead softly as he stands up. 'I better get it. Do you need me to help you get dressed, or will you be okay on your own?'

'Of course, I'll be okay on my own, silly,' I reply, desperate to be alone.

Mark looks back at least three times before he leaves the room. I actually have to flick my fingers in the direction of the door to get him to move forward.

I roll my eyes and shake my head, but I'm smiling as I conjure images of how long it would actually take Mark to put on my clothes and how much more fun it would be if I just took his off instead. But these happy thoughts are constantly interrupted by nasty flashes that appear sporadically from the back of my mind. I can't control how they surface, and I can't suppress them either.

Nothing plays in sequence. It's bright; like hurt your eyes, fluorescent-in-your-face bright. A slim, grey-haired woman is standing beside me. She hands me a plastic cup of water, the kind that comes from the water cooler in a waiting room. I take it, but I don't drink from it. I'm busy watching an elderly man in the distance. There's something oddly familiar about him – a friend or a past colleague perhaps. He's facing away from me, but I recognise his physique. I scratch at my thoughts trying desperately to conjure a face, but my mind is blank. He's speaking to a young blond-haired woman who seems to be crying. I recognise her also, but her trembling posture distracts me from seeing her face. I barely notice the handsome man standing poignantly beside her. He's upset too, but he's hiding it better.

The grey-haired woman continues to speak to me, but I can't pull my stare away from the familiar people at the end of the hall. I'm not listening to a word she's saying to me. Mark is beside me. He's concentrating hard; I can see it in his face. He always presses his lips tightly together when he's listening intently to something. It's a habit I find adorable.

I notice his lips begin to quiver; he's shaking his head. He's shaking his head – hard. His breathing quickens and tears began to fall down his flushed cheeks. Fuck it; why wasn't I listening? The harder I try to hear what's being said now, the more mumbled the words become. The hum of background noise is drowning out the words – the distinctive sounds of teacups chattering in a canteen and babies crying in the distance ring loudly in my ears.

I suddenly feel a stabbing pain deep inside my chest. My ribs chattered so roughly with each racing breath that I worry they might snap. And suddenly the teacups rattle no more and all the babies are silent, and the only sound is a dry, piercing scream. And I know that sound. It's deeps and wallowing and heartbreaking. It's me. 'No, please, God no,' I cry.

I struggled so hard to understand what I've been told. Something so terrible that I've lost all control of my senses. My knees hurt as they jar in place, and I can't move.

Darkness is sweeping in from the corners of my mind, and it's hard to focus on the man in the distance. He's left the couple at the end of the corridor, and I seem to be his target now. He's racing towards me. The pound of his racing feet against the floor tiles emphasises his haste. The closer he gets, the more blurred the image of his face becomes. But, in an instant, he's so close that I can read his name tag that's pinned to his chequered shirt. It's definitely him. It's definitely Doctor Hammond.

~~~

I'm distracted from my eerie thoughts by Mark's voice as he comes back into our bedroom.

'Laura, are you getting dressed or what?' he says. 'You've been here for ages. There's no point in avoiding things. You know you need to come downstairs. C'mon, you'll feel better after.'

Mark tosses some grungy tracksuit bottoms and one of his old football jerseys at me. 'Hurry up. Please?'

I tilt my head a little and wait for Mark to kiss me on the cheek. 'I'll be ready in a minute; I'll call you when I'm ready. Promise.'

I wait for Mark to leave before I pull the jersey over my head, and a familiar smell hits me. Play-Doh? I must have been wearing this jersey recently when I was playing with the kids. A wave of giddy excitement ripples around my belly. I can't wait to wake up some morning and for all my memories to be clear again. Like finding an old photo album I haven't seen in years. I'll reminisce and laugh at bad fashion sense and drastic hairstyles. I can feel myself getting closer all the time, and I know I'll remember any day now. It will be the perfect pick-me-up to have a head full of memories of fun times with the kids. I lie back on the bed, close my eyes, and savour the smell.

Distant family members shake my hand and kiss my cheek. I concentrate on the familiar smell of the Play-Doh, but it's slipping away. A new smell is engulfing my senses. Offensive, cheap incense wafts around me. I follow the scent across my mind. It leads into the playroom, where I find some slender white candles flickering on a small, low table hidden in the corner. I expect to find a floor littered with toys, teddy bears, and the occasional broken crayon or two; but a highly polished, squeaky-clean, red oak timber floor stares back at me. I don't know this playroom. All the toys have been tidied into boxes, labelled and placed too high on the shelf for kids to reach. No evidence that a child has ever played in this horribly melancholic room remains.

The house is full of people, some chatting…some hugging in silence…and some, like me…lost. I shudder as the bitter sting of loneliness clutches at my bones.

I recognise most people. But as I tried to speak to anyone, their image disappears before my eyes. Everyone vanishes one by one until I'm completely alone.

I wander from one empty room to the next, trying to piece together clues to this puzzle that don't fit my life. I find the back door and race towards it. It's so hard to breathe. I have to get out of the house. Fresh air has to reach my lungs before I pass out. I burst through the door and inhale deeply.

Mark is standing alone on the patio. His back is turned to me, but I can see his shoulders shudder. Was he crying? I rush to him and slip my arms around his waist, but he pulls away. I try to embrace him again, but he turns around and pushes me away; so roughly I stumble and cut my palm on the rusty, side gate.

I clench my aching fist and watch as blood trickles past my knuckles.

'It's all your fault,' Mark slurs. 'I hate you.'

Mark's words spin like a crippling, emotional tornado in my ears, around and around, over and over. It was my fault! What was? What terrible thing have I done? I try to walk towards Mark, but he's backing away. I edge forward more, but he's gaining distance. He disappears from my view. I look around. Our small, safe garden has grown to enormity. Our house is a tiny speck far off in the distance. I'm helplessly isolated in a dreary forest, and fallen trees block any pathway home. Dark clouds suddenly fill the sky, blocking out almost all light. The ground beneath my feet trembles furiously as large craters appear all around. I gaze into their never-ending depths and calmness washes over me. The temptation to let go and fall forward is intense and somewhat calming. My body shakes viciously, and I lunge forward.

~~~

'Oh sorry, I didn't mean to scare you,' Ava apologises, as she perches on the edge of the bed with her legs crossed. 'Mark told me to come up and wake you. I think you were dreaming?'

Ava's hand is on my shoulder, and she's gently rocking my sleepy body.

'Yeah, dreaming,' I stutter, shaking my head, struggling to remember where I am.

'You were talking in your sleep, apologising over and over. You've been doing that a lot lately.' Ava bites her lip and turns her head away from me.

It's so unlike Ava to watch what she says, but despite my groggy head, I know she regrets the last words out of her mouth.

'I've been here for ages,' Ava adds. 'I have to go back to work in a few minutes, so I just wanted to say bye before I leave. I'll pop in on my lunch break again tomorrow.'

I rub my eyes and nod. 'Okay, sounds good.'

'You have to actually get up this time, though. Much as I love Mark, he's useless to talk to about wedding stuff,' Ava says with an embarrassed giggle. 'I think I bore him with all the talk about dresses and flowers and stuff. He just ignores me.'

My body finally stops twitching, and my eyes settle on my friend. 'I'll have a word with him about that. I hadn't even noticed he was being rude, sorry. I just can't seem to function properly lately.'

Ava's voice softens to just above a whisper. 'It's understandable, Laura. No one expects you to be okay straight away. Stop putting pressure on yourself.'

I smile, but I don't feel any better inside.

61

'About last night...' I begin.

Ava quickly interrupts me. 'Let's forget about that, okay?'

I smile again, and this time I *do* feel better inside.

'Look, something like this is just going to take time. You can't take an instant problem-solving medicine. But every day gets a little better, yeah? I'm not saying there won't be some super shit days here and there, but I'm still your best friend, and no matter what, that will never change.'

'Thank you,' I splutter, yet again on the verge of tears.

'Ha, listen to me. I sound like a bloody Hallmark card.' Ava opens her arms and hugs me so tightly that my ribs pinch my insides, but I like it.

'Did I say something really nasty to Mark?' I whisper sheepishly, reluctant to spoil the moment, but I have to know.

Ava lets me go and drops her head. 'Why do you ask?'

'So I did say something, then?'

Ava doesn't answer. I knew she was waiting for me to expand on the question and that worries me. I get the distinct impression she's censoring what she'll tell me about the other night, like she's basing what she'll tell me on how much she thinks I already knew. Just because my legs have stopped working doesn't mean my brain has, too. *For fuck's sake!* Everyone has taken to treating me like a child, and it's doing my head in. But there's no point in expressing my frustration; it just makes me look like a child throwing a tantrum. The irony sucks.

'I had a weird dream where Mark told me he hated me,' I say, making a conscious effort to hide how stressed out it makes me feel.

'It was just a dream.' Ava smiles. 'Dreams don't mean anything.'

Yeah, I suppose. Just felt so real, you know. It was horrible.'

Ava gives me a quick kiss on the cheek and stands up. She points to a small white envelope on the bed beside me.

'This'll take your mind off it,' she says with a big, toothy grin. 'Okay, I can't lie. This is the main reason I called over today.'

I open the envelope and inside are four tickets to the annual charity ball in the posh Knightsbridge Hotel in Dublin.

'Oh, I had completely forgotten about this,' I admit, running my finger over the embossed font on the shiny tickets. My head is shaking from side to side instinctively. I haven't actually said no out loud, but my body is screaming a resounding you've-got-to-be-shittin'-me.

'I know, but we haven't missed the ball in the last seven years. C'mon, please. If you could go when you were pregnant and throwing your guts up and couldn't drink, then you can go now. Please, Laura. Don't break tradition. Pleeeeeease!'

Ava is literally bouncing on the spot with excitement. It will break her heart if I refuse to go. We made a pact years ago that even when we were ninety-five and have to have double hip replacements just so we can bend over, we would never miss the ball.

'I'll talk to Mark about it, okay?' I feel a little guilty for the lame-ass attempt to pacify Ava. But I'd say anything right now just to stop talking about the bloody ball.

'I already spoke to him about it. He's totally up for it; he thinks I'll have my work cut out for me convincing you. So c'mon, Laura, what do you say?'

Ava picks up her handbag and begins to button her coat. I close my eyes and sigh deeply, relieved her lunch break is up.

'I'll pop around again tomorrow. That gives you twenty-four hours to think of something to wear. It's going to be great, Laura. I promise.'

Another kiss on the cheek later and Ava is gone. I slouch down in the bed. As if what I have to wear is the biggest of my worries, I sulk. I crumple the tickets in frustration, but my fingers still when I notice the scar on the palm of my hand. The wound has healed and the scar is faded and barely noticeable, but it's nonetheless evidence of a nasty gash. *It couldn't be.* I shake my head. *It was only a dream.*

Chapter Eight

Days begin to pass by more and more slowly. It's been two weeks since Ava asked me about the ball, and I've avoided both her and an answer ever since. I've taken to pretending I'm asleep anytime she calls around, and she never has the heart to wake me. It has also been two weeks since I've seen the children. I miss them so much it's causing a physical pain in my heart; their absence is consuming my thoughts pretty much all the time. The house is an empty shell without them, and it's a depressing reminder that I'm not the person I used to be.

Every time Mark and I plan to visit them, something oddly comes up and we have to postpone. The excuses are becoming more and more far-fetched, as if Mark is intentionally creating a wedge between us.

When I try to discuss my concerns with Doctor Hammond at my appointment, he immediately shoots the idea down, echoing Mark's sentiments. He hands me some bullshit about how my immune system is too weak to handle any sort of virus. *What? Like kids are little cesspools of disease or something? Bollocks.* I'm so upset I actually cry in his office. I'm a complete blubbering mess for a solid ten minutes.

'We are making such good progress,' Doctor Hammond insists. 'Try to remain positive, Laura. The wrongs will soon be right, I hope.'

It doesn't fill me with much hope that my doctor considers a toe wiggle great progress. One-hundred-and-fifty euro an hour for endless physiotherapy sessions, and a twitch is as much as I can muster. We spend more time talking about how I feel than actually trying any physical exercise. It all seems like such a waste of time and money. Despite my best efforts not to be a sulky bitch at each session, it's damn hard to be anything but.

At the end of the session, the part when Doctor Hammond sits behind his desk with his arms crossed over his chest and asks me if I have any questions, I usually close my eyes and shake my head, but today, for the first time, I have a question. I'm confident and certain of his answer. If my doctor says I can't go to the ball, then Ava will *have* to accept that.

'It's a charity thing. We've been going for years. It's a huge event with hundreds of people in a city hotel function room.' I gloat, exaggerating the volume of attendees, waiting for my doctor to shoot down the ridiculous idea at any moment.

'Sounds elaborate,' Doctor Hammond replies.

'Yeah, it is. It's very fancy. Well, it has to be when you have people from all over the country going to it.'

'Wonderful,' Doctor Hammond confirms his enthusiasm with a clap of his hands. 'I think you'll have a great time. You'll have to show me the photos.'

'Excuse me?' I squeal.

'I'm delighted to see you taking steps to reintegrate with society. This is a great idea, Laura. See, I told you we were making good progress.'

'I wasn't aware that I had disintegrated,' I snarl, catching my reflection in the highly polished lamp on his desk. My dishevelled appearance doesn't help my argument.

'You need this opportunity, Laura,' Doctor Hammond advises. 'A chance to dress up and feel good about yourself. I'm sure you'll see many old friends who have been concerned about you. I promise you will enjoy yourself.'

'You shouldn't make promises you can't keep.'

Seriously? I can't understand how it's such a wonderful idea to spend an evening in a function room with a couple of hundred adults incubating all sorts of who-knows-what diseases, but an afternoon with a three-year-old, who might sneeze, would be detrimental to my health. *Yeah, right. Fuck off!* Something is a way off, and it makes me very suspicious about just how genuine Doctor Hammond's intentions actually are.

Hours later, Doctor Hammond's words are still peddling around my head and my efforts to distract myself by making dinner are close to an epic fail. After dropping chicken fillets on the kitchen floor, and then rolling over them with the wheel of my chair, I gave up. It takes me nearly forty minutes of a serious upper body workout, rocking my chair back and forth over the hall mat, to scrape the remains off my wheel. When my energy levels finally bottom out, I take myself and my sparkling wheels to chill out in front of some daytime television.

I snooze my way through reruns of my favourite programmes and wonder if life as a couch potato is the extent of my future. Content that I've gotten my daily dose of self-pity out of the way a little earlier than most days, I turn to stare aimlessly out the window. And like most days, I begin counting down the minutes until Mark comes home from work. He's always late coming home on the days I have appointments. I assume he's making up the time he's spent chauffeuring me there and back in the morning, but he never admits that, and I never ask.

Noticing Mark in the distance, I have to laugh. I watch as he passes our neighbours and stumbles up the footpath towards our house. He's carrying a large box and balancing it forces him to walk with an uncanny John Wayne meets Mister Bean impression. To hold the box steady, Mark rests the side of it against his chest forcing him to hold his chin unnaturally high to peek out over the top. A bouquet of beautiful red roses is wedged under his arm, and I can make out a bottle of champagne hiding in the carrier bag dangling from his index finger. My heart begins to flutter. Mark is a true romantic, but it's been a few years since he's made a gesture this big. I quickly spin my chair around to face the television again and pretend to be asleep. Hoping to make it easier for him to surprise me, I concentrate hard not to smile and ruin the illusion.

Mark comes through the hall door and follows his usual routine. He shouts towards the kitchen to let me know he's home and then kicks his shoes off before taking a step further. The sitting room door creaks open and I'm tempted to sneak a peek, but I don't dare spoil the suspense. The door creaks again, and I hear Mark tiptoe towards the kitchen.

I grow deflated as I wait, and wait…and wait. I wonder if he's cooking dinner, and he is planning to surprise me with that, too. I really hope not. Mark likes to consider himself an expert in culinary arts. His infamous mac and cheese is like eating a blender. It liquefies the contents of my stomach every time.

I wheel myself quietly towards the kitchen, sniffing all the way, delighted when no dodgy smells await me. I'm just about to open the door and wheel through the door when I hear Mark laughing. He's on the phone. I decide to head back to the sitting room, leaving him some space to chat, when I hear him mention my name. Curiosity gets the better of me; I tuck my chair neatly behind the door and listen.

'I'm just home now,' Mark says. 'She's asleep.'

There are a lot of 'yeah, yeah, yeah' and some whispering. I can't make out the gist of the conversation, and I'm ashamed of myself for earwigging.

'No, I didn't get a chance to give her the pills today.'

Pills? What pills? I used the last of my painkillers last week, and I've been feeling fine since. I press my ear against the door.

'I'll try to get them in her tonight.'

The person on the other end of the phone must be in disagreement because Mark's voice grows louder and I can tell he's pacing the floor.

'She's not stupid. I have to be subtle. Just trust me. It's not going to be a problem for much longer.'

I hear Mark slam down the phone. I race back to the sitting room, my arms losing grip on the wheels. A mixture of confusion and fear knots in my stomach. *Would Mark try to hurt me?* I hate myself for even thinking it, but I can't stop. It wouldn't be difficult for him. I'm pitifully helpless, bound to my stupid wheelchair. He could push me down the stairs and say I fell. Or slit my wrists and tell everyone I couldn't take it anymore. The possibilities are endless. If I'm a *real* problem for him, then it won't take a lot of imagination to dispose of me.

I shake my head. *What the hell is wrong with me?* I trust Mark; I love him. But why is he trying to give me medication without telling me? My gut is telling me it's disgusting to doubt my husband; I've clearly seen too many episodes of *CSI*. But my head is telling me there's no harm in being on guard. Mark would never have to know.

I barely make it back to my fake sleeping spot when Mark walks into the room behind me. He places the box he brought home on the couch and lays the bouquet of roses across my knees. He kisses my forehead softly and whispers my name. I pretend to wake up, even throwing in a yawn for authentication.

'Oh, Mark. They're beautiful,' I say, sniffing the flowers. They really are amazing. A dozen long-stem, bright red roses.

'One for every year I have known and loved you,' Mark gushes. 'And two extra for good luck,' he says with a cheeky wink.

I smile, of course, and turn my cheek to accept his kiss. But inside my body is shaking as I remember the advice my mother gave me years ago. "A man only brings home flowers when he has something to feel guilty about," she warned. I can't help but dwell on her advice now. *Especially now.*

'Come on,' Mark says, taking my hand and waiting for me to roll towards the couch. 'Open it.'

I lean forward and examine the long, rectangular box. I have no idea what it could be. I tug gently on the corner of the pink ribbon that wraps around the cream box and ties in the centre. It opens easily. Lifting the lid, a folded, lilac silk meets my eye. *An evening dress.* A dress for the ball that I'm not attending. Purple is my favourite colour and Mark knows that, but I've never actually worn anything that colour before. Not even a scarf.

The giddy excitement of receiving a new and beautiful dress is tinged with a sense of loss. I love the annual day trip Ava and I take into the city to hunt for the perfect dress. We spend hours wandering the streets and only venture into the shops to buy more takeaway coffee. We are usually so busy chatting that we forget to take note of the dresses we see as we window shop. Twenty minutes before closing, we dash in to find something not too florescent, not too expensive, and most importantly, something we can wear to dance the night away. But a girls' day out like that is resigned to just a fond memory from now on. I try to hide my disappointment from Mark. He's gone to such trouble, and he's looking at me with a bright smile and such love in his eyes. It's a huge contradiction to his attitude on the phone.

I stare at the silky bundle in front of me, excited by the feel of soft material beneath my fingertips. I caress the delicate straps and lift the dress into the air. The box slips off my knee and onto the floor. Scented petals of pastel-coloured paper that neatly caressed the dress litter the carpet. The long, lilac gown hangs delicately from my fingertips, swishing from side to side as I gently rock my arms. It's elegant and simple, and exactly the type of style I would choose for myself. I smile, content that Mark knows me so well. I begin to imagine how beautifully the dress would sway as I dance.

I drop the dress, and it falls to my knees. For a moment, I forgot. I forgot how my limp legs betray me. I forgot how helpless I've become. And at that moment, I was happy. *What a waste of a stunning gown*, I think, as reality hits me so hard it knocks the wind out of me. I can't shake it off. I can't walk elegantly into the room turning heads as the silk drapes delicately from my shoulder, hugging my waist as it passes. Okay, so my waist was never enthusiastic about being hugged, probably because it was too comfy hiding under my spare tyre,

71

but at least I had a waist. Now I'm just a blob in a chair. The dress is too beautiful for my unappreciative body to destroy.

'I...I...don't like it,' I shudder. 'Take it away, please.'

'But it's your favourite colour.'

'Just take it away,' I beg, balling the material between my shaking hands and throwing it across the room.

Mark bends down and picks up the crinkled dress from the corner where it landed. I can tell how much he's hurting even with his back to me. He's been so strong up to this, but maybe he's finally at his breaking point. *How can I have ever doubted him?* He would never hurt me. I was turning into a paranoid bitch, and I hate myself for it.

'Mark, honey, I'm sorry.' I wait for a reaction. Mark doesn't move. 'I do like it. I'm just oversensitive. I just...'

There's a long silence before Mark turns around. His bloodshot eyes are too painful to look into.

'No, I'm sorry. I didn't mean to upset you. If you're not ready for this ball, it's okay. I'll understand.'

I sigh, about to thank him and suggest maybe getting a good DVD and a bottle of wine, but before I can gather the words, Mark continues.

'I'll ring my mother tomorrow, okay?'

What? What does a night in front of the telly have to do with Patricia Kavanagh? A spark of excitement ignites inside me. He's going to suggest we bring the kids home. *Oh, my God. Oh, my God.*

'Why do you need to ring your mother?' I ask, trying to play it cool.

'Well, I'm going to need someone to come with me. I hope it's not too short of notice for her.'

My heart sinks. I'm so disappointed about the kids; I don't even think to be upset that Mark intends to go to the ball regardless of whether I go with him.

'Doesn't your mother play bridge on Saturdays?' I snap.

Mark laughs. So hard he snorts unattractively. 'Laura, you're hilarious. I'm hardly going to ask my mother to be my date.' More snorting follows. It's growing louder and more irritating by the second.

'Nicole was only saying last week how exciting the ball sounds. I'm sure she won't mind coming. You guys are about the same size too so the dress won't go to waste either.'

WHAT? *He's taking the piss, right?* Mark's phone conversation flashes through my mind. Maybe he'll drug me up, and I'll just sleep through the ball. *Stop it*, I tell myself.

'I hope purple is her colour,' Mark continues.

Is he still talking? Is he actually serious? I can't believe what I'm hearing. Nicole is a Pilates junkie. Any dress of mine would wrap around her three times, so technically, I should extract the hidden compliment in Mark's suggestion, but I'm too upset that Mark has noticed Nicole has a body of any shape. I snap the dress from Mark's hands nearly ripping it.

'I said I liked it, didn't I? As a matter of fact, I love it. I can't wait to wear it...and I can't wait for the ball. I'm so excited,' I lie, blushing as I pull my arm back down from a dramatic air punch.

'That's my girl,' Mark says in a much calmer tone than before.

Chapter Nine

Time crawls by and days blur. My weekly visits to Doctor Hammond are my monotonous timekeeper. The waiting room in Doctor Hammond's surgery is the dreariest room I've ever had the misfortune of occupying. Subtle, classical music plays in the background; the kind where you wonder if the harpist is plucking nostril hairs rather than strings.

I look around the room. The other patients waiting are as careful as I am not to make eye contact. Every second person looks like a suicidal mass murderer. I freak myself out wondering if Doctor Hammond does actually counsel any reformed lunatics. Maybe the quiet and slightly creepy young man sitting beside me is capable of flipping out at any moment and slitting my throat with his grotesque, excessively long fingernails.

'Laura Kavanagh,' the secretary calls.

Great! I think. Just tell the psychopath my name. Tell all the psychopaths in here my name. Then let's give them my address and an axe and we'll make our own low-budget horror movie back at my house.

I roll my eyes and laugh inwardly at my overactive imagination. I'm sure everyone else is thinking the same less-than-pleasant thoughts about me. But I'm still suspiciously optimistic that I'm the only sane one in here. Even the secretary looks a little off; a bit like a cartoon character, only with more makeup.

'The doctor will see you now,' she says and mumbles something about helping me get past the small fish tank. She's slowly walking towards me, and I suspect she's about to wheel me off. I hate that. It's frustrating enough not to have the use of my legs; I really don't need the embarrassment of borrowing someone else's. I'm already sour enough about being called to visit Doctor Hammond when I was just here yesterday, so I don't need anything else to piss me off even more. I think my vicious glare scares her away because she swiftly retreats behind her desk and leaves me to my own devices.

I bang and clunk my way towards the door and make a less than graceful entrance into the room. Doctor Hammond is sitting behind his desk, but he stands up as soon as he sees me.

There are other people sitting in the chairs in front of his desk. They have their backs to me, and they don't turn around to acknowledge my presence. I blush, decidedly uncomfortable, and begin to apologise for barging in on someone else's session.

'I'm so sorry. The receptionist told me to come on through,' I stutter, trying desperately to reverse out of the room.

'It's okay, Laura,' Doctor Hammond says softly. 'Come on in.'

I wheel forward very slowly as I analyse the back profile of the people in the seats.

Mark and Nicole? I squint and shake my head, certain my eyes are deceiving me.

Mark finally turns around to face me. He looks deathly serious. Nicole doesn't turn around.

How long have they been in Doctor Hammond's office? I was in the waiting room for over forty minutes, and I didn't see them pass. Why are they visiting so long with the doctor?

Actually, why are they here at all? I thought Mark was waiting in the car, and where did Nicole come from?

I feel betrayed, by both Mark and my doctor. I console myself that they can't have been discussing me. Patient confidentiality protected me, didn't it? At least that was one relief.

'Come sit with us, Laura,' Doctor Hammond says.

I don't move or speak.

'Laura. It's okay,' Mark finally says after a long drawn-out silence. There's gentle reassurance in his eyes, but I'm not convinced.

Nicole remains with her back to me.

I wheel forward slowly and tuck my chair beside my husband.

'Do you know why Mark and Nicole are here?' Doctor Hammond asks as soon as I come to a stop.

I shake my head.

'Are you sure?' he questions, in a tone similar to a strict schoolteacher.

'Yes, I'm sure. Do I look like I have a clue what's going on?' I bark.

Nicole suddenly turns to glare at me. Her body language is screaming hatred towards me. *The feeling is mutual, bitch.*

'Mark, why are you here?' I ask.

Mark drops his head and stares at the ground. His knee is twitching and causing a scratching sound as his jeans grate against the fabric of the armrest.

'Laura, do you remember making a phone call to Nicole last night?' Doctor Hammond asks.

'No. If I wanted to check on the kids, I'd phone Patricia.'

'You weren't checking on the kids,' Nicole snaps.

I glared at her. 'I don't even have your number.'

Mark rummages in his pocket and pulls out my mobile phone.

'Where did you find that,' I snap. 'I've been looking for that all morning.'

Mark ignores me. He's scrolling through the call log on my phone.

I try to snap my phone out of his hand, but I can't reach.

'Two twenty- seven a.m.,' he says.

Nicole nods.

'You made a call from your mobile to Nicole's mobile this morning at two twenty-seven for a duration of a little over four minutes,' Mark says, turning the phone screen towards me so I can see the evidence for myself.

'But I didn't call anyone at that time. I was asleep. I didn't even know Nicole's number was in my phone.'

'You did call me,' Nicole insists.

'Why the fuck would I call you?'

'To scare the living daylights out of her by all accounts,' Mark says.

'You made a lot of threats and accusations, Laura,' Doctor Hammond says.

'Oh, really? And how would you know that?' I bark.

Doctor Hammond writes something on the paper in front of him. His making notes of my reply. *Asshole.*

'You were parked across the road from the house watching Nicole,' he continues, putting down his pen.

I laugh. There's certainly nothing funny about the situation, but this is so messed up that my nervous laughter is involuntary. *Are Mark and I really paying this quack good money?*

'In case you haven't noticed, I can't walk. How the hell would I have managed to drive the car in the middle of the night and park it anywhere?'

'Laura, I don't think you realise the seriousness of this matter. Thank God Nicole spoke to Mark and not the police. What were you thinking?' Doctor Hammond's voice is grittier than I'm used to.

Mark can't possibly believe this nonsense. He can't really be this easily manipulated by Nicole. I'm shaking my head so hard I'm making myself dizzy.

'I don't have to listen to this bullshit,' I growl. 'Mark, I want to go home.'

'You do have to listen, actually,' Doctor Hammond says. 'I can keep you here as long as necessary.'

Mark tilts his head. I can't tell if his frustration is directed towards me or the doctor.

'I said I want to go home,' I repeat.

'We heard you, Laura. But you need to listen to Doctor Hammond. What do you remember from last night?' Mark's voice crackles when he speaks.

'Nothing,' I reply honestly. 'We went to bed shortly before eleven, and I woke this morning when your alarm went off.'

Mark's face falls into his hands. Clearly, that isn't the answer he is looking for, but I'm certain it's the truth.

'You are telling me that you didn't make a very nasty and suggestive phone call to Nicole?' Doctor Hammond interrupts.

He had a strange persistence in his voice. He was supposed to be helping me cope with the stress of losing the use of my legs, but at that moment, he could easily have been mistaken for a lead detective probing a suspect for information.

'I'm not telling you anything. I'm speaking to my husband. Mark, baby, you know me. I didn't make any call.'

I look deep into Mark's grey-blue eyes. 'I didn't call her.'

'But you did call me, Laura. How can you sit there and deny it?' Nicole whispers, tears gathering in the corner of her eyes.

Mark leans forward in his chair and places his arm around her heaving shoulders. Damn, she's good. It's a bloody Oscar-worthy performance. The lying bitch has my husband eating out of the palm of her hand.

'Why can't you see she is making this up?' I plead. 'Mark, why do you believe her and not me?'

'Because the proof is on this,' he says, slamming my phone so hard onto the desk the back cover falls off.

Fat, salty tears trickle down my face, but Nicole offers some stiff competition. She wails like a little-lost orphan. Doctor Hammond pulls some tissue from the dispenser on the windowsill and offers it to us both.

I try tirelessly to profess my innocence, but I'm fighting a losing battle. They had their minds made up before I even came into the room, and no one is on my side.

Finally, completely exhausted and the ability to argue any further lost, I fling a snotty apology at Nicole. I snatch the prescription for sleeping pills that I have no intention of filling from Doctor Hammond's hand and stuff it angrily into my handbag. Completely humiliated, I beg Mark to take me home.

Nicole beams brightly; she doesn't even try to hide her satisfaction. My husband and my doctor now suspect I'm less than sane and Nicole is gaining an even greater hold over Mark and *my* children. The woman is dangerous, and I'm the only one who can see it.

Chapter Ten

It's almost a week before I leave the house again, and when I do, I'm hyper aware of my body twitching as we drive slowly through the heavy, evening traffic on our way to Knightsbridge hotel.

I stare out the window and ignore my phone vibrating in my lap.

'Aren't you going to answer that?' Mark asks, taking his eyes off the road to watch me.

'No.'

'It could be important.'

I ignore both Mark and my ringing phone and continue to look out the window.

I recognise the number. It's the chairperson of the Gala Ball Committee. The same person who contacted me three days ago to advise me that the ball's chosen charity this year is the Irish Wheelchair Association. She politely asked me to be the guest speaker for the evening. I suppose she figured it would be politically correct to have the token cripple on stage. I declined, of course, certain I would be admired less as a speaker and more as an exhibit.

Mark was livid. He begged me to get involved, but I point-blank refused. He said he needed the publicity because it would be very good for his business. If people knew how hard things were for us at home, then they would buy their DIY stuff from Mark's hardware shop instead of the chain store down the street.

I spent almost three hours getting ready for the ball, but as I scrutinise every inch of my face in the badly lit mirror of the sun visor, I feel as unconfident as I would if I left the house in my pyjamas. I'm more critical of my appearance than usual, and I know it's a reflection of how much I'm dreading this evening. I stare at the lines and folds that time has patiently embroidered in my skin. Each subtle wrinkle is a reminder of the years of happiness that have led me to this strange point in my life. No amount of concealer can hide the bags under my eyes caused by restless nights filled with too many dreams. I concentrated as I layered on heavy, black mascara to lashes already laden thick with the stuff, in the hopes that the smoky look would distract from the deep, dark circles under my eyes.

I know my over analysing is grating on Mark's nerves. I can hear him clench his jaw. It's killing him not to nag me for poking at myself, but we're not on speaking terms. We haven't spoken all week. I'm still furious with him for his interrogation in Doctor Hammond's office, and he refuses to apologise. He remains a firm believer in Nicole's story. I'm betrayed and hurting and he doesn't seem to care.

I've shown the ultimate restraint and not even asked him how Patricia is coping with the kids. I've phoned the house a few times to ask Patricia myself, but Nicole always answers the damn phone, so I just hang up.

The disabled parking spots nearest the hotel entrance are full, so we drive around the carpark for at least ten minutes before finally finding space at the furthest point from the main doors.

'Just what we need,' Mark says staring out the windscreen at the torrential rain.

I almost reply but catch myself just in time. I absolutely refuse to be the first to back down. Mark will have to come crawling for forgiveness, and even then, I will be hard pressed to offer it.

We sit in uncomfortable silence for a few moments but deciding the rain has no intention of stopping, Mark swiftly hops out of the car. I watch in the rearview mirror as he curses his way around to the boot where he rummages about trying to find the golf umbrella. He struggles to balance the open umbrella while also trying to lift my heavy wheelchair out. Trying to unfold the chair is proving to be a disaster and a sting of guilt pinches in my chest.

Adam coincidentally pulls into a space not far from us, and noticing Mark's struggle, he rushes to help. Mortified, I quickly reach for my mobile. I desperately want to distract myself from the drama at the back of the car. I look at the screen and notice five missed calls from Ava – four text messages and a voicemail.

All the messages are the same 'call me as soon as you can.' I'm just about to press dial when Mark opens the car door.

'Come on,' he orders.

I automatically reach my arms around his neck and wait for him to scoop me out of the car. I've learned how to manipulate my body into a form that makes me easier to carry. Mark is growing very used to lifting me, and I can see the start of some firm biceps developing.

Adam appears in my view from the back of the car and waves. I wave back. However, he isn't walking beside us for long when the atmosphere becomes too uncomfortable for him.

'Oh, I left my ticket in the car. I better pop back for it,' he says. 'You both go on ahead. I'll see you inside.'

'He's lying,' I say.

'Why would he lie about something like that?' Mark snaps.

'Because he's not thick; it's obvious you're fighting with me.'

'I'm not fighting with you, Laura. I just don't understand you, and it's easier to be quiet than risk you exploding at me if you don't like something I say.'

'Is this about the Nicole thing again? I told you I was pissed off about that because you took her side. How do you think that made me feel?'

'Will you please lower your voice? The whole neighbourhood doesn't need to know.'

'No, I won't,' I challenge. 'You lower yours!' I quickly realise how stupid that statement is. Mark is whispering, but I'm so far beyond caring. I'm prepared to air out our dirty laundry in public.

I continue to rant and rave in the hopes of getting a rise from Mark, but I fail miserably. In fact, I manage to push him back into complete silence. His muted stance is almost as infuriating as his taking Nicole's word over mine.

Thankfully, the hotel is very accessible. A long ramp at the front door winds around the main granite steps. However, once inside, I know the rest of the evening will be an embarrassing struggle. The toilets are hidden at the end of a long, very narrow corridor and the main reception area is on a platform with several small, carpeted steps leading towards it. Mark can sense my discomfort and helplessness, and I'm relieved to see the compassion in his eyes.

'I'll check us in,' he suggests casually. 'Why don't you have a look around?'

It's a good idea, and normally, I would be delighted that he took on the hassle of sorting the accommodation, but the fact that I can't approach the reception desk even if I wanted to compounds my distress. I am not angry or upset with the hotel. That's a pointless waste of energy. I'm angry with myself. How could my stupid brain not remember how to work my legs?

Ava appears out of nowhere and wraps her arms around me in a massive bear hug. 'Laura, I'm so glad I found you. Did you get my messages?'

'Yes - all three hundred of them,' I joke. 'Is something wrong?'

'No, not wrong, but…er…I have a feeling you're not going to be too happy when…' Ava stops speaking abruptly when she notices Mark approach behind me.

'Did you get a room sorted?' I ask, completely forgetting I'm not speaking to him.

'I got the last one,' he says with a smile.

There's excitement in his voice, and I'm genuinely delighted that spending a night in the hotel, just the two of us, can spark that reaction. Maybe it's time I called a truce.

I smile in return and Mark leans down and kisses my forehead softly. I sigh deeply, so relieved our feud was over. Fighting with Mark is so alien to me; I had no idea it would be so exhausting.

'Sorry, Ava, you were saying…?' I finally ask.

Ava brushes her hand across her forehead as though she's a secret spy who narrowly escaped being kidnapped and tortured to hand over the information. 'Nothing, it doesn't matter.'

The ringing of a tiny, antique dinner bell summons our attention towards the function room. I cringe as we approach the narrow doorway. Mark navigates the way, and I bow my head in anticipation of the embarrassment that will follow. Ava will have to run off to find some unwilling member of the staff to help manipulate my cyborg ass through the doorway. I feel the hairs on the back of my neck stand as I brace myself.

Mark gently shoves open the other half of the double doors and pushes me inside effortlessly. He even whistles a little tune for optimal dramatic effect.

Inside, I sit as straight as I can and glance around. I've made it to the function room with minimal drama. I'm actually out in public with other people and no one has stared or passed remarks. I'm just another person among the crowd preparing to savour an evening of good food and good company.

I laugh my way through the meal, and in spite of all my doubts, I find myself thoroughly enjoying the evening. I wilt a little from time to time, but I fight the fatigue well even though Mark notices. He's offered to take me upstairs so many times that I've lost count.

'You won't get rid of me that easily,' I repeatedly joke.

He laughs, but I know that fifteen minutes from now, he will again suggest I go for a lie-down. I enjoy the familiarity of Mark's consideration, and I remember what it's like to be a couple in love. A couple without the weight of the world on our shoulders.

I'm relieved to see the waitress approach our table with coffee. The wine has definitely gone to my head. I can feel the room spin, and I'm pretty sure my speech is slurred. I've only had one glass and haven't even touched the top up, but I'm certainly not able for anymore.

'Jesus, Laura, what are you like. If a barman farted, you'd be pissed on the fumes,' Ava teases.

'I know, I know,' I admit. 'It's so embarrassing. I'm usually much better able to hold my drink.'

'You're a cheap date,' Adam jokes.

It's the first time all evening he has spoken to me. It's the first time he's spoken to anyone all evening, actually. He's spent most of the night leaning on the bar chatting to the pretty barmaid. He missed half the meal. Ava defends Adam's behaviour instinctively.

'He had a late lunch today,' she whispers. 'He's just not hungry.'

'Ah, okay,' I say, trying to pretend I don't notice how much his ignorant and rude behaviour is upsetting her.

The band sets up as everyone enjoys the last of the tea and coffee. I call Ava's attention to the girl sitting with her back to us a few tables down from us. She's wearing the same ridiculously expensive green dress Ava wore last year. I distinctly remember it because I talked about it for weeks after last year's ball and made Mark promise if it ever went on sale, I could buy one for myself. Of course, it fell on deaf ears, and after a while, I completely forgot about it.

'Laura,' Ava says pulling me close towards her. 'Okay. Don't flip out, but do you recognise the girl in the green dress?'

'Not really, should I?' I wondered if it's someone we had gone to school with and Ava has some gossip about how her ex-boyfriend died from uncontrollable killer herpes, or some equally juicy story.

'It's Nicole!' Ava states, very matter-of-factly.

'What?' I screech so shrilly I may have confused some poor whale's sonar.

'Well done with the not flipping out thing,' Ava grumbles. 'Damn, Laura.'

'Sorry, you caught me by surprise. What the bloody hell is she doing here?'

'Probably enjoying the evening. Just like we are.'

'Just like we WERE,' I moan.

'Ah, come on, Laura. Don't let it spoil our evening. Isn't it bad enough we brought one child with us tonight?' She points at Adam who is practically drooling over the bar. 'Just ignore her. Okay?'

'Okay,' I agree.

Ava walks away, probably to try to find a lasso to drag Adam back to the table with.

Despite my promise to Ava, I'm stewing with anger and the more I fight to suppress it, the more agitated I become.

'Mark,' I say as I softly tap his shoulder.

He doesn't reply. He's talking to the couple sitting beside him and doesn't hear me.

'Mark,' I repeat.

Again, I get no answer. Paranoid that he's ignoring me, I finally shout his name angrily. Of course, the band would have to take a break at that exact moment so my words ring loudly in the air and the people at the tables beside us turn to stare.

'Jesus, Laura,' Mark says swinging around to face me. 'What?'

'Nicole is here,' I stammer.

'Okay,' Mark replies unconcerned, before swinging back around to continue his previous conversation.

I tugged on the sleeve of his jacket. 'Don't try to pretend you didn't know.'

'I'm not pretending anything.'

'So you knew?'

'Yes. I knew.'

'Why didn't you tell her she couldn't come? The ball is our thing. Me, you, Adam, and Ava,' I stutter as uncontrollable anger pounds in my temples.

'Not anymore, Laura.'

'Well, that's me told,' I snort. 'You've more concern for that bitch than you have for your own wife.'

'My only concern is making sure Nicole has somewhere to stay tonight. I wouldn't dare suggest to you that she could crash with us. We got the last room here, remember.'

'So where is she staying, then?'

'My mother offered to come pick her up, so she's staying there. What could I say?'

'Ever heard of the word...no?' I snap.

'Will you listen to yourself? I can't tell Nicole where she can and can't go.' Mark is beginning to become quite angry. I can tell from the little vein in his neck that's pulsating rapidly.

'Why didn't you tell me?' I ask, not sure if I want to cry or scream.

'Because I knew you'd react like this, and to be honest, my head can't handle any more crap.'

Chapter Eleven

I sit alone in the cold corridor off the main function room for a long time. I need space. I've grown so used to the isolation that being by myself has somehow become synonymous with peace. I'm enjoying the silence. I need to escape the happy couples cuddling on the dance floor as they sway in circles and convince themselves they are dancing. I have to get away from the loud bunch of bachelors whose idea of a good time is suggesting to their already slightly green mate to down his next pint in one. Mostly, I just wanted to get out of the same room as Nicole. Although the dance hall is huge, the idea that the same four walls surround us has me feeling greener than that pint-chugging bachelor.

No one notices that I've left the table. Or perhaps they have but they're too preoccupied to come looking for me. Ava has enough worries of her own with the idiot she's managed to let herself fall in love with. I doubt Mark cares much that I've disappeared. He's probably enjoying the freedom to chat to Nicole without the old ball and chain nagging him. I suddenly feel very out of place. I knew I never should have come. I don't fit in anymore.

If I knew the room number, I'd take myself off to the comfort of fluffy pillows. Although I'm so angry with Mark, I really wished I had some other room to storm off to. I selfishly find myself wishing that Ava and Adam's row escalates a little and then Ava and I can be roommates, just like old times. We can stay awake all night and bitch about Nicole. I wonder if Ava brought any of that expensive face masque that she gets shipped from New York. I begin to imagine a very exciting and relaxing girly night.

I'm startled from my daydream as Adam drunkenly bursts through the large swinging door at the end of the corridor. He races towards the bathroom. He doesn't notice me as he passes. I wonder if he joined in the bachelor's game and is suffering the consequences. I pity anyone else who has the misfortune of needing to use the loo when Adam is finished with it. Judging by the urgency on his face, he isn't going to be able to hold the contents of his stomach much longer.

A tall brunette follows in hot pursuit, wobbling down the corridor in oversized stilettos. She quickens her pace as Adam lunges through the bathroom doors. There's less than a second before she follows him inside, unconcerned that she's heading into the men's bathroom.

My jaw drops as my suspicions are aroused. This is a new low, even for Adam. I recognise the brunette because she sat at our table all night. She's the girl Mark was speaking to earlier. *Thank God, it isn't Mark she's following,* I think. Surely, Ava must have noticed Adam and this long-legged girl leaving together. I throw my gaze back at the function room doors expecting Ava to appear at any moment to investigate. I battle with my conscience, unsure what my duty as a best friend is in this situation. Do I point Ava in the right direction so she will finally know the truth about Adam's antics, or do I say nothing because I know it will break her heart?

I wait and wait, but Ava doesn't appear. Adam and the girl remain in the bathroom for ages. I don't have a watch, but it definitely has a fifteen-minute feel to it, maybe even twenty. It's definitely long enough to get plenty of pleasurable fiddling about accomplished.

The huge, satisfied grin on Adam's face as he leaves the bathroom makes me sick. Poor Ava; she deserves so much better than that cheating prick. I can't be the one to tell her; it will kill her because she worships that bastard. I really don't know what to do, so I decide to head back inside and ask Mark for his advice.

Our table is empty. Adam makes his way straight back to the bar. *Surprise, surprise.* The brunette's coat is missing from her chair as is her partner's. The poor fool must have gone to look for the home-wrecking whore.

I spot Ava in the corner chatting with some old friends, and I'm about to make my way over to join them when I notice Mark and Nicole among the group. Nicole is sitting forward in her seat. Her and Ava are laughing. Mark's arm is draped over the back of Nicole's chair, and his fingertips are barely touching the bare skin of her shoulders. Maybe to an onlooker it's harmless – simply three friends chatting – but I know that soft touch of Mark's hand. It's so gentle you almost don't know it's there. But that's the beauty of it; he leaves you wanting more.

I stare at the three of them until my sight starts to blur. They looked like three old ladies huddled together at a knitting convention. They are genuinely enjoying each other's company, and I can hear their laughter over the band. There's only one problem; it's me who should be sitting among them, not Nicole. Why have Mark and Ava allowed Nicole to slide into our lives so easily? Soon, she will replace me altogether.

The longer I sit in solitude at our table, the more depressed I become. Various acquaintances take it upon themselves to come up and inform me of the others' location as though I have no eyes of my own. Some even throw in a finger point in the right direction. I'm decidedly uncomfortable each time my loneliness is so blatantly highlighted. I want to join them, but my stubbornness won't allow me. Besides, they're so deep in conversation that I'd clearly be interrupting.

My glass is empty and has been for some time, but I still stare lifelessly into it. I barely notice Mark reappear at our table and place a vodka and Diet Coke in front of me. I begin to guzzle the contents of the glass almost choking on the slightly wrinkly slice of lemon that floated to the top. Ava is also back at our table, but there's no sign of Nicole.

'Have you seen Adam anywhere?' Ava asks tapping me on the shoulder.

'No.'

'I wonder where he could have gotten to?' Ava's so concerned where the cheating idiot has strayed off to it's upsetting. Someone has to set her straight. Christ, how I wish I didn't have to be that someone. I take a deep breath and spill.

Colossal speakers vibrate the up-tempo drum beat across the dance floor, but the incessant pounding pales in comparison to Ava's furious rant. Her face is a very unflattering beetroot colour and mascara swells around her eyes before being rubbed into a dirty black paste by her shaking hands.

'You've turned into some bitch,' Ava shouts, so hard her hot breath hits me in the face. 'I'm sorry for everything that has happened to you, really I am. But I just don't know who you are anymore.'

Ava stops abruptly. Maybe she'll hastily retract what she has just blurted, or maybe she was waiting for me to retaliate with something as equally nasty.

I don't speak. There's nothing to say.

Ava throws her head to one side and continues her attack. 'I know you are going through hell at the moment, but you are determined to drag us all along for the ride. It's not fair, Laura. God, I have put up with so much shit. I have stupidly tolerated all the horrible stuff you say that you swear the next day that you can't remember. Bloody selective amnesia.'

She neatly pulls her pencil slim dress just above her tanned knees and crouches down in front of me. Vicious words that are way out of character continue to spill effortlessly from her frothing lips. She rests one hand gently on the armrest of my wheelchair and the other flat across my thigh. She bends in close and places her lips softly next to my ear. She speaks slowly and clearly, and I know she wants me to catch every word. 'It's one thing to change, everyone does from time to time, but the old Laura would be disgusted by the selfish bitch that you have become.'

My hands clasp my face and tears rush past my shaking fingers. Ava ignores my quivering shoulders.

'Look at him,' Ava says. She angrily catches my head and forces me to stare at Mark. 'He is a shell of the guy he used to be and your self-wallowing is destroying him. Is he not as entitled to feel as much pain as you? You are not the only one suffering. Can't you see that? You're so busy worrying that everyone will leave you. Laura, you're the one driving us away. I'm only your friend – I can take it – but you are forcing a wedge between yourself and Mark.'

Ava stands up shakily and neatens out her dress. She runs her fingers under her eyes and wipes away the last remaining tears. She turns on her heels and slowly walks away. She doesn't look back.

Nicole, who I suspect has been watching for some time, finally stops stirring her swizzle stick around some very lonely looking ice cubes in the bottom of her glass. She races over to me like a bulimic greyhound after a runaway sausage. I would roll my eyes, but they're still spinning around in my head after Ava's outburst.

'Is everything okay?' Nicole asks.

I shake my head instinctively, but I understand why everyone likes her so much. She's the stereotypical Hollywood sweetheart – blond, beautiful, pleasant, and always smiling. She even manages to sound genuinely concerned now.

'Everything is just peachy,' I snap sarcastically.

'It's just...I thought I noticed you crying,' she says rummaging in her tiny handbag before pulling out a tissue.

'Well, you would have noticed. You were certainly staring hard enough.' I snatch the tissue out of her hand.

I don't care how rude I seem. This is the woman who is so terrified of me she needs my husband and doctor to protect her. But the slightest sniff of gossip and she's suddenly plucked up the courage to pretend we're friends.

'Piss off,' I growl, so irritated by her lip pouting and false concern that I struggle to suppress the urge to slap her.

'Okay, Laura, I can see you are your usual pleasant self this evening,' Nicole says with a superior smirk.

I don't respond. It's obvious she was trying to spark a reaction. I am not going to give her one. She won't win this time. I won't create a scene.

'I should go look for Adam; he could probably do with a friend right now,' Nicole suggests casually as she turns to walk away.

That's it! Nicole has made one dig too many, and I can't control my temper any longer. I pick up my almost full glass of vodka and forcefully fling the entire contents at her. For someone with dreadful aim, I impressively manage to get almost all the liquid to land in her hair. She yelps like a burst sausage in the frying pan.

Ava re-emerges from the bathroom and races to investigate. Mark, of course, follows the cries of the fair maiden in distress and appears in a flash. Even Adam tears himself away from the new strawberry-blonde he has found at the bar to come and check out the hysteria.

'What the hell happened here?' Mark asks staring angrily at me. I can see that I'm the bad guy in his eyes.

Ava quickly gathers up some crumpled serviettes from the table and dabs the excessive liquid that drips down Nicole's hair onto the back of her dress.

I fling my tired head into my hands. I expected them to be sticky but a grainy texture brushes my cheeks. I try to block out the commotion around me as I slowly examine my hands. A white powder mattes on my fingertips where the alcohol has contacted my skin. *What the hell?* I press my fingers under my nose. It has no smell. I place the tip of my index finger on my tongue and the powder slowly dissolved without a taste. Yuck! The glass was obviously filthy. I'm extra glad Nicole ended up wearing the vodka rather than it making its way to my stomach. Dishwasher powder – maybe.

I suddenly have a horrible flashback to Mark's phone conversation last week. *No. He wouldn't.* I shake my head trying to toss off the disturbing notion as ridiculous. Nicole is crying and I watch as Mark fusses over her like a little-lost puppy. I'm the villain. There's no point in even trying to defend myself when everyone has already reached their verdict.

Nicole is a guest in our lives, an uninvited one at that. I don't want her anywhere near me, my friends, and most importantly, my children. Mark has forced her upon us all without ever checking if it was okay first. For someone who's apparently so great with the children, she seems to be spending less and less time with them, and more and more time with my husband and my friends. She's slowly trying to replace me and everyone seems happy to let her. Everything changed when she arrived. Everything was fine before that. I begin to wonder just how far Nicole was prepared to go…far enough to cause a horrible car crash?

Chapter Twelve

The cold of the night air stings my damp cheeks. I need the bed so badly waiting for me inside, but I refuse to share a hotel, never mind a room, with Mark. I doubt anyone will miss me. Everyone will still be swarming around poor defenceless, Oscar-winning Nicole.

I never once look back as I make my way to the end of the road. I don't want any reminders of the disaster that this evening has been. I come to a sudden stop at the end of the side street that leads to the usually busy main road. But all is very still now, eerily so. The only noise is coming from a group of rowdy teenagers perched on a low wall outside the service station a few paces down from me. They're drinking cheap cider from an old lemonade bottle and shouting at each other for taking mouthfuls too large. They're clearly no strangers to the loitering thing as they take turns standing guard on the corner. I wonder who they're watching out for. A rival gang perhaps, or more realistically, they're on guard from a surprise attack by a concerned parent. They make me incredibly uncomfortable.

'Here, Missus,' one of the younger boys among the group shouts while clicking his fingers at me. 'What's a loner like you doing all dressed up?'

I pretend not to hear them, but it is obvious their boyish laughing and sarcastic wolf whistles are intimidating me.

'No need to be alone tonight. I'll bring ya home and show ya a good time,' another much older boy jeers.

'Yeah. WUP! WUP!' comes supportive shouts from his buddies.

'Piss off, assholes,' a familiar voice from behind me yells. 'Go home and shag your pillow like you did last night.'

I turn around to find Ava standing behind me. I begin to cry, much to the amusement of the group of youths. Ava grabs the handles of my wheelchair and pushes me across the road out of earshot of the group. It's the first time she's ever wheeled my chair, and although I thought it would be weird, it isn't.

'What are you doing here?' I ask shakily.

'Someone has to teach you how to return some profanity,' Ava jokes.

'But I was horrible to you. Why did you come after me?'

'Because that's what best friends do. Besides, you were right. Adam is an arsehole, and I do deserve better.'

'Ah, Ava I'm sorry. Did you split up?'

Ava doesn't answer.

'He couldn't tear himself away from looking up Nicole's skirt long enough to listen to anything I have to say. Anyway, he's not worth wasting my breath on.'

Ava's voice is breaking, and it's obvious she's hurting a lot more than her convincing cover-up hides.

'You're right. Us single ladies have to stick together,' I say.

'What? How much wine did you have, woman? I think you'll find that little bit of gold wrapped around your finger means you're married,' Ava says, spinning my wedding ring around on my finger.

'Someone should tell that to Nicole. Apparently, she likes to pretend Mark doesn't have a wife.'

'Well, as long as Mark remembers, that's all that matters,' Ava assures, but I detect some hesitancy in her voice.

'You don't think there is anything going on with them, do you?' I ask, shocked that suddenly somebody shared my suspicions. Suspicions I never admitted out loud until that moment.

'No, no, of course not,' Ava says, shaking her head.

She's lying, I can tell. She's nervously opening and closing the clasp on her handbag ten times a second.

'Ava, please don't lie to me. If you know something, then you have to tell me.'

'Laura, I don't know anything. There is nothing to know. Mark loves you; that's all I know for sure.'

'That's all you know for sure? Right, now I'm more worried about what you know for unsure.'

Ava falls silent.

The teenagers across the road begin heckling us again and my patience with their rudeness is wearing thin.

'Fuck off,' I roar in a deep voice that I didn't know I had.

They respond with more inappropriate comments and name-calling. Eventually, when they're getting little reaction from us, they began with the cryptic sexual hand gestures.

Ava and I both shake our heads, slightly amused at their silliness.

'Ah is the little cripple all confused,' one of the small ones at the back shouts. 'Billie no mates is Billie no legs, too.'

They all laugh hysterically. Ava's about to shout something wonderfully colourful and no doubt probably far too intellectually challenging for their tiny brains to understand, but before she has the chance, I dart across the road in a fit of temper.

I notice a lonely gathering of small chippings of cement lying on the ground. The group must have scraped them off the wall as they climbed up. I bend down and pick up several. Ava races after me.

'Laura, no,' she shouts.

'You freak,' one of them yells as I pelt them viciously with the little chips of rock.

My temper is completely out of control, and I can see my reckless behaviour. It's as clear to me as if I am a stranger on the street watching my own actions play out. I know how unnecessarily aggressive I am, but I'm powerless to stop my anger.

'I'm normal,' I screech over and over. 'Do you hear me? I *am* normal.'

'Laura, stop! Jesus Christ, Laura, just stop it.' Ava screams so loudly that my ears ring.

I look at the stones in my hands. I feel all the strength that came with my rage leave my body. I'm suddenly exhausted. I let my arms fall lifelessly beside me. Ava quickly grabs my hands and shakes the pebbles from my grasp.

I stare at the startled row of teens in front of me. Not one of them has moved from the wall. It's obvious the small stones haven't physically hurt them. They glare at me, but they aren't staring at me in anger. They have a strange look in their eyes. I've noticed the same look from Mark and Nicole. They're afraid of me. I really am a freak, and everyone knows it. My eyes weigh heavy, and like I do every time a situation becomes too intense, I pass out.

Semi-conscious, I see one of the girls in the group help Ava to lift me to sit back up. Ava apologises to the group for my outburst. I worry soon Ava will grow tired of tidying up my messes, as Mark has.

'For the spilt drink,' Ava says offering a tenner to the girl, but she doesn't take the money.

'She's a freak, you know,' the oldest youth says. 'Stay away from her.' He bends down and pulls the girl away from me as though a contagious disease riddles me.

'I don't think she's well,' the girl defends me.

'She's a fucking freak,' he protests.

The girl doesn't reply. She gets to her feet and rejoins her group. Ava grasps the handles of my chair and pushes me away. I slouch forward, my arms struggling awkwardly to grab the wheels of my chair to help push my heavy body uphill. Ava is walking so fast her calves are almost buckling beneath her, and I know she'll have to stop from exhaustion soon.

We gain quite a bit of distance before I finally drop my hands off the wheels. We come to a stop.

'What the hell just happened?' Ava asks stepping out from behind my chair to face me.

'I was hoping you could tell me,' I answer genuinely.

'Were you trying to get us killed? What if one of them had a knife or a gun or something?'

I don't know which scared Ava more; the prospect of how horrible that scene could have played out, or how out of my mind I had momentarily become. Ava is still shaking uncontrollably even when we are well out of view of the group, so I know the latter has her truly terrified.

'I'm sorry,' I apologise, breaking what has become a very long silence.

'It's okay,' Ava says. 'It's not your fault.'

'I don't know what came over me.'

'I think I do.'

'Wine?' I ask, trying and failing to hide my embarrassment.

'I don't think the wine was the problem. More whatever was in it.'

I look into Ava's eyes. She's not looking at me; she's staring blankly at the road ahead. We've walked far, and we're very isolated. Ava doesn't seem to notice. She looks as though she has the weight of a small wrestler sitting on her shoulders.

'Ava,' I call.

'Mmm?'

'You think maybe there was something wrong with the wine?'

'I think Mark poured something into your wine this evening.' She rushes her words together as though it hurts her so much to say it she can't leave the words in her mouth for long.

I snort and shake my head as I once again think of Mark's phone call. 'Mark wouldn't do that.'

'I know; that's what I thought when Adam told me but...'

'Hang on,' I interrupt. 'Adam saw Mark do this?'

'Yeah, Adam was at the corner of the bar. Mark didn't know he was there. Laura, I was as shocked as you when I found out.'

'I'm not shocked,' I assure my delusional best friend. 'I just can't believe you would fall for any of the crap that comes out of Adam's mouth. The guy is a compulsive liar. The only way he would know the truth was if it was tattooed on the tanned ass of some sexy blonde. Even then, he wouldn't recognise it. He'd probably just think it was a birthmark. I was genuinely worried for a second. But if your only source is Adam, then I know I've nothing to be concerned about. Jesus.'

'Laura, don't you think I know how ridiculous this sounds? But you're the one who is convinced Nicole is trying to get you out of the picture. Is it so hard to believe that maybe she has an accomplice?'

'Mark loves me,' I snap.

'Yes, okay, Mark loves you, but why was there undissolved powder all over Nicole's hair when you threw your drink at her?'

I hadn't noticed the powder on Nicole; I thought it was just the little bit on my hands. I was so busy storming out that I'd just focused on the door.

'I thought the powder on my hands was from a dirty glass, or maybe something I picked up on my wheels,' I explain.

'I'm sorry, Laura. I think you might be right after all. Maybe something is going on with Nicole and Mark.'

Ava bends down and hugs me, so tight it's hard to breathe. I know she really believes Adam.

Large fat salty tears run heavily down my cheeks. My makeup that's sat so flawlessly at the start of the night is streaky and smudged and feels like tar on my face. I can handle my doubts of Mark when it was just a niggling theory in the back of my mind, but being hit with the evidence to prove that theory is more intense than if those teenagers had fired a bullet straight through me.

'I'm here for you, you know that, yeah?' Ava assures.

'I know,' I whisper.

'Do you want to stay with us tonight?' Ava offers.

'No, it's okay; you and Adam have your own problems.'

'Ah, don't worry about that.' Ava brushes it off as though they had a slight argument over who ate the last biscuit.

'You guys aren't breaking up, are you?' I ask in confusion.

'No. No, we're not,' Ava says almost apologising. 'I just needed to talk to you, and I knew you wouldn't listen to me if Adam was here.'

'Well, where is he now? You been missing for well over an hour, and he hasn't come to look for you or ring your phone even once. I don't think he has even noticed you're gone,' I moaned. 'Typical.'

'He's been driving about fifty feet behind us the whole time. I'm sorry. It's really dark and creepy out here. I was too scared to chase after you on my own. Please don't hate me,' Ava pleads.

I stare at the ground as Ava twitches nervously waiting for a reply.

I grab Ava tight and hug her so hard I hear a snap. I know I'm lucky to have someone who could lie so convincingly just so they could help me discover the truth.

'Well, can we stop and wait for him to catch up?' I finally suggested. 'I'm freezing.'

Adam revved the engine of his soft-top, vintage sports car as he pulls in beside us. The bonnet is so shiny that the slightest glimmer of moonlight lurking out from behind a cloud reflects impressively off it. I always wonder if his new flashy car is compensating for something, but I'm never crude enough to ask.

It's a relief to sit in the backseat of the car.

'Should you be driving?' I ask remembering that Adam has spent most of the night lounging over the bar counter.

'If you would prefer to use your own wheels to get home, then please, be my guest,' Adam growls.

'Adam, leave it out,' Ava warns as she slapped her hand gently against his thigh.

'Excuse me,' I squeak disgusted at Adam.

'Nothing, Laura. It was a joke,' Ava says jumping to Adam's defence.

I don't find it very funny. But I say nothing. I caused enough trouble between the two of them earlier, so this time I'm going to keep my mouth shut. Besides, I have more pressing concerns on my mind.

'We should go straight to the police,' I suggest.

'Ha,' Adam snarls. 'Like I'm really going to drive you to the cop shop so you can give them a demonstration of my drunk driving.'

'Not about you, you idiot. I mean about Nicole trying to kill me.'

'Whoa, whoa, whoa! Who said anything about attempted murder?' Adam shrieks, his eyebrows rising ridiculously high.

'You did!' I insist. 'You said Mark and Nicole put something in my drink.'

'Yeah, probably prescribed meds. It could have been fucking sherbet for all I know.' Adam pauses. 'I certainly never said anything about anyone trying to kill anyone else.'

'Ava, you think we should go to the cops, yeah?' I ask.

'I don't know. I mean it's all a bit hasty. I think maybe we are a little paranoid,' Ava says, squirming in her seat.

I'm so frustrated I could scream. Why is she retreating now? Does she have to agree with Adam on absolutely everything?

'Jesus Christ, what is wrong with you?' I yell, way too loud for the confined space of the car. 'She wants me out of the picture. Don't you get it? Nicole is winning. She's taking everything from me. She has my kids, my husband, and now she wants my life.'

'I know you're scared because everything has changed lately, but I think you need to start thinking more rationally,' Adam explains. 'Let's just go home. You can sleep it off back at my place.'

'Sleep what off?' I sob. 'The drugs I've been tricked into taking, the two sips of alcohol I drank, or the paranoia that I'm clearly irritating you with. I thought you were on my side.'

'I am on your side,' Adam says, sounding genuinely supportive. 'But you can't try to destroy an innocent woman's life simply because you don't like her.'

'I hate her,' I correct. 'And I'm not destroying her life. I'm trying to stop her before she destroys mine. But no one will help me.'

I cry myself to sleep that night. I'm no stranger to tears lately, but this was a new sensation. Fear has replaced the self-pity – horrible, uncontrollable terror.

Chapter Thirteen

I have mixed feelings about finding Mark's car parked nearly in front of the door as we pull into my driveway early the next morning. Deep down, I'm relieved Mark came home. Visions of him and Nicole enjoying our hotel bed together haunted me all night. At least that was one less horror to face now. But I'm still nervous of the conflict I'm certain lies on the other side of the front door.

Adam helps me out of the car, and as we approach the house, my nerves begin to multiply. The door is slightly ajar, and I figure Mark is expecting us. Strange emotions tease me. Fear is my primal instinct but many sub-emotions squirm around inside me, but I'm too afraid to process them. It's like a scene from an old black and white horror movie. The mad axe man waits patiently behind the door for his victim. I get the impression Adam is nervous too as he pushes me along by the grass verge leading to the door. He isn't intentionally tiptoeing, but his shoes make no sounds as they graze the ground. Ava lags behind. If Adam is right, and Nicole and Mark are no threat, then why are we all so reluctant to go inside?

The walls in the hall have been stripped of family pictures. The sparse scenic canvases occupying the space where the kids' smiling faces should be felt alien and offensive in my home. I want to rip them off the walls. Neatly stacked cardboard boxes sit under the stairs; they're all individually labelled. I read through as many as I can see. 'Attic Stuff' one reads. 'Baby Toys' is scribbled on another. 'Katie's Clothes' is written neatly on a third box.

Confusion replaces my fear now as I rush through to the kitchen. The messy poster paint pictures are missing from the fridge. The piles of laundry that I haven't gotten around to folding have been neatly placed in a large suitcase that lies open on the table. I feel a chill run down my spine. The house is naked of all memories.

I catch Ava's gaze. She's as much in disbelief as I am. Mark hasn't come home to wait for me. He has come home to leave me.

I hear footsteps on the stairs.

'Mark?' I call as I plunge myself back into the hall.

Mark walks silently down the stairs carrying more boxes.

'What are you doing?' I ask unable to disguise the desperation in my voice.

He ignores me, walking straight past to stack the boxes with the others.

'Are you leaving me?'

'I'm leaving this house,' he finally replies.

'But this is our home…the kid's home. What will we do without you?'

'This is just a house, Laura. It hasn't been a home in a long time. I need to get away while I still have some happy memories of this place.'

His tone is cold and unloving. He speaks to me the same as you might a stranger on the street simply enquiring the time. There's no hatred in his voice, just indifference. That hurts the most; to be indifferent means he lost the will to care. He doesn't just no longer love me; he no longer acknowledges that he ever had.

I know he has firmly made up his mind. There's no point in arguing because it won't change anything. I've lost him. I've no idea how it's all gone so horribly wrong, but somehow, we've become strangers. I won't fight to save our marriage, but I won't let him take my kids away.

'I want to see the children,' I demand.

'No, Laura. We're not going over this again,' he protests.

'We haven't discussed anything. I've just been told that I can't see them. Well, I'm telling you now I can. And I want to right now,' I spit through an angrily clenched jaw. 'I want to see the children today. I am going to your mother's and don't even think about trying to stop me,' I warn.

'I won't stop you. But you're wasting your time. They aren't there.'

Mark's face is a blank canvas; there isn't a hint of emotion. It's as though he's rehearsed this very conversation and could recite it like a poem well learned.

'Where are they?' I ask softly. 'Please tell me.' I know I'm degrading myself by begging, but I can't bear not knowing.

'Laura, stop it; you're upsetting yourself,' a voice from behind me says.

I turned around to find Nicole behind me. Katie is sleeping in her arms, with her little head resting on Nicole's shoulder.

I reached my arms out to take my baby girl. Nicole walks forward, about to hand Katie to me, but Mark shakes his head. My heart sinks.

Bobby appeared bright and cheery from behind Nicole's legs. He has a small toy car, and he crouches on the hall carpet and begins driving it up and down in line with the pattern.

'Vroom, vroom,' he chirps, happily unaware of any conflict around him.

'Hi Bobby,' I say.

I startle him. He looks up for a moment but then looks straight back down to where his car is waiting.

'Aren't you going to say hello?' I ask him.

He shakes his little head. Tears well in my eyes. I miss the kids so much, but Bobby has been just fine without me.

'Bobby, it's me. It's Mommy. Please say hello to me?'

'Hello, Mommy,' Bobby says like a little robot.

He doesn't look at me or even smile. He's simply being a good boy and doing what he's told. He clearly has no interest in talking to me.

'Can we go to Mc Donald's now, Nicky?' he asks with excitement.

His bright blue eyes sparkle as he looks at her. I know that expression. He shares it with me every day when I pick him up after his morning playgroup. He's too young to understand the words I love you, but his eyes tell me those words every day. Today, they tell Nicole.

'Bobby, I can take you to Mc Donald's. Would you like to go with me?' I ask, my tone less sweet and a lot more anxious now.

'No, I want to go with Nicky.' He drops his cars and stands up to hold Nicole's hand.

Frustration fills me.

'Bobby, come here,' I command.

'No,' Bobby shouts as he backs away to hide behind Nicole's legs.

'Bobby, come here right now,' I say angrily.

Bobby begins to cry and calls for his father. His tears are strong, and I can see his little body shake as he rests his head against Nicole's thigh. Katie wails. All the commotion is upsetting her. I desperately want to reach for her and kiss her soft forehead, but as I move forward, Nicole quickly distances herself.

Mark is so distant that he doesn't acknowledge how upset the children are. He doesn't take Bobby in his arms and rock him back and forth, as he used to. I hate Mark at that moment, but I still want him to hold our little boy. I want Bobby to feel safe and loved, but Mark is cold and unfamiliar. He's ignoring our children as if they don't even exist, and I know he doesn't want them; he's only taking them to hurt me.

'Go on out to the car. I'll be there in a minute,' Mark instructs.

Nicole nods and both children go with her.

'Bye, sweetheart,' I say at one final attempt for recognition, but Bobby just sobs harder.

'You're acting scary,' Mark insists angrily.

'I didn't mean to,' I protest.

'Of course, you didn't. Your screaming and shouting were actually a warm and friendly gesture.' Mark's sarcasm cuts through me like a knife.

'Nicole is taking my place. How do you think that makes me feel?' I cry.

'No!' Mark growls. 'She is just being a good friend. A job you clearly resigned from long ago.'

'What the hell is that supposed to mean?' I snap. 'I would give my life to make you happy.'

'Well, not so long ago that's exactly what you tried to do.'

I look at Mark, almost lost for words. 'What the hell are you talking about?'

'Stop playing games, Laura. I can't pretend anymore,' Mark says. 'You cost us everything. Every. Fucking. Thing.'

His tone has changed. He was so angry moments before, but now there are tears glistening in his eyes.

'It was an accident. You know it was,' I stutter. 'I didn't see the other car coming.'

'Can you see it now?' Mark softens.

'What?' I shake my head.

He's confusing me. Is he doing it on purpose?

'Can you see the other car, now? Maybe then you might find some answers.'

'Stop being so cryptic; I don't understand what you are talking about.' I can barely speak I'm crying so hard.

'You're not the only victim, Laura. Open your goddamn eyes.'

'I have my eyes wide open, and I don't like what I see,' I reply hastily.

'You only see what you want to see,' Mark whispers as tears swell in his red eyes. 'I wish it was that simple for me.'

Mark is guarding his emotions, I could tell. He was hiding something. And now I know his secret.

'I see that you and Nicole tried to kill me.'

There's sudden silence. I scan the hall for any sign of Ava. I'm afraid now that Mark knows I'm aware of his plan he might fly into a furious rage and hurt me.

'If you honestly think that, then you need a lot more help than I thought,' Mark replies. His body is hunched so far forward I think he might fall to the ground.

He's a broken man. *But it's just an act.* He's distraught that I know about his vicious plan to dispose of me.

'Stop lying to me,' I yell.

His helpless stance is pathetic. He can't convince me that he's anything other than a liar.

'You're lying to yourself,' he whispers softly, dropping his head and sighing deeply.

'Go on. Walk away. I'm better off without you,' I cry. 'I hate you.'

'I know you do, but you can't push me away. I will always come back for you,' Mark says without lifting his head.

I instantly extract the hidden threat in his sentence. It's a warning. If I try to follow him to take the kids, then he will come after me and finish the job he started last night.

I hurt inside. Pain knots in my stomach and aches in my brain. Every time Mark speaks, it's in a tone foreign to his personality. He's changed drastically, and I don't know or like the man he's become. He's hurtful and frightening. A stranger hides inside the shell of my husband's body.

I look through the glass pane of the front porch. Nicole is waiting in the passenger seat of *my* car. I don't see my babies through the tinted back windows, but I hope they're strapped safely into their car seats and blissfully unaware of the hell tearing their family apart.

Mark's still speaking to me, but I don't hear a word. Heartache is engulfing me.

The next few moments play out in unimaginable slow motion, although, in reality, it's only a matter of a few short minutes. I can feel the loss of self-control sweep over me. A relentless rage surges through my body. It isn't new. I've experienced temper like this before, and I recognise the warning signs. I know the pattern the rage will take. I knew I was losing control, but this time I embrace it. This time it feels good to rebel. I'm empowered by my fury, and I allow it to devour me completely.

Mark's staring at me strangely. Perhaps he can see the anger brewing in my eyes. He almost looks frightened. For a moment, I suspect he recognises the warning signs, too. Maybe he knows what's coming. He remains unmoving, but his eyes admit he's desperate to back away.

I lean towards the edge of my chair, and with undeniable strength, I lunge viciously forward. I knock Mark helplessly to the ground. He lies still for a few moments pinned by the weight of my lifeless frame. He's shouting. I can see his lips moving, but I choose to block out the sound he forces into my ears. I'm the powerful one now. I'm commander and chief. He can't hurt me now.

My bubble quickly bursts. I'm wrong. Of course, he can hurt me. He's by far the stronger opponent. He shows no remorse as he forces his large hands against my shoulders and pushes me upright roughly. I struggle to catch my breath, but before I can react, he catches my rigid waist and flings me off his bucking body.

I don't know what expression I'm expecting to see on Mark's face as I cower in the corner where he has thrown me. I'm waiting for hatred to appear in the tired lines that rest around his eyes, but instead, I see sadness – unbearable sadness. I recognise the expression. It's heart rendering. Hatred would have been easier to bear.

Mark's still carrying a secret; something more I still didn't know. It's scribbled in the contorted wrinkles of his face. He's thirty-three on his next birthday, but lately, he wears the tired face of a man twenty years his senior.

I use my exhausted arms to pull my legs into a neat ball that I stuff under my chin. I remain a quivering mess in the corner as I watch for any sign of Mark backing down. I want so badly for him to kneel beside me and tell me it's all a misunderstanding. That he loves me and we would work it out. But I know that's an unrealistic fantasy.

Mark approaches me and I pull my knees closer to my chest. I begin to scream for Ava. I realise at that moment that more was lost than I first thought. We aren't two people who have fallen out of love. We are two people driving each other to the point of insanity.

I scream and scream but Ava doesn't appear. Mark gets close enough for me to see his chest heave with each heaving breath. I reach my hand over my head and use my elbow to protect my face. As long as I've known Mark, he was adverse to violence, but in that terrifying moment, I think he's going to attack and I have no will to fight back. However, I never suspected he would use someone else to do his dirty work for him.

The quiet footsteps on the stairs seconds before failed to register in my mind. I was concentrating so hard on Mark that I dismissed the noise as quickly as I had heard it. Doctor Hammond reaches the final step just as I turn to face him. The large syringe in his hand is terrifying, and I scream so loudly I hurt my own ears. It's too late. The sharp, cold metal of the needle penetrates my neck and all lights banish from my view.

Chapter Fourteen

I gradually open one eye and then the other. The light stings as it burns into my dilated pupils. I'm lying flat on my back with my knees bent. I try to stretch out, but there's no room to manoeuvre. I'm cramped and uncomfortable. I can't see enough to determine where I am. I think I'm frightened, but I have so much on my mind that I don't indulge the feeling. I can sense jerky movements flinging me from side to side. My inability to focus irritates my groggy brain.

There is noise. A voice or voices. Someone is speaking to me, but the words run too quickly together. Staccato tones blur sentences into a low hum in my mind. Engine noises quietly purr in the background. I lie still and listen. I listen for a long time. I'm in a car. I'm obviously lying across the backseat. For a brief, terrified moment, I worry that Mark and Nicole are the couple in the front of the car, but I gradually realise the voices I hear are jumpy and agitated. They're as frightened as I am.

'Ava,' I call.

I hold my breath as I wait for an answer.

'I'm here,' Ava replies softly.

She's only sitting in the passenger seat, but her voice seems to travel miles before it reaches me. I have to concentrate so hard to decipher each simple word from the other that I can feel my brain pound against the back of my skull.

'Thank you,' I whisper as I close my weary eyes. 'Thank…you…'

I have no idea where we're going, but I know it needs to be far away.

'I'm sorry,' Ava apologises stirring me from a fitful sleep.

'For what?' I mumble, my eyes still closed.

'For not believing you.'

There's such remorse in Ava's voice that it saddens me. She shouldn't have to feel guilty about anything. She has been more than wonderful, and I almost pushed her away.

'Don't be,' I insist, opening my eyes and staring at the roof as I speak. 'I didn't believe it to start with, either. Who would? Even now, I keep wishing I could find something to prove me wrong.'

'I don't think you're wrong,' Ava says. 'It's taken over two hours for whatever that freaky doctor shot you with to wear off. But you're okay now. We have you. You're safe with us.'

Ava tries hard, but her words are of little comfort. Everything I've ever loved has been cruelly stolen from me, and I fear I might never get it back.

My eyes close again, and for the first time in weeks, I sleep without the fear that the opportunity to wake up may be denied to me.

'We're here,' Adam proudly announces as he stops the car outside what looks like a little barn.

'Is this it?' I ask as I rub my sleepy face.

'Think so,' Ava replies, sounding just as surprised as I am.

I scan the small, almost isolated building on the outskirts of a quaint village. It doesn't look anything like a police station. There's a very old four-by-four with no back bumper parked in front. Adam's attempts to convince us it's an unmarked police car fail miserably, but it does lighten the atmosphere.

I'm too nervous to go inside. I don't really know what I should say. I'd been very assertive when I spent the last hour and a half insinuating that Nicole is out for blood – my blood. Ava nodded along, and I knew she believed me. Adam, however, was more sceptical. But I naïvely hope he will come around to the theory. After all, it was his suggestion that we retreat to the safety of his grandmother's old house in west Cork. He thinks I'm in a fragile state of mind, and a couple of days retreat in the country is just what I need. I suspect Ava threatened all sorts to get him to offer his help, but I'm not in a position to take offence.

'Will you come in with me?' I plead as I finally work up the courage to open the back door of the car.

'I don't think that's such a good idea,' Adam says before Ava has any chance to reply.

'Why not,' I snap, immediately on the defensive.

If looks could kill, then Adam would be six feet under with a wreath on top as Ava's stare cuts through him like a sharp blade.

'Yes, Adam. Why is it not a good idea?' Ava echoes. 'I can't let her walk in on her own.'

'Laura, you are about to make some very serious accusations,' Adam explains. 'I don't think anyone else should get involved.'

'Why on earth not?' I ask, unsurprised by Adam's lack of support.

'Well, for one thing…there's no evidence.'

'What more evidence do you want, Adam?' I bark. 'My corpse!'

'Don't be so dramatic,' he snaps. 'I'm just saying you're big enough to fight your own battles; you don't need help.'

I actually admire Adam's attempts to protect Ava. I'm almost impressed. Ava however looks disgusted. She's Ms. Independent and has been as long as I've known her. She doesn't take orders very well from anyone.

'This isn't a simple argument over who left the porch light on all night,' Ava retorts. She doesn't bother to hide her agitation. 'Her husband's mistress is trying to kill her.'

Ava's words send bile twisting around my stomach. Although I've suspected Mark's unfaithfulness for a while now, hearing it come from the mouth of someone else means I can no longer hide in denial.

'He really is trying to get rid of me, Adam,' I assure.

Adam doesn't bother to look at me as I speak. He stares out the window. His actions seem eerily familiar and a sense of suspicion fills inside me. If I struggle to convince someone who's witnessed Mark's odd behaviour that I'm in danger, then how can I expect a stranger to believe me? Maybe Adam is right, maybe I shouldn't get the police involved. After all, right now I'm just some silly women in a dirty ball gown on a Sunday afternoon with a crazy story about an angry husband.

I can't stop thinking about my children. I know Mark wouldn't hurt them, but I remember a time when I was certain he wouldn't hurt me either. I miss them. I missed them so much my body aches. I miss the smell of Katie's soft baby curls. I miss Bobby's slobbery kisses. But most of all, I miss how good being their mother makes me feel. I don't feel good now. I'm failing as a mother because I am not protecting them. I realise I have to save them far more than I have to save myself. I have to talk to the police.

Adam's eyes are glassy and tear stained. His mixed signals are confusing the shit out of me.

'I really don't think this is a good idea,' he reiterates. His hungover expression dilutes his argument. 'Let's just take a few days of chilling out time and see how you feel then.'

'Chill out?' Ava mumbles, disgusted. 'Come on, Laura, let's go.'

Ava swings her exhausted legs out the car door and turns her attention to assisting me.

'Thanks.' I smile as I fumble to get myself into my wheelchair in a minimum number of awkward movements.

'No problem,' Ava chirps falsely enthusiastic. 'Can I tell you a secret?'

I nod and try to smile.

'I'm scared,' she says.

'I'm not scared,' I lie very unconvincingly as we reach the tattered timber door. 'I just want to do this and get the hell out of here.'

'Good afternoon,' Ava shouts into what appears to be an empty station.

There's a lonely mahogany table just inside a small porch area. It sits in the middle of the floor and although there's nothing to suggest against it, Ava and I are reluctant to enter past the desk.

'There's no one here,' Ava says disappointedly.

'What will we do?' I ask, beginning to panic.

I know it's unrealistic, but I'm terrified that Mark has secretly followed us. I've seen a few too many horror movies and my nerves are in overdrive.

'Hello,' a husky voice finally says.

'Hello, Sir,' Ava replies shakily taking control of the situation. It's obvious she's a good, law-abiding citizen. Just being inside a police station is enough to have her quaking in her very fashionable Ugg boots.

I notice her eyes widen in delight as a tall, attractive guard appears from a small room at the back of the station.

'It's a beautiful day out there,' he says. 'What brings you to this part of the world?'

Ava turns subtly towards me and rolls her eyes. Is it that obvious that we're intimidated city folk released to the wilds of the country for the day?

'We want to report an attempted murder,' I say, having second thoughts before the sentence even leaves my mouth.

'Yes,' Ava concurs pathetically, with excessive nodding.

The guard's mannerisms change completely, and he suddenly becomes impressively official and professional.

'Attempted murder,' he echoes.

'Yes,' Ava replies, a stammer creeping into her voice.

The Garda quickly looks behind him and beckons for a colleague's assistance.

'All right, I'm going to need you to make a statement,' he explains kindly. 'Have you been hurt?'

'No,' I quickly answer. 'He hasn't actually done anything, yet.'

'Yeah, but he wants to,' Ava is fast to insist.

'Who?' the guard asks, sounding confused.

I nod. 'It's my husband.'

'Your husband is an attempted murderer?' the second guard states as he reaches us. He's a humourous cliché of a long-serving, country-stationed policeman. He's well built but carries a few noticeable, extra pounds. A fresh, yellowish stain dots on the collar of his uniform. I can smell fried eggs, and the culprit, a half-eaten breakfast roll, rests on the desk. It's hard to take his sloppy appearance seriously. He stands beside the handsome, young guard, his bald head almost in line with the young guard's shoulder. They're a comical pair. They look like they've just arrived back from a Laurel and Hardy look-alike convention. It's obvious they don't get many serious crimes reported in their station, as they both looked as uncomfortable as we are.

I glance at Ava to see if she has noticed their strange appearance also, but she's too busy drooling over Officer Dreamy. I smile sadly to myself as I realise how much I miss Mark. He would have been silently laughing along with me. My chest tightens as the stark realisation that I will never share another joke with him again hits me. After this, there is no hope for us ever recovering. No one likes a joke that starts with 'do you remember that time I had you arrested for attempted murder...'

'Okay, love,' the shorter guard says after an exaggerated, awkward silence. 'So, firstly can I have your name please?'

'I'm Laura Kavanagh.'

'Pleased to meet you, Laura. I'm Sergeant David Clancy.' He smiles and extends his hand.

I reluctantly shake his greasy hand. He has kindness in his eyes and his subtle smile puts my shattered nerves at little at ease.

'Okay, Laura, can I have your address please?'

'146 Ballyview road, Lucan, County Dublin.'

'Laura Kavanagh?' the younger guard says, questioning my name oddly. He repeats my name at least twice more as if he needs to clear a bad cough from his chest. His eyes are burning into me, and I feel horribly self-aware.

'Yes,' I confirm irritated and uncomfortable by his approach.

'I recognise that name,' he says.

The sergeant doesn't say a word as he takes his attention from me and turns it towards the younger guard.

'Yes, I remember now,' the young guard says finally. An exaggerated smile pulls his lips into an unflattering position. Suddenly, I don't find him attractive anymore.

'I remember reading your story in the papers not so long ago. I'm very sorry for your troubles.'

'Thank you,' I reply, surprised.

I didn't know the accident had been reported on. It must have been a slow news day. I turn to Ava who is shaking her head. I guess I must have been in a coma for my five minutes of fame.

The sergeant's eyes narrow and his expression sours. And, without words, he tells the younger guard that he'll take it from here. The young guard takes the not-so-subtle hint and walks away.

'Sorry, love,' the sergeant says, turning back to face me. 'I swear that young fella's gob is the biggest part of him. Please continue. Tell me why you are so concerned about your safety.'

'My husband is having an affair with our neighbour, and they've tried to poison me,' I blurt without drawing a breath.

The sergeant nods sympathetically.

'Okay,' he says softly. 'This is a very serious matter.'

124

'I know,' I eagerly agree.

I caught Ava flirting with the younger Garda out of the corner of my eye. She's rubbing one foot on the back of her opposite calf and twirling a soft curl around her baby finger. She's the textbook opposite of helpful. In fact, she's a bloody distraction.

'Has your husband regularly shown signs of violent behaviour in the past?' Sergeant Clancy continues. 'That's a nasty gash on your hand.'

I clasp my hands together instinctively. 'No, Mark's not like that...' I pause for a moment and wonder why, after everything that's happened, it's still my natural instinct to defend my husband. *Why am I here?*

'I mean, no, this is the first time he has tried to hurt me. But I overheard him talking about poisoning me before.'

'Did you report it then?' the sergeant asks.

'No.'

'Can I ask why not?' the younger guard asks rejoining the conversation to the humorous annoyance of his superior.

His tone is accusatory, and I dislike him very much now.

'I'm not sure if that's exactly what he meant,' I explain.

'You're not sure if he wanted to poison you or not?' Sergeant Clancy says. The kindness is slowly fading from his eyes, replaced with frustration.

'He didn't actually say he wanted to poison me...but...but...but I know that's what he was talking about.'

I'm embarrassed by how pathetic my story sounds. I'm struggling to take myself seriously; how can I expect anyone else to? I know my panic is becoming noticeable as my jaw starts to twitch.

'Okay, Laura,' Sergeant Clancy says. 'We'll get a toxicology report to see what poisons we are dealing with and then take an official statement.' He's still smiling but not as kindly as before. I get the distinct impression neither policeman believes me.

I don't reply. Neither does Ava. She's too busy watching the young guard who actually snorted out loudly moments before and walked away.

'Does that all sound okay to you?' the sergeant asks. He's obviously noticed I'm distracted.

I hang my head in embarrassment before I continue. I knew how hollow my theory already sounds. If I admit that I haven't actually ingested the poison, then I've lost all hope of being taken seriously.

'Love,' Sergeant Clancy says loudly. His voice is rough and cranky now. 'Are you happy to have a blood test?'

'There's no point,' Ava says beating me to it.

The sergeant stares through me.

'I spilt it,' I admit.

'You spilt the poison?' the younger guard repeats from behind the desk before offering his attention to his breakfast roll.

'Yes, I spilt it,' I snap, furious about very obviously becoming the butt end of a joke.

'Do you think I'd be standing here to tell the talc if I had drunk it?' I threw in a rough huff at the end for dramatic effect.

'All right, Laura. Calm down. We believe you,' Sergeant Clancy says.

'Thank you,' I sob as I let my face fall tiredly into my hands.

'Yeah, but you might have a bit of trouble convincing a jury though,' the younger guard snorts.

'Stop laughing at me,' I shout abruptly.

'All right, Mystic Meg, no more laughing I promise,' he continues.

'Why don't you come back tomorrow with your tarot cards; that'll really convince us.' 'Enough,' the sergeant bellows. He tries to remain professional, but I can't miss him look away and support his stout belly with his hand as he shoulders shake from laughing silently.

'Look, Laura,' he says. 'I'm very sorry that the terrible accident has caused such a strain in your marriage. It's understandable, and I wouldn't wish something so horrible on my worst enemy. But I can't arrest your husband for attempted murder just because you are having domestic problems. I need proof. Can you get me that?'

'No,' I reply shaking my head sadly.

'Well, then I'm sorry, love, but I can't waste any more valuable police time on this nonsense.'

'Valuable police time, my arse,' I groan to Ava as we reluctantly walk towards the door. 'Helping Little Bo Peep to find her sheep and lashing into the donuts isn't a valuable use of police time.'

'Oh, did they have donuts?' Ava giggles in an attempt to lighten the atmosphere. 'I'd love a donut. I'm starving.'

It doesn't work. Nothing is going to take my mind off the fact that I'm a sitting duck. I'm certain Mark and Nicole are rethinking their strategy. It's only a matter of time before they find me. I've nowhere to hide, and no way to protect myself.

We're sluggishly reaching the car when the young guard appears, racing up behind us waving with a sheet of A4 paper in his hand.

'They must be going to help us after all,' I say with a relieved smile.

The smile is quickly wiped when I notice a blurry, black and white photo of the children and I on the page in his shaking hand. Their faces have been blacked out but mine is as clear as day.

'I knew it. You're the Lucan School Stalker,' he accuses loudly.

The what? I can't take my eyes off the page.

Ava's hands fly to her face and tears stream down her cheeks. It's not shock upsetting her, it's familiarity. *She knows this picture.*

'Well, it is you. Isn't it?' The guard stutters.

'That's my picture.' I point. 'But I really don't know why you have it or what the hell you are talking about.'

Ava is almost hysterical it's embarrassing. *What the fuck is going on?* More secrets. I suddenly felt completely alone. Is there no one I can trust? Not even Ava.

'Ava, please. Talk to me,' I plead.

She looks at me so sadly that I think her heart was going to break right there on the spot.

'It says here that you attempted to snatch a little boy from the local primary school, and you assaulted your friend when she tried to stop you.' the officer explains, running his finger over the article printed below my picture.

'Where did you get that?' Ava snaps.

I realise she's not surprised to see the photo, but she is surprised to see the guard with it.

Maybe she's on my side after all.

'All charges were dropped,' Ava continues, shaking in temper. 'How dare you use hearsay to frighten my friend? Tabloids will print anything to sell the paper. No cop should use that as evidence. You know that.'

'Hearsay?' I echo, dry retching on my own words.

Ava turns to me and takes my hands in hers. The gesture is familiar, and I know she's preparing me for some bad news.

'The papers wrote a nasty article saying you and Nicole got into a nasty argument,' Ava says softly.

'That's stupid,' I shout, flinging Ava's hands away from mine so roughly she staggers and almost falls over.

'Why would the papers care about a nobody like me? There's more to it than that. Why is everyone lying to me?'

So many different emotions grip me all fighting for space inside my body. My eyes weigh heavy. But I won't let my body fall limp just because my mind doesn't want to comprehend my reality. I shake the dizziness from my limbs. A tingle buzzes so strongly in my fingers, it stings and my knees tremble...but this time I win. I fight the darkness and push it away. Something is happening around me, and I need to understand. Everyone knows what it is, even strangers. I'm the only clueless one. It hurts to be lied to on so many levels.

'You stalked her with threating emails and texts for days and then attacked her outside your house with a piece of broken fencing,' the guard says quoting more text from the vicious article.

Ava glares at him furiously.

'That's what the papers said, but Nicole denied it all,' Ava promises.

'How could an article like this have made it to the national papers and I have no memory of any of it?'

'It was printed just days after you left the hospital. We didn't tell you about it because they printed a retraction within hours. You had enough on your mind without the stress of that added to your plate,' Ava explains.

'Is Nicole setting me up? I have a strange feeling that she was watching when the crashed happened. Like, every time I think of it Nicole is there in my mind too.'

'I don't know,' Ava admits. 'It's possible, I suppose, but I don't think she's that cunning.'

'She is. I know she is. God knows how long she's been planning this. You have to give her credit; it's very clever. She takes her time and brands me as a psycho-bitch, and then just as she has everyone convinced, she kills me off claiming self-defence. Christ, it's genius; the perfect crime.'

'Psycho-bitch?' the guard repeats. 'Well, it wouldn't take much convincing,' he tuts under his breath.

I doubt he intended for either Ava or myself to hear him, but Ava has ears that would hear a rugby player fart in an arena of chanting spectators.

Ava calls him all sorts of degrading names, but he ignores her. He's clearly much more angry that I've ripped the paper from his hands and crumpled it into a ball before throwing it back at him.

'I could have you arrested for that sort of carry on,' he bellows.

I shake my head. I can't believe squeaky-clean, super-good girl Ava has just disrespected a policeman.

'And I could complain about you badgering us. I wonder what the department would have to say about you taunting my friend here,' Ava said sternly. But it was obvious to me she was shaking inside. I really appreciated her standing up for me. I'm usually the strong one, but I'm too shocked to string two words together.

'Go on, get out of here before I really get annoyed,' he stutters like an intimidated schoolboy.

Ava and I quickly scamper into the car, knowing he's dashing inside for the support of the sergeant. We lie down on the backseat and scream dramatically at Adam to drive away quickly. Our heartbeats are beginning to slow to a normal pace when Ava's phone rings loudly and startles the hell out of us. She fumbles for what seems a lifetime in her leather jacket pocket and finally pulls out her fancy new iPhone that has given up ringing.

'Who was it,' I ask?'

'Mark,' Ava says.

My hands fly to my face. 'Do you think he's looking for us?'

'Of course, he's bloody looking for us. Adam and I literally kidnapped you.'

'You can't kidnap someone who goes with you of their own free will,' I reassure.

'But you didn't,' Ava says shaking her head. 'You were unconscious when we took you.'

'You saved me.'

'It doesn't matter if we did or not. Doctor Hammond was about to take you back to the hospital and we got in the way of that. Adam, you were right. We never should have come near a police station. I'm surprised they didn't arrest me. Oh God, Laura, I'm so scared.'

'Stop it, Ava, you're freaking me out.' My lips quiver and I hold my mouth open a little, aware that if I close it my teeth will chatter. 'We're not the ones who need to be arrested.'

'Yeah, you and I know that but the cops don't. Jesus, Laura, Mark has a doctor on his side. We're never going to win. We have to get the hell out of here.'

'Where can we go?' I whisper.

'New York,' Ava says.

Chapter Fifteen

At the country cottage, Ava paces the floor in an attempt at wearing the carpet threadbare. Adam is sitting in an armchair by the fireplace. His left ankle is resting on his right knee and his thumb and finger are stroking his chin. He's studying me insistently. Gaging my every breath. I'm certain he detests me for dragging Ava into this mess. What he doesn't know is that I hate myself just as much.

'What good is running away going to achieve?' Adam finally says. 'America is a crazy notion. A pipedream.'

Christ, I hate him so much that I just want to slap him across the face. But I don't, of course. For Ava's sake.

'Laura isn't safe here,' Ava explains surprisingly calmly.

'Laura, c'mon. See sense, for fuck's sake,' Adam says. He obviously wants to pick his argument with me and not Ava.

'What's your problem?' I snap no longer able to control my frustration.

Ava places her hand firmly on my shoulder, and I know it's not my place to say more.

'This doesn't have to be your problem, Adam. You can walk away now. No one gets hurt.' Ava replied softly.

'My problem?' Adam snaps, ignoring how his anger makes tears pour down Ava's cheeks.

I stare at the ground. I'm too embarrassed to make eye contact with either of them. Ava and Adam may not have the best relationship in the world lately, but I hate being the cause of another argument between them. It seems lately that no matter what I do, World War III breaks out around me.

'Laura has always been there for me. I'm going to be there for her now. I have to do this,' Ava insists as she flings her arms around me. She shakes and quivers, and I soon realise she needs the hug more than I do.

'New York,' Adam says. 'Of all the places, you want to go there. Are you looking for trouble?'

What's wrong with New York? I suddenly realise I'm missing the deeper point behind the heated conversation. Adam isn't angry with me. I am not privileged to the reason why he is upset. I can't help shaking my head.

'That's my prerogative,' Ava snaps. 'I have a mind of my own, and a body of my own, for that matter. I choose what I do with it and where I take it.'

Adam throws his arms in the air and glares at me. 'You know what? Fine! Go to damn New York. You always do what you want anyway.'

I didn't intend to interrupt their *War of the Roses* moment, but I can't listen to any more of their nonsensical rubbish. The tiny, insignificant matter of my husband trying to kill me is pressing slightly on my mind.

'Adam, if you're worried I'm putting Ava in danger, then why don't you come with us?' I suggest. I cross my fingers behind my back that he won't take us up on the offer to tag along. Seven hours flying across the Atlantic beside that insufferable jerk and I would beg Mark to kill me at the other end.

'Laura, don't talk such crap,' Adam growls.

'Excuse me,' I yell, waving my finger widely in his face like an enthusiastic guest on Jeremy Kyle. 'I'm not talking crap, Adam. Thank you very much. I'm freaking the fuck out here, and I'm just trying to be polite, when all I give a shit about is getting the hell out of here alive.'

'Oh, shut up,' Adam rudely instructs.

Ava glares open mouthed at him. Resentment boils in her eyes. This obnoxious attitude is a new low, even for Adam.

'I'm very sorry if my survival is an inconvenience for you,' I blurt out.

'Are you for fucking real? Can you think of anyone other than yourself for just one minute? Maybe other people have stuff on their mind. Maybe we don't give a shit that you think your husband is bonking some blonde bombshell.'

I recoil in shock. I'm too upset to retaliate. Heartache churns in my stomach, and if I could be physically sick all over his granny's hideously floral couch, I would be.

'I'm surprised the poor bastard has put up with your high-maintenance ass for as long as he has,' Adam continues.

Ava grabs her coat off the couch. 'Let's go,' she says as she wrestles with my limp body in a pitiful attempt to help me into my chair. Adam doesn't offer to help. He stares at us. His face is as puce as a well-slapped backside.

'This is completely crazy,' he says pointing towards me. 'Just crazy. Look at you. You can't even get up off the couch, but you're going to manage to run away to America.'

Ava doesn't respond. She's too determined to get the hell out of there; nothing is going to delay us any longer.

'If you leave now, then I won't be here when you get back,' Adam shouts after us.

'I won't be coming back here,' Ava snorts.

Adam looks around the cluttered old cottage and stomps his foot in frustration when he realises how wrong his attempt at a dramatic ultimatum has gone. 'I won't be back at my apartment either,' he says with an arrogant toss of his head. 'I can't do this anymore. I can't pretend as if everything is okay.'

'Okay, Adam. Goodbye,' Ava snorts dryly as she slams the sitting room door behind us leaving Adam standing alone with his mouth gaping. This time she means it. This time I know they're finally broken.

'Damn it,' Ava grumbles loudly. 'Damn it to hell.'

'What's wrong?' I ask, feeling stupid for asking such a general question at that moment.

'I left the bloody car keys on the coffee table. How can I go back for them after that outburst?'

I start to laugh. I laugh so hard I worry I'll lose full bladder control. Perhaps it's a combination of fear and just plain exhaustion, but the laughter continues to spill loudly out of my mouth. I'm bordering on hysterics. But I'm laughing alone. Ava is motionless. It's almost annoying watching her stand like a zombie. I wait for her to snap out of it, but after five minutes into her trance, I'm begging to worry that her heart was breaking on the spot. Oh God, she's going to change her mind. She'll stay and Mark will find us. *Oh God, oh God.*

I can hear the muffled sounds of the television coming through the door. Adam had obviously finished sulking and sat down to relax. I wish we were still sitting in front of the nice cosy fire. Even though we are in the hall of the old cottage, I feel incredibly vulnerable and exposed without Adam beside us to protect us. The vertical glass panels framing each side of the front door are large enough to make hiding almost impossible. I shudder at the thoughts of who may be outside watching and waiting for us.

'Just go back in and get the keys,' I say.

'No,' Ava snaps, clearly furious that I would even suggest such a thing. 'There's a spare set somewhere. Let's just look for those.'

'Fine.'

'By all means, Laura, if you have a better idea, I'd love to hear it. Maybe we'll just hitch a lift to town on the back of a Massey Ferguson.'

I ignore Ava's sarcasm. She's entitled to be pissed off because I'm dragging her into hell. She just lost her boyfriend because she was trying to protect me.

Ava races into the small, cluttered kitchenette and begins upturning pots and pans and slamming cupboards. *Is she making noise on purpose?* Adam turns the volume on the telly to an uncomfortably loud point and chooses to completely ignore Ava's dissection of the kitchen.

Seconds seem to tick by like hours as I wait in an alcove between the hall and kitchen. I can't edge any further to help Ava's search as the step connecting the two rooms is just too steep to navigate. I constantly keep one eye on the frosted glass by the front door that exposes us. I can't focus properly because of the nervous twitch that's causing my eyes to blink so fast I think they'll fall out of my head as they break the sound barrier. I stare at the blurry cows in the field opposite. They seem to look at me with sympathy. If only my life was as simple as theirs was. Then again, chewing grass all day and walking around in each other's shit can't be much fun. That's when it crystalizes in my head. There's just no pleasing me. Adam is in some ways right; I *am* high maintenance. But I'm not the total bitch he's making me out to be. I'm a great mother and no matter what my faults are, no one has the right to take my children away from me.

I notice the handle on the sitting room door creak, and in a blind panic, I force my chair down the rickety steps that have held me back until now. I manage to clear it in one swift motion and I take a moment to look back and commend myself for the achievement. I startle Ava and she drops a large frying pan on her toes.

'Ouch, ouch, ouch,' she cries as she hops around gripping her foot in her hand and strutting like a one legged chicken dancing to The Black Eyed Peas.

'Adam's left the sitting room,' I whisper. 'We should grab the keys now.'

'Yeah, good idea,' Ava agrees and darts past me.

I'm alone again. *Damn this bloody chair.* I curse under my breath as I look at the steps that tease me. Going down was one thing, but I have no hope of getting back up.

Ava arrives back beside me within seconds. I don't like her expression.

'Did you get the keys?' I ask.

'The keys?' she echoes.

'Yeah you know small little silver things. They open doors, start cars, that sort of thing.'

'Oh, the keys. I forgot the keys.'

'What? You just went to get them.'

My heart sinks. Without the keys, were we going nowhere. I wonder if deep down Ava doesn't want to go. Forgetting the keys might be her way of attempting to repair things with Adam. But the lines in her face scream more than just heartache. She has fear in her expression. I recognise it because I see that same face every time I look in the mirror lately.

'Ava, are you okay? You're acting weird.'

Ava shakes her head.

'Did you see Adam? Did he say something to upset you?'

'Yeah, kind of.'

'What did he say?' *Christ, that guy is such a dickhead.* 'Whatever it was, it wasn't worth the breath he wasted on saying it. Don't let him get to you.'

'He wasn't talking to me. I overheard him on the phone.'

'Who was he talking to?' I ask reluctantly, remembering the last time I overheard a phone conversation.

'I don't know, but whoever it was he was giving them the address of the cottage and some very detailed directions.'

I start to quiver. At first, I think it's the cold finally gnawing its way through my tweed jacket, but deep down, I know it's panic. It's a feeling that's unfortunately becoming way too familiar.

'Oh Christ, you don't think he called the cops, do you? They're already pissed off with us over earlier. If Doctor Hammond has reported me missing, then they'll think you kidnapped me.'

'Laura, stop. That won't happen. You're not missing. You're a grown woman. You can go where you like. This has nothing to do with the police.'

'Well, who was he talking to then?'

'I'm not sure. Somebody he knows, I think.'

Mark?

Ava bends down to be close to me and takes my hand in hers. I know I'm not going to like whatever I hear next.

'I think he was talking to Nicole.'

I close my eyes. *He wouldn't do something like that*, I reassure myself. Even Adam isn't that big a bastard. Unless he's in on it, too. *Oh God*. 'Are you sure?'

'No.' Ava shakes her head. 'Not one hundred percent, but I overheard enough to know we really need to get out of here. Now.'

Ava flings open the door off the kitchenette and the sting of the icy outside air blasts us in the face. I glare down the long country lane. It winds like a corkscrew. In the hours we've spent at the cottage, I've only seen one tractor and a lonely lost sheep pass by. It would take us at least an hour to make it back to the village by foot, and by that time, Mark and Nicole may have reached us.

'Oh God, Laura,' Ava says between loud terrified sighs. 'Adam has just landed us a death sentence. I don't see how we can get away now.'

She sits on the wet ground and begins to cry.

'Oh no, please don't fall apart on me,' I beg. 'I can't be strong on my own.'

'I'm sorry,' Ava cries shaking her weary head. 'I tried so hard to help you. I just want to be a good friend, and I have only made things way worse for you.'

'You are a good friend. I love you to bits. We'll be okay, you'll see.'

Loud vibrating rings from my phone interrupt my courage-building speech. I fumble in my pocket to find it.

'It's Mark,' I say, almost dropping the phone.

I clutch my chest and tug my clothes away from my skin. I'm suddenly way too hot and breathing is hurting my throat. 'What will I do?' I yelp.

'Answer it,' Ava insists.

'No way.'

'Answer it,' she shouts. 'We can find out where he is.'

'As if he is going to tell us that.'

What the hell did Ava think Mark was going to say? *'I'm just coming off the main road; I'll be there to kill you in about five minutes. Stay where you are.'*

The ringing stops and eerie silence hangs in the air.

'There's a voice message,' Ava announces, interrupting my thoughts.

I can't listen. I offer Ava my phone. She doesn't take it, and I know she's freaking out just as much as I am.

'Put it on speaker,' Ava suggests. 'We'll listen together.'

My fingers quiver as I struggle to press the digits on my phone.

'You have one new message.
To delete messages while listening press five.
Received today at four fifteen pm…'

'Hey…' I cover my ears with my hands as soon as I hear Mark's familiar voice. And I watch as Ava listens inventively, her face falling.

'What did he say?' I ask

'Nothing much,' Ava says, her pale face and whitish lips belying her.

'You were listening to him say nothing for a very long time,' I say.

141

I can feel the familiar toil of suspicion grab hold of me. Ava is a threat, again. I dismiss the foolish notion as quickly as I think of it. She's not lying to me; she's protecting me.

'It was lies, just lots of lies,' Ava says unconvincingly. 'It's good you didn't hear that crap.'

I grab my phone tight in my hand and stuff it back into my handbag so roughly I hurt my fingers. 'Fuck him,'

Ava flings off her high-heel boots and winces as the ice-cold ground stings through her socks. She doesn't falter. She takes position behind my wheelchair, and we both prepare ourselves to charge down the laneway. We're not giving up without a fight.

We've barely passed the gate when Adam is fast catching up with us from behind.

Ava stops and stands still as he repeatedly calls out my name. We both know there's no point running; he's faster and stronger than both of us combined.

'You called Nicole, you jerk,' I scream in a frightening display of temper. Just like last night outside the hotel with the teenagers.

'Nicole called me.'

'It doesn't matter who called who,' I argue. 'You told her where to find us.'

'I had to tell her.'

'No, you fucking didn't. Whose side are you on?'

'There are no sides, Laura. I just want to help you.'

'You're a liar. Have you any idea what you've done? Why aren't you taking this seriously? They'll kill you too,' I warn. 'None of us are safe now.'

'Are you really that stupid?' Adam asks, inappropriately bordering on laughing.

What the fuck?

'You're the stupid one,' I cry with childish retaliation.

'How do you think you were going to get your passport if Mark and Nicole are still hanging around the house? I had to draw them out somehow, didn't I?'

I stare at Ava. Suddenly, Adam is making sense again. I'd completely forgotten about needing a passport and a visa. Ava had hers from her business trip to Boston a few months ago, but I've never been to the States before. I didn't have one.

'Do I have to sign papers or do something online before I can go to America; isn't there some form you need to sort out?' I blurt as if I'm the first tourist to ever enter the United States.

'That's all sorted,' Adam assured. 'But you need to leave now if you don't want to bump into Mark and Nicole. They aren't far from here, and your flight leaves tonight.'

I want to argue that my problems are a little greater than the awkwardness of bumping into my cheating husband, but Adam is doing me a favour here. One he really doesn't have to. I hold my tongue, and Ava doesn't say anything either. For the first time in her life, I think she's actually at a loss for words. She kisses Adam and wraps her arms around his neck, but he must still be angry and hurt because he doesn't hold her or kiss her back.

Chapter Sixteen

I look at the cluttered kitchen island. Half a spilled smoothie, some randomly scattered cornflakes, and a few spoons of uneaten raspberry yogurt line the worktop. A couple of pairs of pyjama bottoms were lying on the kitchen tiles and a lost runner peeks out from underneath the corner of one crumpled leg. I know the countertops would never clean themselves, but every morning, I relentlessly stare for ages at the mess and hope it will just disappear in the next blink. And every morning, after a million and one other chores take precedence, I clean the filthy kitchen, all the while wondering what my life would be like if I still had my career. I daydream about office chats around the water cooler and about dressing in flattering pencil skirts with flawless makeup. My reality is very different; reruns of *Oprah*, an old pair of oversized tracksuit bottoms, and some dried porridge instead of eye shadow.

When Mark and I found out that I was pregnant for the first time, we raided our savings account. We made a mad dash to the nearest baby store and bought all the most ridiculously overpriced baby gadgets we could pack into the car. It was an exciting time. Even though I was scared shitless that I didn't have a clue how to be a mother, I was embracing the role. However, three months of nonstop puking, swollen ankles, and stretch marks later, I knew I wasn't going to be one those women who earned the yummy mummy title.

I was initially horrified by Mark's suggestion that we should hire a nanny, and the implication that I couldn't hack it alone.

But the lack of sleep and few too many headaches had me eagerly agreeing to accept help. A little to my disappointment, the interview process was long and drawn out. I was hoping for someone with a flying umbrella, who sang songs that magically sucked you up the chimney. Instead, I was facing a cranky headmistress in a dodgy black suit who looked like she could eat children for breakfast. I needed Mary Poppins not Mrs. Trunchbull. When Ava agreed to take a morning off work and go over an interview trial run with me, I could have kissed her.

'I'll just observe this morning,' Ava says, giggling as she struggles to stay in character.

'Come in, come in,' I insist, ushering her through to the hall.

'Oh, watch the Power Ranger on the floor...sorry...and the mashed banana there by the radiator,' I say, embarrassed by the clutter paving the way to the kitchen.

'It's not usually this messy,' I lie, knowing full well Ava is used to seeing my house exactly like this. 'I just slept it out this morning.'

'Not bad.' Ava smiles. 'I almost believed that.'

'Stop it.' I laugh. 'You don't know me, remember.'

Ava winks. 'Got it.'

Mayhem at a climax, we are finally ready to leave the house. I quickly swing the door shut behind us leaving my scarf sacrificed in the hard slam. I didn't have the time to go back to rescue it. It would have to remain dangling there signalling to the neighbours that another Monday morning has gotten off to a shaky start. I drive out the gate running the usual morning checklist over in my head.

Kids in the car - check

Seat belts fastened - check

School bag — check

Lunchbox – check

No time to wipe yogurt stain from leg of trousers – check

Excessive high-pitched shouting from uncooperative children – check

Sanity almost lost – check

And we are ready for another day of madness.

*I kiss a grumpy little boy goodbye and wait at the school gates until I
see him go in the classroom door. I sigh heavily before the usual procession
of a nod and wave to the other equally flummoxed parents making a last-
minute dash to the classroom door. A sneaky smile creeps across my face
with the relief of watching others race by, even later for school than we are.*

*I sit back in the car and breathe a sigh of relief. Another morning
started well but, as usual, slid quickly downhill. I grip the steering wheel
tightly and bang my forehead gently against the cold leather. Tomorrow will
be different, I promise myself. It's the same promise I make to myself every
morning.*

~~~

But this time, it's a promise that's kept. Tomorrow was
different, so different, in fact, that it has changed my life
forever. Guilt thunders through my veins. Every cross word
spoken, every missed opportunity for a hug, every time I was
apart from the kids for five minutes is deeply regretted. A
glimpse of a very lonely future filled with the pain of missed
opportunity eats away at my aching heart.

'Laura, Laura,' Ava calls as she tugs at my jumper.

I looked up from the spot I'm staring at, possibly without
blinking for a long time. My eyes finally focus, and I remember
we're in the airport and the morning of the accident is just a
distant memory now.

'Laura, snap out of it,' Ava says tugging harder. 'You're
daydreaming, again.'

'Sorry,' I quickly apologise. 'I was miles away.'

'I can see that. Is everything okay?'

'Not really. I was thinking about the kids.'

'Oh.'

'It's okay. I'm okay.'

'Look.' Ava points towards the flight check-in desk in front of us. 'We're next in the queue and soon we'll be thousands of miles away from Mark and Nicole.'

'And thousands of miles away from the kids, too.'

Ava sighs. 'Yeah…but only for a little while.'

I close my eyes. *Only for a little while, only for a little while.* I repeat the mantra as I return to staring into space.

'God, I just love the airport. Do you?' Ava says sounding giddily excited about our sudden adventure to the Big Apple.

I wish I could share her enthusiasm.

'I miss them, Ava. I miss them every second of every day.'

Ava's face falls. 'I'm so sorry, Laura. But leaving is the only way. You know that?'

'Yeah, I know, but it doesn't make it suck any less.'

'I *do* understand how hard it must be for you being apart from the kids,' Ava says gently rubbing my back.

I know she's trying to be supportive in an impossible situation, but it's the opposite of helpful.

'I don't mean to be rude, but please don't patronise me by saying you understand. You don't have any kids; you couldn't possibly begin to know what I'm going through.'

'I…I…I'm sorry, Laura. I just don't know what to say.'

'I understand,' Adam interrupts. 'I always wanted kids.'

I'd drifted so far into my imagination that I had almost forgotten he was there. I turn my head to look up at Adam

147

who's standing beside me. Adam is a tall guy, at least six one or two, but today he looks shorter, as if the stress I'm causing has chipped a couple of inches off him.

'I really appreciate your help. I know I am not making it obvious, but I am so grateful to you. But honestly, no matter how hard I try to explain, you will never understand how I feel,' I insist, forcing myself to use as gentle a tone as possible even though I just wanted to scream until my throat was raw and no more sound comes out.

'A baby isn't always easy,' Adam says. 'Ava and I were trying for ages before…'

I'm so shocked that I cut across him before he finishes. 'A baby? Really?'

Ava smiles brightly and nods.

'That's great news,' I say genuinely delighted and perhaps a little worried about how Adam's genes will come out when inflicted upon the next generation.

'Why didn't you tell me?'

'I wanted to, but you had a lot of your own stuff going on. I didn't want to throw my problems at you, too,' Ava explains a little unexpectedly sad.

'What problems?' I ask confused.

Ava stares at the ground. She distracts herself from the seriousness of the conversation by pointing her toe and squiggling imaginary circles on the floor with her foot.

'A baby is not a problem. A bit of a shock to the system, but so is a bad haircut and you've had more than your share of those,' I tease. 'I'm sure you guys will cope just fine.'

'Well, Adam wasn't sure he was ready to be a dad,' Ava stutters.

I glare at Adam. Sometimes, I wonder if Adam is sure he even wants to be a grown-up. He returns my glare and doesn't flinch. He clearly isn't even remotely intimidated. Luckily for Adam, a twitch is all the strength my leg can muster. It wants so badly to take on a life of its own and wedge itself smack-bang in the middle of his crown jewels.

I'm delighted Ava is going to be a mother. She adores kids and a little baby would be very lucky to have a mother that wonderful. I have to put my disapproval of Adam aside and be supportive. After all, he has been a great help to me in the last few days. He's proven he can be resourceful when necessary. Maybe the news that he's going to be a father soon has finally helped him to mature.

'Laura, I really don't want to talk about this,' Adam snaps, strangely upset. 'It's, it's just too hard.'

Adam's attitude annoys me. I can discuss anything I want to with my best friend. He doesn't own her. I can just imagine how controlling he will be once the baby arrives. It's little wonder Ava is so eager to flee to New York. She needs some space, maybe now more than ever.

Suddenly, everything adds up in my head. 'Oh God,' I stutter. 'Is that what you were arguing about back at the cottage? The baby?'

'Arguing?' Adam repeats sounding coy.

'I thought you were arguing about helping me,' I say. My cheeks sting scarlet, and I'm mortified. I completely misread the situation. I look at Ava and take a moment to process. Is she leaving Adam? 'I don't think running off to New York will solve any problems,' I say. 'What if something happens?'

'Exactly,' Adam agrees enthusiastically. 'You're finally taking sense.'

'I'm not going to listen to either of you. I'm only three months along. Somehow I don't think we have to worry about me going into labour on the plane.'

I smile. Ava is determined to save me, and I know I would regret it if I denied her the opportunity.

'Okay, but I'm not holding your hair back if you puke your way across the Atlantic,' I joke.

Ava returns my smile, and in spite of everything, at that small moment, I was happy. Of course, when I realise I'm smiling, guilt immediately thunders in and I'm forced back into pouting and feeling miserable.

'Lorcan,' Adam adds, cutting through the silence that has fallen over us. 'That's a name I like.'

'Pardon?' I say, briefly startled by a strange familiarity of the name.

My concentration levels are pitiful. I'm constantly battling to keep up with my overactive imagination, and the reality around me is slipping by unnoticed.

'Adam, don't,' Ava says slapping her hand roughly across his chest. 'We haven't decided on any names yet. We don't even know if it's a girl or a boy.'

'Lorcan. Do you like it? Lor-can,' Adam asks, his eyes narrow as they glare at me like glazed almonds.

'Adam, please? I asked you to leave it,' Ava reminds him.

'I'm just curious to see what you think, Laura. You're a mother; I wonder if you would use that name yourself.'

His face is strangely contorted and there's an odd, almost overly enthusiastic forcefulness hanging on his every word. His simple words are indirectly vicious. But I am at a loss to unravel whatever nastiness his sentences hides.

'It's lovely,' I finally say, brushing off this nonsense as I pick up my almost empty bag and follow Ava's lead to the check-in desk. I long for a brick wall to beat my exhausted head against, but I will have to settle for a pillow on a transatlantic flight.

'Laura. Oh, my gosh, how are you?' the smiling lady behind the check-in desk asks, as she glances over my passport.

'I'm very well, thank you, Bernadette.' I reply glancing at her nametag. I'm too exhausted to add a smile.

'How's everyone at home?' she asks.

I'm not too exhausted to frown. *What the hell kind of question is that?* It's almost ten pm, and I haven't eaten all day. I'm in no mood for this shit.

'Are you getting a little holiday?' she continues. 'You're dead right. A few days away is probably just what you need right now.'

I turn to Ava. She's looking at me blankly, waiting for an explanation. Or an introduction. Ava must think with Bernadette's strange questions that we're acquainted.

I roll my shoulders.

Bernadette finally abandons her plan to be friendly and stops chatting to me like a giddy schoolgirl. She professionally runs through the standard security questions and weighs and tags our bags.

'Thank you,' I murmur, my throat as dry as an unbuttered cream cracker.

I smile at Ava as I watch our suitcases trundle along the conveyor belt and out of sight. It's hard to decipher between worry and fear, but to my surprise, there's a hint of excitement bubbling about in my tummy, too.

'Take care now, we're all thinking of you,' Bernadette says at one final attempt to extract a smile from my expression of cold stone.

'Who's we all?' Ava whispers subtly.

I shake my head. 'I have no idea!'

'Tell Mark I was asking for him, won't you? I haven't seen him since I heard about your terrible loss. If there is anything I can do, then just please let me know. The whole community is here to help,' Bernadette adds. 'I tried to call you a few times. I thought maybe we could grab a coffee, but Mark said you weren't up to talking to anyone. I totally understand.'

A chill runs the length of my spine. *Who is this woman?* How does she know so much about me? She even knew about my miscarriage. *Jesus.* Nobody knew about that besides Ava. Unless Mark told people. Why would he talk about something so personal? *Oh God.*

I've been housebound for so long that I have no idea what else he may be telling the neighbourhood. Is he telling people that I'm ill? If I am not taking anyone's calls, then there would be no one to notice when I disappear. There's so much more to Mark and Nicole's plan than I first thought. I'm once again terrified that I have yet to discover many more layers to their plot.

I scrutinise every inch of Bernadette. She's pretty in a conventional sense. She's my age, maybe a year or two older, and she looks like a genuinely nice person. The type of person you could easily make friends with, but she isn't my friend. *Is she?*

I concentrate hard for a few moments, searching for any hint of recognition. A brief familiarity flickers in the depths of my mind. Her cheeks; I know her rosy cheeks. We've laughed together – I think. Yes, a few times, over coffee and wine. I eagerly begin conjure a foggy memory when my entire body starts to shake mercilessly. *Not again.* At the prospect of unravelling the slightest hint of a past I have forgotten, my brain panics and instantly shuts down, refusing me access to the information. *Fight it. Fight it this time.*

'Laura, wake up,' Ava commands as she lightly slaps each of my cheeks in turn.

My face stings and I groggily rub my cool palms over the ache.

'Oh God,' I say as I opened my eyes.

'You fainted again,' she explains.

Again.

I rub my eyes and look around. My wheelchair is on its side, the upper wheel spinning slowly. My knees are curled on my chest, and I'm slouched so far forward the ground is only inches from my face. Adam's arms are firmly in place underneath my shoulders. His strength is the only thing preventing me from colliding with the floor. Bernadette has left the check-in desk and is standing beside us. A noisy crowd is gathering around us, attracted by the commotion. Awwing and gasping as though my helplessness is a show for their entertainment.

'Are you okay?' Bernadette whispers softly.

'I think so.' I nod, too confused to be embarrassed.

It is a physical struggle to sit upright, and I could feel the eyes of every onlooker burn into my wilting spine.

I noticed Ava's face fall as a pair of security guards approach to investigate the scene. I turn to Adam for reassurance, but the men's arrival has equally shaken him. My heart pounds. Any small security delay could mean the difference between our successful escape and the terror of being found. I haven't done anything wrong, but I feel like a fugitive on the run.

Bernadette must have sensed our anxiety because she presses her hand supportively on my shoulder then calmly walks forward.

'It's all right, guys. This lady is my neighbour. She's just a bit nervous about flying. I think it all got the better of her for a moment. Nothing to worry about,' Bernadette explains to the men who are now uncomfortably close to us.

'Thanks.' I smile, grateful that Bernadette has so easily defused the awkward situation.

'No problem.' She winks. 'But I'm holding you to that coffee, okay?'

She bends down, takes both my hands in hers, and lifts them close to her chest. I don't flinch. The gesture feels strangely familiar.

'Please take care of yourself. Don't be a stranger any longer?' she pleads with tears glistening in her eyes.

I convincingly promise to keep in touch, although I still have no idea who she is.

I desperately race to retreat from the drama of the scene I've caused. I lunge the full force of my body into my arms as I churn the metal wheels of my chair forward. Rushing awkwardly through the door of the disabled toilet, I will my shaking fingers to cooperate as I bolt the door behind me.

I fling my large handbag across my knee and search for my phone. I can't find it. I catch the leather strap in frustration and swing the bag upside down, angrily shaking the contents to the floor. My lipstick case shatters in the fall and light pink smudges across the other items littering the ground. I stare at the mess before me. It's like a mocking symbol of the hysteria my life has become. My phone sits innocently on the pile and I reach to grasp it, falling awkwardly to the floor. I don't notice the pain of landing crumpled with both my knees twisted behind me. I just concentrate on the screen of my phone. I scroll through my contacts not sure what clarity I'm expecting to find. There it is. Bernadette Joyce +353867697440.

'Christ,' I say out loud as I nearly drop the phone. We really are friends. How can I so easily forget someone I know? What other memories have been stripped from my mind? I shake my head pitifully. *What is happening to me?* I'm actually losing my mind... or is it being stolen from me? What has Mark done to me? I forget more and more of my past with each passing day. If I can simply erase a friend from existence in my mind, then what's next? Will I wake up some morning and just no longer remember who I am? Or even more terrifyingly, will I suddenly forget the children? Will I let Mark and Nicole win without any memory of the fight?

I ignore the knocking on the door as I stare at myself in the slightly dirty mirror. I hardly recognise the reflection. I've become a stranger in my own body. Something awful is happening to me and I don't know how to stop it. The knocking grows louder and faster.

'Ava?' I call as I reach to unlock the door.

'Laura?' she shouts back.

'Yeah, it's me. I'm in here.'

'Thank God we found you. What the hell were you thinking running off like that? We didn't know where you went.'

Ava sounds weary. I'm very aware of her pregnancy now, and I know I have to put her first. I can't have her chasing me all over the place every time I flip out.

'I'm okay,' I lie. 'I was just bursting to pee. Couldn't hold it. Sorry.'

'Your flight leaves in less than hour,' Adam shouts. 'Are you still sure you want to do this?'

I glance at my watch. He's right. I've locked myself away within the confines of the bathroom for at least an hour. No wonder they're worried, and from the tone of Adam's voice, he's angry, too.

I reluctantly swing the door open and look at what I expect to be frustrated faces. I am not expecting to find them open mouthed with shock etched into their gaping jaws.

Adam passes me my ticket reluctantly. He looks as though he has a thousand things he wants to say, but every time he opens his mouth, no words come out.

'Let's go,' I say with a smile so forced that I hear my jaw crack.

Ava stands motionless in front of me, blocking the way. She's pointing and staring.

I glance back into the bathroom to check I haven't left my bag behind or come out with loo roll stuck to the leg of my trousers or something.

'Laura,' Ava squeaks.

'What?' I snap uncomfortably. 'Why are you looking at me like that? It's freaking me out.'

'Look,' Adam stammers, copying Ava's pointing. 'You're standing up by yourself.'

Chapter Seventeen

I lap the ground floor of the airport twice and actually skip my way up the escalator to take in a lap of the first floor also. Adam and Ava lag behind in unison. They are united in shock. Shock is the last emotion I'm prepared to entertain. I'm too busy basking in glorious euphoria. I can walk. Real, unaided walking. One leg in front of the other, actually propelling my body forward like a regular person, walking. It's marvellous, and I never plan to stop. I begin daydreaming. I'm one step closer to getting my old life back, and I can take those steps with my own two feet. I'll have to get the kids back now. Everything is going to be okay.

After nagging me endlessly to hurry up, Ava takes what feels like forever to say goodbye to Adam. She lays her head on his shoulder and takes deep breaths. I know she's savouring his smell, but her expression is so poignant it seems like she's saying goodbye - forever. She must have kissed him at least twenty times before she finally drags herself away with tears in her eyes and an obvious lump in her throat. It's really rather upsetting to watch Adam's blasé reaction to her affection. He's too busy watching me to pay Ava any attention. He doesn't even kiss her back. But she doesn't notice, and I fight the urge to lend my unwarranted opinion. I hope it's because he's overcompensating. I understand he's worried. Anyone can see it. Stress is screaming from the tense lines of his forehead. His attempts to remain cool backfire, and he actually ends up coming off as superior and condescending.

'First sign of trouble…' he warns. 'Just pick up the phone.'

'I know, baby. I promise I will call if there's anything to worry about.' Ava smiles.

'I'll make sure she's a good girl,' I joke, hoping Adam will accept my gesture to lighten the atmosphere.

Adam rolls his eyes.

I couldn't blame him for being concerned. I'm tearing his pregnant fiancée away in a mad bid to escape my murderous husband. I feel selfish and so incredibly needy.

'Take care,' Adam says before grabbing me by the elbow and hugging me tight. It catches me off guard. My feet actually leave the ground a little bit as my body jolts back, but my arms automatically wrap around him in return and it feels good to hug him. I've spent so long consumed by indifference towards Adam that I've never allowed myself to like him or to be liked by him. It all feels so foolish now. His hug is so genuine and warm, and I've never felt such honesty from Adam before. This is the Adam Ava loves. This Adam is a million miles away from the sleazy womaniser of late. And, for a brief moment, it feels like Adam is my friend. A real friend who cares about me – not just my best friend's boyfriend who puts up with me.

Chapter Eighteen

Ava is adamant that I sit back in my wheelchair for boarding. I'm reluctant but the temptation to skip the queue is enough to convince me.

'I'll take it as far as the departure gates, but I want to walk up the steps myself,' I insist. 'It'll be a pleasant challenge for me.'

'That's fine by me, just so long as you don't exhaust yourself too much.' She smiles kindly.

I know she means well, but I'm full of energy. I don't think I will ever be tired again in my life. However, I do experience a sharp pins-and-needles sensation in the backs of my thighs, but I refuse to yield to it. In fact, I almost enjoy the uncomfortable tingle. Unpleasant as it is, it's a million times better than no feeling at all.

'Your chair will be waiting for you as soon as we land, Ms. Kavanagh,' the air hostess says as we board the huge plane.

I smile. I don't tell her that I hope I never see that piece of clunky metal ever again. 'Thank you. That's great.'

Ava and I sit on the runway in complete silence. We're both too busy pondering over all the changes in our respective lives to make conversation. I watch the air hostess wave her arms about as she stands in the aisle going over the usual flight safety precautions and exit locations. I don't pay much attention. I have an overwhelming sense of guilt; guilt because for the first time in months, I feel happy. *I shouldn't feel happy when my children aren't with me*, I tell myself. But I can't stop smiling because I have my body back. My children will be my next conquest then

I will be whole again. Now the only thing left to wish for is patience.

We shake a little in our seats as the plane thunders down the runway and smoothly ascends into the air. There's no turning back from this point. I'm officially running away. I occupy my overtaxed mind by staring out the window and challenging myself to recognise land masses below the scattered clouds.

'Something's not right,' I say suddenly, breaking sharply into Ava's daydream.

'Hmm?' she mumbles, paying little attention to me as she fiddles with her seat belt.

'There's something wrong,' I repeat.

'With the plane?' Ava squawks. Her nostrils flare instantly and her eyes are as wide as if someone is trying to shove an open umbrella up her backside.

I quickly apologise for my bad choice of phrase, remembering Ava has a fear of flying.

'Shit. No. Sorry. I mean with me, something is wrong with me,' I stutter, embarrassingly on the verge of tears.

Ava doesn't reply. She has her eyes closed, but I know she's listening.

'I've changed.'

'We all change from time to time, Laura. It's just the way life goes. You've dealt with a lot of crap lately. But look...' Ava points at the window. 'We're on our way now. It'll all be better soon.'

Ava seems so convinced that there's an easy fix to all my problems. I wish I could share her positive attitude.

'No.' I shake my head. 'There's more to this. I can't really remember who I used to be, but I know I am not that person now. I'm not normal anymore.'

'What? What do you mean? Of course, you're normal. Don't be silly.'

'I'm not. I'm so not. Normal people don't just suddenly stand up from a wheelchair and start walking again. Shit like that just doesn't happen in real life. You're either paralysed or you're not.'

'Miracles do happen, Laura.'

'Bullshit. It's not like you get up some morning, decide you've had enough of sitting on your arse and put your dancing shoes back on.'

I only stop speaking because I've run out of air. I force a huge lump of air down my throat and I'm about to continue with my rant but Ava looks bewildered. It's a long flight, and I'm aware that I'll drive Ava crazy if I moan my way across the Atlantic.

We're halfway into the flight, and I'm well into munching through my second packet of salt and vinegar Pringles before I finally give in to the discontentment of the silence. Something is holding Ava back from congratulating me on walking again, and I have to know what it is.

'Aren't you happy for me?' I ask.

Ava ignores me and continues looking past me and out the window. There isn't much to see except for the middle of big white fluffy clouds and the odd glimpse of blue sea below, but Ava stares as though she would find the answer to all life's problems spray-painted by the angels out there somewhere.

'Ava,' I call, knocking my shoulder against hers.

'I am afraid to be happy for you,' she says softly, drawing her eyes back to meet mine.

'What does that mean? Why on earth would you be afraid to be happy about anything?'

'I don't know what reaction you want from me, Laura. And if I give you the wrong one, I'm afraid you'll totally flip out at me like you do with everyone else.'

My fingers begin to twitch as though they have an independent mind, and I can't stop them. Have I really become such a bitch that people are actually watching what they say around me?

'I'm happy for you every time you walk,' Ava finally says.

Ava closes her tired eyes, turns her back to me, and prepares to drift off to sleep.

'Every time?' I ask, almost spraying a mouthful of soggy crisps at her.

Ava shoots up to sit straight and rubs her tired eyes. She obviously realises what she just said and tries to backpedal. It's no good. My mind has jammed on her words. Nothing is going to take my mind off it.

Ava's cheeks flush and she looks as though her body temperature has risen by ten degrees and is still climbing. Delicate beads of perspiration gather on the edges of her forehead.

'I was being sarcastic,' she says. 'Sorry, I know it was inappropriate. I was just trying to be funny.'

'Yeah. Fucking. Right,' I spit. This time the wall of crisps stands no chance of remaining confined to my lips. Slightly chewed crumbs project forward and hit the man sitting in front of me directly in the back of the head. I imagine he's furious as he unfolds a tissue and begins to wipe away the mess. His wife turns around to investigate. I apologise meekly and politely tolerate the long rant she throws at me. I cross my fingers that she won't call the air hostess. I'm so fragile the thoughts of a further telling off churn my stomach. Thankfully, she finally accepts my grovelling and turns back around.

I'm ready to continue interrogating Ava, but she's fallen asleep. She looks as peaceful as a baby does. I know she's pretending; when she really sleeps, she snores as loudly as the purring engine of a Formula One car.

'Ava, please? So many people have lied to me recently. I never thought you'd be one of those people . Please, I'm begging you. Just tell me?'

'This isn't the first time you've remembered how to walk. Okay!,' Ava growls without opening her eyes.

'Okay.' Her words cut through the air and hit me like a blunt knife twisting in my gut. I don't know what explanation I was waiting for. Or what explanation would have made sense, but it certainly wasn't that.

'That doesn't make any sense. Ava, please? I need more. I need to know more. I feel like I'm losing my mind here.' I exhale sharply through closed teeth. 'Where's the air hostess. Fuck, I need wine!'

'See, this is why I didn't tell you. I knew you wouldn't believe me.'

'How can I believe that?'

'Easy. You believe it because it's the truth. I'm your best friend and the person putting my neck on the line to help you. You asked me not to lie, yeah?'

I nod.

'Well, I'm not lying. Simple as.'

Her expression promises me she's being honest, but my head just won't accept something so unrealistic. *What am I supposed to say?*

'Anyway, it doesn't matter if you believe me or not. By the time this plane lands, you will have passed out at some point and not only will you forget having walked today, but you'll also forget this conversation ever happened. You always do, Laura.'

'No. That won't happen,' I shout forgetting the limited confines of the plane. 'I'm never getting back in that fucking chair again. Never.'

The familiar feelings of temper and confusion swirl around my body like a cyclone too powerful to escape. I feel darkness creep over me, and I'm afraid to blink. I don't believe Ava. I just don't. But something is screaming at me from inside not to rule out her theory. If I let myself fall asleep, then I may never get this close to an answer again. I'll just rest my eyes. I won't fall asleep. *I won't fall asleep.*

Muddled memories shoot around my head bringing with them a crippling headache. I press the palms of my hands against my aching temples; fanning my shaking fingers across my head, I softly stroke my hair. It's almost metaphorical as though my fingertips are scratching away the dark soil that buries my memories. I concentrate hard and tightly grip hold of any tiny clue I've unearthed. I cement it to my mind and scrutinise every detail before it breaks away from me and I risk forgetting all over again.

My first recollection is the night of the ball. I was distraught as I waited alone on the dark road. I remember losing my temper, and the teenagers jeering me. I was furious. A strange and overwhelming emotion had swept over me. I wasn't in control. Anger was a powerful strength and I had no desire or ability to stop it. I had somehow conjured the ability to physically run across the road to attack the group.

I bow my head. The memory is flooding my senses now, and it hurts. It crushes my chest and my lungs ache beneath the weight of my thoughts.

They called me a freak. Of course, they did because I am one. I make a mockery of paralysis. Even a group of dysfunctional teenagers could see how disgusting my behaviour was. Seeing it play out, I disgusted myself. Was I always suppressing the ability to walk? Or, was I lacking the capability to without an explosive surge of adrenaline? Either way, something is drastically wrong with me.

Next, I remember spilling my drink on Nicole. God, I was vicious. *That's not me. And if it is, it's not who I want to be.*

My hand covers my mouth. I don't want to know any more. I don't want to remember any more. But now I can't stop. My thoughts are an out of control hurricane in my mind, and there is nowhere to hide.

I remember standing in the hallway of my house. I was screaming. It scratched my throat. It was directed at Nicole. I wanted her to leave. Ava was there, too. I reached for the picture frame from the wall, grabbed it, and flung it at them. I was trying to hurt them. On purpose. I shake my head gently from side to side and pull my mind back to the here and now.

'Oh, Ava, I'm so sorry,' I apologise, turning awkwardly to look at her. 'I never meant to hurt you.'

'It's okay,' Ava whispers, half asleep. 'I know you never mean it. Anyway, I'm kind of used to it by now.'

I giggle a little at first and try to turn it into a real laugh, but it doesn't work. I'm not sure which is worse – the fact I've viciously attacked my best friend or the fact I've done it so often Ava can laugh about it now. I remember lots from the past. I've wanted memories for so long. I've waited for this moment; I've prayed for it. But now that it's finally here, I wish so hard it would go away. I'm unravelling a monster. Maybe Mark isn't so wrong to want to be rid of me. *Maybe Mark isn't the bad guy*, I think. Perhaps getting rid of me is his attempt to protect our children from the freak I've become. But I would never hurt them. No matter how frustrated I ever become, I would never take it out on the children. *Would I?* I don't recognise myself, how can I expect anyone else to understand me?

More memories seep from my brain. It's like a leaky tap inside my head, and I can't turn it off. I hold my breath as if it will save me from the horror before my closed eyes. If I don't breathe, then I don't exist. Time will stop with my lack of oxygen, I hope. And it helps for a moment. For a moment, there is only darkness. But I give in to my body's desire for air, inhale deeply, and brace myself.

I remember Mark rushing down from upstairs to protect Nicole, but it only heightened my furious rage. I caught the expensive Waterford Crystal frame from the shelf and aimed straight for him. It shatters into hundreds of tiny pieces as it collides with the timber floor. The jagged pieces of glass sparkled as they dotted across the picture of our wedding that had been dislodged from the frame in the fall.

'Am I crazy?' I ask shaking my head.

'No.' Ava turns her whole body to face me. 'You're just struggling. That's all.'

'Do you think it's whatever drugs Mark gave me? Do you think that's why I lose control?'

My desperation is obvious, and my eyes silently plead with Ava to agree with me. I need her to blame Mark, too. I need to know I am not crazy. I need Mark to be responsible for the mess I'm in because I can't deal with it if it's my own fault.

'I don't know what the answer is,' Ava admits sadly, 'but that's what we're going to New York for. We won't leave until we know all the answers, okay?'

'Okay.' I nod.

Chapter Nineteen

'Go on, Ava,' I encourage, 'I reckon you can take her down.'

Ava smiles and shakes her head. A fifth person has cut in front of us and grabbed the next available taxi while we freeze our asses off, waiting.

'See, this is why I wanted you to keep the wheelchair. We'd never have to queue like this if you were still broken.'

I grab Ava and hug her tight. A small part of me is just after her body warmth, but the majority of me is just so glad I'm still standing upright. I didn't forget our conversation on the plane, and even better, I didn't forget how to use my legs. *Progress.*

'What's this for?' Ava asks, hugging me in return.

'Just thanks.'

'Thanks for what?'

'Thanks for always being a great friend, even when I'm a pain in the ass.'

'You, a pain in the ass? Never!' Ava playfully winks and sticks her tongue out. She retracts it quickly, either embarrassed that the attractive man across the road is staring or worried that it'll get frostbite and fall off.

I look around at the sea of yellow cabs stretched out for miles on the road ahead. Layers of thick snow hide the ground, but the weather doesn't slow the hundreds of people rushing about. It's such a busy place and nothing like I'm used to, but I feel a strange sense of belonging.

I'm thousands of miles away from my life. I can be anyone I want to be here. I can be outrageously eccentric or simply slip under the radar; there are no limitations. I'm free. *But I don't want freedom.* I long to be laden down with buggies and changing bags. I want tired, screaming children racing around me 'til my head pounds. I want all the things I so often long to get a break from.

Ava doesn't notice my wallowing, and I'm glad. I promised her so many times that we would go on a girly adventure to this amazing city, but it was just another broken promise on a long list. I wasn't intentionally letting her down, but it was just that something always came up. An unexpected bill would land our way, or Mark would be swamped with work. The time was never right. The timing is most definitely worst of all now, yet here we are.

I can't feel my face. The only sign that I'm still breathing is the fog coming out my nose every few seconds. My extremities are completely numb. As an Irish person, I'm born with a God-given right to bitch about the weather, but even I don't have words to describe this degree of cold. The icy wind finds its way inside my clothes and burns into my bones. I cross my fingers that we will eventually learn the technique needed to hail a cab and actually manage to sit in it before another yuppie chatting on an unbelievably slim mobile phone plonks themselves in it first. Ava is used to traveling for work, so I can't understand why she's acting like a stunned rabbit in the headlights now. She's leaving all the negation of this place up to me.

Every time I glance across the road, I make brief eye contact with the attractive man opposite me. I quickly turn my gaze towards the ground. But I know he hasn't looked away. He's studying us with concentration. *What the hell is his problem?*

I look back up, determined to outstare him, but it's hard, since he looks so damn familiar. He's tall and seriously well dressed. Clearly money is no object for him. Maybe he's a movie star incognito or a successful Wall Street banker. I am about to call Ava's attention to him when he crosses the road and begins to walk towards us. He must have decided a taxi would be easier to get from our side. In fact, he was probably just going to take ours.

'Hi,' he says stopping right in front of us.

'Hello,' I mumble.

'You look great,' he adds.

'I'm married,' I say shakily.

He laughs.

'You look great, too,' Ava says, dropping her bag and flinging herself full force into his arms.

He must be made of titanium or something because he doesn't as much as flinch. But he does smile; there's something reassuring in his bright eyes, and despite the icy cold, I feel warm. 'Laura, do you remember Nigel?' Ava says, untangling her arms from around his neck.

I shake my head, slightly embarrassed. I spent the last ten minutes subconsciously admiring his chiselled jawline and sparkling emerald eyes. He's the nearest thing to perfection I've ever seen. If we've met before, it would be almost impossible to forget a face that beautiful.

'I'm sorry,' I apologise. 'I can't place you.'

I hoped to God that we aren't good friends or, even worse, past lovers. Maybe this man is another memory erased. Although the idea that I may have made love to such a stunning man isn't such a hideous thought.

'Don't worry,' Nigel assures. 'I've changed a lot in recent months. But I remember you, Laura. It's really good to see you.'

I blush. I'm relieved Nigel thinks I'm forgetful rather than rude, and I'm very flattered that he remembers me. I instantly like him. He's friendly and polite. I wonder why Ava hasn't mentioned him before now. Although maybe she has and, like everything else, I've simply forgotten.

'Nigel is living here in the city,' Ava explains. 'I thought we could stay at his place and save a fortune on hotel costs.'

I look at Ava with more than a little concern evident in my crumpled eyebrows. As nice as Nigel seems, I don't fancy shacking up with a stranger – especially when we don't know how long for.

'Hotels are pretty expensive here,' Nigel explains, 'and the exchange rate isn't in your favour at the moment. You're more than welcome to stay with me.'

'Laura, come on. It'll be fun. Nigel is going to take us dancing tonight,' Ava says, jumping up and down on the spot with excitement.

'Please?' Nigel asks. 'I've a nice two-bed apartment. I seldom admit this, but it can get very lonely sometimes. You'd be doing me a favour and keeping me company.'

I smile. With a face like Nigel's and a body to match, I doubt he ever gets lonely. But surprisingly, there's nothing dishonourable about him, and I find myself comfortably wanting to be his guest

'Great stuff,' Nigel says, and I think I can hear a hint of an Irish accent buried underneath his New York twang. 'This will be fun.'

I really hoped it would be. *I can have one night of fun*, I tell myself, but it's straight to work tomorrow as I start formulating a plan to get the kids back.

A shiny, black limousine pulls in close to the edge of the footpath in front of us. Ava nearly tramples me as she dashes by. She nods to the driver who has left his place behind the wheel to open the rear, passenger door. She looks back at Nigel, shrieks happily, and jumps inside. Before I have time to gather my thoughts, Ava pops her head out the door again.

'Thanks, Sam.' She giggles and ducks inside once more.

The driver doesn't reply; he just smiles.

'Come on, Laura,' Ava shouts from the comfort of what I imagine is a very spacious backseat.

I look from Nigel, back to the driver, and back to Nigel again.

It's all a little too surreal. People like me don't travel around famous cities in the back of stretch limousine. People like me take the bus because petrol prices are crippling. People like me don't flee their life, their country, their marriage. *People like me*, I tut. *I don't even know who I am anymore.*

'Please, go ahead,' Nigel politely suggests as he takes my hand and helps me to sit inside.

The car is stunning. Cream leather seats, so soft it feels like my bottom is being kissed by cotton wool. A miniature mahogany bar with a dim blue neon light acts as a confident centrepiece. Two crystal champagne glasses rest on the polished timber and beg to be drunk. Ava is sitting with her legs crossed and arms stretched out, draped over the backseat. *No wonder she loves New York.*

'It's the real stuff.' Ava chuckles, dropping her eyes to the label on the champagne bottle. 'Not like that horrible sparkling wine Adam gets on offer in the supermarket.'

I laughed. She's right; that stuff is terrible. I never know whether to drink it or use it to clean the loo.

Nigel finally scoots in beside us and joins our joking. He's easy to talk to, and I find myself chatting as though we are old friends.

'Are you hungry?' Nigel asks.

I was starving, but I didn't know whether to admit it or not. I'm afraid Nigel will suggest we stop at some outlandishly expensive restaurant and my credit card will be maxed out after half a slice of pizza.

'I'm peckish.' Ava rubs her tummy.

'Well, I'm starving,' Nigel says. 'How about we drop your bags off at my place and then grab a bite to eat?'

'Sounds good to me.' Ava nods.

I just smile. I'm too busy worrying about my finances to actually speak. A fancy restaurant would be no bother for Ava. She practically prints money herself since selling her PR company last year. Perhaps that's how she knows Nigel so well. Maybe they are involved in investments together. I'll have to ask her later.

The car stops outside an impressively large hotel, and I realise I have no idea where I am. I was so busy sipping champagne and nibbling on appetisers that tasted and smelt a bit like dirty football socks that I had completely forgotten to look out the window and admire the sights.

I enjoy the view now. The hotel is at least twenty stories high, if not more. The whole front wall is flush with the reflective glass and the view of the entire street radiates in its reflection. A large fountain centred in front sprays several jets of water high into the air every ten seconds or so.

Two porters in top hats and tails wait to greet us at the marble steps leading to reception. I cringe as I gaze at my scuffed ankle boots that badly need a polish and my comfy jeggings that have seen better days. I looked across to Ava for reassurance. She sits cross-legged, unintimidated by her lavish surroundings, sipping her champagne like a diva. She's wearing a simple navy tracksuit that's probably a one-off by some famous designer I've never heard off. Her gel nails radiate manicured perfection and not so much as a hair in her sleek ponytail strays out of place despite just getting off a plane. Although we left Ireland in a fit of blind panic, Ava still looks as though she's stepped off the pages of *Vogue*.

I shiver as I suspect we've abandoned the idea of dropping the luggage off first and are obviously going to head straight for lunch in this offensively expensive hotel. Sam opens the limo door, and I thank him as I step out, hoping the others will follow quickly behind.

'Good afternoon, Sir. It's a lovely day out there today,' one of the porters says with a grin so false he could have held a feather between his teeth and it wouldn't budge as he spoke.

'Perhaps it's lovely if you were a polar bear, but it's freezing the arse off me,' Nigel jokes.

The man's face turns bright red, and for a moment, he looks as though he's choking on the hypothetical feather.

'You're going to get me in trouble with the boss someday, Nigel,' he says between laughs and snorts.

'Nonsense,' Nigel insists. 'If the old farts who own this place can't have a laugh, then I'm not sure I wish to reside here any longer.'

'Aren't those old farts your parents,' Ava teases.

I look around in astonishment. Nigel winks cheekily at me. I couldn't tell if it's a strange joke or if he genuinely is the heir to this enormous building. It does, however, explain Nigel's opulence.

I walked through reception, slowly spinning around a couple of times to take a mental picture of the grandeur. The finely polished marble floors sparkle as they catch my reflection. Pale porcelain statues hide in subtle alcoves dotted every few meters along the walls. They are seriously ugly pieces of art, so I know they must be expensive. The lobby carpet is so thick it attempts to polish my boots as I wade through it. The slightly shrill recording playing over the lift speakers wishes us a nice day. I wonder how long it would take before listening to that every morning would start to really grate on your nerves.

'This is us,' Nigel announces as the lift stops with a slight jolt when we reach the top floor.

I follow Ava and Nigel, lagging behind.

'It's this one here,' Nigel says as he turns the key in the only door at the end of the long corridor. I wonder why Nigel's room is the only one on the entire floor. I feel decidedly uneasy about being so isolated in a strange man's hotel room. If Nigel is aware of my apprehension, then he certainly hides it well. He's an expert in politeness.

In spite of my less than fervour attitude, Nigel remains fresh-faced and enthusiastic as he swings the door open and stands back allowing Ava to enter first.

'It's okay,' she calls back beginning to get impatient waiting for me to follow. 'He won't bite, you know.'

Nigel silently follows Ava inside and leaves the door ajar for me to enter in my own time.

Deciding I feel even more anxious waiting alone in the hallway, I quickly follow the others inside and close the door behind me.

'It's a penthouse.' I gasp as the sheer class of the room I find myself in hits me.

'Yeah, well, what else did you expect to find on the top floor?' Ava asks as she ducks her head into a large diner-style fridge in the open-plan kitchen.

'It's so beautiful,' I admit.

Nigel doesn't say a word. I wonder if my reaction amuses him. He's obviously been around grandeur his whole life. I'm sure most women have a similar reaction to mine when they walk inside, so my shock is probably old news for him. The floor area is enormous. It's sparsely furnished, but tastefully so. All space is utilised to its best airy potential without appearing bare. Several different living areas are defined by a change in tile colour or a step or two leading to what is essentially a different room. The steps are small and almost unnoticeable. The only blemish on the pristine beauty of the apartment is large metal ramps. They sat noticeable and ugly at the right, extreme corner of any raised floor area. They were a vivid, dark grey, and obviously not a regular feature of the magnificent décor.

'Ramps,' I say, almost disgusted.

'Oh yes, I almost forgot about those. I had them fitted recently for you, but it looks like we won't need them after all,' Nigel explains cheerfully.

I'm painfully embarrassed. Ava obviously took the time to discuss a lot with Nigel. She managed to organise for us to be his guest and to inform him I was confined to a wheelchair. However, I am horribly disappointed that not once, not even when we struggled for conversational topics on the long flight, did she mention so much as Nigel's name to me.

'Would it be okay to freshen up?' I slur, trying to hide my temper.

'Of course,' Nigel says gently. 'Your bag should arrive up shortly. There are clean towels in the bathroom, and I can leave your stuff in the guest room when it comes up.'

I smile and nod. I'm beyond words. Anything I do say, I worry will tumble from my stuttering lips as gibberish. I walk straight into the bathroom. Despite the size of the apartment, I don't have to ask for directions. The bathroom is one of the few rooms in the open-plan penthouse to actually have a door.

I must spend close to an hour in the shower. It's wonderful to stand upright and feel the light, silky water gently massaging my shoulders. It's the first time I have washed unaided in weeks. I have forgotten how refreshing a simple shower can be. Baths are fine, but when you have to be lifted in and out, it kind of defeats any relaxing element.

I lather and rinse my hair at least five times. The shampoo smells like a summer meadow, and I wouldn't be surprised if the tiny rough grains exfoliating my scalp were actual chips of gold. I even find a new pack of disposable razors on the windowsill and shave my legs. My luggage is beyond limited, so

I doubt I'll be showing off my smooth legs in a fancy dress anytime soon, but just knowing I'm less of a werewolf boosts my confidence.

Ava repeatedly bangs her fist hard on the bathroom door. 'Come on, Laura. I'm starving, and I need a shower, too. I hope you haven't used all the hot water.'

I grab a large, white towel from the top of the neatly folded pile in a wicker basket beside the sink. I cocoon my long dripping hair in a second equally fluffy towel and reluctantly open the door.

'Jesus, take your time why don't ya,' Ava snaps. 'Sam's been waiting ages to drive us to the restaurant.'

I must look concerned because Ava smooths her cross brow and musters up a smile. 'Wear something nice. Nigel says dinner is his treat, and we are going to hit a club after.'

Now I know I look worried. I don't have something nice to dress up in. A few pairs of jeans and some baggy jumpers are all Adam managed to grab from the house for me before we ran away.

'Borrow something from my stuff, okay?' Ava chirps as she breezes past me.

She catches me lightly by the elbows and spins me out the door locking it behind her. I'm mortified as I stand in the hallway with just a towel wrapped around me. I've no idea where the bedroom is, and I really don't fancy walking into the kitchen where I can hear Nigel chatting on the telephone. I'll just have to navigate my way around the apartment myself and hope I find the bedroom before Nigel finds me, half-naked.

The bedroom is actually conveniently located almost opposite the bathroom, and I dash quickly across the corridor into it. The room follows the theme of minimal furniture. A king-size bed and two simple bedside lockers are the extent of it. I fling myself onto the bed and sink deep into the soft mattress. I have to fight the urge to jump up and down like a giddy child.

I search every inch of the room for Ava's ridiculous oversized case. There's no sign of it, so I resign myself to the disappointment of wearing something shabby from my own bag. Unfortunately, I don't see my case anywhere either. I realise the concierge probably hasn't carried them up to the room yet, and I'm relieved. Now Ava can't blame me for delaying the evening. How am I supposed to get ready when I have no clothes?

I become bored quickly, so I decide to pass the time by examining my reflection in the full-length mirror opposite the bed. I haven't seen myself standing yet, and I'm actually excited to see if I still look the same as I remember. I stand almost in awe of my reflection. I scrutinise every visible inch of myself. My neck is still the same, long and with three little freckles just under my left ear. My toes are still short and stubby, and my chipped nail polish is badly in need of removal. My hands, arms, and calves all look the same, slightly chubbier from lack of exercise. Now the real test; I have to peek at my bum. I imagine the cheeks will be less than their usually perky selves after suffering the brunt of my entire body weight bearing down on them constantly. I hold my breath, close my eyes, and drop the towel.

'One…two…three,' I say out loud and open my eyes. A loud shriek escapes my lips as I see Nigel standing in the doorway with my case in his hand and his jaw on the floor.

'I...eh...oh...I'm sorry,' he mumbles.

I quickly reach to the ground and grab the corner of the towel in a panicked attempt to regain my dignity. It doesn't work, and I'm beyond embarrassed. My face stings like a million vicious wasps have just attacked me.

'Oh, God,' I stutter. 'I didn't know you were there.'

Nigel's eyes avert to the ground. 'I'm sorry,' he apologises again. 'I should have explained earlier. This is my room. You are at the other end of the hall?'

I didn't think it was possible to be any more humiliated, but Nigel's simple words have managed to push me that way.

I don't say another word. I pull the towel so tight around me that I almost cut off circulation below my neck, and I race out the door to find Ava. Of course, I can't even manage that right, and to my surprise, I find myself standing in a massive walk-in wardrobe. It's the size of a small drapery shop. It has ceiling to floor shelving on one side and on the other hangs too many beautiful dresses to count. Hundreds of pairs of stunning stilettos are stacked in open-ended boxes. I've never seen anything like it in my life. It's every woman's fantasy right before my eyes.

I back slowly out the door, all the while staring at the rainbow of silk and satin dresses.

'Do you like them?' Nigel asks from behind me.

I jump, almost dropping the towel for a second time, but my reaction is fast enough to grab it and hold on tight even though my fingers are trembling.

Nigel must sense my discomfort because he keeps a firm distance between us as he speaks.

'They were my wife's,' he explains.

Were?

'Perhaps you would like to wear one to dinner this evening?'

'Oh, no. I couldn't.'

I imagine myself trying on each and every one and parading in front of the mirror for hours.

'I couldn't,' I repeat trying more to convince myself than Nigel.

'Nonsense; of course, you can.'

Nigel ignores my nervous twitching and reaches for a royal blue silk maxi dress. It's stunning, the beading on the front, breast sparkles under the bright wardrobe lighting, and I can't help but gasp a little.

'This one would be perfect for you.' He smiles.

I reach out to touch the soft fabric. The price tag is still attached to the side. It has never been worn.

'It's beautiful,' I admit, 'but I really can't wear it. I don't think your wife would be too happy about me wearing a dress she hasn't even worn herself yet.'

'My wife isn't too happy about most things, unfortunately. Besides, I doubt she will be coming back for her dresses. I'm sure she will screw me out of enough in the divorce settlement to buy herself a whole new wardrobe…and a mansion to put it all in.'

I stare at Nigel blankly. I decide that my first impression of Nigel is spot-on. He isn't just handsome and rich, he's also a genuinely nice person – he's perfect. I can't help but wonder what kind of complete fool would want to divorce him?

'I'm sorry,' he apologises. 'You don't need to hear my sob story.'

I look into his big, unbearably sad eyes. I understand his pain. It was almost therapeutic to stand opposite him and empathise. For a brief moment, my own stagnant worries are pushed to the side of my brain. I want to listen to his story. I want him to open up and confide in me. And most of all, I want to feel the ability to care about something outside of my obsession with getting my kids back. Only for a moment, of course; I can't stop thinking about the kids for longer than a moment.

I take the dress from his hand and hold it against me. 'You think this one would suit me?'

'I think it would highlight how beautiful you are, yes.'

I smile. I am not sure if he's flirting or if it's an innocent compliment. It really doesn't matter; I just enjoy being caught up at the moment.

Before I know what I'm doing, I find my lips pressed to Nigel's cheek.

'Thank you,' I say.

'You're welcome.'

Nigel hugs me, and I allow myself to be completely swallowed up in the comfort of his warm arms and strong chest. It feels surprisingly calm and soothing. However, when the hug lasts a little too long, I find myself shakily breaking away. It isn't because I'm uncomfortable being close to Nigel. In fact, it's the opposite. I enjoy the closeness a little too much. If we stay that close, then I can't be sure my lips won't want to touch more than just his cheek.

'Where have you been?' Ava asks crankily as I walk into the bedroom we are sharing.

She's staring at her watch and tapping her foot like a mother scolding a disobedient teenager.

'What is that?' she asks, pointing at the blue dress I clutch.

'Do you like it? Nigel said I could borrow it.'

'Oh, he did, did he?'

Ava is smirking. 'You two seem to be becoming very good friends, very quickly.'

'He's a nice guy,' I say

'He *is* a nice guy,' Ava agrees, 'but just how nice are we talking?'

'Ava, stop it.'

'Stop what? I'm only asking how nice you think he is.'

'I know exactly what you are asking. Anyway, he's married.'

'He's getting divorced.' She smiles; a giddy giggle muffled by her hand over her mouth.

'I know. He told me.'

'He told you?' Ava asks a little too loudly.

'Yeah. It's not as if it's a secret or anything, is it?'

'Well, it is kind of a secret. He asked me not to tell anyone.'

'But you just told me.' I tut.

'That doesn't count. I tell you most things. I just don't know why he wanted me to keep it hush-hush if he was going to go blabbing to the world himself.'

'I'm only one person, Ava. I think the rest of the world is still in the dark on this.'

I glance at Ava hoping for a smile, but she isn't looking at me. She's gazing into the distance with a frown so firm no amount of Botox could prevent. She isn't blinking. I can't be sure, but I don't think she's breathing either.

'Ava, are you okay? You're acting a bit weird.'

'I'm not weird. I'm just surprised. He's really upset about the split. I didn't think he was ready to talk about it yet.'

'Well, maybe he thinks I can relate…you know, with everything I have going on.'

'Oh, come on, Laura. I think Nigel knows you better than that. You're about as compassionate as a wet tea towel. Look how you disapprove of Adam and me.'

'What do you mean Nigel *knows* me? I thought we're barely acquainted?'

A sudden creepy déjà vu sweeps over me, making the hairs on the back of my neck stand like fine wire bristles. If I concentrate, I can hear music coming from Nigel's room. I know the song. It's the heavy metal stuff that I hate, but Mark loves. I remember years ago putting Mark through a serious interrogation when he and some college buddies went missing after a rock festival, and I found them two days later hungover and getting off the boat back from Holyhead. For a moment, I wonder if Nigel is one of those influential college buddies. Nigel could be a friend of Mark's. This could all be a setup. I shake my head. I've only forgotten recent memories. That festival was at least ten years ago. I haven't forgotten anything from that far back. At least I don't think I have. *I'm just paranoid.*

'I didn't mean it like that, Laura. It's just an expression, you know.'

I shrug.

'C'mon. Let's get some food and then some sleep. It's been one hell of a day.'

Chapter Twenty

After all Ava's moaning at me to hurry up, in the end, she takes an hour longer than I do to get ready. I've drunk two glasses of wine rather quickly while waiting. I must have fallen asleep because I'm groggy and not really listening when Nigel shakes my shoulder and asks me if ordering pizza is okay instead of going out. I mumble something incoherent, and he leaves me alone.

It's late the next morning before I finally wake up. My cheek is cemented to the armrest of the sofa. A gooey streak of lipstick and dribble marks the spot where my face has spent the night. I have a horrible crick in my neck and my tongue feels as furry as a sheepskin rug. I'm still wearing the blue dress. It's twisted around me awkwardly now, and a dark stain somehow made it all the way down the front in a large, obvious splash. I'm horrified at the state of myself. I'm a disaster. I destroyed the beautiful dress and the couch all in one subconscious motion. I dread to think how Nigel will react.

I peel back the blanket that I assume Ava was kind enough to cover me with and dash to the bathroom. I cross my fingers that I won't bump into Nigel or Ava on the way.

I emerge a new woman. Well, a new woman in some old clothes. I wear a pair of skinny, grey jeans and a loose Tommy Hilfiger t-shirt that has shrunk in the wash and doesn't fit Mark anymore. I ball up the dress in a towel and stuff it into the laundry basket. I assume with Nigel's money he sends his laundry somewhere to be washed for him. There is no washing machine in the penthouse, and he doesn't seem the type to

186

hang out in the local laundrette on a Saturday afternoon. I hope the dress will come back as good as new and it will be one less embarrassment for me.

I rummage my way around the kitchen presses, hoping to find something that I can use to clean the couch. There's nothing. Not even washing up liquid. The presses are bare of food and the fridge houses just a few bottles of white wine with very fancy labels and a tray of strawberries. I smile as I confirm my suspicions that Nigel isn't the domestic type. He must eat out – always, or get an unhealthy amount of room service.

I sit on the couch for what feels like an eternity. I flick through all the television stations at least twice. I can't find anything to watch. I wonder how late Ava and Nigel plan to sleep in. Maybe they're sleeping off an even worse hangover than mine. I looked around for any evidence of a drinking session last night, but the only bottle on the shelf is the white wine I lashed into last night.

My tummy bubbles angrily. I squirm on the spot when I realise I was the only overindulgent one. Of course, Ava wasn't drinking. I snort at myself for forgetting her pregnancy. Even the smell of wine probably drove her morning sickness crazy. I used to hate the stuff when I was pregnant. And Nigel is some sort of finance investor, Ava finally told me. High flying businessmen didn't dabble in midweek binges, I'm sure.

I've made a fool of myself. I hope I haven't pissed Nigel off. It's not often you invite someone into your home and then they streak naked across your bedroom, get drunk and destroy your wife's dress, and mash seventy-five liters of foundation into your beautiful, cream leather sofa. *Jesus.*

'Oh, you're awake,' Ava says as she and Nigel walk through the front door of the penthouse.

Nigel is carrying several heavy shopping bags. They walk past me and into the kitchen. I follow.

'Why didn't you wake me?' I ask, bordering on moaning.

''Cause you looked wrecked,' Ava said.

'It's only a few groceries,' Nigel explains. 'The store isn't far from here. You weren't alone for long.'

He seems on edge, and I wonder if he's embarrassed that there's nothing to eat in the fridge.

'It looks like there's more than a few there,' I say pointing to the extreme volume of food that Nigel is unpacking.

'I didn't know what you liked, so I decided to get a little of most things. If there's anything I've missed, then just let me know, and I can go back out for it,' Nigel says.

His eyes smile, and I relax once more.

'There was no need to go to so much trouble. A slice of toast would have been more than fine,' I say politely.

Nigel's face falls disappointedly. He's enjoying treating Ava and me like royalty, I can tell, and now I seem to be completely unappreciative. I hurry to rectify the situation.

'Everything looks yummy. I'm so hungry.'

It's true. The fresh fruit looks as tasty as if he handpicked it straight from the farmer's garden himself. There are so many varieties of bread and pastries that my tummy aches just thinking about how delicious they will taste.

It's a test of my patience to wait until the food is placed on the table. My fingers twitch a couple of times in the direction of a bright red raspberry or juicy kiwi from the fruit salad bowl.

I haven't eaten properly in weeks, so as soon as we sit, I rudely refrain from making conversation as I tuck into the delicious breakfast. Nigel glances in my direction every time he hears the peculiar sound of my stomach growling as it enjoys the delicious meal.

'Are you sure you don't just want to spend the day resting? The city will still be here to see tomorrow when you are less tired,' Nigel suggests between sips of cooled coffee.

I feel a little uncomfortable as I suspect it's his way of politely suggesting I need to sleep off my hangover.

'We're not tired,' Ava insists. 'Anyway, we don't know how long we'll be staying for so we want to make the most of it.'

I'm disappointed. I don't like the idea of facing the freezing cold outside. I'd much prefer to spend the day researching custody cases on the internet. My head is pounding, and I feel as though I've been kicked in the back of the skull with a football boot. But I can see how much Ava wants to hit the city so I smile brightly and act excited.

'If you insist; then shopping it is.' Nigel smiles as keen as ever to please. 'Will I have the car ready in…say…an hour or so?'

'Nope,' Ava replies completely adamant. 'We'll get the subway.'

'The subway?' I squeak.

'Okay, if that's what you'd prefer,' Nigel says.

Ava loves her luxuries. She would never give up leather seats and suede cushions for a chewing-gum-infested polyester seat on an overcrowded train. She must have been really worried that Mark would find us if she wanted this badly not to draw attention to us.

'I want Laura to experience the real New York, and you only get a rich man's perspective from the back of that fancy car of yours. Poor people have much more fun.'

I scrunch my nose and glare disappointedly at Ava. Her idea of a poor person is slightly off. Unless you own five pairs of Louboutins and spend the summer on a yacht, you are poor.

'More fun, my arse,' I mumble biting my lip to muffle the sound.

Real people like me, poor or not, hate the bloody subway.

I look at Nigel and shake my head. There's no point in arguing with her; she'll only win eventually anyway.

'Stop being such a pessimist. It'll be fun.' Ava smiles.

I really hope Ava isn't going to keep saying fun all day.

'At least let me give you my work mobile number?' Nigel says.

'Work number?' I ask, taken aback.

'Of course,' Nigel replies dismissively. 'You can get me any time on that line.'

'Of course,' I playfully mimic without thinking.

Thankfully, Nigel sees the funny side and smiles. I punch the number into my mobile and promise to call if we get lost.

'Unfortunately, it turns out I won't be able to join you in the city for dinner this evening. Something has come up at work,' Nigel explains.

'Oh no, that's a pity.' I say, genuinely disappointed.

'I'm terribly sorry. Perhaps, I can still join you for a drink after. Although it may be a little late and if you're tired...'

'I'm not tired.' I nod eagerly.

Ava laughs at my enthusiasm, as does Nigel.

'You've changed your tune,' Ava whispers.

Nigel smiles and I'm certain he heard her. I'm also certain he notices me blush a little because it was true.

Chapter Twenty-One

I barely notice the sharp cold of the November wind as we walk away from the hotel. Ava assures me the entrance to the subway is just a couple of blocks away. I don't care if it's around the next corner or fifty miles away; I'm too busy enjoying walking around with my head in the air staring at giant buildings that line the streets like a giant game of dominoes.

'Yep, it's definitely obvious you're a tourist.' Ava giggles pointing at me. 'You'll get a crick in your neck.'

I already had a crick in my neck, but it was worth it.

'If you think this is impressive, just wait 'til we get to Fifth Avenue,' Ava says excitedly.

I feel my heart skip a giddy beat. Ava was right all these years; New York is amazing. I hold my breath in anticipation of seeing more. I also hold my breath as we descend into the subway. It stinks. An unpleasant combination of stale body odours and old rubbish mixes with hot sticky air. We grab our one-way tickets quickly from the machine and dash to squeeze on the train with all the other mashed commuters. I stop mid hurry and don't run any further.

My attention is drawn to a young woman sitting cross-legged in the only quiet corner of the busy terminal. She can't be more than twenty-five. She has her back firmly against the wall and she's tucked into a neat ball. A small boy shivers as he lies sleeping curled up in the crook of her filthy arm. He's skinny and unwashed, just like the woman. I assume she's his mother. A lump rises in my throat just looking at them. Hundreds of busy people rush by as they execute their daily routine. *It's the city that never sleeps, but people must walk around with their eyes closed,* I decide. How else can they ignore the heartache that's dotted on the corner of every block?

I root in my oversized handbag and pull out ten dollars. I know it's pitifully insufficient, but it's hopefully enough to make some small difference to the young woman. It's enough for at least a cup of coffee and a packet or two of crisps for her little boy.

I bend down close to her and stuff the money into her shaking hand.

'Thank you…thank you…thank you,' she repeats over and over.

I don't know what to say; the lump in my throat has swelled so huge that I doubt I could speak anyway. So I just smile and slowly walk away.

'You're too soft for your own good,' Ava says once we are out of earshot.

'Excuse me,' I say, trying hard to get the image of the shivering little boy out of my mind.

'She's only going to spend that on drink, you know.'

'You can't say that,' I insist, disappointed in Ava's cynicism.

'I can. I just did. How can I say that? Because that's what they all do. That's why they're in that situation in the first place.'

'People can't choose what awful direction life takes them in. Some people are victims of circumstances, you know,' I say sharply.

I know I'm no longer talking about some poor, homeless woman. I'm drawing on my own misfortune, and Ava chooses not to argue the matter any further.

'Well, let's hope I'm wrong,' she says. 'That poor little mite looks like he hasn't seen a decent meal in weeks. I'll keep my fingers crossed that your money buys him some food and doesn't go to feed his mother's habit.'

The streets of central Manhattan are thronged with busy people rushing about their daily lives. We blend in with the crowd and were blissfully anonymous. I'm not Laura the overwhelmed mother trying to be supermom. I'm not a wife or lover trying to look somewhat attractive in the face of pure exhaustion. I'm not a career woman who gave it all up to raise her children. I'm not even Laura whose life has been stolen without her knowing how.

'How did I let this happen?' I ask out of context as we walk up the subway steps and onto the street.

'Let what happen?'

'My life,' I clarify. 'How did I let it become such a mess?'

'You're just going through a really tough patch. Everyone has them. Okay, yours is worse than most people's, but I think you're doing great.'

Ava never seems to grow tired of me reiterating the same old sob story. She always tries her best to cheer me up.

'I'm falling apart,' I admit.

'You're not. But your wardrobe is. Jesus, Laura, what the hell are you wearing? First stop Macy's.'

Normally, I would have been jumping for joy at an offer like that, but I'm not in the mood.

'I'm serious, Ava. I think I'm losing it.'

Ava takes me by the hand and leads me to a little bench at the edge of the footpath. She winces a little as the cold metal seat hits the backs of her thighs. Under different circumstances, I would have laughed hysterically.

'Are you ready to talk about everything.' Ava smiles.

'I don't even know what it is I'm talking about anymore,' I explain. 'I'm so confused all the time. Every time I remember something and think I'm getting close to understanding why everything has changed, I realise I've just scratched the surface.'

'Well, let me help you scratch. What are you thinking right now?'

Ava has a heavy sadness in her eyes. She's struggling to hold back tears. I hope she won't cry. If she crumbles, then I will fall heavy, too.

'My life is ruined,' I sob.

'Why do you say that?' Ava asks. 'Is it because you miss him so much?'

'Miss who? Mark?'

Ava doesn't say another word. She's just nodding and listening.

'Yeah, I really miss him. It's not because I'm in New York and he's back home. I've been missing him for a long time. We've been growing apart for ages now, and it really hurts.'

'Is it since Lorcan?' Ava whispers, tears rolling down her cheeks etching pale lines into her otherwise perfect makeup. She's fought it as long as she could, but she's lost the battle to contain her emotion.

'Lorcan?' I ask surprised.

It's sweet that Ava was referring to her baby by name already, but I can't understand what that has to do with me missing Mark.

'Mark doesn't know you're pregnant, does he?

'No. Of course, not. You and Adam are the only ones who know.'

'Oh okay,' I say, still confused. Maybe Ava thinks I'm upset about her baby because of my miscarriage. It makes sense. That must be why she waited so long to tell me she is pregnant.

I slide to the end of the bench so Ava and I are squashed together in a tiny space usually only occupied by one super-skinny person.

'I'm not upset about your baby,' I say.

'Okay,' Ava whispers, wiping her eyes and blowing her nose loudly.

'I did find the miscarriage hard, and it would have been lovely if we could have been pregnant together, but with the state of my marriage, I don't think a baby would be a good thing. Not right now anyway.'

'Adam and I don't exactly have the perfect relationship either, but I'm hoping the baby will bring us closer.'

I look at my best friend. 'Babies really do change everything,' I say. I remember gazing into the beautiful blues eyes of my new baby, who was a carbon copy of Mark. Life was so blissfully perfect in that moment. It isn't fair that time has made such a cruel difference to how happy we were.

'Do you think you and Mark can come back from this point?' Ava asks. Her voice shoots through my daydream and it sadly shatters.

'I don't think so. He tried to kill me because he's having an affair. Yeah, if it was *Eastenders* or *Coronation Street*, I'm sure we'd kiss and make up, but unfortunately, real life is a little different.'

'Do you think it's because your loss has changed you so much?' Ava whispers. It's almost as if she's afraid to admit out loud that I was different.

'No. I think it's because he's shagging someone else,' I spit as if the words taste disgusting in my mouth.

We are both silent for a while. There isn't much that can be said in response to that.

'Anyway, he's replaced me with *her*,' I finally say. 'Maybe it's time I do the same.'

'Nigel?' Ava asks, a touch of disapproval streaked between her frowning eyebrows. 'Now that would be weird,' she adds.

'Why? I'm single; he's single. What could be weird about that?'

'It just would be.'

'Why, Ava? Just because I've spawned little people out of my lower half doesn't mean my bits have shrivelled up and fallen off. I still have feelings, and hormones, and needs.'

'I know,' Ava defends. 'I just mean it would be a bit weird with all the history and stuff.'

'Not this again. What history? You said Nigel and I didn't know each other, remember?'

Dammit. I feel a dizzy wave build again. Ava's lying to me; I know it. My subconscious has a built-in sense about it. Maybe my own head is trying to protect me. *Is that even possible?*

'Nothing. Forget about it. I've already said too much,' Ava says.

'What do you mean you've said too much? You haven't said anything at all.'

'Good. Let's keep it that way.'

'No. Ava, if you know something, you have to tell me. Please?'

'Remember how we always promise that we will never push the other person to talk about something that they're not comfortable with?' Ava asks trembling slightly.

I nod.

'Well, I'm not comfortable talking about this.'

I slouch on the bench a little and turn to face her. 'I'm not asking you to confess a drunken fumble with some random stranger in a bar. This is my life we're talking about.'

'I know,' Ava says sympathetically. 'I wish we could talk about it, but I've been warned not to discuss this.'

I jumped up powerfully. I'm sick to the pit of my stomach. 'You've been warned?' I screamed.

'Shh,' Ava says. 'People are staring.'

'I don't care who's watching. I couldn't care less if a camera crew pulls up alongside us and airs the whole ugly scene on a big screen across Times Square. I will scream all I want. Now tell me. Who warned you what? Nicole? Mark? Who? Did Nicole threaten you? Or was it…?'

Ava jumps up from the bench even faster than I did. Her face has changed completely. She almost looks angry with me. 'You've got this sooo wrong, Laura. Mark is the one person fighting, all this time, to protect you.'

'What? No. What are you saying? We ran away because we are in danger. Now you contradict all that and say that Mark is trying to protect me? His idea of protecting me is shoving me six feet under.'

Ava's face falls into her hands, and she flops back onto the bench as if someone has just sucked all the air out of her body. 'I thought you were starting to remember.'

'I'm trying to remember. If you would just tell me what you know...then I could understand.'

'Don't you get it yet?' Ava asks trembling.

I can't tell if she shakes with frustration or if she's just too upset to contain herself.

'You have to remember for yourself. I can tell you all the gory details 'til I'm blue in the face, but the next time you pass out, you'll just forget all over again. We've been there before. You only retain what you remember by yourself.'

Ava's words hurt, and I want to poke holes in her far-fetched and unreasonable theory, but there's honesty in her sad eyes and her words resonate with me. I run my hands over the top of my hair and pat down any strays. I dab my fingertips against the corners of my eyes and wipe away the stray tears. My spine cracks as I pull myself up as straight as my messily five-foot-two allows.

'So, are we going shopping or what?' I say.

Ava grabs my hand. She's still shaking but not as noticeably, and a delicate smile replaces the chewing of her lips.

Chapter Twenty-Two

We walk around Macy's until we both have blisters. Ava's arms are laden with pretty cocktail dresses, expensive jeans, and tailored blouses. None of which is maternity wear. She insists they're her inspiration outfits. She's determined to fit back into her regular size after the baby is born. I didn't think it will be any problem for her. If anything, her regular clothes will be too big for her. She's lost a lot of weight since getting pregnant. Her violent morning sickness has her looking pale and gaunt, like a ghost. I'm sure the stress I've dragged her through isn't helping either. And I try to curb my constant questions about whether she thinks Mark and Nicole will find us here. Although watching her shop like there is no more material left in the world, she looks deceptively at ease.

'C'mon; you should get yourself something small, it'll make you feel better,' Ava suggests, picking up a hideous floral silk scarf and passing it to me for approval.

'Yuck,' I grumble and neatly tuck the scarf back on the shelf.

'Oh, c'mon. Treat yourself.'

I shake my head. 'I don't want to use my credit card. Mark takes care of the bill and when the transaction shows up in the States, he'll know where to find us. No manky scarf is worth the risk.'

'You've been watching too much *CSI*.' Ava snorts.

I glare at my best friend. I wish Ava would take this whole mess a little more seriously.

'Use my card. I never got around to getting you a gift when Katie was born, so this can be my treat now. Look, there are loads of nice skirts over there,' she says pointing in the direction of some stylish mannequins.

I'm really not in the mood to try anything on, but Ava has flung a small trolley load of clothes at me and dragged me giddily in the direction of the changing rooms.

I gaze lifelessly into the mirror. The satin pencil skirt and soft silk blouse are beautiful, but I don't care much for the person underneath. I used to dress like this all the time before I had the kids, but now I look like an imposter playing dress-up. My mousy brown hair is dull and lifeless as it hangs clinging to the contours at the side of my face and stops just shy of my shoulders. The grey that sweeps over my ears is not as subtle as it was just a couple of months ago. The bags around my eyes are so prominent it looks as though the smoky eye effect has gone horribly wrong, and my whole frame is a lot pudgier than I ever remember. I hate this reflection. All my life, I've been meticulous about my appearance. I'm no supermodel, but I did stand out in the crowd. I still stand out in the crowd but now for the wrong reasons.

I twist my head around the changing room door. 'Okay,' I say catching Ava's attention. 'I'll buy these.'

'Just those two?' she asks disappointedly.

I pull a face.

Ava twitches her nose and flicks her hand back and forth. 'It's a start,' she chirps. 'We can shop more tomorrow.'

I have to admire Ava's positive attitude. Although it's not quite contagious, it stops me from completely breaking down.

I enjoy the day in spite of myself. But dragging heavy bags around busy streets is exhausting, and I long for the comfort of my own bed in my own house.

'We should get back,' I suggest, completely out of breath and stopping to have a rest for the third time in less than ten steps forward.

'No, this is too much fun.'

Ava is trying hard, but buying a few new bits and pieces does not make up for my life shredding at the seams. It's not fun! I inhale so hard my nostrils burn.

'Walking around smelly streets in minus a million degrees is not more fun than sipping champagne in the comfort of Nigel's?' I know exactly how to speak Ava's language. 'C'mon, please; I'm freezing and wrecked.'

Ava nods. If I'd known she'd agree that easily, then I would have pleaded my case ages ago.

I rummage in my bag for my phone, but before I have a chance to dial, it beeps at me. 'Dammit.' I snort. 'I missed a call from Nigel.'

'Okay, so call him back.'

I already have the phone to my ear, listening to a voicemail.

'He's had to go upstate for the evening,' I explain. 'Looks like he can't meet us or pick us up after all.'

Ava looks offensively smug. I'm going to experience *real* New York living whether I want to or not.

I frown at the bags in my hand and sigh, taking in a deep breath and the smell of something greasy and delicious. I dash across the road to a dodgy vending stand and come back with two messy hot dogs and a can of Diet Coke.

'Here,' I say biting into the messy snack. 'I'm starving, so you must be famished, too. You'll get sick if you don't eat something soon.'

'Sure.' Ava nods.

'E. coli is part of the real New York experience too, don't ya know?' I giggle, munching into the surprisingly delicious snack.

We sit on the rusty bench eating in silence for a few moments. We're too tired to waste any valuable energy on talking.

'You okay?' Ava asks when we both have our hunger under control.

'Yeah, just that déjà vu thing again,' I say.

'Again?'

'Yeah. I know. It's weird. That's like the fourth or fifth time today.'

I've had déjà vu so often since we arrived in New York that I'm beginning to feel strange when I don't have it. The last bite of my hot dog brings with it my most vivid feeling yet.

'Such and awesome game, wasn't it?' Ava says.

'Yeah.' I laugh, poking my ear with my finger. 'I think I'm still a little deaf from all the screaming.'

'Yeah, the crowd were crazy.'

'I meant your screaming, actually.' I knock my shoulder against Ava's as we sit on the steps of Grand Central Station, eating pretzels and coming down from the buzz of the stadium.

'Well, it's not every day the Yankees kick the Cubs' asses.'

A guy walking by bends down to shake the giant rubber hand I'm waving about, high on team spirit.

'Goooo, Yankees,' he chants.

~~~

'Have I been here before, Ava?' I ask, closing my eyes trying to hold on to the fading memory.

'Where?'

203

'America…New York…right here, this very spot.' I open my eyes and find a street sign. '42nd Street. Have I been on 42nd Street before?'

'I told you this place is great. It's like a home away from home,' Ava mumbles.

I agree. It felt a lot like I could belong here. I notice Ava hasn't answered my question, but I think I already know what she would say.

We trundle our way tiredly from one subway station to the next. Ava can navigate the underground system like a pro. I, on the other hand, am clueless. If I lost Ava down here, then it would take me days to find my way back. We hop from one train to another and then another. I drag my bags up so many steps my shoulders pop from their sockets, and it drags me down an equal number on the opposite side of the tracks. Every time I cough, I feel like I'm losing a little piece of my lungs from the stench of carbon monoxide and minimal ventilation. It's as warm as a sauna down here, and I can feel small beads of perspiration trickle down my spine and land unflatteringly just above the waistband of my jeans.

I can't count on one hand the number of times I'm tempted to let the large steel doors of the train savage the bag and drag it far away from me.

Finally, we reach the last station. We've successfully survived the day without any major drama. My neck doesn't even strain from the weight of carrying my pounding head. I smile to myself as I realise this is what it feels like not to have a headache. I've grown so used to the constant throbbing that when it's absent, I almost feel like I could float.

I yank the bag up the final few steps leading above ground. The plastic nibbles mercilessly at the backs of my fingers as it pinches me. I string an impressive list of profanities together and mumble them coarsely under my short breath. I curse Ava for forcing me to buy crap. I curse Nigel for promising a lift and then pissing off. And I curse Mark. I curse him and I curse him and I curse him. I hate him for abandoning me when I needed him most. I hate him for not loving me the way I loved him. I hate him for getting me pregnant, letting me fall in love with being a mother, and then snatching that all away from me. But mostly, I curse myself because, in spite of every horrible thing, I still love him, and I don't know how to change that.

I'm distracted out of self-pity by the scene I notice on the street corner. I call Ava to look. She stands beside me and drapes her arm around my neck and over my shoulder.

'You were right,' she says happily. 'There is good in this miserable old world after all.'

We stand in silence as we watch the young homeless mother from earlier that morning. The woman and her son are sitting huddled together, leaning against a lamppost for support. Someone has given them a blanket, and the mother has a little colour in her cheeks that wasn't there this morning. The little boy is contently gulping a carton of fresh milk and eating a cookie almost as big as his own head. His mother smiles and nibbles on the crumbs he drops. Ava is right; there truly is good in the world, and today, I played a part in creating it. I only wish I could do more.

Chapter Twenty-Three

My heart pounds against my chest as wildly as a starving tiger trying to escape from its cage. I can't believe I've succeeded. I'm actually there. I have found them.

I park the car neatly behind some small bushes on the grass verge at the side of the little laneway. I can barely hear the engine purr over the sound of my own deep breathing. I had followed them halfway across the country. She didn't notice me tailing her with just a couple of cars between us the whole way. There were times when I bravely snuck up directly behind her and I had to really fight with myself not to press my foot onto the accelerator and push her off the road. I wouldn't, of course, because my children were in the back of her car. But my temper was so savage that the children were her only saving grace.

I sit alone in the darkness peering out over the steering wheel and try to view as much as I can between the gaps in the hedging. Nicole opens the rear door of her car and lifts a sleeping Katie out of her car seat. She looks like a beautiful, cuddly teddy bear in her big furry coat. Her little body tucks up into a neat ball and her tiny head rests on Nicole's shoulder. Bobby hops happily out the door after them. He reaches his gloved hand up to hold Nicole's and the three of them huddle together as they head into a beautiful house I have never seen before. They are the perfect little family. Only they're not Nicole's family, they're mine. Nicole is a thief and she has stolen my most precious items...my children.

I duck quickly and cower in my seat as Mark's car passes by. There's only room for one car in the driveway and Nicole's small hatchback already occupies the space. I realise I'm foolishly parked where a second family car would fit nicely. Mark has to settle for a space further down the street, but he walks back towards me. He's obviously coming to investigate the car that was rude enough to hog his regular spot. Shit. Shit. Shit! A few more steps and he is certain to recognise my car. Thankfully, he's suddenly distracted and dashes towards the house. Bobby has fallen on the front porch and is crying loudly. My hand grabs the door handle and I want to open it and race to pick him up and wipe away his tears. But I can't reveal myself. They can't know I'm here. Not yet.

Mark scoops Bobby into his arms, hugging him tight, and Bobby stops crying. Mark leans forward and kisses Nicole on the cheek. The picture perfect family all go inside and close the front door behind them. I swing the car door open and barely manage to twist my head out before I throw up.

I struggle to get my limbs to cooperate with me. My fingers shake as they fiddle with my seat belt. There is hardly enough strength in them to press it open. My jelly legs wobble awkwardly as I finally force them to lift me out of the car. I catch a quick glimpse of myself in the wing mirror. The khaki oversized trousers and Army camouflage coat are Adam's Halloween costume that I've taken without asking. Wearing them may have been a bit extreme, but I have to be certain I'm not seen. If I'm going to steal my children back, then the mission has to be executed with military precision. I have to be invisible.

I crouch down and hide in the shadow of the car as I begin to crawl along by the outside of the hedge. The cold of the cement path stings my knees as I creep slowly forward.

'Have you lost something?' a voice from across the road shouts just as I reach the gateway.

I turn around to find an old man with his head leaning out of an upstairs window of the house opposite. I ignore him and hope he'll soon lose interest.

'Do you need some help, love?' he asks.

I shake my head. He continues to shout at me, and I know if he doesn't shut up, I'll have to abandon my plan. Nicole and Mark are sure to hear him and come to investigate. The old man is messing everything up.

'I'm fine. Piss off,' I bellow.

He retreats as if my voice has just taken him out like a sniper. I breathe a sigh of relief. But it's short-lived. The old man has probably gone to phone the cops and report a weirdo lurking in his neighbourhood. I'll just have to hurry even more.

The front door opens unexpectedly, and I panic before dashing around to hide at the side of the house. I glance at my watch. By my calculation, Mark shouldn't be leaving for his kickboxing class for another fifteen minutes. But I'd forgotten to factor in the extra distance to the gym from this new house.

'Bye bye,' Bobby's sweet voice chirps from just inside the open door. Mark waves as he walks away from the house.

Nicole swiftly appears behind Bobby. Ugh.

'I won't be late,' Marked promises.

'Take your time. Try to enjoy yourself, okay?' Nicole says, smiling.

'Thanks, Nicky,' Mark beams. 'What would I do without you?'

Now's my chance. Nicole is alone with the kids. I will win. I will save the children. If I could just get my excessively fast beating heart to calm down a little, then I can have my family back.

It's pitch dark and eerily quiet. But I continue to crawl along the edge of the grass all the way around to the back of the house. The back of the house overlooks a large golf course. No one plays at this time of night, I think gratefully. There is no one to see me here. If no one can see me, then no one can assist Nicole if she tries to stop me.

The light of the kitchen shines brightly and causes a foggy hue to illuminate a window-size square of the back garden dimly. I'm careful not to step into the light. The blind is up so I have a clear view of inside.

Nicole is standing on the other side of the island preparing dinner. Bobby sits contently at the table colouring a picture. He occasionally hops down from his chair and brings his colouring book over to Nicole for her approval of his masterpiece in progress. She ignores him as she continues chopping carrots. I would never ignore him like that. I can't see Katie, but I assume she's sleeping in her bassinette in some quiet room. I watch for so long the grass stained wet patches on my knees begin to harden as they turned to ice. I can't feel the tips of my fingers numbed by the cold wind, but I have a wonderful, warm feeling inside. I watch Bobby smile. I could stay at this moment forever. But I know if I follow through with my plan, then these moments will be a regular thing. The only difference will be me standing on the other side of the window and Nicole out in the cold.

I lay myself out flat on the freezing grass. The cold bites into my kidneys, but I ignore the ache. I stretched out, tucking my arms tightly against my sides and my legs press flat and together. I line the edge of my body up with the edge of the bright patch of the garden. I count backwards from five then roll in one fast, continuous motion until I'm on the other side of the brightness. I stand up and stay very still for a few moments. I felt like my heart is lodged in the back of my throat. My legs shake like a wrecking ball has hit me in the back of the knees as I wait, holding my breath. The back door doesn't open. Nicole hasn't seen me. I'm one unnoticed step closer.

I brush off the excess wet the damp grass has left on my clothes. I'm shivering wildly and I have to keep my mouth open a little to stop the noise my teeth make as they chatter. A distracting combination of nerves and cold shakes my bones. I do my best to ignore it and continue to creep towards the back door. I spend ages trying to open the door without letting it creak. The heat of the house is glorious, and I sigh as feeling attempts to return to my extremities. I'm still alone, but the intensity of the impending

209

conflict is overwhelming. I take a moment to compose myself in the utility room.

The happy voices inside tease me. They laugh and joke, blissfully unaware of my secret presence. I burst through the door between the kitchen and utility room; my legs are walking me forward, but my head is roaring at me to turn back. Even my own mind knows I've lost all control of myself.

Nicole screams loudly as she turns ghostly white. Her shrill cry scares Bobby, who in turn bursts into tears. Katie, who had been playing contently on the floor mat in the adjacent sitting room, becomes hysterical. There's so much noise. This was not part of the plan. I'm terrifying them, but it will all be worth it. It will all be worth it.

'Jesus, Laura,' Nicole shrieks. 'You scared the life out of me.'

'Sorry,' I say. 'I didn't mean to frighten you.'

It's partially true. I knew sneaking up on her like that would scare her, but my intention was only to get into the house. If I scared her in the process, then that was an unavoidable necessity.

'What are you doing here?' she asks barely able to string her words together.

'I think that's obvious,' I snap.

Bobby jumps down from the table and races to Nicole. He buries his head in the material of her jeans and refuses to look at me. She doesn't comfort him, but I suspect she refrains because she knows that it will make me jealous.

'I thought you were in the hospital,' Nicole says.

'I was,' I admit.

'How did you get out?'

'I was in the hospital, Nicole, not prison.'

I wasn't in prison, but I wasn't in the hospital of my own free will either. Doctor Hammond, the bastard, held me trapped in a psychiatric

210

ward and then he refused to release me until I admitted I had a problem. I wouldn't admit it. How could I admit to something I don't have? And even all the drugs they pumped me with wouldn't force me to say it either. I told the doctor every day that Mark and Nicole were setting me up, but he wouldn't believe me. And I know a lot of money is exchanging hands; I've seen Mark write cheques with my own eyes. Doctor Hammond isn't my doctor; he's Mark's lapdog and a goddamn prison guard.

'You scared me half to death sneaking up on me like that,' Nicole repeats herself. She's still afraid, but her tone is laced with anger now. 'Mark is in the shower. Do you want to wait for him?'

I glare at her. She lies so effortlessly. I hate her more for it.

'No, he's not,' I shout. 'I saw him leave.'

Nicole recoils in terror. And I can't help the sadistic grin that curls my lips. Nicole is afraid of what I might do knowing that Mark isn't there to protect her. I have the upper hand for the first time, and it feels so fucking good.

'Well, he'll be home any minute.' She squirms.

'No, he won't,' I yell. 'It's Wednesday; he goes to the gym every Wednesday.'

Bobby begins to cry again, and I immediately soften my tone.

'It's okay, sweetheart. Mammy isn't cross with you,' I assure him. I reach my hand out to hold his, but he jumps with a fright and steps away from me.

'Laura, please. Stop this nonsense. You're scaring me.'

I flick my eyes away from Bobby's sweet face to growl at Nicole. It's a message not to fuck with me. She steps back, and I know she's taken the hint.

'I'm cross with Nicole,' I explain to Bobby. 'She's a very bold girl.'

'She is a good girl,' Bobby shouts. 'I hate you, go away.' He kicks me hard in the shin then runs away to hide in the sitting room.

Nicole is deathly pale and very still. She's obviously afraid of how I will react to Bobby's outburst. I'm so hurt by Bobby's reaction, and I know it's because Nicole has poisoned his innocent mind.

'Please don't hurt me,' Nicole begs as she backs her way around to the opposite side of the island to me.

Nicole is fucking my husband and mothering my children. She has all but erased my identity and filled the void herself, driving me close to the brink of insanity, but the most she has ever hurt me was in those five simple words. She said them with such genuine concern. Does she truly believe I'm a monster? Or is she an expert in reverse psychology? I'm so confused.

The light of the oven door reflects off the shiny steel behind Nicole's back to reveal a large chopping knife grasped tightly in her hand. I realise the dangerous situation in which I've put myself. I'm not the monster here. I'm an intruder in her home, and anything she does now is self-defence.

I reach for the only sharp object in view. I pull a meat cleaver out of the open drawer beside me. Nicole loses her battle to remain composed, and she begins to scream and cry.

'You really are crazy,' she cries.

I nod. At that moment, I feel it. I am crazy. Crazy with anger and resentment and bitterness.

'If I am,' I say, 'then it's all your fault.'

'I know, and I'm so, so sorry,' she says hanging her head shamefully. 'Can you ever forgive me?'

'No,' I answer without having to think. 'No, I can never forgive you. Not ever.'

My emotions change so often it's a constant battle to know how I feel. Hating Nicole is the only constant. I could never let go of that familiarity.

'Mark.' Nicole smiles as she focuses on something behind me.

I turn around to face my husband. There's an empty space. I feel a sharp pain in the back of my head and all lights and sounds are banished from my mind. I'm drifting out of consciousness, and I have no idea what Nicole has done to me. Perhaps I'm dying.

Chapter Twenty-Four

It hurts to open my eyes. Seeing light maximises the pounding of my skull. I run my hand over the back of my head. The swelling around the huge bump is subsiding. It feels like a small golf ball is hidden under my skin. Nicole is surprisingly strong for such a petite person. When she packs a punch, she goes all out.

I carefully analyse the familiar sights and smells that jumble before my eyes. I sink down deeply in the chair as I realise I'm in Doctor Hammond's office. I've come to hate this room. Not only for the dreary décor, but also for the equally dreary questions that Doctor Hammond insists on asking repeatedly. It's as if every time he asks, he's hoping for a different, better answer. But my reply is always the same. I'm not the crazy one. Nicole is. That's of course on the rare occasion that I choose to speak. Most of the time, I just sit in silence and stare out the window.

'Are you with me?' Doctor Hammond asks growing increasingly weary of the silent treatment.

My response is nothing more than a deep sigh.

'You gave us quite a scare running away like that,' he says. 'What were you thinking?'

'I was thinking that I want to see my children.'

'I know you do.'

'I've done nothing wrong, so why am I being forced to stay here as a prisoner? If I am crazy, then it's because being trapped here has driven me to it. It's not fair.'

'I agree.'

'You do?' I mumble.

'Yes, I do. You're right. It's not fair and I want nothing more than for you to return home, so if you would just let us help you...'

I catch the delicate vase of flowers from the coffee table in front of me and squeeze it so tight I think it will snap in my hand. I recognise this speech. I know what he's going to say next. He will fill me with elaborate lies and then sit back hoping I accept his tall tale. I will never believe him.

The vase in my hand finally shatters under the pressure and nicks the soft flesh of my palm. I drop the sharp pieces of porcelain to the floor and watch as several small beads of blood run down my fingers. Doctor Hammond immediately stands up to come to my aid. I pull my hand away. I snatch the tissue he offers and begin to dab the light bleed. He watches me for a few moments and then continues talking. He appears glad I'm distracted. I am not giving my full concentration to blocking out every word he says as I usually do.

'Laura. Are you listening,' he asks.

'Um-hm,' I groan concentrating on my hand.

'You have been living in your own imagination for the last few months. We have gradually been drawing you back to reality.'

I shrug. This is certainly a new approach. Next, he will be telling me we had lunch with the fairies and danced naked around the bonfire after.

'Of course,' I say. 'Do tell Fifi-Twinkle-Bell that I was asking for her. I love her new, purple wings. I wonder if I should get a pair like that before my next flying lesson.'

I can tell my sarcasm infuriates him. I shrug again.

'You haven't made it easy for us, Laura.'

What the fuck did he expect?

'You haven't made it easy for yourself,' I growl. 'I just want to be left alone. How is that too much to fucking ask.'

'You are very stubborn, aren't you?'

I shrug again and make a face this time.

'But you really must accept what I am telling you. You need to move forward now. This must stop.'

215

I agree. For once, I actually agree with this man. This. Must. Stop!
'Do you understand?' Doctor Hammond asks.

My insides are turning to jelly. Something in his words forces the cogs in my brain to turn faster than they should. I don't want to believe him, but the cogs are slowly piecing together what he's saying and I am starting to see a pattern that makes sense. I take my medication like a good girl. I pass out. I can't remember shit. Repeat. My stomach heaves and I throw up on his dull, grey carpet.

Oddly, he looks pleased. 'It's a lot to take in. I understand that.'

The taste of vomit burns my mouth. 'May I have a drink, please?'

He leaves the room, leaving the door wide open behind him, and walks to the water cooler across the hall.

I begin to scan the room for signs of weakness. Any little hint that it was all an elaborate scam. A prescription, a box of pills, falsified medical notes. Something. Anything. Christ, Nicole is a genius. I'll give her that. It all makes so much sense now. Killing me would be way too obvious. She'd never get away with it. Instead, she's trying to convince the world that I'm crazy. Either she's doing a bloody good job of it and Doctor Hammond believes her, or he's in on the plan.

'Can't you see, Doctor Hammond? She hates me,' I say as soon as he returns.

He hands me a glass of cool water. I don't drink it. I can't take the risk.

The doctor shakes his head disappointedly. 'I had hoped today would be the day we finally made progress. Maybe it is too soon.' He sighs.

'I want a blood test,' I say. 'That will prove I am right.'

'Blood test,' he echoes.

'Yeah.' My eyes widen, irritated. 'For one thing, it'll show all the drugs in my system. Won't it? If you won't help me, then I'll ask a doctor who will.'

'I'm offering you my help, Laura. But you won't accept it,' Doctor Hammond says with genuine regret.

'Please just give me the test, and then you'll see. You'll understand then,' I promise.

I begin rolling up my sleeve and shoving my arm towards him.

He catches my hand and holds it gently in his.

'Laura, we've already given you every test imaginable. You just forget.'

'Stop saying that,' I shout, pulling away from him. 'Every time something doesn't make any sense, people just tell me I've forgotten. There is nothing wrong with my memory. I know you're all lying to me. It's all part of the scam.'

I'm speaking so fast that my words are tangled, but it felt good to simply say my theory out loud. I am tugging on the cuff of his shirt, but he doesn't bother to free himself from my grip.

'Let's get a few things straight, okay, Laura?'

I nod. I'm sceptical that he will say anything believable, but I'm curious to see what elaborate story he conjures up this time.

'I am trying to help you. We all are. If I do a blood test, then all it will show is the sedative I have personally administered.'

My heart jumps in my chest. Finally, I hear something I actually believe. Doctor Hammond admits he's a willing accomplice. Christ, can I trust no one?

A light knocking on the door as it creaks open distracts me. I can hear Mark's voice. Why is he here? Has he come to join the witch hunt for my sanity?

I straighten out my clothes and run my hands over my hair. I'm incredibly nervous. I almost begin to giggle. Doctor Hammond stands up and slowly turns to face Mark. The look of concentration that he wore for the duration of his conversation with me is imprinted heavily on his face. The smile Mark entered the room with quickly fades. The two men exchange a handshake before Doctor Hammond leaves the room, leaving the door slightly ajar behind him.

I grip the arms of the chair until my knuckles whiten and my eyes drop to the floor and onto the pieces of broken vase still scattered on the ground. The jagged porcelain is there if I need it. Oh my God. Oh my God.

'Hi,' Mark says softly. He reaches his hand out to hold mine. 'How are you feeling?'

I want to slap his hand away. I wonder how often he has run those same broad palms over Nicole's body. I shudder at the thought. But I don't want to piss him off so I accept his touch and take his hand. I twitch and shake as his fingers slip between mine. His palm is hot and clammy. He doesn't want to be here; it's written all over his face.

'I miss you,' he whispers.

Fat, salty tears run down my face. Mark slides his finger under his nose and sniffles. I miss him, too. I ache to hold him or to feel him in bed beside me. But I wish more that I didn't cry myself to sleep most nights, pining for the life we shared not so long ago. Nothing would ever be the same again. I so desperately want to reach out to him, but I don't know how. Mark has always been so strong. A bright mind on strong shoulders. But right now, he's a shell of the man I fell in love with. I could normally read Mark like a book, but the man before me is a stranger disguised by a familiar face.

'I want to go home,' I whisper. 'Please, can we just go home?'

Mark shakes his head.

I close my eyes trying to accept the pain of his rejection.

~~~

I slowly opened them again to find myself sitting on a train rattling quickly along the dark tracks of the New York City subway.

218

'Well, hello there!' a bubbly, young African American woman sitting beside me says.

She is scrutinising me like a hawk, but she's smiling. A huge, wide gummy smile that reveals plenty of missing teeth. The remaining few are as tarnished as dried tea leaves.

'Excuse me,' I say rubbing my sleeping eyes.

'You don't have to apologise to me, girl. You just sleepin'. The driver's gonna be none too keen on you riding on his carriage all day, though.'

'All day?' my words rattle in my throat. 'What time is it?'

'It's nine thirty now, but you been on this same train since ten this morning.'

'Nine thirty pm?' I squeal, jumping stiffly up from the seat.

'Yeah?' she says looking at me as though I've just landed from another planet.

I shake my head in disbelief. Where has the whole day gone? Where has Ava gone? And most important of all, where the hell am I?

'You're new to this, aren't ya?' she says, still smiling. 'You're gonna have to learn to work the system better. You can't stay on the same train all day. They'll notice. You gotta move around. Anyways, the exercise is good for you.'

Tears swell in my eyes, and without warning, they begin to fall softly down my face.

'Don't cry, honey,' she says. 'Hell, I know it's tough when you first start sleeping rough, but it does get easier. I had me a good day today. Found a perfectly good cheeseburger thrown in the trash. Only two small bites gone from the side. People throw away good stuff all the time, doncha know. You know where you're sleeping tonight? I'm goin' to the park; there's a group of us there. You can come along if you like?'

'I'm not homeless,' I stammer.

'You ain't fooling anyone, girl,' the woman replies snappishly. 'Look, they're a good bunch of people I hang out with. We take care of our own when things get hard. You gonna be very lonely on your own. You look like you need a friend.'

'I have friends,' I explain.

'Yeah, yeah, I believe you. And your friends just let you be wandering around down here for the last two days all alone. With friends like that, girl, you don't be needing no enemies.'

My hands fly to my face. How could I possibly have been down here for two whole days? Ava and I were just chatting a few moments ago.

'Do you know where we are?' I stutter beginning to accept the fact I'm completely lost.

'You been drinking? Or taken somethin'? You don't even know where you are. Next stop is Thirty-third Street. What does it matter anyway, all the streets look the same from down here.'

She's right. In the artificial light, I could be anywhere.

'How do I get to Macy's from here?'

'Why? You gonna to do a bit of shopping?' She laughs loudly. She holds her hand up and rubs her thumb and fingers together without clicking them. 'Don't you need some of this stuff?' she teases. I guess she's symbolising money – or the lack of.

Her patronising is really starting to irritate me.

'I know my way home from there...I think?'

The woman looks at me with real concern. I confuse her, I guess, but I really don't care.

'You bang your head or something? I think you need to see a doctor. You don't seem right in there.' She taps me on the temple.

I didn't want to hear any more. She scares me. She scares me because a tiny part of me thinks she might be right. I slap my hands over my ears and shake my head from side to side. A sudden image of Doctor Hammond pops into my mind and I'm terrified. I looked around, paranoid that he's coming for me. He'll find me and drag me back to confinement. So many suppressed memories rush to the surface that I think my head will explode like a firework on the fourth of July. I remember the clinical, white walls of the hospital. The stillness of my isolation room. The torture of all the grilling questions. The psychological trap they have laid for me. I scream; I just open my mouth and let the pure frustration spill. I scream and scream and scream.

Everyone stares at me. Even people in the next carriage peer through the glass of the doors to catch a glimpse of my meltdown. A young mother sitting opposite cradles her son tightly in her arms turning his head into her chest and away from looking at me.

'What's wrong with the strange lady,' he says and points.

'I'm not strange,' I roar. 'I'm not crazy.'

I lunge through the doors as soon as the train stops, almost knocking several people over with my excessive forcefulness. I calmed quickly after my outburst, and now I'm drowning in mortification. I can feel the shocked eyes of every commuter burn through the hopelessly transparent shield with which I try to protect myself.

I have to go back to Nigel's. Ava will be terribly worried. I can't understand how we separated when I was so careful not to let her out of my sight.

I'm very proud of my navigational skills as I walk towards the exit at the final station just before Nigel's house. It's as if the journey was routine. I didn't even have to think or stop to read the subway map. My legs just began walking in the right direction all by themselves. They automatically knew when to change trains and which train to catch. My fingers understood which route to select on the ticket machine. It's all so incredibly familiar.

I can smell the fresh air battle to reach me, drawing me outside. A giant, relieved smile creeps across my face as I inhale deeply, filling my lungs with actual semi-fresh air. I'm just about to start ascending the steps when I notice a little boy wandering around behind me. *He's lost.* I turn around to face him, and I recognise his gaunt face and grubby blond hair immediately. He's the little homeless boy.

'Where's your mommy,' I ask, imagining his poor mother would be blind with panic.

He hangs his head and doesn't answer. I stretch my hand out to hold his, but he winces and jerks away. Perhaps my approach is too strong.

I bend down on one knee and bring my head level with his.

'Are you lost, sweetheart?' I ask as softly as I can.

I root in my pocket and find a half-eaten packet of fruit gums. I offer them to him, and he nearly snaps my hand off as

222

he quickly grabs them. *Maybe he isn't so shy, after all.* He stuffed one after another into his little mouth without taking the time to chew. I'm afraid he'll choke, but he savages the jellies before they have a chance to lodge anywhere near his throat.

'Will we go find your mummy?' I ask hoping the sweets have sealed our friendship.

He shakes his head sadly.

'Do you know where she is?' I ask.

He raises his grubby, little hand and points to some freestanding bins in the distance.

'Is your mommy down there?'

'She's asleep.' he explains.

I smile at hearing his sweet voice.

'Let's go see if we can wake her?' I suggest.

I hope she's still there. If she's woken to find him missing, then I'm certain she will be searching for him and we may miss her.

I walk quickly almost forgetting the size of his small legs. He trots beside me, struggling to keep up. He wraps his small hand tightly around mine. His fingers are sticky and cold. He has no coat and one of his shoes is missing half its sole.

A pair of skinny legs lay knotted together and peek out from behind the large bins. The smell from the rubbish is positively foul. My stomach retches as we get closer. I pull the little boy in close to me shielding his eyes from the disturbing scene we find.

The young mother is unconscious on the ground. An offensive smell of urine stings my nose, and I automatically hold my breath. Her face is mashed into a puddle of her own vomit. She grips an empty bottle of cheap vodka in her hand and another broken bottle lies beside her.

I don't know what to do. I can't abandon the child. I can't leave him alone with his disastrous mother. I scoop his light, frail body into my shaking arms and hug him tight.

'It's okay,' I promise. 'I'll take care of you.'

He snuggles his tired head into the crook of my neck, and I savour the warmth of his little body.

'If I remember correctly, you like cookies. Is that right?'

'I've never had a cookie,' he says.

'But just earlier…I saw…'

His body tensed in my arms. And I realise I'm scaring him again.

'Okay, well, cookies are yummy. And I think you'll like them a lot. Would you like to try one?'

His grip around my neck loosens, and I can breathe again.

'I'll take that as a yes,' I say. 'Would you like to come to my house? I have some cookies there. Strawberry milk, too.'

His head bobs up and down, and he actually seems excited.

'What's your name?' I ask not expecting to get an answer.

'Lorcan,' he whispers softly as if the two syllables are too big for his mouth.

'That's a lovely name.'

A couple of police officers pass us on the steps, and for a brief moment I freeze as the gravity of what I'm doing shoots up my spine. I pull Lorcan tight against me, but it doesn't ease the horrible fear that the officers will try to take him from me.

'There's a woman passed out down there. She's in a bad way,' I say, trying to distract attention from the scared little boy in my arms.

'Okay ma'am, we'll take care of it,' one of the officers says as they walk away. They don't acknowledge Lorcan. I know I should have told them that he's the drunk woman's son, but I can protect him. I can save him. I want to. I want to keep him.

Lorcan shivers as the cold night air bites through his flimsy jumper. I stand him in front of me, and he beams at me with an adorable smile. I take off my heavy, winter coat and drape it around him. It overlaps, cocooning him and he snuggles against the soft material. I pick him up once more and begin running towards Nigel's apartment. I almost trip a couple of times because I'm paying more attention to looking over my shoulder than watching where I'm going. I can't shake the feeling that someone, anyone, everyone, will snatch him from me and I will be alone again.

I swallow a lump of nervous bile as I walk boldly past the main reception area of the hotel. I slam my fingers against the buttons in the lift and my legs twitch nervously as I wait for what feels like hours for the doors to open. I punch in the code instructing the lift to take us to the private top floor. I didn't even question how I knew the correct combination of numbers because I'm running on autopilot. I won't breathe properly until we are safely inside the confines of Nigel's apartment.

I bang on the penthouse door so hard I feel my hand bruise as it connects with the solid oak.

Nigel opens the door and his jaw gaps unattractively. 'Laura. Oh, thank God. We were so worried.'

'I'm sorry; I don't know how I got lost,' I say as I barge past him, taking the door and slamming it shut behind me.

I press my back against the door, barricading it with my shaking body in case someone bursts through after me.

Ava races to me from the kitchen, wearing rubber gloves and a damp tea towel draped over her shoulder.

'Jesus, Laura. Where have you been?' She throws the gloves off and stretches her arms out wide preparing to hug me.

She stops abruptly just meters in front of me and slowly begins to back away. 'Who is that?'

She points towards Lorcan, her finger twitching as if I'm holding a grenade in my arms.

'This is Lorcan,' I say proudly.

'Lorcan,' she echoes. It's not a question. She hasn't misheard. 'Lorcan. Don't you think that's a little too coincidental?'

'Yeah.' I smile. 'It's a sign; you definitely have to call your baby Lorcan now.'

'Whose kid is this?' Nigel asks smiling at Lorcan. It's obvious he likes children.

I ignore their questions and, double-checking the door is firmly closed, I walk to the couch. I set Lorcan between some fluffy cushions and turn to the first children's channel I can find on the huge, flat screen television.

'Whose child is that?' Nigel repeats following me through to the sitting room, frustration creeping into his voice. 'Do you know this child?'

'It's the little boy from the train station,' Ava announces. 'Does his mother know he's here?'

'Of course not,' I snap.

'Oh Christ,' Ava says beginning to shake. 'Did you kidnap him?'

I don't answer her.

'I knew this was a bad idea,' Ava whispers quietly to Nigel, but I heard her.

'Shh…' Nigel says placing his finger over his lip. 'We don't want to scare him.'

'How can I shhh…she has stolen a child. I think we have to face the fact we have a problem.' Nigel clasped his hands and presses them down on the top of his head. 'I knew this would never work. You should still be in the hospital.'

'Excuse me?' I growl, my attention still focused on Lorcan.

Nigel's nose twitches and his feet shuffle. His edginess dents his usual perfection.

'Nothing,' Ava snaps. 'Never mind.'

'We have to take him back to his mother.' Nigel's stiff upper body attempts to soften, but it's a fail.

I shake my head.

'Don't be ridiculous, Laura,' Ava shouts.

'I'm not stupid,' I retaliate angrily.

'No one is suggesting you're stupid, Laura,' Nigel whispers.

'Not stupid, my arse. Only stupid people steal children,' Ava adds.

Nigel ignores Ava. Maybe he thinks she's being rude, too.

'I didn't steal him,' I explain dryly. 'I saved him. His mother is a drunk.'

'Okay, okay,' Nigel says calmly. The crackle of his voice dilutes his fake composure. 'Maybe you did save him, but we have to take him to the police now.'

'No way,' Ava screeches. 'We can't get the cops involved. You know that.'

'The cops don't care about him as I do,' I say, sitting on the arm of the sofa and stroking his matted hair with my fingertips.

'We have to take him back down to the train station,' Ava says coldly.

'Christ, he's a little boy not a stray puppy. We can't abandon him,' I scold.

'We don't have many options here,' Nigel interrupts. 'His welfare has to come before all other crap, Laura. We have to take him to the police. They can trace his mother or put him into care if necessary.'

'No cops,' Ava bellows.

I shake my head repeatedly at every word that passes Nigel's lips.

'There is no other way,' Nigel bellows, finally showing signs of temper.

Lorcan begins to cry, and I pull his head onto my knee and stroke his cheek to comfort him.

'He stays with me,' I say. I mean it. I have no intention to leave him. Ever.

Nigel throws his arms in the air and lets them flop lifelessly by his side, pulling his tall frame down with them until he's hunched like an old man. 'I don't know what to do anymore, Laura. I just don't know.'

There's a scratch in his voice, and I suspect he is referring to more than just the boy.

'I'm his mother; I know what is best for him,' I snarl.

Nigel's finished arguing. He looks at me with pain in his eyes. *I prefer his arguing.* His stare hurts my soul. It's an expression I know because I've seen him wear it before. A burning headache ignites in my skull. More memories race around my mind like pages of a scrapbook flicking open. I rock my head roughly from side to side, hoping to shake them away. I don't have time for this crap now. I have a child to care for.

Nigel says just one word. 'Mother?'

My heart stings, and my head feels too hot. 'I mean, I *am* a mother. I know what's best.'

'He can stay for the afternoon. We can get him washed up and get something for the poor little lad to eat. But after that, Laura, we have to take him to the police, okay?'

I know Nigel is no longer making a suggestion. He's decided on a plan and his tone makes it clear he'll tolerate no further discussion. I agree to his kind offer even though I do not intend to stick to it.

I take Lorcan to the bathroom to get cleaned up, but I don't miss Nigel grabbing his phone as soon as he thinks my back is turned. I need to move quickly.

Lorcan loves the silky bubbles of the bath. He splashes and laughs, and on a couple of occasions, he worryingly dives head first into the water. The bath water turns a murky greyish blue. I can hear Nigel pacing outside the bathroom door on his phone. I'm enjoying Lorcan's excitement, but I hurry to get him out. I reach for a large towel and cradle his painfully thin body in the soft cotton. He smells as good as fresh cut grass in springtime, and I find myself kissing his little head with affection. He beams from ear to ear and a twinkle of innocence sparkles in his big, blue eyes. I feel his dependence; his need to be cared for. He needs me, but I need him more. I ache to fill the void in my heart. A happy little smile from a content child is the perfect fit.

His own clothes are too soiled to even attempt to wash so I bin them. Thankfully, jeans, jumpers, and even a pair of air-cushioned trainers litter the couch where Nigel has laid them out. I didn't ask him to pick up clothes for Lorcan, but I appreciate his help. I've no idea how he managed to do it so quickly. I didn't even notice that he left the penthouse.

I enjoy rummaging through the bright colours to find an outfit that would highlight Lorcan's soft curls and long legs.

Lorcan helps examine the clothes for a short while, but his attention is easily drawn back to a plate of biscuits and loud cartoons. He's content. I guess it's possible that for the first time in his short life, he's not hungry. My heart aches as I stare at him. He's a rather attractive child. With his big eyes and a chiselled chin, he could easily have passed for my own son. In fact, if I didn't know better, I could well believe he was mine.

I sit for a long time on the couch with him – one eye on Nigel and one eye on the television. I laugh along at the silly antics of the fictional characters of the colourful cartoons and eat so many chocolate chip goodies that I think my stomach will explode. I hadn't smiled so genuinely in a long time. As darkness fell, Lorcan laid his head on my lap, and within minutes, he was sound asleep. I changed the channel on the television and prepared to relax for the rest of the evening.

I ignore the noise coming from the kitchen. I suspect Ava and Nigel are arguing about what to do with Lorcan. I don't care what either of them suggests because it's irrelevant. By tomorrow morning, the problem will no longer be of their concern. I map out my escape plan in my head and smile happily as I kiss Lorcan's sleepy forehead. We will leave before dawn. I know that Lorcan and I will be safe together; everything else I can worry about later.

Chapter Twenty-Six

It's been a long time since Mark and I shared the same bed, but the loneliness of waking up in our bed without him stings even more than usual. I toss and turn in the solitude. Every fibre of the mattress irritates my exhausted body. I know it's early. It's still dark outside, and the street is absent of any activity. I hope I'll drift back to sleep, but my mind turns to thoughts of Mark sleeping in the spare room. I forcefully pin myself to the bed. I'm afraid that if I move, I'll lose the battle I have with my heart that begs to be beside him. I imagine lying with his arms around me. I ache so much to feel him. Missing him is becoming a physical pain and it is overwhelming sometimes. I torture myself with the same futile thoughts as yesterday morning and the morning before. *Why has everything gone so wrong? How have I let so much slip away from me? How could I repair the damage I know I'm causing?* I'm alone. I'm so horribly by myself, and I hate it.

I scrunch my eyes tight and run my hand back and forth over my aching head. I try hard to concentrate on happy memories. I want to go to my feel-good place that Doctor Hammond and I spoke about, but my brain is refusing to cooperate. Images of a little, white box with shiny, blue handles begging to be opened parades across my mind. I want so desperately to open the box, but I can't raise my arms to lift the lid. I realise I see this poignant, little box more and more often. Maybe it's time I told Ava about the strange box? Maybe she would understand what it means.

I look at my watch. It's eight thirty. I shoot from the bed and jump onto the floor. We're late – as usual. I face the unflattering prospect of dropping Lorcan to school with my pyjamas still bulging out from under the grubby tracksuit I pull on over. I wander around the room in circles a few times looking for my slippers. When I've spun around so many times I feel dizzy, I decide to give up and sit on the bed. I allow myself to relax for a moment and savour the silence. Once I wake the kids, the house will buzz with noise and a headache will be an instant certainty. This is my favourite part of the day. It's the only five minutes of the twenty-four hours in a day when I can hear myself think. I crave a little more me time.

I wander into the hall and begin to walk with my eyes still half closed towards the kids' room. I swerve automatically to avoid the mule post of the stairs that I've banged my hip on way too often. Unfortunately, my manoeuvring is a little overenthusiastic, and I began to trip. I reach out to grab the post, hoping to break my fall, but I feel the hard smack of the floor when it meets my jaw. I shake off the pain and look around. There was no post to grab, there were no stairs to navigate, there's nothing familiar. I'm not at home in the comfort of my own house preparing for my daily routine. I'm standing in striped pyjamas in the centre of Nigel's posh bloody apartment with my children stolen from me on the other side of the ocean. A giant, golf ball-size lump forms in my throat and tears blur my vision.

I race back to my room and shut the door behind me. A horrible darkness creeps over my eyes, and I know I am going to pass out. I'm beyond tired now, so I embrace the feeling. I lie down on the soft cream carpet and close my eyes. Maybe

I've been wrong to fight it all this time. Maybe I'm fighting the truth. Perhaps if I face the darkness, some light will follow. Maybe I'm thinking bullshit now, but I just don't know. I don't know anything anymore. Everyone around me scares me. *Hell, I even scare myself.*

Ironically, this time I remain awake and I continue to think of a happy morning at home with the kids. A light knock sounds on my bedroom door and a small hand struggles to twist open the handle. Lorcan pops his little face around the opening door and his bright smile makes my heart jump happily.

'Breakfast is ready,' he says cheerfully.

'Okay,' I say, returning his smile. 'I'll be there in a minute.'

'Okay.'

I can hear his little legs barely graze the tiles as he happily skips away. I glance at my watch again. Eight forty-five. I can't tell if it's Irish or New York time. I realise with stinging eyes that no amount of rubbing them will clarify the time for me. A few stubborn rays of light break through the heavy fabric of the curtains. It's morning. My plan of escape has failed to materialise. I will have to reformulate.

I can smell freshly baked bread as I enter the hall, making my mouth water. Nigel is standing in the kitchen proudly sporting an oversized *Everybody loves the chef* apron. I can't help but giggle. At first, I worry that I'll offend him, but I relax when I hear him snort, revealing a muffled laugh.

'Fancy a scone?' he asks.

I nod eagerly.

Lorcan sits contently on a tall stool at the end of the countertop. He's dressed smartly and his hair has been brushed.

He has one of the cushions off the couch under his bum to give him some extra height. The side of the cushion is covered in sticky blackcurrant jam in the distinctive pattern of little fingerprints, but Nigel doesn't seem to mind. I'd been quick to judge Nigel when we first met. I assumed he was a sumptuous bachelor and ladies' man. He may have been all those things, but he was so much more, too. He is kind and thoughtful and wonderfully at ease with Lorcan. An ease rarely found outside the bond of father and son. Nigel really seems to be enjoying the challenge of caring for a five-year-old.

'You'll make a great dad someday,' I say as I sit on the stool next to Lorcan and begin to dust away the scattered crumbs from around Lorcan's plate.

'Thanks,' Nigel mumbles, reluctant to accept the compliment. 'Butter or jam?'

'Sorry?' I say distractedly. I'm almost unable to pull my stare away from Lorcan's beautiful eyes to look at Nigel.

'For your scone. Would you like butter or jam? I have strawberry, blackcurrant, raspberry...' Nigel trails off noticing I'm not listening. 'Laura?'

'Sorry.' I apologise again. 'Strawberry would be lovely, thanks.'

Nigel places a hexagon-shaped plate in front of me. The warm scone sits beautifully presented in the middle with a few fresh strawberries resting on the side.

Lorcan announces quite loudly and with a mouth full of half-chewed pastry that he's full. He hops down from his chair and trots away to watch more cartoons. He has become a master of the remote control and can find all the kid's entertainment channels with the flick of a button. I feel myself grow increasingly uncomfortable with his absence. My legs tremble as I force them to remain still instead of racing after him. My head tells me to mind my manners and politely eat breakfast. My heart tells me to grab hold of Lorcan and never let him out of my sight. I settle on a compromise. Forgetting to excuse myself from the table, I pick up the fancy, china plate and carry it towards the sitting room.

'Where you off to?' Nigel asks.

I point towards Lorcan.

'Don't tell me you're a massive *Tom and Jerry* fan, too?' Nigel asked excitedly. 'I've loved them since I was a kid.'

I pause for a moment. An overexcited love for an old television show is far more admirable than a possessive obsession with a little boy.

'Yep, you've found my darkest secret. I'm a huge *Tom and Jerry* fan,' I lie.

'Really?' Nigel continues, more than a little unconvinced.

'Yes, really,' I snap. *What the hell does a stupid cartoon matter? Why does he care so much?*

'Who's your favourite then, Tom or Jerry?' he quizzes.

'Tom.'

'Oh, me too. I love that mouse.'

'Yeah, he's a great mouse?'

'Wrong,' Nigel moans. It was a new, almost aggressive Nigel. A Nigel I didn't know existed.

'Excuse me?'

'Tom is the cat. Jerry is the mouse,' he says sternly.

'Okay, thanks for the education.' I frown, not following where his strange questions were leading.

'You're a huge *Tom and Jerry* buff, yeah? So much so that you can't sit at the table and enjoy a meal with me because you might miss an episode. It's just funny that you don't know which character is which, that's all.'

I've no idea what I've done to irritate Nigel so much. Perhaps he's a stickler for breakfast etiquette. He's certainly not as transparent as I first thought. I think I like this three-dimensional Nigel more.

'Sorry.' I apologise, embarrassed. 'Let's eat?'

I place my plate back on the table and sit down. I hope my edginess isn't painfully obvious. My fingers tremble as I spread the jam over the crisp, white scone. I hate raisins, but I try to ignore their shrivelled brown heads peeping at me from the corner of the otherwise delicious treat. I bite deep, filling my mouth completely. My stomach heaves as I try desperately to force the lump down my throat. I'm going to be sick. I can't contain it any longer.

I cover my mouth with my hand and force my chair back quickly. As I turn my back on him, Nigel catches the plate containing my nibbled scone and flings it to the floor. The shrill smash startles me. I forgot the woes of my temperamental tummy and turn to face the mess.

'What the hell?' I shout, more angry than shocked. He's broken the plate solely to get my attention. It's irritatingly dramatic. Nigel isn't a threating person, but fear begins to boil inside me nonetheless.

'What the hell is right,' Nigel bellows, his face puce with temper. 'What the hell are you playing at?'

I scan the room for any hint that the commotion may have woken Ava. I wait and wait but everything is eerily still. Nigel catches my pathetic glances. His eyes soften. He picks up the stool he's also knocked to the ground and offers me the seat. I reluctantly sit down.

'She's not here,' Nigel says very matter-of-factly.

I look at him almost cross-eyed. 'Who?'

'Ava! That is who you're looking for, right?'

I nod.

'She's not here.'

I shake my head. I don't know why.

'Jesus Christ, Laura, she's not fucking here. You can't use her to save you. Save your goddamn self for once.'

I don't understand what Nigel means, but the cruel resentment in his voice brings me close to tears.

'Enough,' he snaps. 'I've seen enough tears to last me a lifetime.'

His anger just makes me cry more.

'Why are you doing this?' he asks.

'Doing what?' I don't understand.

'Torturing everyone. I know it's hard. Of all people, I know. But damn it, it hurts for everyone. You're not the only one in pain and you're making it worse for us all.'

Nigel hits a nerve. For a second, a flash of guilt radiates brightly in my mind, but it dims quickly. I have nothing to feel guilty for; I'm the victim. My life is destroyed. I'm entitled to sulk if I want to.

'Where is Ava?' I stammer.

'I told you already. She's not here.' Nigel slams his hand so hard on the counter all the cutlery shakes. He's making it very clear that he doesn't appreciate my asking.

I try not to let his fury intimidate me, and I continue to quiz him about Ava's location.

'You know exactly where she is, Laura,' Nigel insists.

What? Ava didn't tell me she was going out. I don't bother to contradict him. This is yet another side to him. And this side isn't nice like the others. If I ask any more questions, then it might make him even angrier.

I take a scone from the basket on the counter and stuff it roughly into my mouth.

'There,' I stutter through the dry crumbs. 'I ate breakfast with you.'

Nigel rolls his eyes. 'Drama queen.'

The insult is strangely familiar, as is choosing to ignore it. I hate him at that moment. *Who is he to judge me?*

I exhale a couple of times, each large breath calming my frayed nerves. I'm finished with this pointless argument. Nigel's opinion is uninvited and doesn't even make any bloody sense. I know he is judging me. He probably started the minute I stepped into his place. But I don't care. I don't need him. After today, I won't need anyone… just Lorcan.

I hop down from the stool and away from Nigel like a sulking child. Thankfully, Lorcan hasn't heard Nigel's outburst. Or, if he had, it didn't bother him. He's happy to remain curled up on the couch watching television.

'You can't keep him,' Nigel says, following me.

Oh, fuck off.

I shrug my shoulders dismissively and continue walking.

'You can't replace one child with another,' he adds.

238

I spin around. Ferocious temper seeps from my every open pore. 'You bastard. How dare you?' I scream. 'I love my kids. I would never replace them. NEVER.'

Nigel falls silent and hangs his head.

'I'm leaving. Now,' I say, my heart working like a jackhammer against my ribs.

'Honey, time to go?' I call, catching Lorcan's attention.

A small, sad frown curves his cherry lips. He's clearly unimpressed that I'm interrupting his viewing, but he gets up and begins to walk towards me. I grab his petite hand in mine, my knuckles whitening from the tightness of my grip. Lorcan yelps softly and pulls his hand away. I hurt him. It was an accident, but that's a useless excuse, especially to a crying little boy.

'I'm so sorry,' I say bending down to kiss the reddened tenderness around his palm. 'I didn't mean to hurt you. I would never hurt you.'

Lorcan gazes at me with his big, beautiful eyes. The adorable sparkle that had shone so brightly yesterday is faded now and patched over with fear. My heart sinks so deep it rattles around my ankles.

'Was I naughty?' Lorcan asks sadly. No tears form in his eyes, but his bottom lip quivers. *Is he too afraid to cry?*

'Of course not,' I explain, hugging him against my chest.

He doesn't lift his arms to wrap them around my neck as I hoped he would. 'My mommy says I'm naughty all the time. That's why she throws things at me. I make her angry.'

I glance at Nigel. Any hint of anger is missing from his face. He's pale now and upset.

'Is that why your back hurts?' I ask softly. I'd noticed some old bruising on Lorcan's back when I bathed him. I assumed he'd taken a fall, just like five-year-olds do every so often. I should have realised sooner.

'I spilt my mommy's special drink. She was very angry.'

'Your mother hurt your back?' Nigel asks walking slowly towards us.

'She was very cross,' Lorcan repeats tears finally falling from his eyes. 'Do I have to go back now?'

Nigel stares at the timid little boy. Sad disgust contorts his face. He smiles at me and nods. Relief sweeps through my entire body. I could keep him. Nigel would help me save him.

'No, Sam, you don't have to go. You can stay watching the cartoons,' Nigel softly assures as he playfully tosses Lorcan's soft curls.

I scowl at him. 'Sam?' I say. *Who the hell is Sam?*

'This is Sam,' Nigel explains pointing towards where Lorcan climbed back up on the sofa

I shake my head confidently. 'No. That's Lorcan.'

'No,' Nigel says, 'I promise you, the scared little boy sitting on the sofa is Sam.'

I follow Nigel into the kitchen where he makes two very strong cups of black coffee. He takes a large mouthful from one and places the other at the end of the counter.

'Drink that,' he orders.

'I don't like coffee,' I lie, resenting Nigel's bullying.

'I know damn well you're addicted to the stuff,' Nigel says.

It's a clear accusation, but there's no harshness in his tone. It's a simple matter of fact. He does know I'm a coffee lover. I begin to wonder if Nigel knows a lot more about me than I realise. I dismiss the silly thought. I don't have time to play cryptic mind games with myself. We have a frightened little boy to look after.

I pick up the coffee and savour the smell of the rich blend before drinking half the cup in one large gulp.

'What now?' I ask, twitching from the caffeine rush.

Nigel stares into his cup and doesn't look up.

'What are we going to do about Lorcan? I think I should take him home to Ireland with me.'

'Are you mad?' Nigel snorts, spilling his coffee all over his crisp white shirt. 'How would you even get him past airport security?'

'I would…I would…I eh…'

'Exactly,' Nigel snaps as he grabs a cloth from the drawer and tries to minimise the coffee damage to his clothes. 'We have to take Sam to the police station.'

I slam my cup on the counter and prepare for an argument. Nigel doesn't allow me the pleasure.

'You can protest all you like, but he is an abused child and he needs the state to protect him, not some silly misguided woman with her own selfish interest at the forefront.'

Nigel throws the cloth into the sink and stares at the stain with disgust. He blames me; I can see it in his burning glare. He seems to blame me for many things, none of which I understand. But his anger is blunt and obvious and there can be no misunderstanding there. He really dislikes me. Nigel gathers up Lorcan's scattered clothes and stuffs them into a couple of carrier bags. He throws in a couple of large chocolate bars and a few cans of ice tea also. He holds both bags in one hand and scoops Lorcan up in the other arm.

241

'Time to go, Sam,' Nigel says kissing Lorcan on the head. 'Say goodbye to Laura.'

'Bye bye,' Lorcan says like a trained parrot.

'Please, Nigel, don't do this,' I beg, crying hysterically. 'Don't take Lorcan away from me; he's all I've got.'

'Bye bye, Laura,' Lorcan says once more.

My legs give way beneath me, and I fall to the ground with a rough thump. I'm desperate to scramble up again, but my lifeless limbs are no longer under my control. I want so badly to kiss Lorcan goodbye, but I remain in a disgruntled heap. 'Please,' I continued to plea, 'don't do this.'

Nigel rests the bags beside the front door and stands Lorcan beside them. 'Wait here, Sam.' He smiles.

Lorcan does as he's told. No matter how much I call out to him, he remains by the door. Nigel paces towards me, catches my slump body, and lifts me roughly upright. I slouch forward. My full weight draped over his strong arms. 'Stand up,' he shouts.

'I can't.'

'Stand. The. Fuck. Up.'

I try. I really do. I know what to do, my brain knows I should simply wiggle a little and place my feet on the ground with the rest of my body resting on top, but I don't remember how.

Nigel lets go and I fall in a painful heap. *Ouch.*

'I'm not soft like Mark,' he scowls, his jaw clenched in temper. 'I'm sick of your selfish crap. I have a friend in a precinct downtown. I'm taking Sam there.'

I begin to cry uncontrollably, but it only makes Nigel angrier.

'Clean yourself up, we're having guests later.'

I run my fingers under my tear-soaked eyes and wipe away large clumps of last night's mascara.

'Can I at least kiss Lorcan goodbye,' I ask.

'Of course,' Nigel says, 'just walk over to the door and kiss him. I'm not stopping you.'

A tearless cry scrapes the back of my throat. Nigel is cruel. He knows I can't find the strength to carry myself forward. I shake my head – defeated. Nigel also shakes his, but his is a shake of disapproval.

'Goodbye,' he says as he pulls a photograph out of his back pocket and drops it on the coffee table. It's close enough for me to see the various colours of the people's clothes but too far to make out their faces.

'Sam and I are leaving now. If you want to see Lorcan, walk to the table. Goodbye.'

He slams the hall door behind him.

Chapter Twenty-Seven

Time ticks by in slow motion. Hours feel like days. The cold of the floor has worked its way through my fluffy pyjama bottoms and numbed the cheeks of my bottom. I strain my eyes to see the photograph on the table, but I have no further success in making out the images. I do however manage to cause a headache that pounds in my skull like butter in a churn. It takes hours for me to realise that the light tapping sound I originally suspect is a leaky tap in the bathroom is actually the tapping of the sole of my slipper off the edge of the coffee table. My legs are shivering as the cold drives down my calves and into my feet. I have feeling – sharp pain from the icy floor, but I'm delighted. The shock from Nigel's aggression has worn off and my body is once more prepare to surrender itself to my brain's commands.

I scarper shakily towards the table. Pins and needles pinch the backs of my knees, and I want to yield to the pain and sit back down but I don't. I grasp the unframed picture from the table and drop it just as quickly. It lands upright and stares at me. I slam my eyes shut, convinced that if I can't see it, then it isn't real. But the brief second I stare at the picture is long enough to burn the images into my mind. I can't escape from the faces I know are resting on the ground. I peel open one eye and then the other. A cloud of disbelief hazes over the image, and I have to squint to make sure my eyes aren't playing tricks on me. I pick the picture up between my shaking fingers. *It can't be,* I tell myself. *It just can't be.*

Two little boys smile happily in the centre of the print. They wear matching superhero costumes. Their arms are draped over each other's shoulders, and it's obvious they're the best of friends. They're a similar build; like brothers. Their defining features are their different hair and slight height difference. The smaller, younger of the two has a thick mop of raven dark hair and his face is hidden behind a Batman mask. The elder boy's face is framed with soft, blond curls. A happy birthday banner hangs in the background just above their heads. I'm in the picture, too, sitting beside the boy with blond hair. I can't take my eyes off his perfect face. *It's Lorcan.* I can tell his smile a mile away. He's a lot thinner now and his greeny-brown eyes in the photo have faded to a light blue, but it's still him. *I'm sure.* My heart pounds so fast it almost blocks air from circulating around my chest.

I recognise the room in the background. How could I not? I'm standing in that very room now. The colour of the walls has changed, but it's definitely Nigel's sitting room. It's undeniable evidence that I've been in this place before.

Mark stands behind me in the picture; one hand on my shoulder and the other reaching forward to hold my hand.

Nicole is on the opposite side of the picture, looking fresh-faced and pretty. The Nicole I know is gaunt and drawn. *Why has she changed so much?*

She stands behind the raven-haired boy; her arm snuggled against his waist affectionately. It's just a strange mix of people. And we all look so genuinely happy, and so at ease in each other's company. *Is this some fucked-up Photoshop joke? But why?*

I turn the print over and examine the handwritten words on the back. It's my writing. *Lorcan's 4th birthday!*

I catch the corner and begin to tear. I rip the picture to shreds and leave the pieces on the ground where they fall, stomping my foot on the scattered pieces.

Even ripped up, the picture is freaking the shit out of me. I jump onto the ground and try to piece it back together; I want to hold it close to my heart. I piece the jagged edges together and Lorcan's face peers up at me, smiling. I flick my hands across the pieces and they swirl in the air and rain down like confetti. I open my mouth to scream, but no sound comes out.

The picture has opened a window into my past, and I can't get away from this. Closing my eyes doesn't help. The photograph is painted across the back of my eyelids like a mural. My thoughts map out like a giant jigsaw puzzle in my mind. Except all the most important pieces are still missing.

I know I've been to New York before, and I've obviously been in Nigel's apartment. So, Nigel knows me better than he's letting on. And he knows Nicole. That's too weird. Why didn't he ever say anything? They're friends, obviously. And his loyalties might lie with her and not me…maybe he's even helping Mark and Nicole. Reporting in with them regularly, telling them where to find me. *Fuck, fuck, fuck!*

The phone rings and I jump. I try to ignore it, but it's incessant. Whoever is at the other end isn't going to give up. I wait for the answering machine to cut in, but it just rings and rings and rings.

'Hello,' I bark, finally.

'Laura.' The voice on the other end twitches.

'Ava?'

'Yeah, it's me. Is Nigel there?'

'No, he left a few hours ago.'

'Really?' Ava asks sounding unusually drained.

'Everything okay? Where are you? Are you still at the airport?'

'Airport?' Ava echoes.

'Yeah, Nigel said he had guest later. He didn't say, but I just assumed you'd gone to pick them up or something. Where else would you be?'

'Oh, right. I didn't know he'd mentioned the guest. What time are you expecting him back? I really need to speak to him, and I can't get in touch on his mobile,' she explains.

'I dunno.' Just thinking about Nigel is pissing me off. 'He was really angry when he left. I was hoping you'd be back before him. I don't like being on my own with him. I wish you hadn't left without telling me.'

'Angry,' Ava says, like repeating my words is a habit that she's struggling to break. 'Why was he angry?'

'Long story, I'll tell you later. What time will you be back?'

'I don't know,' Ava mumbles.

I feel something is very off, but I can't put my finger on what. It's like speaking to a stranger on the other end of the phone. 'Everything okay?'

I know the honest answer is no, but I wait to see what Ava will say. She's sniffling. I can hear muffled sobbing through what I imagine is her hand covering the receiver.

'Ava,' I say sharply. 'Is something going on? Where have you been all day? Nigel has been gone a lot longer than I expected, too. Hours. What is going on?'

I glanced around the apartment. My eyes dart from wall to wall. The stifled conversation resurrects strong paranoia, as if

I'm a mouse in a cage, racing frantically on a spinning wheel but going nowhere.

'Ava, please tell me?'

Ava takes a deep breath. I hold mine.

'Nigel has gone to collect Adam from the airport,' she stutters.

I don't say a word. I've lost track of how long we've been in New York now, but it's understandable that Adam would come to see Ava. In fact, the only thing that surprises me is that he wasn't on the first flight out after us, or that he let her go at all. I wonder why she seems so reluctant to share that harmless nugget of information with me.

'I thought they would be here ages ago, but there's no sign of them,' she explains.

'You thought they'd be where? You still haven't told me where you are.'

Another large pause fills the air, and the habit is becoming exhausting. Ava is so silent I worry that the line has dropped.

'Ava,' I called breaking the calmness. 'Hello…Ava?'

'Sorry,' her meek voice answers. 'I'm in the hospital; I started to bleed last night.'

I almost drop the receiver.

'Oh no, not that baby,' I cry. 'Oh Ava, this is all my fault. I stressed you out and now you might lose your baby. I'm so sorry. I wouldn't blame you if you hated me.'

Suddenly, all Nigel's anger makes sense. He blames me for Ava's situation. If I had never brought Lorcan here, then Ava wouldn't have been so stressed. And it was all for nothing. I've already lost Lorcan. And now Ava might lose her baby, too. I feel sickeningly guilty.

Ava begins to laugh. I am not sure if it's to disguise her own worry or if she really thinks my panicking is funny. *What the hell?*

'You're as bad as Nigel. He's so freaked out, too,' she snorts. 'Everything is fine. I'm just here for observation. The baby is perfect. Ten little fingers, ten little toes. I even got my first scan picture last night. I can't wait to show you.'

'I'll come visit,' I say without hesitation. 'I'd love to see it.'

'I'm really tired, Laura.' Ava sighs. 'I'll be released tomorrow, and I'll show you then.'

Ava's reluctance to see me is worrying. Maybe she's more pissed off than she's letting on. She's alone in a hospital in a foreign country. She needs a friend.

'Okay,' I find myself agreeing. I don't want to upset her any further.

She must notice my disheartenment because she throws me a long-winded explanation about strict visiting hours and about how dangerous crossing the city is for a woman to navigate on her own. 'You might get lost again, Laura.'

'Yeah, you're right,' I say, crossing my fingers behind my back. 'I'll wait here until Nigel gets back. I don't think he'll be much longer.'

Ava's worrying about my poor sense of direction is a wasted effort. I know the route to the hospital as if I was there daily, and I know it's just another memory from my past that has dusted itself off without me even searching for it. I grab my coat and Nigel's spare set of keys. Racing out the door, I don't leave a note and I catch the bus on the street corner just in time.

A little over an hour later, I pause outside the automatic doors of the dauntingly large hospital. A nervous quiver forces the hairs on the back of my neck to stand spiky and straight. I don't want to go inside. It's not my first realisation that the accident has affected me badly, but it still freaks me out. I harbour a bitter distaste for the clinical sanctuary confined within the walls of the hospital. I consciously associate it with hurt and misery.

I refuse to tolerate my squeamish misgivings. I allow myself one giant shiver and force myself to walk inside. I read the information board in the reception area at least five times, but I still have no idea where the maternity unit is. It's marked clearly on the board, but I just can't concentrate long enough to get the words to resonate in my head. I give up and decide to wander the corridors instead.

For such a large, busy hospital, the corridors are eerily quiet. I'm almost alone apart from the odd nurse or clerical administrator passing by. I've never spent so long admiring my shoes before as I keep my head down. I memorise each stitch in the leather. But my pathetic effort to avoid eye contact is having the reverse effect and compounding how ridiculous my jitters are.

I wander around hopelessly. I'm deep within the bowels of the hospital now but none the wiser about what direction I should be heading. The lift doors open beside me and a mother and her little girl step out. The child is six or seven, I guess. She holds her mother's hand and hugs a tattered teddy bear under her chin. I imagine he's so threadbare from seven years of little hugs. She's small for her age and too thin. She wears a sparkly pink bandana on her head. Although it is pretty and suited for her small face, it's obviously not a fashion statement. The mother's face is pale and her bloodshot eyes spoil her pretty features. They walk slowly, almost tiptoeing. The little girl wilts after a few steps, and her mother stops walking to lift her daughter into her arms.

I can't bear to watch them any longer. It's breaking my heart; *no mother should have to know that fear.* But when the little girl drops her teddy, I find myself racing to pick it up for her.

'Thank you,' the mother says struggling as she tries to smile.

'You're welcome.'

The little girl grabs a grateful hold of her teddy and kisses and cuddles him with love.

'I hope you get better really soon,' I encourage.

Tears well in the mother's eyes and her shoulders shake as she tries to fight back tears, and I instantly regret my words.

I watch them walk away. The mother's arms wrap around her daughter's back. She's brave and defiant, but she knows they're cheating death and soon will be outsmarted. I empathise with her pain. I recognise it. I understand her fight against it; her desperation to protect and save her child.

I clench my chest and tug at my clothes. It's hard to breathe, as if the weight of my blouse against my skin is crushing me. It's too hard to be here. *I can't, I can't.* I want to turn around and run back to the sanctuary of fresh air, but I have to do this for Ava. *I have to.* It's just this place…the stench of disinfection and the undertone of death… I lean back against the wall, and breathe. *Just breathe.*

In less than a minute, I have my racing pulse and closing airways under control. Turns out Doctor Hammond knows some shit because his meditation technique has just calmed me down. Relieved that it worked but pissed off that I needed to draw on his advice, I begin to wander around some more. I peer into corridors and rooms that tell the story of others' lives. We're all just strangers surrounded by bricks and mortar. But there are so many stories unfolding under the one roof. I can't help but wonder how many people will be affected today by the news that someone they love is never coming home.

An only child prays over the bedside of her aged father; maybe once his life light fades out, she will be all alone in the world. A young, pregnant woman cradles her neat bump in her hands, aching for the loss of a father who will never meet his baby. A teenage boy with a mild concussion and a broken wrist wrestles with the guilt that his showing off in his new car has cost his passenger, and best friend, his life. All these innocent people have entered the hospital whole, but they've been broken by their loss. Their lives are changed forever. Time will heal their wounds, but their emotional scars will never fade.

My own scars are slashed all over my heart. I can't always see them, but every time a shocking memory surfaces, the wounds are ripped open once more.

Chapter Twenty-Eight

Finally, I stop outside the maternity unit. My fingers shake as I press the release button on the double doors, and without a word, someone buzzes me through. The nurse's station is vacant when I reach it, and I feel horribly self-conscious as I wait. A busy nurse in blue scrubs approaches me with a friendly smile. 'Are you looking for someone?'

Her kind face puts me at ease and I manage to return her smile. 'Ava Cassidy,' I say.

The nurse shakes her head. 'I don't believe we have an Ava Cassidy.'

I stare blankly at the wall behind the nurse. *What the hell do I say now?*

She must take pity on me because she pops behind the station and clicks a couple of times on the computer mouse.

'Silly technology.' She smiles. 'I miss the good old days of a pen and paper.'

'I know, right?' I say, remembering I haven't checked my social media in ages.

'I can't find anything here, but I'm on my way to the ward, if you want to follow me…I'll take a look around there for you.'

I follow so closely behind her that I almost step on her heels a couple of times.

'It's been a busy day and we've had a lot of admissions. Maybe some aren't in the system yet,' the nurse continues. 'Are you a relative?'

I nod.

She must feel as awkward as I do because she quickly fills the silence with small talk. 'We've had so many visitors today that I can't see straight,' she says.

I don't respond. I'm embarrassed as I wonder if that's her way of calling me a nuisance, but her kind smile is still bright and I decide I'm reading too much into it.

'Just wait here for a moment,' the nurse instructs as we reach the sliding doors of a four-bed ward. 'The doctor is with a patient. I'll call you when he's finished.'

She disappears behind some drawn curtains, and I'm once again alone in the hallway. I was used to being the patient and having Ava, and everyone, come visit me. It feels strangely surreal to now be in the very reverse of that situation.

I'm not alone for long. A frantic looking young man races towards me, almost skidding on the finely polished floor. As he grows closer, I realise it's Adam. I drop my head and stare at the floor as I prepare to face a seriously awkward conversation. I needn't have worried. Adam sees me, makes brief eye contact, and just as I'm about to say hello, he blanks me and walks straight past. His rudeness is upsetting, but I imagine he's distraught with worry. Nigel follows shortly behind him. He's less distracted. He throws a subtle nod my way but also continues to rush past me without a word.

A third man appears in their shadow, but this time it's me who instigates the ignoring. A nervous twitch causes a vein in my temple to pulse uncomfortably fast. I focus on the same floor tile for so long it begins to sway and bend under my watch, but I don't dare look up. I can feel warm breath fall on my hair and I almost feel violated. I begin to count backwards from ten. Doctor Hammond's meditation isn't working quite so well now.

He's uncomfortably close now as he reaches for my hand. I jump, hitting my back against the wall. The thud slaps a deep, ugly groan out of me.

'Oh Christ,' I yelp looking up to see Mark standing before me.

'Hello, Laura,' he says, his voice gritty and sexy as always.

My top teeth dig into my bottom lip.

'Can we go somewhere to talk?' he asks.

My head thrashes from side to side.

'Please, Laura? There is a lot to say.'

'I don't want to hear anything you have to say, Mark.'

I stare into his eyes expecting to see hatred, but all I see is pain, and it catches me off guard. He grabs me roughly by the arm and attempts to drag me through a swinging door and into a dark corridor.

'Please, Laura. It's not appropriate for you to be here.' Mark sighs.

I press hard into my feet and lock them against the floor. 'You can't bully me as easily anymore,' I snap.

Mark lets go and I almost fall on my arse, but I gain my balance just in time.

'I bet you're surprised to see me walking,' I snipe. My words are laced with hate.

'It's great to see you walking. I was so excited when I heard. It's real progress, Laura.'

Nigel and his big mouth. *I knew it.*

'I'm really proud of you.' Mark smiles.

I catch myself smiling back. I love hearing those words from my husband. They resonate deep within my heart, and for a moment, I almost believe him. His eyes sparkle as he watches me stand in front of him. The temptation to drop my guard and wrap my arms around him is overwhelming. *Christ, he's good.* He's a more cunning player than I ever thought possible.

'Where is Nicole?' I ask, certain the mention of her name will quash how drawn I am towards Mark.

'She thought it would be best if she stayed at home.'

'Of course, she did,' I snarl. Thinking of my children alone with that bitch makes me sick.

'She thinks we need time on our own to talk about everything.' Mark softens.

'There's nothing to talk about. I told you,' I spit. I'm lying. There's a multitude to talk about, but what's the point. Mark will just lie to me, and I've lost the will to entertain any more bullshit. 'You stole my life and gave it to that bitch. What more is there to say?'

'No, Laura. That's just not true. I didn't take anything from you. You are standing before me alive and well; after everything, I'm grateful for that.'

I roll my eyes. It's the best response I can come up with.

'Laura, you're being so unfair. Nicky is a rock. We'd be lost without her. We are lucky to have a friend that considerate.'

'Do you get lucky with her in bed, too,' I shout.

Mark backs away. 'Fuck, Laura! Is that what you really think?'

'No. It's not what I think. It's what I know.'

'Then you obviously don't know me at all,' he says, his eyes beginning to glisten as tears form.

Mark's pain feels so genuine, but I know I'll regret allowing myself to believe him.

'I thought coming home would help you, but I was wrong. You haven't changed. You still blame me,' he says.

'How can I not blame you? You're having an affair.'

Marks bottom lip curls downwards.

'Did you think I didn't know? Is it not working? Is that why you're here? Do you think we can move on now that you're finished fucking Nicole?'

Mark's pale face only irks me more.

'You tried to kill me, for Christ's sake. I think we are a bit past a kiss and a hug to make up, don't you?'

'Oh, Laura. I didn't know things were this bad,' Mark says with his eyes closed.

'Well, then you're not just a cheatin' bastard; you're thick as a plank, too. '

'Laura…' Mark tries to hold my hand, but my nails scratch him as I jerk away. 'You know I love you, and I could never hurt you. We've been through hell and back; you just don't remember.'

I toss my head back and stare at the ceiling.

'Once you remember what's happened, you'll wish that the pain you feel *is* because I'm having an affair. Then at least you'll have someone else to blame.'

What? I grab the sides of my head with my hands.

Part of me actually believes him. Dammit! On top of everything, now I have a niggling doubt about my theory. I'm *still* afraid of Mark, but that feeling isn't as strong as wanting him back.

'I don't understand,' I say shaking my head.

'I know,' Mark replies. 'I remember everything you don't, and I still don't understand.'

'Tell me?' I shout. 'Please, tell me whatever it is I've forgotten. Please. It's driving me crazy.'

'Shh,' Mark whispers as he reaches into his pocket and places something into my hand. 'Laura, try to calm down. There are sleeping babies here.'

I blush. Seeing Mark has messed with my head, and for a second, I almost forgot where I was. He must sense my unease because he takes a couple of steps back.

'Just look at it, Laura. Please?'

I glance down. It's the photograph I destroyed back at Nigel's apartment. It's held together with lots of sticky tape, and it wobbles in the middle. I look at the writing on the back. It's not mine. This time it's Mark's penmanship. *Mommy and Daddy's little princess.*

I stare at the words for a long time. *Too long.* When I look back up, I want to tell Mark that I still don't understand. The photo makes me sadder than I ever thought it was possible to feel, but I didn't know why. I want Mark to explain. But he's gone. He's getting too good at becoming invisible. Just like Ava.

The nurse reappears on the corridor. 'Did you get lost?' she asks softly.

I concentrate on folding the flimsy photo and gently push it into my pocket. I don't want to damage the repair work.

The nurse repeats herself a couple of times, but it's not until she clears her throat loudly that I give her my attention. She must notice I'm frazzled because she offers me a tissue. I grab it and dab away the patches of water-streaked makeup around my eyes.

'I'm sorry. I can't find your friend,' she explains.

'It's okay,' I find myself saying. It isn't, obviously, but the energy to argue eludes me now.

'Perhaps she's registered with a maiden or married name?'

I shake my head. 'It's just Cassidy. Ava Cassidy.'

The nurse asks some more questions hoping to be helpful. She even rings some other wards to try to locate Ava, but I'm too distracted to assist in her search. I'm trying to remember which door Adam and Nigel disappeared through earlier. That will lead me to Ava. I walk away while the nurse is still on the phone.

The ward is quiet. Most of the curtains are closed, and I don't dare to peek my head around any. I call Ava's name softly and hope I don't wake anyone who may be sleeping.

'Down here,' I hear Ava's voice.

I follow the sound to the end bed. Ava sits propped comfortably up with a couple of fluffy, white pillows. She has half a candy shop sitting on her locker and enough Diet Coke to float a small boat. Someone has certainly been looking after her. My cheeks flush realising I haven't brought her anything. I root in my bag for the bottle of orange juice I took from Nigel's this morning and add it to her collection of unopened bottles.

'You look good,' I lie as I lean forward and kiss her cheek.

She grabs my shoulders and hugs me tight for a long time. I can feel her fear. I know that feeling, and I hold her for as long as she needs.

'So,' she says finally letting go of my aching neck, 'you came anyway. I knew you would.'

I pull a sheepish smile and snort a little. Yes, I turned up at the hospital against her specific request not to, but I know her like the back of my hand. I wouldn't have come if I thought she genuinely didn't need or want me here. It's one of the things that makes Ava such a great friend; she always puts everyone else's problems ahead of her own.

'You managed to get here without getting lost then,' Ava teases. 'Your sense of direction is improving in your old age.'

'Yeah, I just seemed to know where I was going. It was really weird, actually.'

Ava drops her eyes to the ground. I shrug off her lack of interest; she has far more on her mind than me turning into a human sat nav.

We chat for a while about how she's feeling, and I share in her excitement as she shows me the scan picture. I lie and say the baby looks gorgeous even though all I can see is the shadow of her insides and a couple of obscure blobs. I find it hard to play the good friend role when deep down I'm seething with frustration. I've so many questions I need her to answer. But she's pale and her eyes are bloodshot from trying to keep them open. If I leave, then she'll get some much-needed rest. I have to consider her best interests above my own insecurities. I've waited this long for answers. Although another day will feel like an eternity, I'll just have to wait.

A rare, uncomfortable silence falls over us, and I suspect Ava has something on her mind but she won't dare say it. I debate whether to tell her I saw Mark. I should warn her to be on guard, but if the news scares her, it could be bad for the baby.

I decide to keep my mouth shut. She risked everything to help me, and now I have to do the same for her. Mark doesn't scare me as much as before. But maybe that's an even bigger reason to stand alert. He hasn't come all this way to tell me that Katie is sleeping through the night. He has an agenda. But New York has been good for my head. I'm in a better place to outwit Mark now.

I need to find Nigel even though I doubt he'll listen to anything I have to say. I've grown to be a thorn in his side, and he's never tried to hide his misgivings about me. His tuts, sighs, and finally his blind temper are far from a subtle hint that he has learned to detest me. No matter how little value he places on my opinion, he'll have to listen to me now. He needs to know that Mark has followed Adam and found us.

I'm about to say my reluctant goodbyes when I notice Ava's eyes widen and her fingers twitch nervously.

'Oh Christ,' I say as my hand covers my face. 'He's here, isn't he?'

I turn around expecting to find Mark standing with a weapon of some sort in his hand and all the lights to dim before the pandemonium began.

Instead, I find a very timid looking Adam lurking in the doorway with a giant bouquet of red roses in his hand.

'They're gorgeous.' Ava smiles.

Adam holds the flowers so high he almost hides his whole face. He's so on edge, I can see it from here, and I'm certain I'm the reason. I begin talking gibberish hoping to dilute the awkward situation.

'I don't think flowers are allowed here for anyone,' I say. 'Something about allergies and all that.'

Adam's lips quickly press together to form a narrow, straight line. 'You're not serious. That must be why they were left in the corridor. What am I supposed to do with these now?'

'Jesus, Adam. For a second there I thought you'd turned into a romantic.' I laugh.

Adam blushes and shuffles from one foot to the other as he sets the flowers down next to me at the foot of the bed.

'Leave them in the apartment for me. They'll be something to look forward to tomorrow when I get out of here,' Ava suggests, winking at me.

Although it makes sense, it hadn't dawned on me that Adam would be staying with Nigel also. My stomach bubbles uncomfortably at the thought of being under the same roof. I'll be sharing the apartment with two men who do little to disguise the fact that they can't stand me.

'Visiting hours are over in five minutes,' a nurse says as she walks around the ward and nods at all the visitors.

I realise I've been sitting on Ava's bed for the past ten minutes or so completely zoned out. I didn't hear a word either Adam or Ava said.

Finally, when Ava drifts to sleep, Adam places his hand on the small of my back and tilts his head towards the door. 'It's time to go,' he whispers. 'We shouldn't be here.'

I kiss Ava softly on the forehead. Adam doesn't, but I guess it's less about hiding his affection and more about concern that he'd wake her. For the first time, I actually believe he loves her. The worry of seeing her ill has brought out a new side to him, and the more time I spend with him, the more I realise that this is going to be one very lucky, little baby with two great parents.

'C'mon,' Adam says draping his arm over my shoulders. 'I'll give you a lift back.'

'Thanks.' I smile, genuinely grateful. Not so much for the lift but for the effort he's putting into being nice to me.

'See you tomorrow, Ava,' I whisper, painfully reluctant to leave.

She doesn't hear me. But it doesn't matter. I'm only trying to reassure myself anyway.

Chapter Twenty-Nine

Adam and I chat in the car like old friends. It's nice. There are no uncomfortable silences and no snide insults on either part, just conversation for the sake of conversation. We talk about Ava and my shopping spree and about Nigel's love of cooking. We joke and even laugh. We never mention Ireland, or Mark, or my kids.

Adam knows his way back to Nigel's place surprisingly well. I wonder if he's been there before, too. Maybe he visited with Ava at some stage. I'm tempted to ask, but there's something else I'd much rather know. 'Why are you being so nice to me?' I whisper, dropping my head and pressing the button as we step into the lift.

'Because it's what friends do and Ava would never forgive me if I didn't look out for you.'

I look up and notice Adam's eyes are glossy and tear stained. Neither of us bothers with any more small talk.

Nigel opens the door before we even knock and I brace myself for the foul stare I'm certain he'll throw. Nigel and Adam exchange some sort of strange wiggle your fingers and slam your knuckles together handshake, follow by a hard thud of their left shoulders knocking together, finishing with a pat for each other on the back. It certainly answers my earlier question. Adam has definitely been Nigel's guest before. They are good friends.

'How is she?' Nigel asks suddenly becoming less of a giddy fifteen-year-old and more a concerned friend.

'She's doing well. Showing definite signs of improvement,' Adam assures.

'That's great news. God, she had me worried there for a while,' Nigel says.

'It certainly was a wake-up call all right. I never should have let her come here, I just thought…' Adam sighs.

'This isn't your fault, man,' Nigel insists, staring convincingly at me. 'You're doing your best. Ava would be proud of you.'

I swallow the large lump in my throat and shuffle on the spot. God, I wish Ava was here. I don't think I can cope with the negative atmosphere until tomorrow. Maybe I should check into a hotel, but I decide against it. I can't afford to stay indefinitely in some hotel, no matter how cheap and dingy. I would eventually have to come back to Nigel's. If I think right now is awkward, then returning with my bankrupt tail between my legs would be ten times harder. I have to suck it up.

'Have you eaten?' Nigel asks.

'Yeah, I grabbed a sandwich at the hospital,' Adam says sticking out his tongue.

'That tasty, eh?' Nigel jokes. 'Come into the kitchen, and I'll fix you something real quick.'

Both men walk away. I lag behind. I wonder if it's okay to go to the bedroom I've been sleeping in. But Nigel still hasn't actually acknowledged my presence, and I'm beginning to feel like an intruder.

'You coming or what?' Nigel asks looking back at me.

'Me?'

'No, the invisible woman beside you. Yes, you. I assume you're hungry? If you want dinner, then you're going to have to help. You've been here long enough; you've officially lost guest status. You're part of the furniture now. C'mon.'

I smile so hard that I think I sprout a fresh wrinkle. It's such a relief not to be exiled. Both Nigel and Adam are making an effort to accept me. It's weird, but I'm grateful.

Nigel gives me a heavy, timber chopping board and some red and green peppers.

'Fajitas okay?' he asks.

'Yum,' both Adam and I say together.

'You were right, by the way,' Nigel says passing me a sharp knife.

I jump as the overhead light catches the stainless steel blade; dramatically magnifying its sharp point.

'It's okay,' Adam says dropping his eyes to the peppers in my hand. 'Just chop 'em into thin slices.'

When my heart stops beating frantically, my face flushes as I realise how ridiculous my reaction was. Adam is smiling understandingly at me; it's as if he expected me to flinch. *Weird.*

Nigel doesn't acknowledge my mini meltdown and continues to chat. 'Like I was saying, you were right. Sam was in danger. His mother had snatched him from his foster home a week ago. The cops were looking for him.'

A tingle ran up my spine. 'What?'

'You were right, Laura.'

I heard him the first time, but I don't think I'd ever grow tired of him saying that.

'You really did rescue him. Well done.'

I drop the knife almost reducing my foot by a shoe size. I can't believe Nigel is congratulating me. I was sure he thought I was crazy.

'Thanks,' I say. 'Where is he now? Can I see him?'

Nigel moves close to me and takes my hands in his. 'No, Laura, you can't see him.'

I nod as fat tears run down my cheeks. I had known the answer before I asked the question, but it still pinched in my heart. 'Is he happy?' I swallow hard.

'He's back with his foster family on Long Island. He's very happy,' Nigel says, his voice crackling.

Nigel's harsh exterior has been rocked by the little boy, and Nigel is about to show emotion. If I blink, I might miss it.

I grab some kitchen towel and dab my eyes. Nigel copies and then passes a sheet of the tissue to Adam who also has tears in his.

'Oh, these bloody onions,' Nigel sniffles.

Just under an hour later, the smell coming from the kitchen is gorgeous and my tummy rumbles as I wait impatiently on the couch. Nigel has tried hard to work with us, but he eventually got terribly agitated with Adam cutting the chicken breast too small. He told me off for stirring the sauce clockwise instead of counter clockwise. He kicked us out of his workspace, banning us from returning until he served dinner.

'Tada,' Nigel says as he carries a hot plate towards the dining table. His luminous, orange oven gloves complement the delicious colours of the crunchy vegetables.

'Tuck in,' he says proudly.

I rush to the table and take a large bite before I take the time to sit.

'I thought Ava wasn't coming home 'til tomorrow,' I say filling my plate.

Adam doesn't reply. His mouth is full. He shakes his head instead and swallows so hard I see the lump swell in his throat.

'Who's sitting there, then?' I point a plate resting in front of a vacant seat.

Nigel scowls across the table at an oblivious Adam. 'I thought you told her.'

'I thought you did.'

'How could I tell her? I haven't seen her all day,' Nigel snaps.

'Well, I couldn't tell her,' Adam says between more mouthfuls. 'I didn't want to upset anyone.'

'Will someone please tell me what's going on? Who was supposed to tell me what?' I groan.

'You could have told her on the way back from the hospital,' Nigel says, tossing his head towards me.

Adam lowers his eyebrows, scrunches up his nose, and stops short of sticking out his tongue.

Jesus, these two are worse than a pair of squabbling kids. If I wasn't so pissed off that they were keeping something from me, I'd probably laugh.

'Okay, Laura,' Nigel begins, and his tone instantly puts me on edge.

'Hang on,' Adam interrupts as he reaches across the table and takes the knife and fork out of my hands and places them at the far end of the table, then he reaches back and does the same with my glass of water and plate, leaving my area of the table completely empty.

Eyeing up my empty place setting, he says, 'Go on.'

Nigel nods at Adam as if to say, *good job*. He takes a deep breath like what he's going to say next will hurt.

'It's Mark,' he splutters, followed by some more deep breaths. *Ugh!*

I watch him, waiting for him to say more. But that's all I'm getting.

'He's here. I know.'

'You do?' Adam snorts spraying a mouthful of chewed up carrot across the table Nigel.

Nigel looks at the sticky patch on the table with disgust. 'Ugh, Jesus, Adam. Say it, don't spray it.'

I can't hold in my laughter any longer. Adam laughs and snorts, too. Nigel doesn't laugh.

'So, you're okay?' Nigel asks.

I shrug my shoulders. 'S'pose. I saw him at the hospital. It was a bit weird, but I'm okay now.'

'Oh, thank God,' Nigel says his shoulders falling and rounding. 'I was dreading telling you.'

Adam begins to laugh again, but this time I don't see the funny side. 'Oh yeah, Nigel. No wonder you tried to leave the dirty work for me,' he says.

Nigel shrugs and slugs Adam's arm.

'I thought you'd react a bit differently,' Nigel says.

'What do you want me to say?'

'Dunno. Just thought you'd be shocked,' Nigel adds waving his hands about a bit neurotically. He doesn't seem to know whether to hold my hand, offer me a hug, or simply give me a good ole slap on the back. He settles on none of the above and rests his hands on his lap.

The toilet down the hall flushes, and I hear footsteps approaching.

'Holy shit,' I shout as I jump into the air. My chair flies back and cracks loudly off the false fireplace sending a huge crack across the marble mantel.

Mark stands sheepishly in the corner, his jaw quivering.

'Lau-RA,' Nigel scolds, racing over to examine his damaged fireplace.

A loud buzz is attacking my ears and darkness is falling over my eyes. *Don't you dare faint*, I warn myself. *Not now*.

'What's wrong now?' Adam asks. 'You said you knew Mark was here.'

'I meant here, New York, here. Not here, the apartment. Oh God…oh God.'

My knees turn to jelly, and I have to grab the table to remain standing.

Mark steps forward to catch me, but the closer he gets, the more I tremble. He backs away again quickly.

'Grab her,' he shouts to Adam.

I can't fight it any longer. My eyelids feel like they weigh more than the rest of my body and they slam shut.

I wake lying on top of the bed. My head is resting on a soft pillow and my feet are elevated on two even more fluffy pillows. My skirt is tangled around my knees and my lifted legs expose polka dot oversized granny knickers.

Mark is sitting beside me with one arm on each side of my waist. He hasn't noticed I'm awake. I can feel his chest heave wearily with every breath. He leans over me and kisses my forehead softly. I want so desperately to feel his lips move lower and touch mine. *What the hell?* I'm so angry with myself that I begin to shake. Why am I weakening? Why am I savouring his smell and enjoying studying the contours of his face? I'm still so damn attracted to my husband that it's infuriating.

I wriggle beneath him and he freezes. It's as if he's embarrassed that I've caught him showing his affection. I pull myself up to a sitting position against the pillows. Mark stands up, looks at me, and then sits back down. He does this a couple of more times before finally settling on remaining seated.

'You're looking well,' he says fiddling with his fingernails.

I smile, remembering when he was so nervous on our first date that he had almost pulled the nail off his thumb.

'Thanks, you look good, too. Nicole must be looking after you.'

I'm not purposely bitchy. It's a genuine compliment. Nicole is obviously good for him. He looks less thin than I remember and less pale. But he does look like he's aged ten years.

'Everyone misses you,' Mark whispers.

I drop my guard and let my rigid shoulders soften. I needed to hear that. *I miss them.*

'They haven't forgotten me?' I ask begging for reassurance.

'Of course, not. They could never forget you. I think they just want you to come home. We all do.'

My shoulders tense again, engulfing my neck. I want to believe him, so badly. My bottom lip trembles, and my nose scrunches tightly as I wear my feelings on my face. 'I thought you wanted rid of me?'

'No. You decided I wanted rid of you. And you know as well as I do there's no arguing with you when you make your mind up on something.'

I roll my eyes. *He's right.*

'Have you looked at the photo?' Mark asks, trying to sound casual but failing miserably. No amount of smiling can hide the twitch in his lip.

I rummage in my pocket, but all I pull out is a flaky tissue and a couple of dimes.

'It's gone,' I quiver.

'It's okay,' Mark dismisses. 'Don't worry about it.'

Tears sweep across my eyes and race down my cheeks as my whole body heaves. These aren't the delicate tears that I so often find myself shedding lately. These aren't like the salty tears that fell when Nigel took Sam to the police station, or the tears that trickle when I think about how much I missed the kids. These are very different and very raw. They are uncontrollable, sting your face and blind your vision tears. I let them fall and fall, as the hours, days, even weeks of exhaustion flow out of me.

'It's okay, it's okay,' Mark whispers, gently rubbing my back.

'No, it's not,' I snort as I wipe my nose with my sleeve. 'It's really, really not. You think I'm crazy, don't you?'

Mark drops his head and doesn't say a word.

'I don't blame you,' I admit. 'I think I'm crazy, too.'

Mark slips his finger under my chin and tilts my head a little until my eyes are looking into his. His sparkling blue eyes have faded, and dark circles hang under his eyes like heavy baggage. I know something so terrible has happened that his usual shine has been wiped away and may never come back.

'Can I ask you something?' I ask finally, as my crying dilutes to heavy sobbing.

'Of course.' He smiles. 'You can always ask me anything.'

I drag some air between my teeth and force it back out with a muffled hiss. 'Did you really try to kill me?'

I don't disguise the intensity of the question with any frilly language. I'm not sad or apologetic when I speak. Neither am I accusatory. They are just six words strung together to form a painfully serious question. Nonetheless, they stick in my throat like specks of shattered glass. I know mad, murderous villains don't usually go around confessing to unsuccessful slaughters. But I have to ask. I know in my heart that I will believe the answer Mark gives.

'No, Laura; I never tried to kill you.'

I sink back against the soft pillows and breathe. I have to actually tell myself to draw breath in and let it back out or I might just stop. *I can ask about the kids now.* Mark knows I'm a good mother. Even if he doesn't love me anymore and wants to be with Nicole, he won't stop me from seeing my children. My heart still hurts that things between Mark and I will never be the same, but people separate. It happens. We can still be good parents together. Mark takes my hand in his, and I don't pull away. I close my heavy eyes.

'Are you going to stay until I fall asleep?' I whisper.

Mark squeezes my hand. 'Sure.'

Later, when we've been alone in silence for a long time, Mark lets go of my hand, but I don't stir.

'Laura? Laura, are you asleep?' Mark asks softly.

I groan, but I'm too tired to form words.

'I had to let you think you were in danger,' Mark whispers. 'It was the only way.'

I don't move or even breathe. Mark must think I'm asleep or he'd never confess something that horrible. *Oh, my God.*

Chapter Thirty

The next day wind pinches my ears as I stand outside the gates of a large apartment block. It's taken us over an hour on the train to reach the quiet area in the suburbs and another twenty minutes of walking in arctic-like conditions to find the large, intimidating tower.

Mark talked the whole journey like an excited child rambling off his Christmas wish list. I didn't say very much. I couldn't stop thinking about his strange revelation the previous night. I don't understand why he worked so hard to mess with my head. I desperately want to quiz his callous efforts, but I can't find an approach I'm comfortable with. Just being alone with him is challenge enough for my frayed nerves. But I didn't want to stay in the apartment with Adam and Nigel either. I glance at my watch, counting down the hours until Ava will be released from the hospital.

Mark continues to natter speedily, unaware of my serious reservations about his sincerity. He fills me with short stories and little anecdotes from a life he swears we once lived in New York.

'It's just more stuff you don't remember, Laura,' he says. *Bullshit.*

Mark follows every sight and sound along our way with an enthusiastic, 'Do you remember this?'

It's exhausting trying to scratch my brain to recognise the shabby paint stripped door of a little bakery or the special of the day outside an Irish bar. I just don't know if I'm trying to remember something that really happened or something Mark wants me to think happened. Every now and then, a little glimmer of a something lights up in my head and Mark gets all excited and literally jumps up and down. But just as often, I realise I've seen something similar back in Dublin and I'm actually revisiting that.

Mark takes my hand, and even though I want to pull away, I don't. He leads me up short steps towards a slim revolving door.

I jerk instinctively.

'C'mon,' he insists dragging me forward.

'We can't go in there,' I stutter.

'Of course, we can,' he says holding up a small, silver key.

'What's that for?'

'You'll have to come inside to see.'

I shuffle along so close to Mark that I accidentally step on the back of his heels. I hang my head and brace myself to be manhandled by security back out onto the street. Mark breezes past the large glass reception desk in the corner of a huge hallway with finely polished porcelain tiles and elegant marble pillars. The girl behind the desk glances up briefly, waves, and turns her attention away from us. The crossword in front of her appears to be of far greater concern than our trespassing. Before I realise it, we're standing in the lift heading for the sixth floor. *Christ, that's high,* I think, once again worrying about the murderous tendencies of my husband.

'Here we are,' Mark announces as we step out of the lift and onto a long corridor with three different coloured doors spaced evenly along the wall. A red, a green, and a blue door face us, and I stroll towards the red door without hesitation and wait for Mark to follow.

I stare at the gold numbers on the door, scrunch up my nose, and shake my head. 'Number twenty-one M,' I ponder out loud.

I lift my arm sluggishly and twist the 'M' ninety degrees. 'Ah, number two-one-three; that's more like it,' I say standing back to admire my handiwork.

Mark laughs.

'What?' I snort, looking back at him.

'You always do that,' he says happily. 'And it always just falls back down again.'

Mark's right. As he speaks, the last gold digit considerately backs up his story and swings back to its original spot.

Mark places the key in the lock and pushes the door open to reveal a very spacious and beautiful apartment. *Damn, that's impressive.* I often fantasise about a life like this. I imagine myself a busy office executive complete with tailored suits and fabulous shoes coming home in the evening to my impressive New York apartment. It's elegance and class meets contemporary comfort.

Mark convincingly plays the patronising actioner as we wander from one impressive room to another. He introduces each room by their respective title and waits gleefully for a reaction. I play up to his enthusiasm. *It's fun.* I politely admire the choice of bold wallpaper and heavy suede curtains. I love it. It's as though I've chosen every inch of the décor myself. There's not one thing I would change.

When we've toured the whole apartment at least three times, Mark's excitement dwindles slightly. He drops my hand for the first time since we've entered the hall and leaves my side to sit in the cream window box inside the large bay. I follow swiftly. I can't bear to be alone. A potent smell of mothballs and stale, eucalyptus air freshener lingers in the air. Something about the distinctive combination of fragrances presses on the already knotted ball bouncing around my stomach. A subconscious presence seems to be chasing me, and I can't shake the feeling that the apartment may be haunted. A sharp ache stabs my temples. I slam my eyes shut and pray for the pain to stop.

The lighting is blindly dim and a few solitary candles struggle to create ambiance as they dot strategically around the room. I stub my toe off the kitchen table and serenade Mark with colourful profanities as I make my way to sit beside him. He looks horribly disappointed, and if my toe wasn't swelling to compete with the size of my ankle, I'd make an effort to admire the romantic atmosphere.

Mark kisses my hand lovingly and waits for me to shut up before handing me a long-stem red rose with a note attached.

'Read it,' he suggests, ignoring my violent fit of sudden sneezing.

'Stupid hay fever,' I sniffle, balancing on the edge of the window seat with one hand on my nose and the other massaging my aching toe.

'Just read it, Laura! Please?' I see less of Mark's romantic smile and more of his gritted teeth.

I nod to agree and unfold the moist page that I suspect has been doused in my very expensive, designer perfume.

'Margarita,' I ask, confused as I read the smudged letters. I wonder if we're going to play an exciting guessing game and I tingle with excitement.

'Marry me?' Mark snaps. 'It says fucking marry me.'

I laugh. Mark hops up from the window seat and stands in front of me stomping his foot on the ground. It clearly isn't the sensuous proposal he was hoping for, but the disaster only makes me love him more.

'Yes,' I say standing up to face him. 'I would love to marry you.'

Mark kisses me. It's a real Hollywood-style kiss. He even flings me back over his knee and drops me close to the ground as he presses his tongue softly against mine. Unfortunately, I don't have an A-Lister's makeup crew on hand and I come back up looking a lot more like Medusa than Jennifer Aniston.

Mark playfully teases my adventurous 'up do' and kisses me once more. And I'm happy. So very bloody happy. There's only one thing that could make the moment more perfect, and I hope Mark will feel as excited about it as I did.

'I'm pregnant,' I blurt.

Mark falls painfully quiet.

'I did a test this morning,' I explain cutting into the thick silence.

'Are you sure?' he asks shakily.

'Well, I wasn't too sure at first, but by the fifth positive test, I was pretty convinced.'

'A baby?'

'Yeah, a baby.' I smile. I really hope it's okay to smile.

Mark isn't saying anything. His exaggerated sighs and strange facial expressions are making me nervous.

'What about work?' he says sounding almost disheartened.

'What about it?' I reply walking to the dining room table and picking up a pile of paper as thick as a dozen encyclopaedias. 'Ava and I will work something out. She can take on the bulk, and I'll be a silent partner.' I lift the pages above my head and let them scatter to the ground.

Mark stares at the mess.

'You don't sound pleased,' I say sadly.

'I'm just a bit shocked, that's all,' Mark confesses. 'You've always been a career girl. You said you never wanted kids!'

'I did. I know…and I meant it at the time. But I have your baby growing inside me now. No job in the world could make me feel as happy as I do right now.'

Mark bends in front of me and untucks my blouse from my slim, pencil skirt. He slowly opens the bottom buttons and exposes my quivering tummy. He runs his hand across my bare skin and kisses it softly.

'Hey there,' he says speaking very seriously to my belly button. 'I hope you know how lucky you are. You have got the most amazing mom in the world.'

Mark pulls himself up again and kisses me once more. 'I love you,' he whispers. 'Thank you for making my life so perfect.'

We make love for hours on the soft carpet inside the window. In hindsight, it may have been a good idea to close the curtains, but the city lights shine beautifully and I can't imagine a better setting to realise that Mark is no longer just my best friend and lover; he is my family.

~~~

'Laura…Laura…Laura,' Mark calls repeatedly.

I can hear him clearly, but my lips aren't moving to respond. I look around. I'm lying on the ground in a twisted heap. Mark is sitting beside me with my head resting on his knee.

'You okay?' he asks running his fingers through my hair. 'You banged your head really hard that time.'

I try to sit up but fall back quickly, almost feeling sick from the reeling of my head. 'What happened?'

'You fainted,' Mark explains. 'It was my fault. I'm so sorry. I was pushing you too hard to remember stuff.'

Mark continues to run his hands gently over my face.

'I remember,' I admit groggily.

Mark's holds his breath and I can feel his knees tremble as they shake my aching head.

'You do?' he asks. *He doesn't sound convinced.*

'Yeah,' I say, staring into his bloodshot eyes. 'You proposed to me here, didn't you?'

A sparkle ignites in Mark's eyes, and he jumps up with a burst of energy I wasn't expecting. He reaches his hand out, seeking mine, and pulls me to stand up, too. My legs are wobbly, but I force them firmly onto the ground. I want to be beside him.

'This is amazing,' Mark says. 'You have remembered something all by yourself. I knew this would work. I knew it.'

I tilt my head to one side, intrigued. 'You knew what would work?'

'Coming back here. I knew coming back to our old lives would fix you.'

I pull away from him. 'I didn't know I was broken.'

Mark's excitement fades as quickly as it began, and he looks horribly sad once more.

'We're all broken, Laura. But once you remember that then we can heal together. I love you,' he says wrapping his arms around me.

I fall into his warm hug and smell his sweet aftershave as I enjoy a familiar comfort. I need him. The more I remember from my past, the more I fall in love with him all over again. I'm still afraid, but not of Mark anymore. I'm afraid of what else I will remember. *Maybe I drove him away? Maybe it's my fault he loves Nicole now and not me?*

Chapter Thirty-One

'We're late,' Mark shouts back at me as I struggle to keep up with him.

We race down the street trying to grab a taxi.

'Ouch…ouch…fucking ouch,' I whine as I curse Ava and the stupid new shoes she made me buy. My feet are like a shrine to a blister god and each tiny step is a little sacrifice.

Mark jumps into the back of a yellow cab and slides across the leather seat to make room for me.

'La Rivista on West Forty-sixth Street please,' Mark says like a seasoned New Yorker.

'Special occasion?' the driver asks.

'Yes, very special.' Mark smiles.

'Nigel is going to kill us,' I say looking at my watch. 'We're almost an hour late already.'

'Nigel needs to lighten up,' Mark snorts. 'He always kept me waiting in college, so it's payback.'

My lips curl and my whole face pulls into a smile. The revelation that Nigel and Mark were college roommates for years washes over me as easily as if Mark had just offered me a stick of chewing gum. I'm just embarrassed that I forgot and have been unable to jog that memory. It must have been head wrecking for Nigel that I treated him like a stranger. I'll apologise when I see him.

I enjoy peeking into the fogged up windows of my past, and I look forward to the next little snippet of information. Soon, I will be a whole person again, and I can't wait to know how that feels.

I recognise the outside of the charming Italian bistro. My mouth salivates as I think about their carbonara with a rich creamy texture that will cripple me with indigestion for the next two days.

Once inside, the friendly waiter takes our coats and informs us politely that we should expect at least a twenty-minute wait. I'm about to take a seat in the waiting area, but Mark rolls up a twenty dollar bill and not-so-subtly slips it into the waiter's palm.

The waiter stuffs the note into his pocket and pretends to look around the busy restaurant once more. 'Ah yes, Sir, I believe we have managed to make some space at your friend's table. If you would like to join them, then I'll have someone follow you with menus shortly.'

'Thank you,' Mark says patting the young man firmly on the back. It was written all over Mark's face that he would rather be patting with his fist and using a lot more pressure, but he remains a gentleman and smiles falsely.

'Thank you, Chad,' I add.

Mark's smile becomes genuine. 'Wow, I can't believe you remember the waiter's name; I don't even remember that guy. You're really starting to get a grip on your memory.'

I giggle as I point to the discreet nametag attached to the lapel of the waiter's uniform.

Mark laughs too and turns a little red.

We are still sniggering as we reach the table. Nigel stands and offers me a kiss on each cheek. Adam copies, although I can tell the practice makes him uncomfortable. Ava doesn't stand. I assume she's still tired after her ordeal, although she looks great. Her makeup is flawless, as always, and she's wearing a tightly fitted black polo in a clear attempt to emphasise her bump. Classy and undoubtedly expensive as the top was, her newly expanding waistline looks more like she's had one bun too many at lunch and doesn't reveal itself as a bun in the oven just yet. But it doesn't take from her sheer healthy glow, and I tell her how wonderful she looks.

'What's so funny?' Adam asks, Mark's laughing catching his attention.

'Nothing.' I shrug.

'Yeah, nothing,' Mark snorts pathetically unconvincing.

I look lovingly at my husband. It feels so good to share a private joke with him. And for a moment, I forget the dents in our relationship.

'I hear you went to visit the old apartment,' Nigel says.

'Yes, we spent a long time there actually,' Mark says.

'Oh, say no more.' Nigel winks. 'We get the picture.'

'Nigel, you have a filthy mind,' I scold. 'Nothing happened. Some of us are actually able to control ourselves.' A sudden memory of a very promiscuous, college years Nigel pops into my head.

'Nothing did happen, Nigel. I'm sorry to disappoint you,' Mark insists.

Mark is stern and indignant, and I wonder if he's worried a rumour might spread back to Nicole. *Maybe I should tell Nigel I fucked Mark's brains out in the old apartment.* But the waiter arrives to take our order just in time, and thankfully, the subject of conversation switches to the food.

Good food and good company make for a very enjoyable lunch. Well, mostly enjoyable. Adam is like a thorn in my side, constantly drawing the conversation back to the apartment.

'Is there something you want to ask?' Mark says finally unable to ignore Adam any longer.

Ava nods her approval to Adam, and he launches into a very obviously rehearsed speech.

'I've decided to sell back in Ireland and move over here. Business is going down the drain. It has been for a while. You know what it's like there at the moment.'

No one says a word. The revelation has shocked us all. It's Adam's party piece to moan about how a city upbringing in the States can't compete with the open fields and fresh air of the Irish countryside.

'It's no place to raise kids,' he always says and now he plans to raise his own child here. *Seriously?*

'I'm going to invest anything I get for the company into something smaller over here.' He fiddles nervously with his napkin. 'And hopefully build a better life. You guys were right all these years. I do love it here.'

I find myself agreeing. Even though the minute I found out I was going to be a mother, all I wanted was to give up my job and get away from the intensity of the city and head back home to the bad weather and pot-holed roads of Ireland. But Ava is different; she's a city girl through and through, and I know life in New York is more here than me.

'There's more…' Adam says still smiling. 'Ava and I got married the morning of the accident. Laura, I wanted to wait until you got your memory back to tell you.'

A stagnant hush falls over everyone. Ava looks disappointed with the response.

'Well, say something,' Adam requests crossly. 'I thought you'd all be delighted. We saved you a fortune in wedding presents.'

'It's very sudden,' I stutter not realising I'm stating the blatantly obvious.

'I know. I know…it was sudden for us, too. But we knew we were going to get married sooner or later. You just never know what's around the next corner, and we wanted to be husband and wife. With everything that happened after, I'm so glad we got to say I do. You understand, right?'

'Yes.' I smile throwing my arms around Adam's neck. 'I do understand. It's great. Congratulations.'

'Congratulations,' Mark and Nigel echoed following my lead.

Nigel calls the waiter to the table and orders a couple of bottles of the restaurant's most expensive champagne.

'There's a bit more,' Adam says.

'More?' Mark snorts, his eyes two round circles in his head. *He's clearly out of practice drinking wine,* I think, and try not to laugh.

'Are you still looking for tenants?' Adam asks.

I looked at Mark with confusion. Mark's nodding.

'Well, look no further.' Adam smiles. 'Just until my business takes off. Then I hope there'll be some cash for me to purchase something nice.'

I don't speak. I don't know what to say. I didn't know we owned the apartment, but it's a pleasant revelation. Although I've only just found out about the place, I feel affection for it that's evidence of years of happy memories. I'm not sure I'm ready to share that.

'I don't know,' Mark admits. 'I'm thinking of selling the place.'

'No,' I suddenly shout. My legs twitch so hard, they bang on the table causing our plates to shake noticeably. My jaw quivers and the people at the next table turn around to stare. 'We can't sell. I don't want to.'

'Okay, Laura. It's okay,' Mark says softly. He seems to manage my strange panic effortlessly. 'It was only a suggestion. We won't sell if you don't want to.'

My eyes roll in my head, and I'm certain I'm going to black out again.

Mark drops two little white pills onto the table in front of me and places my glass of water beside them. 'Take them,' he orders.

I shake my head viciously, almost pulling myself off the chair.

Mark rummages in his pocket and slams a box of paracetamol in front of me. 'Please, Laura,' he says, and I can tell he's agitated.

Maybe I'm embarrassing him. I'm embarrassing myself.

'If you don't take them, then you'll be sorry when a headache kicks in,' he adds.

I stuff the pills into my mouth, almost dropping them because my hands tremble so much. I slug huge mouthfuls of water and wash them down.

Nigel lifts the second, still full, bottle of champagne from the table and places it back in the cooler beside him. He's as subtle as a constipated elephant. My cheeks sting with embarrassment.

My chair squeaks loudly as I stand up and excuse myself from the table. Marks eyes plead with me to sit back down. I don't. Instead, I fumble my way towards the bathroom. People stare as I pass their tables. Some even voice their disapproval under their breath in ill-disguised comments. It's late afternoon, and I play the part of a drunken disgrace convincingly.

I stagger through the swinging door of the ladies' room and glare at my reflection in the mirror. I hate losing control like that. Fear is my worst enemy, and once again, I feel I'm losing a battle to be normal.

Ava appears and finds me slumped over the sink like a haggard old witch. She grabs a tight hold of me and slides carefully downwards until we're both sitting on the floor. I hug her tight and cry.

'I'm really sorry,' she says sadly. 'Adam and I didn't mean to upset you. We'll find a different apartment, okay?'

'It's not the silly apartment,' I admit. 'It's the life that goes with it.'

'An apartment is just four walls. You and Mark can have a happy life anywhere.'

'But I remember having a happy life there.'

'That's great. I'm so glad you remember that.' Ava smiles. 'But you'll remember being happy in lots of places. Just wait, you'll see.'

'I hope so.'

'I know so.'

Ava drops her eyes to the back pocket of my skirt. I reach around and pull out the paper.

'This is Nigel's photo. He'll be furious when he finds out I tore it. I had no right to.'

287

'He'll understand.'

'I wish I could understand,' I say beginning to cry again.

'Do you want to talk about it?' Ava asks.

'Not really. I don't know what there is to talk about it. It's just a picture of some fancy dress party with some kids I don't know,' I snap. 'Why is everyone so concerned with the damn picture? Mark wanted to quiz me about it, too. I told him I couldn't find it.'

'And why do you think you told him that, Laura?'

Ava sounds strange. I stand up and shake my legs out, as if I can shake off this conversation.

'Just look at the picture, Laura. Look at their faces and then tell me again you don't recognise them.'

Chapter Thirty-Two

A teary-eyed little boy tugs the sleeve of my cardigan and begs to stay home from school. He's tired and clingy and insists the school is smelly and yucky.

'You have to go to school, sweetheart,' I say straightening his red tie and tucking it neatly behind his navy school jumper. He looks so smart; I just want to smother him with kisses. I won't, of course; I don't want to embarrass him in front of his school friends.

'I'm not going,' he repeats and adds a defiant foot stomp this time.

'You are,' I say sternly. 'No tantrums, okay?'

I have an appointment for a wash, cut, and blow-dry a half an hour later. I haven't been to the hairdresser in months. I don't even have to rush back because Ava is picking him up. I'll make it up to him later. I plan to meet Ava in the park later, and we will go for a walk or check out the playground. We could get a kite maybe. He loves kites. It will be a good day. I don't tell him. I don't want to spoil the surprise. I just smile and attempt to tame his hair before bending down to kiss his forehead softly. He wipes his head with his sleeve and shakes his arm after, clearly throwing away my kiss. I press my lips tightly together and hold in my laughter. His sulking is a trait he picked up from me, unfortunately. I kiss him again and promise him we will do something fun together later. He nods and I watch as he plods drearily in the direction of his classroom.

~~~

Mark and I sit in silence. The only sound is the angry roar of the engine as we race up the hard shoulder of the busy motorway. I've never been in a car traveling so frighteningly fast before yet at that moment it isn't marginally fast enough. I will the engine to work harder, the wheels to spin faster and get us there sooner. I feel like we're crawling. Other drivers

289

flash their headlights at us, angry that we have the cheek to dodge the traffic. They wouldn't be so fast to disapprove if they knew the terrible phone call we had just received. Not one driver would dare to begrudge us a clear path if they knew that a little boy was fighting for his life in the hospital, and we were on our way to find out if he had won or lost his battle.

We burst through the doors of accident and emergency. I immediately see the small mahogany framed window of the reception desk. There's a queue.

'Excuse me,' I say as I shove past the other patients forming an orderly line.

'Excuse me, excuse me,' I continue, beginning to really use force to push my way forward. 'Get the hell out of the way,' Mark finally shouts at the last few agitated people who refused to allow us to skip ahead of them.

A seemingly friendly, pretty woman leans out from behind the reception desk. She makes obvious eye contact with the two security guards manning the main entrance, warning them to be on guard.

'Calm down, Sir,' she warns. 'Is there something I can help you with?'

I try to explain, but even though I move my lips as usual, I can't manage to get a sound out. Every inch of my body trembles, and my breath is too big for my chest and attempts to choke me.

Mark is rambling, his words are jumbled and slurred, but thankfully, he remains steadier than I do. I place my hand firmly on his shoulder. To the startled patients in the waiting room, it must look like a compassionate gesture, but it's strategic. Without the support of Mark's firm body, I would almost certainly crumple in a distraught mess on the floor.

'Miss, can I help you?' the woman asks indifferently. We must be an inconvenience in her busy day. Some of the others in line are beginning to complain and shout abuse at us.

'Please help us,' Mark stammers as he points at me and then back to himself. 'We got a call to say there's been a serious accident.'

The angry voices behind us are no more. I prefer the noise. The hush is intense. It's unbearable.

'Lorcan Kavanagh,' Mark says quietly. 'Can you tell me where his is?'

The woman peers over Mark's shoulder to find my face.

'Mr. and Mrs. Kavanagh,' she says, her whole body softening.

Mark nods. 'Yes. Mark and Laura Kavanagh.'

'We've been expecting you,' she says.

'Can we see him? Can we see Lorcan now?' I interrupt.

She nods and smiles. She quickly abandons her desk and comes to stand beside us. 'Follow me…I'll take you through to the doctor,' she promises.

I smile with a sense of some relief. The minutes after we got the horrific call, the race to the hospital, and rushing through the emergency doors had all ticked by in teasing slow motion. But we are finally here. We've made it. We're seconds away from seeing Lorcan. I plan to wrap my arms tight around him, and no matter how bad it is, I will whisper to him that it will be okay. He just needs me to comfort him. Then, he will get better.

We walk through the swinging doors that lead to the examination rooms. It's surprisingly quiet and still. There's no drama to see. A couple of nurses are dotted along the hallway and some junior doctors walk around wearing scrubs and holding a patient file or two. The receptionist passes them and leads us to the end of the corridor. An elderly female doctor in a starched, long white coat steps out from behind a cubical curtain. Her frozen smile disappears as soon as she sees us. It's obvious she's expecting us. She knows who we are, but the receptionist introduces us anyway.

'I have Mr. and Mrs. Kavanagh,' she says politely before nodding once at the doctor and then nodding again at Mark and me, in turn.

291

'Thank you,' the doctor replies and dismisses the receptionist with a wave of her hand.

I notice the tears glistening in the receptionist's eyes as she turns to walk away. Her shoulders are rounded and drag her upper body forward and down. I can't imagine how difficult her job must be, every day facing parents of ill or dying children. It must eat you alive after a while. I've only been in this place a few minutes and I already know it has left an eternal mark on my soul.

'Please step this way,' the slim, grey-haired doctor says, stretching her arm out and offering us the comfort of a small, intimate room across the hall. I can't hide my agitation. I do not intend to spend half the evening waiting around in a glorified shoebox with no information. They asked us to hurry, the least they could do is offer us the same courtesy.

'Please, can I just see him?' I beg, refusing to step into the room.

Mark doesn't speak. He catches my fisted hand in his and leads us as requested into the small room. We all stand in silence for a few long, drawn-out seconds.

'I'm so terribly sorry,' the doctor says.

I feel Mark stagger as though standing on the one spot suddenly becomes a challenge for him. The doctor passes me a plastic cup of water she kindly filled from the water cooler in the corner. I take it, but I don't drink from it. I want to fling it across the room and watch as it creates a puddle on the floor. But I hold my composure as shakily as I hold the cup. I try to block out every word coming from the doctor's mouth. If I can't hear it, then it isn't true. If she just stops talking, then everything will be okay. It will be okay.

I watch another doctor in the distance. He's short and stern, and I decide straight away that I dislike him. He's speaking to a petite, blond-haired lady who's crying hysterically. She's standing with her back to me, but I recognise her immediately. It's Nicky. She's trembling, and I hear *her loud tearful cries carry down the corridor. I cover my ears with my hands and toss my head from side to side, begging her cries not to confirm what I'm concentrating so hard on denying. I barely notice the handsome man standing poignantly beside her. He's also upset but not as noticeably so. He's more refined. The only small hint of his emotions is the uncontrollable twitching of his left eyebrow. He hides his pain well, even from himself – perhaps.*

The grey-haired doctor continues to speak to me, but I can't pull my stare away from Nicole and the man beside her. They haven't noticed Mark or me yet. I'm glad. I continue to ignore everything being said to me. Mark is listening though; I can see it in his face. His lips press tightly together in concentration. Every painful word is registering in the contours of his distraught expression. I want to shout at him to cover his ears too, not to let the doctor's words reach him, but it's too late. He knows.

His lips part and a deep, throaty roar falls out of him. He's shaking his head so hard I think he might fall over. His breathing quickens and heavy tears begin to race down his flushed cheeks. He believes the doctor. It's true. It must be true.

My ears rang loudly, and now when I try to hear the words being spoken to me, I cannot. I can hear background noise, teacups chattering in a canteen, and babies crying in the distance. I can see the doctor is still speaking. Christ, she has a lot to say. Her lips definitely move but no sound reaches my ears.

My hands grip my chest, and I feel a stabbing pain in my heart. My ribs chattered so hard inside my chest that I worry they will snap. I scream, 'No, please, God no.'

She's going to say it. I'm going to hear her and then there will be no going back. Nothing will ever be the same again.

'He didn't make it,' she whispers. 'I'm so very sorry.'

The four simple words shoot around my brain like treacherous bullets. He didn't make it? He didn't make it where? Where was he going? He didn't make it on the school football team; not to worry, he can try again next year. He didn't make a mess; well, of course not, he's a good little boy. What did she mean that he didn't make it? She couldn't possibly be telling me that he didn't make it out of the car without a chance. She couldn't be telling me that the little boy I love so much has been stolen from us. She couldn't possibly be telling us that Lorcan is dead.

'I'll give you a moment,' the doctor says, slowly edging away. 'Do take all the time you need; our family room has somewhere to sit and water if you need some.' She stretches her arm towards the tiny room behind us again.

The pain of my heart breaking is almost physical. It's sharp and strong and I wish I could succumb to it. I want to die, too. My knees hurt as they jar in place, and I can't move. I know then that Hell exists because I have been plunged full force into it.

Nicole races towards us and flings her arms around me. She's shaking hysterically, but I barely feel her tremble. I'm beyond numb. I've aged a hundred years at that moment. I'm frail and weak and no longer myself. That hideous moment would define the rest of my life. I would never be the same again. Laura is gone, and this shell of a woman, the new me, stands in her place.

'This is a nightmare,' Nicole cries. 'A horrible fucking nightmare.'

It's worse. So much worse. A nightmare we could wake up from and it would be over; this horror will never end.

Nicole's partner moves to stand beside us silently; his head is facing the ground. I carefully examine the lines and folds that time has patiently etched into his face. They are more deeply indented than I remember. His incredible good looks strain under the sorrow. He shakes hands with

Mark. No words are exchanged, but the long, firm handshake speaks volumes.

'Thank you for calling us,' Mark says choking back tears.

'We thought you'd make it in time to say goodbye,' Nicole sobs.

'Did he…did he feel pain,' I ask.

Nicole's blank expression tells me my words are washing over her. She's as hollow inside as I am.

'Please tell me?' I beg. 'Was he scared?'

'Laura, don't,' Mark says.

'Don't what,' I snap. 'Don't ask if such a beautiful little boy was afraid of dying. Don't ask if he cried. Don't what, Mark? Don't freak out because this is all so fucking wrong.'

'Don't torture yourself like this,' Mark says. 'Not now, not like this.'

'I'm not torturing myself. It's that stupid doctor. She doesn't know shit. He's not dead; I don't know why she is lying to us. Lorcan is fine. He's fine!'

I wait for someone to back me up; someone to agree that the doctor is just a lying bitch. Everyone is silent.

'I'm going to find her. I want her to admit she is lying. Lorcan is fine.'

I begin to run down the long corridor.

'Laura,' my name echoes in the hall as Nicole shouts after me.

I turn to face her. She's shaking her head again. I fall on the spot, my legs weak and no longer able to support my weight as my heart finally catches up with my head. I know he's gone. The silence screams it at me, teasing me that I will never see him again.

We left that very hospital five years ago with such joy in our hearts as we admired the gift of a precious baby. All too soon, the gift of that little life had been taken away from us. It's not fair. No child deserves to die.

~~~

I wake lying tangled in the duvet and with beads of perspiration dotted across my distressed forehead. I lie still for a few moments digesting my surroundings. I take a while before sliding my legs off the edge of the bed and forcing myself to get up. What a nightmare, I think. It's left me physically shaking. I throw on my dressing gown and quickly make my way to the landing.

I slowly creak open the bedroom door, but before I look inside, I slam the door shut again and stand with my arms hanging and heart pounding.

'Oh my God,' I whisper. Oh my God. Oh my God. Oh my God.

Mark races up the stairs. He stops dramatically when he reaches the top step and sees me standing zombie-like outside the bedroom door. The look on his face shoots a bolt of sorrow through my veins. If I open the door in front of me, then I will find an empty bed, and I can't see it. I'm not strong enough.

The pain that has all this time confined itself in a foggy vapour circling around the back of my mind now solidifies in torturing pain. An ache in my heart pulls me to the ground like a powerful magnet. I can't pull against it. I don't want to. I want to embrace the hurt. The hurt makes me feel human. I've hidden from the pain for so long it's emotionally empowering to grieve. The raw heartache attacks all my senses until I'm stripped bare of all thoughts. Grief is the predator, and I surrender myself a willing victim.

A deep moaning sound catches my attention. It echoes all around me until I can hear nothing else. There's no music playing from the radio in the corner. No cars drive by on the usually the busy road. No children play happily on the street below. The world, for me, has frozen. Nothing exists now except for the hollow cry. I look at Mark. His eyes are closed and his body sways back and forth like a fragile leaf blowing in the wind. I know he can hear the cries, too. He rocks faster and harder as the howling grows louder. I hear the unbearable pain behind the cry. I know that pain. I

296

know it, and I hate it. I put my hands over my ears. I want to scream,
'Shut up!' I want to tell whoever cries so loud that I can't hear myself
think, and that I'm grieving, too. I want to tell them that their tears will
not erase the pain – nothing will.

Finally, when I can't take it any longer, I shout out. But no sound
comes out. No more sound can come out of me; I'm already using my voice.
The horrible, heart-wrenching screams are coming from me. They're
involuntary and unstoppable. It's the sound of my heart begging to rewind
time. Begging for one more cosy cuddle before bedtime. Begging for one more
day in the park. Begging for just one more kiss good night. Begging to go
back to that last morning when I dropped Lorcan at school and run a
million miles in the other direction.

'Please,' I cry, looking towards the sky. 'Please, give him back to us.
I'm so sorry for what I've done, so sorry; but I don't deserve this.'

~ ~ ~

I rub my sleepy eyes, bordering on delirious. I'm not at
home in the comfort of my own house. I'm lying in a contorted
heap on the cold tiles of a restaurant bathroom. Ava has
disappeared, and I'm alone and cold. My head is pounding, and
I feel like I'm going to vomit. *What the fuck was in the pills Mark*
gave me? My mouth foams and shaking my head makes it worse.
Memories bubble in my mind like a pot boiling over on the
stove. Images spill over the edge and tell me the cruellest story.

I try so hard to put the lid back on the pot and stuff the
memories once again into the unsearched archives of my
bewildered brain. But I can't find any mental hiding spots. I
remember everything, and Mark is right…I truly wish my only
worry was my husband trying to kill me because he's having an
affair. How easy that would be to deal with in comparison.

I find my way back to the table. Everyone has finished dessert, and they're polishing off some coffee. A bowl of melted ice cream waits in my place.

'Jesus, Laura, what were you doing in there?' Adam says. 'God help whoever has to use the loo after you. Maybe stay away from the lasagne next time, yeah.'

'Lorcan,' I say, my lips dry and barely able to form the syllables of the name. 'How could I forget, Mark. How could I?'

Mark stands up and helps me to my seat. The lines of his face soften and years instantly melt away from his tired expression. 'You remember now, Laura. That's all that matters. You remember now.'

My eyes plead with Mark to tell me everything will be okay. But there's still no sparkle in his once bright eyes, and I know he's just as broken as I am. No one can say anything now. It's all just words and none can ever make this right.

Chapter Thirty-Three

I stare monotonously out the penthouse window. The imposing large buildings and busy crowds of New York's streets don't intimidate me anymore. Nothing scares me now, not since I remember who I am. I'm a successful entrepreneur who chose love over my career. I lived in New York for eight years, building my textile company. I sold up, making a hefty profit, and invested the money into getting Mark's hardware store off the ground back in Dublin. I'm a mother who put the love of my baby above all else. I'm not a frumpy old housewife stuck in a rut. I embraced the rut with open arms, threw in a leather recliner and an HD television, and sat back to admire my handiwork. I was happiness personified. But a jealous grim reaper had bulldozed my lavish rut and left me to sieve through the pieces of dirt and clay to find any remains of happiness with which to rebuild my life.

Mark approaches me silently from behind and kisses my neck. He startles me, and I jump a little before enjoying his soft lips against my skin.

'You ready, honey?' he asks.

I exhale roughly and turn around to press my lips against his. I feel safe at that moment. I've finally found who I am and I actually like her. Going home to Ireland will rock my emotional boat once more, and I'm not sure if I will sink under the pressure or not.

'Can't we stay here?' I plead with one last attempt to change Mark's mind.

It's been over a week since my memory returned, and I've spent almost every minute of every day since then begging Mark to rip up the plane tickets.

His answer is always the same. 'You know we can't. Our lives are in Ireland now. We have to go home. You know that.'

'I do know it, but knowing it and actually accepting it are two totally different things and I'm struggling with the latter.'

Mark's smile lightens his whole body.

'But we threw up our lives here to move to Ireland in the first place. Let's do the same again. Let's forget about our crappy existence in Dublin and come back here. It'll be so much better. I promise.'

Mark places his hands firmly on my shoulders and presses hard. 'Stop this, Laura. Don't make promises you can't keep. We are going home and that's final. Okay?'

'Can we at least stay another few days,' I plead. I smirk to myself as I think of a plan. We could stay another few days. A few days would turn into a week. A week would turn into a month, and when a month turned into a year, we would be back to our happy lives here in the city. I cross my fingers behind my back and pray that Mark agrees.

'We don't have anywhere to stay. Adam moves into our apartment tomorrow, and Nigel needs his space back. He must be sick of the sight of us at this stage.'

'We could stay in a hotel,' I suggest passively. 'Just for a few days, Mark. Please?'

'We are going home *TODAY*,' Mark says firmly. 'Our flight leaves in four hours, so now is a good time to start your goodbyes.'

'Fine,' I snap tossing my body away from Mark. 'But I'm not talking to you on the plane.'

'Fine by me,' Mark says unable to hide his smirk. 'I need some sleep, anyway.'

Three cups of coffee later it's time to leave.

'I'll miss you,' I whisper to Ava as we stand beside the front door of the penthouse.

'I'll miss you, too.' She smiles. 'But I'll be home in a few weeks to pack up my stuff and organise shipping etcetera.'

Tears smudge in the corner of my eyes. My ears clearly hear what she says, but somehow on the way to my brain, the words jumble around and I end up with 'Goodbye, I'll never see you again.'

'See ya,' Adam says placing two fingers on his forehead and saluting me sheepishly. That I heard with no confusion. My reply is the simple repetition of the same two words. But I know if he hugged me, I'd grab on tightly and say another tearful goodbye.

Nigel appears from his bedroom and passes me a folded piece of white paper.

I open it and try hard to read the almost illegible words scribbled in blue ink.

'It's Sam's address. Apparently, he's been asking his foster mum about the nice lady who helped him, and I thought you might like to write to him.'

I carefully refold the page and place it safely behind my credit card in my wallet. I then put the wallet into the secret zipped pouch at the back of my bag where I keep all my important stuff like my passport and lip balm.

'I don't care,' Nigel snaps, his words laced with a dull panic. The strange behaviour is completely adverse to Nigel's usually dignified demeanour.

'We can get a taxi,' I suggest hoping to calm the situation.

Nigel ignores my suggestion.

'I can drop you at the airport instead,' Adam offers looking at his watch.

'Thanks,' Mark says.

Nigel continues to jump on the spot.

'It's okay, man. Adam is driving now,' Mark says, grabbing Nigel by the arms trying to get his attention.

But Nigel continues to ignore everyone. He pushes his weight firmly against the ground and uses the pressure built up in his legs to push himself impressively into the air.

Mark staggers back grasping his nose and groaning loudly. His face has accidently met with the full force of Nigel's moving elbow. Blood trickles between Mark's shaking fingers, and I rush to grab hold of him before he falls over.

I help a very shaky Mark sit on the couch, and Adam races into the kitchen in search of a tea towel and some ice. He arrives back a few seconds later with a packet of frozen, organic green beans and a flimsy dishcloth.

'It's all I could find,' he admits sheepishly.

'It'll do fine,' I say as I wrapped the frozen vegetables in the cloth and offer the pack to soothe Mark's throbbing nose. He accepts the homemade ice pack gratefully. He tilts his head back and lets the cold ease the pain. Ava sits beside Mark and sympathetically rubs his back. Adam makes some light-hearted jokes about how Mark could enter a *Shrek-lookalike* competition and win.

'I'll be back in a minute,' I say as I walk back into the hall to confront Nigel. I'm disappointed he hasn't bothered to apologise to Mark or even check if he's okay.

Nigel has changed his tactics and is now attacking the light shade with the end of the sweeping brush. He's acting even more crazily than I usually do.

'Can't you get someone from maintenance to come get the keys for you,' I ask.

'Those guys take all day,' he barks.

'So? They'll be here by evening. You don't need the car before then, do you?'

'I don't care about the stupid car,' Nigel snaps angrily.

'Really? Look at yourself. You're freaking out over silly old car keys.'

'Shut up,' Nigel shouts.

He swings the brush hard, and for a second, I think he's going to hit me. I'm wrong. It isn't me who bears the brunt of his temper. It's the light shade. It shatters into millions of tiny crystal pieces that fall from the ceiling like little drops of sharp rain. They dust over my hair and clothes and pinch at the exposed skin of my face and hands. Nigel's cheek bleeds where a piece of the crystal has caught his face, but he doesn't seem to notice. He's smiling happily as he bends down and picks up the keys that have fallen to the ground. He sits in the spot among the dust and shattered glass. I'm about to warn him that he will hurt himself, but I decide against it. I don't stand any chance of gaining his attention anyway.

His eyes are transfixed on the colourful keyring that he runs his finger across. It looks like a homemade, yellow sun with a disproportionate smiley face stuck in front, possibly fashioned with bake-in-the-oven clay of some sort. It's simple and obviously the masterpiece of a child. Nigel clearly adores the little charm.

'Can I see?' I ask reaching out my hand and hoping he will share with me.

'Sure,' he replies and places the bundle of keys into my hand.

He's calm now, back to his normal dignified self. I realise the keys don't concern him; it's the key ring he was worried about.

'Be careful,' he suggests. 'They're hot.'

The bright light has heated the steel of the keys enough for them to sting to the touch. I don't care. I want to hold them. I want to examine the little sun that meant enough to Nigel to turn him into a quivering mess at the prospect of losing it.

'It's very cute,' I say pointing to the smudgy black eyes and wobbly, curvy, red line that makes a smile.

'Thanks,' he says.

'Is it special?' I ask, careful not to attach any tone to my words. I don't want to upset him by appearing to have any impression, positive or not, about the key ring. At least, not until I know how he feels about the little craft himself.

'Yes. It's very special.' Nigel is close to tears.

I don't know what to do. He never shows emotion. I like Nigel, I do. But sometimes I really suspect he's made of stone. For something to move him this much, it must mean the world to him.

'Someone very special gave it to me. That person isn't in my life anymore, so I keep this to remind me of them every day.'

Wow. When Nigel dips into the pool of emotion, he really dives in headfirst. I wasn't prepared for a heartbreaking revelation. I decide not to ask any questions. If there's anything more Nigel wants to add, then he can, in his own time. If not, then maybe it's lightened his load just to share that small piece of information with me.

After a long time, the silence becomes uncomfortable. I give Nigel back his keys and help him to his feet.

'You okay?' I ask, knowing the honest answer is no.

'Yes. Of course,' he replies.

He calmly dusts off the last of the shattered glass from his clothes and looks at his watch. 'Oh dear, we need to get a move on. You'll miss your flight.'

I nod. I know that's the last time we will speak of the key ring. That's okay; Nigel wasn't the sharing sort. But at least now I know he does possess emotion, even if showing them is still a battle.

'Good Lord, man, your face looks terrible,' Nigel says apologetically.

Mark's two blackening eyes and raw red nose are glowing like a beacon. He cups his face with his hand as we walk down to the car park and slide into the car.

'I'm so sorry,' Nigel admits.

'It looks worse than it feels,' Mark lies as he tried to minimise his painful blinking.

'I hope they still recognise your passport photo,' Adam jokes.

Ava laughs. So do I. Mark tries to laugh, but his giggles shake his head and he ends up yelping in distress instead.

I find myself cruelly wishing that Nigel had hit Mark a little harder. Maybe a few more bruises and Mark would have been too dishevelled to travel. If we only had a couple more days, I know I could convince Mark to stay.

At the airport, Ava, Adam, and Nigel walk with us as far as they can until security won't let them go any further. We huddle together like wild animals sheltering from a storm and say our goodbyes for the millionth time.

'Come with us?' Mark suggests hugging his old friend.

'No. I want to, but I can't,' Nigel replies.

Similar to the energy I'm putting into convincing Mark to stay in New York, Mark is pleading with Nigel to agree to come to Ireland with us. I don't mind either way. Nigel seems lonely sometimes; maybe a holiday would be good for him.

'There's nothing there for me anymore. Too much water under the bridge. It's much better if I just stay here.'

'That's not true, and you know it,' Mark insists.

'Leave it, Mark, please,' Nigel asks softly. 'I've made my decision.'

Mark shakes Nigel's hand. I can see he's disappointed, but he respects Nigel's choice and doesn't ask again.

Chapter Thirty-Four

The plane is small and cramped and looks more like something that should only be used to island hop. It certainly doesn't appear to be capable of transporting a couple of hundred people to the far side of the ocean. I voice my concerns to Mark, but he thinks it's simply another stalling technique on my part. The closer we get to boarding, the more reluctant I become.

As I expected, the flight is horrendous. The passengers are packed together like sticky marshmallows on a skewer and the in-flight meal is obviously something they've bought in bulk after seeing a dog food commercial.

'Are you excited to be going home?' I ask.

Mark raises his head slowly from leaning against the window and rubs his eye. He's clearly unimpressed that I've disturbed his cat napping. He shrugs his shoulders and punches his jumper into a neat ball to form a pillow. He lifts my hand to his lips and kisses it softly before preparing to drift back to sleep.

'I am looking forward to you being back home. I really missed you,' he says with his eyes closed but with a large smile that lights up his whole face.

I snuggle close to him hoping that the next time I open my eyes will be when we're on the ground in Dublin.

Hours later, the wheels have barely touched the runway when Mark turns his phone on. The loud string of beeps from unread text messages are embarrassing as the distinctive noise reminds all the other passengers to find and fiddle with their phones. I guess it's work trying to get in touch. I realise I hadn't considered Mark's business when I tried to relocate us to the other side of the pond. I'm not sure if I should apologise for my stroppy attitude or not. I decide to say nothing unless he brings it up first.

Mark listens to his voicemail as we wait for our bags to come through. Some messages make him smile and others worry him because he frowns as if someone has just squirted him in the eye with lemon juice. He dials a number I don't recognise and asks me to watch out for our luggage as he walks away to find a quiet area to talk.

Our bags appear quickly and I load them onto the trolley and fight to push it in a straight line against the stubborn defiance of a wobbly front wheel. I can't find Mark anywhere. He's taking ages, and I begin to wonder if he has headed into the arrivals area and is waiting for me to follow him through. I'm just about to push the crippling trolley through the automatic doors when Mark taps me on the shoulder.

'Sorry about that,' he says as he kisses my cheek.

'Who were you calling?'

'No one,' Mark mumbles.

'Well, no one is very chatty,' I joke.

My effort at indifference is disastrous. But Mark is so familiar with my nosy nature it washes over him.

'I need to go to the loo. Will you wait here for me?' Mark says.

'Sure.' I shrug.

Mark throws his heavy jacket and carrier bag on top of our other luggage. 'I'll only be a minute.'

Mark isn't thirty seconds gone when his phone vibrates inside his coat pocket. I pick it out and I'm about to answer but almost drop it when I see the name that appears on the caller ID. It's Doctor Hammond. I press the reject button immediately and stuff the phone back into Mark's pocket. I wait a while nervously tapping my foot on the ground. The temptation to check his call log is overwhelming. I scan the baggage area like hunted prey. Checking to see if someone, anyone, is watching me. I roll my eyes at my ridiculousness.

I feel guilty, but not enough to stop. My fingers tremble as I run through Mark's recent call activity. He has made a call to his mother from the airport in New York and one to an unknown number shortly after. His last dialled number is Doctor Hammond, and he made the call just moments ago. I quickly shove the phone back into his jacket and try to calm my wobbly nerves. I'm shaking uncontrollably. It's my own fault. I know I shouldn't have gone snooping. Now that I have, I need to deal with the confusion that comes with what I've found.

I wonder why Mark refused to tell me that he was speaking to my doctor. Why was that the first call he made as soon as the plane landed? I comfort myself with the explanation that Mark was telling the doctor that I have my memory back and I no longer require his services. *But isn't that right reserved for me?* What about doctor-patient confidentiality? Shouldn't I have had the pleasure of telling the assuming and irritating doctor to get lost? I can't help but smile anyway. Either way it doesn't matter. As long as someone has told Doctor Hammond to piss off, I'm happy.

We drive straight from the airport to the graveyard. I insist…against Mark's best advice, of course. The journey is silent apart from the occasional rev of the engine. Each bend in the road is a painful reminder of the day of the funeral. Various images from that horrific day flash inside my head like scenes from a desperately poignant television movie. The sights and sounds of the journey are just as blurred now as they were that day.

The melancholic memories are so strong that they all but transport me back to that moment in time to experience the heartbreak all over again.

I walk silently behind the hearse. My feet can't feel the concrete of the ground beneath them, but the sound resonates in my head like the beat of a loud drum. Mark's hand is tightly wrapped around mine, but I don't feel that either. My whole body is numb. I find myself rubbing my eyes often. They're irritated and sore. A combination of salty tears and disbelief stings between every blink.

Lorcan's tiny white coffin sits on display in the back of the hearse. The timber is finely polished and simplistic as it cradles its sleeping angel inside. The baby bluebells and ivory lilies that hug the tiny white box lovingly spell out Our Son.

Adam organised most of that kind of stuff. I can't remember now if I thanked him or not.

I can't take my eyes from looking through the window of the hearse. Family and friends' wreaths litter all around. Flowers in every colour of the rainbow fill the gaps in the back of the hearse where the coffin is too small to occupy. It's like a packet of Lorcan's favourite fruit pastels have spilled all over the back of the hearse. But all I can focus on is his tiny coffin. Once I can see it then he's still here.

Breathing is no longer a voluntary action. I have to consciously force myself to suck air into my lungs, and every so often, I forget to exhale, but soft whimpers release trapped air from my body.

Cars slow down as they pass by us. Drivers automatically bow or shake their heads as they notice the lonely, little white coffin. However, they will soon forget the sombre scene as they carry on with their lives. I hate them for that luxury. For us, the pain of this day permanently carves into our souls.

The headstones as we walk through the graveyard tease me. Men of ninety lie resting in the ground; some with wives beside them who have lived full lives and died in old age. Lorcan was just a little boy and he was stolen from us, condemned to join them in the cold earth. My mind screams in anger at God, the world, and everyone in it.

I stand at the edge of the open grave. Blackbirds fly overhead. How dare they, I think. How dare they fly today? Today the world should stop and mourn. Mark's cousin stands beside us. Her antique violin trembles under her shaking chin. The sound of Eric Clapton's Tears in Heaven soars as pallbearers lower the tiny white box deeper and deeper into the cold ground. It's a beautiful song, but I hate the music with every fibre of my being. I force the full weight of my body into my feet, firmly cementing them to the ground. I'm losing composure, and I don't care. I'm not going to say goodbye to our little boy. Not now, not ever.

I lunge forward, forcing anyone beside me out of the way. I viciously throw the violin out of the young girl's hand and knock her to the ground after it. Everyone gazes on; some throw their hands on their face, others gasp or whisper, but no one tries to stop me. I charge at the pallbearer. I tug the ropes from his hands in some naïve attempt to rescue Lorcan from the cruel hand that faith has dealt him.

Mark's arms wrap around my waist and pull me backwards. I kick and scream. The full force of my desperation thrashes wildly against him. He's weak against my fight, and I feel his chest heave as he cries. We fall to the ground together, our bodies tangled, one as broken as the other.

~~~

'We're here,' Mark says, parking the car outside the gates of the graveyard.

I follow reluctantly as we walk through the graveyard until we find a lonely headstone. It's cold and uninviting. Some stubborn weeds creep up and around the bottom of the granite. *Lorcan wouldn't like this*, I think. Of course, he wouldn't like it. *What am I thinking?* No five-year-old should have to like their headstone. God, it is all so wrong. He was just a little boy.

I look at the grave to my left. It's beautifully maintained with fresh flowers and lots of teddies and toys. It's obvious some broken-hearted mother visits every day. I wipe the heavy tears from my eyes and try to read the loving caption engraved. The names are hard to make out as so many flowers block my view and I don't dare touch them.

Aoibheann Louise O'Rourke
Died 3rd Nov 2014 age 29.
Beloved wife and devoted mother.
'Forever loved, never forgotten'

Another inscription is engraved just below.

Robert David O'Rouke
Died 3rd Nov 2014 aged 3.
'Sleep soundly in Heaven with Mommy, little man.
Daddy loves you.'

I can't take my eyes away from the words. I read and re-read them.

Maybe that baby boy has made a new friend. Maybe in some playground up there, Lorcan is joining in a fun game. Maybe he isn't alone.

'Oh, Lorcan. I wish it were me and not you. I wish I were dead. I don't want you to be alone,' I whisper as I kneel on the cold ground.

I look back at Mark. He's nodding. I know his heart is just as broken. I know this is what he wants; he wants me to talk to Lorcan.

'I know how afraid of the dark you are, Lorcan. I hope you're brave and not scared. I miss you. Do you miss me? Can you see me? I want to hold your hand. I wish you could come home because I need a cuddle… I need a cuddle,' I whisper to the grave as if the little boy can hear me through the soil.

'I don't like it,' I say as I turn to face Mark.

He steps closer to me and grips my hand, squeezing it so tight it pinches.

'The headstone, I mean. It needs Mickey stickers. Lorcan loves Mickey Mouse. You know that.'

'We can get some stickers,' Mark says with a sad smile. 'We can go to the shop for some now, if you'd like?'

'You go. I can't leave Lorcan alone. He's afraid of the dark, remember?'

Mark tugs on my hand, and I know he's going to try to guide me away. I pull against him. I don't want to leave; this is the closest I can ever be to Lorcan again, and I plan to stay here forever.

I visualise myself tearing away the clay, opening the tiny box where he lies and wrapping my arms tight around his precious little body. God, it hurts; breathing is physically painful. I never knew it was possible to ache so much for something. All your senses tell you how much you want something and your head cruelly reminds you that you can never have it. I just wanted to take Lorcan home.

When Lorcan was born and I held him for the first time, he had instinctively wrapped his tiny little hand around my finger. I was so incredibly happy at that moment. I kissed his soft forehead and promised him that I would love him forever. Forever wasn't meant to be this short.

Mark gently places his hand under my chin and turns my head towards his.

'Laura.' He pauses, maybe waiting for me to answer or maybe just waiting to gain my attention. 'We have to go home. It's time.'

'I can't leave Lorcan.'

'I can't do this alone anymore, Laura,' Mark admits. At nearly six foot, I have never seen Mark so small before. He's hunched forward like a little old man. 'I lost my baby, too. I hurt, too,' he spits through a clenched jaw. I know he isn't angry with me, but for a moment, it feels that way. I wouldn't blame him if he hated me. It was my fault. I caused this. I had taken everything away from him.

'I want to go to bed and just not wake up because maybe then the unbearable pain I feel every day will go away. But I can't. I have to be strong. So many people depend on me. I can't fall apart. I want to. Every single second of every single day, I want to. Mostly, I have to be strong for you.' Tears hang heavy in Mark's every word. 'I am crumbling and I need help, Laura; please help me.'

I stand up and take Mark's hand. 'I'm sorry,' I say.

It's a broad-spectrum apology, but I know by the way that Mark squeezes my hand that he understands.

'I want to show you something,' Mark says.

Mark and I walk hand and hand to the back of the graveyard. I watch Lorcan's grave until it's out of sight. Mark doesn't stop me. He just leads the way, and I follow. We reach a smaller, less well-kept grave that stands alone beneath a large weeping willow. The grave is just a slightly raised mound of clay that has been all but levelled over time. A delicate timber cross marks the head of the mound. There are no flowers or teddy bears here. But the square of ground is small. This is also a child's grave.

I wonder what kind of mother could leave her child in the cold ground and never return to visit the grave. Some poor child cruelly forgotten.

I try to read the faded inscription painted in white on the cross, but too many letters have succumbed to the hardship of the weather. The wind and rain have erased them. There's no name, just a date. A newborn baby lies resting in the forgotten grave.

'Why are you showing me this?' I ask

Mark looks at me blankly.

'Have we not suffered enough? We don't need to see this, Mark.'

I turn to walk away, but Mark places his hands on my shoulders and spins me back around.

'Look,' he says.

'I am.' I soften. 'Are you trying to show me that others have suffered like us? I know they have. We are not the first people to lose a child, but that doesn't make it hurt any less.'

'You're not looking, Laura. Not really.'

'I want to go,' I say trembling. A combination of bitter cold and heartache challenges me to remain upright, and I contemplate giving up. I want to fall to the ground and just never get up again.

Chapter Thirty-Five

Mark and I sit in silence in the driveway at our house. It's dark outside. The thick grey clouds completely hide the moon. The sitting room curtains are closed and no lights are on inside; the house is miserable and uninviting. It's obvious that the house has stood unoccupied for a while now. Mark must not have been back since I ran away. I wonder why. I guess the memories inside are too painful for him too, and I dread to think how I will feel as I walk through the front door. I try to be brave and convince myself that I'm finally ready. We can face it together, and hopefully, time will help us move on.

A light comes on in the hall, and I freeze. I turn towards Mark and wait for him to panic at the thoughts of an intruder, but he doesn't flinch. The light on the porch flickers a little before deciding to remain on and illuminates most of the driveway. The hall door creaks open and it's time to accept we have company.

Nicole sticks her head around the door and smiles. I'm about to explode into a lecture directed at Mark when my mother-in-law's head appears close behind her. A flock of millions of tiny butterflies gather in my tummy. *The kids must be inside too*, I think with giddy excitement. The fluttering increases and my delicate butterflies became more like hungry pelicans trying to fly to freedom through the wall of my stomach. *What if they don't remember me? What if they have learned to love Nicole more?* I should never have left. I make myself feel sick as I continue to berate myself with the regrets of a bad mother.

Mark climbs out of the driver's seat and walks around to open my door. The vicious December chill fights with the comforting heat inside the car. He reaches his hand out to me.

'You ready?' he asks softly, and I sense his enthusiasm.

I nod, but my contorted face is protesting. I'm so far from ready. I can't wait to hold my children, but I can't do that without going inside, and I really, really don't want to go in the house. My heartstrings aren't being tugged at; they're clumped together like sticky spaghetti.

'Come on. No one will bite, I promise,' Mark assures, tugging me by the hand.

It's easier than I think it will be. I just put one weak leg in front of the other and soon I'm standing inside the hall door with Patricia hugging me and crying. I'm taken aback by her lack of composure. I was never in the running for daughter-in-law of the year, but standing there, with the air being squeezed from my lungs as her arms wrap tightly around my neck, I could be forgiven for thinking she is actually glad to see me.

Nicole stands with her back to the wall, and I know that's because I'm making her uncomfortable. And even though I know my hatred for her was misguided, I still can't bring myself to like her.

Mark takes my coat, hangs it on the end of the stairs, and ushers me into the sitting room to sit by a roaring fire. Nicole potters towards the kitchen and mumbles something about making a pot of tea. I sit back against the soft suede of the couch. If I close my eyes for longer than a second, then I'll fall asleep, so I didn't allow myself to relax completely. It isn't difficult; I'm sandwiched between Mark and his mother.

Patricia's hand is on my knee and she's patting it gently as she speaks. 'I'm so glad you have your memory back, sweetheart. Mark has been out of his mind with worry.'

I smile lovingly at my husband. It's a relief to know that all the time I was convinced he didn't love me anymore; he was actually just hurting and just struggling to show it.

'When did it all start to come back to you?' Patricia asks.

Mark takes my hand in his and strokes the back of my palm with his other hand. 'Mom, Laura is tired. I think we should leave the questions for another time.'

'I'm not tired,' I assure Mark. 'I remembered when I saw the photo. As soon as I saw Lorcan's face,' I say.

Patricia grabs me for an unexpected hug, and my spine cracks in protest.

'Aww, that's beautiful. I'm so glad you finally decided on a name. Lorna is a pretty little name,' Patricia says, still holding me.

Mark glares at his mother through squinted eyes. He's desperate for her to shut up, but she's on a roll.

'Did you visit the grave?' she asks, finally releasing me to blow her nose into a fancy, embroidered handkerchief.

Mark hops up from beside me and waves his hands crossing one over the other. 'No, no! This is a happy day. Laura is home now; we don't want to spend the evening talking about things that are going to upset us all.'

'It's okay, Mark,' I say with a sniffle. 'I want to talk about it. It helps me deal with it.'

Mark sits reluctantly back down. He's decidedly uncomfortable. *Just because I'm coming to terms with all this doesn't mean he is.* Maybe I'm upsetting him.

320

Patricia continues to ramble on and my eyes weigh heavy as I try to stay awake. I'm not listening to a word she's saying, but I'm enjoying the company. Nothing matters more to me now than family time, no matter how tedious the conversation.

Nicole rattles back into the room as she carries a large silver tray I didn't know we had with four teacups, some milk, sugar, and even some inviting chocolate chip cookies.

She pushes a couple of magazines off the coffee table and lets them fall to the floor before placing down the heavy tray.

'Biscuit, Laura?' she offers timidly.

'Yes, please,' I say reaching out to take one. I look at Mark; certain he will commend my effort to be polite. I'm right. His eyes smile happily at me.

I bite into the cookie happy to be offering my growling tummy something at last.

'Ugh, yuck,' I say spitting the flaky, soap-tasting cookie into a serviette I grab from the tray. 'Where did you get these? I think they may be stale.'

'I baked them myself,' Nicole stutters.

My face flashes bright red. I hope she doesn't think I'm rude on purpose. She slams her cup down on the coffee table. Some tea spills over the edge and leaves a brownish-yellow circle on the pine table. Mark races after her with Patricia following soon after.

The heated conversation from the kitchen filters through to the sitting room where I sit staring at the ceiling. I can't understand the muffled sounds, but I imagine Patricia and Nicole are giving Mark an earful. I'm tempted to press my ear against the kitchen door, but I decide against it. Patricia is still my mother-in-law. The once a month family dinners at their house are hard enough already – with the five hundred pieces of cutlery that I never know which to use, appetisers with names I don't understand, and Patricia watching me with beaded eyes as I try to swallow something that I often suspect is made from sour milk. If I hear Patricia say something cruel and unforgettable, then I will never be able to sit opposite her at the table again.

I decide instead to creep up to the kids' rooms and check on my sleeping angels. I'm almost at the top step when Mark runs into the hall calling after me. His mother and Nicole follow irritatingly behind.

'What you doing?' he shouts. 'You okay?'

'Shh,' I say placing my index finger over my lips. 'You'll wake them.'

'Wake who?' Mark asks ignoring my request for hush.

'The kids, you wally. Who else?'

Patricia's hand covers her mouth, and she stumbles back almost falling against Nicole. 'I thought you told her,' she says angrily, staring at Mark. 'You said everything was okay now. You promised, Mark. Nothing has changed, has it?'

Mark is pale and silent.

'Has it?' Patricia screams.

Nicole holds Patricia tightly in her arms and strokes her hair softly until she calms. It's all so over that top that I want to slap someone.

'Will someone please tell me what is going on?' I say beyond irritated.

Mark looks from Nicole to his mother and then at me. He opens his mouth, and I pause waiting for what I assume will be his answer, but he closes his mouth again.

Nicole finally speaks. 'They're not here,' she says. She steps back towards the kitchen dragging Patricia with her. It's as if she was expecting me to have some sort of horrid reaction and she was preparing to protect herself.

'If they're not here, then where are they?' I snap.

Again, an annoying silence falls over everyone, and I notice they all appear to be holding their breaths involuntarily.

'Where in the hell are my children?' I bellow so loudly I give myself an instant headache.

'They're in my house,' Patricia says finally passing Mark her handkerchief to wipe the tears swelling under his eyes.

A small twitch has made its way into Mark's body and it jerks him back and forth on the spot. If I blink, I'll miss it, but I see enough to know Mark isn't coping. And I know Patricia sees it, too.

'I thought you would need your rest after the long trip, so I suggested that I keep them with me tonight. Okay?' Patricia says.

I want to shout that of course it's not okay. I want to tell the interfering old woman that it's a stupid idea; that I miss my kids more than I can bear and another day waiting to see them is a lifetime. But I don't say a word. Anything I say now might tip Mark to the breaking point.

'Well, I best be off,' Patricia says nervously as she reaches for the front door handle. She can probably sense the vibes I'm shooting her way, and I don't blame her for wanting to leave.

'I'll drop you home,' Mark suggests.

Nicole's bottom lip begins to quiver. I know we're never going to be the type of friends who sip tea in the afternoon while chatting about the latest celebrity scandal, but I honestly never realised that I intimidate her quite so much. She almost seems afraid of me.

'No, Mark, I'll go,' Nicole says gripping Mark's arm and silently pleading with him.

'That okay, Mom?' Mark asks sweetly.

'Why don't you all go,' I suggest. 'I'll be fine by myself. I think I'm just going to head straight to bed. You're right, Patricia. I *am* exhausted.'

I step off the bottom step of the stairs that has taken me a long time to descend and lean forward to kiss Mark.

Nicole shudders a little as I stand beside her and the damsel in distress act is doing my head in. Nicole mumbled goodbye and flings her handbag over her shoulder almost knocking out my front teeth. I notice the tattered key ring that hangs from the zip. It's a silver crescent moon with a pretty painted face. It's handmade. The giveaway is it looked a lot more like a squashed silver banana than a moon. Nicole must have always had it, but I never noticed it before. It only catches my eye now because it reminds me so much of the little sun that Nigel is so endearingly attached to. The key rings share the same wobbly, bright red smile. I wonder if Nigel would have had the same meltdown had he known it wasn't lovingly handcrafted after all, and more likely a buy-one-get-one-free offer from a corner brick-a-brack shop.

Chapter Thirty-Six

'Bye,' I say as I stand on the porch and wave at our car pulling out the drive. Mark was ridiculously reluctant to leave me alone. But I couldn't wait to be alone. I have an extensive amount of snooping to do. Even though I'm back in my own home, it has changed so much since I was last here that I need to research every nook and cranny. I have a weird feeling there's something I need to find, even though I have no idea what.

The house has been stripped to skeletal remains of what I remember. The chocolate handprints dotted along the bottom of the doors are no longer visible. No scribbles in brightly coloured marker wiggle up and down the walls. It's as if Nicole called in pest control. The cleaners have fumigated the place, removing any evidence that children once lit up the house with giddy laughter and playful games. It really pisses me off that Mark would allow the messy slate that is our family life to be wiped so clean.

I decide to investigate the playroom first. A painful ice filters through my veins and into my heart as I stand looking in from the door arch. The room has been completely redecorated. A large and impressive dining room stares back at me. A solid oak dining table and six chairs replace the large plastic train set in the centre of the floor. All the colourful storage shelves are absent and a large, built-in unit housing scented candles and shiny picture frames stands tall at the back of the room. It's a beautiful room. Homely yet stylish, but it's wrong. It doesn't belong in my house. Where are the messy toys and biscuit crumbs that usually litter the floor?

Memories of the day of the funeral rush back to me. No fog covers the images anymore. There's nothing to protect me from the pain. I can remember clearly, and God, how much I wished I couldn't.

Distant family members shaking my hand and kissing my cheek. The offensive, cheap incense wafts around me. It engulfs the whole room. Slender white candles lit on a small table hidden in the corner. There's a picture of Lorcan in a pretty, silver frame. He's only a few days old in the shot, and I wonder why we've chosen that photo instead of a more recent one. I remember how precious it felt to hold his tiny body as a baby. I long for the touch of his soft wrinkled hand or another chance to inhale the distinctive smell of his newborn skin. I miss him so much that I think my grief will choke me. I wouldn't fight it if it does; I wouldn't want to.

I shudder as the bitter sting of loneliness grabs me. I see the house full of people, some chatting and laughing…some hugging in silence…and some, like me…standing alone. I recognise most people. My parents console each other in the corner. My sister tries to busy herself cutting apple tarts and offers a piece to anyone who's brave enough to make eye contact. People tell me they're sorry for my troubles and that they will pray for me. Others avoid me completely because they don't know what to say. Everyone hurts, but no one hurts like me. Remembering is hell.

I wander from one empty room to the next. The house is so silent. I hate being here. I want to be back in New York. Everything is better there. There are no demons there. I resent Mark for making me come home to this. It's not even a home anymore. Now it's just a poignant house that teases me with thoughts of what could have been. I find the key to the back door and race towards it. It's becoming increasingly hard to breathe, and I have to get out of the house. Fresh air has to reach my lungs or I feel I will explode. I burst through the door and inhale deeply.

Every step I take now brings with it a torrential downpour of memories. It's bordering dangerously on a mental overload. I drop my head and tuck my face into my hands as the images of the past parade across my mind.

I remember standing alone on the patio. It's raining, but I don't notice the cold wet soak of my clothes and it makes me shiver. My back is turned, but I can feel Mark's presence behind me. He's crying. He reaches his hand out to me, but I pull away. He tries to embrace me, but I push him back so roughly I stumble and tear my palm off the rusty side gate as I attempt to keep my balance.

'It's all your fault,' I shout. 'I hate you.'

'It's nobody's fault,' Mark disagrees sadly.

'I hate you,' I scream over and over. 'I told you I never wanted kids. I told you.'

Mark looks at me blankly. He's already suffering so much, but my hysteria is making it even harder for him to cope.

'But you wanted to be a mother,' Mark says.

'I did, so much. But now our little one is gone, and I want to die. If you didn't get me pregnant, then the baby would never have been born and would never have died. I would never have to hurt like this. I hate you for it. I will never forgive you.'

I close my aching fist and watch the blood trickle past my knuckles. Mark's words ring in my ears, over and over again. It wasn't my fault! What wasn't my fault? Mark tries to walk towards me, but I back away. He has such pain in his eyes.

~~~

I want to stop the memories now. They're too vivid and awful, but I my head is reeling and I can't make it stop. They continue to pop like hundreds of pins attacking shiny balloons. I pull out a chair from the dining room table and sit down. I fold my arms and drop my head against them.

I was the one who pushed Mark away. I was cold and out of character. I'm surprised he still loves me at all. I've destroyed our marriage because I blame him for something he had no control over. But now I know the mistakes I've made. I won't make them again. I can fix everything, and we will be okay.

Oh my God. Oh my God. The back of my chair cracks loudly as it collides with the floor. I can't get up the stairs fast enough. I dash into the spare room and frantically pull everything out from the wardrobe. Black sacks full of Christmas decorations, an old hand-knitted cardigan, and a duvet cover spill out on top of me. I push the heavy pile to one side and stare at the little metal box that hides at the back of the empty wardrobe. It's just as I remember; a small white box sealed with some yellowing adhesive tape. The dark blue handles are tattered and close to falling off, but to me, the precious little chest is beautiful. I sit cross-legged on the floor, my fingers quivering as I tug at the edges of the tape. I lift the lid and gasp at the treasure inside.

My eyes first light up as I stare at the delicate pink baby booties and a tiny white baby vest, barely big enough to fit a doll. A small, white hospital bracelet is also peeking out at me. I try to place the bracelet on my index and middle fingers, but it's too tight to fit. I remember stroking my new baby's little hand as the bracelet spun around on the tiniest, most fragile wrist I had ever seen. There's a note stuffed inside one of the booties and I pull it out and read it out loud.

Dearest baby,

Happy 21ˢᵗ Birthday, my princess.

As I write this letter to you, my paper is resting on my enormous bump and you're kicking up a storm inside. You're due in less than a week and your dad and I are so excited to meet you. I can't wait to hold you in my arms, kiss your little forehead, and tell you how much I love you. I can't wait to be a mom. Your mom.

I hope I've done you proud over the years. I hope that at twenty-one years of age, you love me as much as I loved you even before you were born. I hope that we are not just family but friends and I hope that every day of the last twenty-one years I've made sure you know how very special you are.

I struggled with the decision to give up my career in New York and move back to Ireland. Did I ever tell you that? But day after day, feeling you grow inside me, I am so grateful for the decision I made to become a mother.

Today is one month to the day until Ava and Adam's wedding, and if you don't hurry up and pop, I'm going to be the world's most heavily pregnant bridesmaid.

I hope you and Bobby have grown up to be great friends. Just like Ava and I. Adam once told me that his family aren't just in his heart, they are his heart. I didn't understand at the time, but I do now. You are my heart, little one. You're not even born yet and already you are the centre of your dad's and my world.

We love you so very much, princess.

Mom x

I fold the paper neatly and place it back in the bootie. There's something else in the box, a folded sheet of newspaper. I don't remember putting that in. The edges of the pages are rough and it appears the article was ripped from a larger page. I unfold it carefully and my eyes struggle to remain in focus as I read the black and white print.

A five-year-old boy, Lorcan Kavanagh, has died today after last Wednesday's car crash on the M50 North Bound. Lorcan, a pupil of St. John's Primary School in Lucan, County Dublin had been on life support since the accident.

This brings the number of fatalities in the two-car collision to four. The driver, a close family friend of the boy, was pronounced dead at the scene. Her three-year-old son also died later at The Saints Children's hospital. The heavily pregnant driver of the other car is reported to have been discharged from the hospital in recent days. Her baby girl died as a result of her injuries.

Police are continuing to investigate the cause of the accident at the notorious black spot. Lorcan's mother, speaking outside the hospital, has requested that the family's privacy be respected at this tragic time.

A short, sharp scream escapes my mouth, so loud it leaves my ears ringing. I crumple up the paper and fling it in the corner. I think about tucking my knees into my chest and rocking back and forth on the spot. *But what good will that do?* Instead, I take out my phone and hit speed dial. The phone rings twice before I hang up. I forgot the time difference. It's the middle of the night in New York. I desperately need to hear Ava's voice, but I will have to wait.

Vomit swells in my mouth as I stand up. My head is shaking so hard from side to side that I lose my balance and scrape my shoulder off the corner of the radiator. I'm grateful for the pain it causes. It takes my mind off the article, but only for a second. There's something familiar about the piece of paper; something my body knows but my head doesn't. A sharp pins and needles sensation pinches my skin.

'It's just a joke,' I shout out loud even though I know there's no one there to hear me. I need noise, any noise. This silence is unbearable.

My shaking is getting worse. I lie on the ground. My eyes close, but I can't escape the words that spell out a cruel, alternate reality. *Faint, goddamn it*, I tell myself. It doesn't work. *Faint, you stupid bitch…just faint.* My eyes remain closed, and I remain awake.

I scurry to the corner in pursuit of the article and read it again and again and again. I hate myself for reading it. I hate my eyes for seeing the words, and most of all, I hate my brain for believing them. I reach for my phone once more, dropping it several times. Time anywhere in the world is no longer of consequence. My trembling fingers try hard to cooperate, but it

takes numerous attempts before I manage to dial the correct
digits.

'Hello,' a sleepy voice answers.

'It's me,' I explain. 'I know the truth.'

I hang up and stuff the article into my pocket.

Chapter Thirty-Seven

The front door slams announcing Mark is home. I rub my eyes; I must have fallen asleep. My legs beg me to stay still as they try their best to anchor me to the spot. But my head is in control now, so my body will have to cooperate. I hold on to the banister and descend two and three steps at a time. I'm shaking so much I can feel the knobbles of my spine pulsate together.

I try to reach the dining room before Mark, but I don't make it. He stands and waits for me. Some of the cardboard boxes were ripped open, odds and ends lie scattered on the floor like jigsaw pieces from our life. He has a silver picture frame in his hand.

'Looking for this?' he asks casually waving the frame.

I don't know how to react.

'Nigel called me,' Mark says, stiffness creeping between his frowning brows. 'You know?'

I nod.

'Ava?' he asks.

I nod again.

'How long?' Mark wipes his eyes. 'I mean when? No, I mean...'

'It's okay,' I say taking his hand.

Mark cries. I do, too. He drops the frame onto the ground. It falls face down, hiding the picture it contains. Mark wraps his arms around me, and I grab him so tight in return my knuckles crack. We hold each other and slide to the floor. We sit together for a very long time just cradling each other.

Hours pass and we drift in and out of sleep. Neither of us wants to break the embrace and be the one who suggests we go to bed. But it's starting to get very cold as icy morning fog attacks the world outside the window, and we're both uncomfortable. Mark stands up first and stretches his hand out to pull me to my feet.

'Hang on,' I suggest as I reach for the now buckled frame.

'No, Laura. Don't,' Mark says, pulling on my sleeve like a child. 'Not tonight, please?'

There's an ache in his heart; it reveals itself in every phonic. He has such urgency and panic in his stance. I can't figure out what he's afraid of now because I already know the secrets of the past; there's nothing left to be afraid of.

I pick up the picture and his fear turns to sadness. I fiddle with the back of the frame; the glass releases the photo into my hands. It's strangely surreal to stare at the beautiful, happy family. Smiling faces beam at me from the confines of the print. I recognise the image straight away. It's strikingly similar to the picture Nigel showed me in New York. Nicole stands with her arm around a handsome dark-haired little boy. I sit next to her sporting a huge baby bump and Mark stands behind me with his arm draped over my shoulder. But Nigel's apartment is so different in the backdrop to the blissful domestic scene. The granite behind our shoulders doesn't sparkle and the kitchen cupboards are more cheap MDF than solid timber. And it looks far more homely than Nigel's bachelor pad. It looks like a real family belongs there. I wonder whose house it is.

'I'm so sorry,' I cry. 'I'm a monster. All this happened because I wanted to get my stupid hair done. I never should have asked Ava to collect Lorcan from school.'

Mark shakes his head. Months of intensity spill forcefully from his exhausted body like the lid popping on a pot of cracking popcorn.

'I miss them,' Mark says softly.

'Me too,' I sob. So many heavy tears heave from my body that it's almost impossible to get enough oxygen to remain conscious.

I run my finger over the picture that I can't stop staring at. It was like a map, leading me from my comforting place in deep denial to the poignant reality that I should be accepting.

'It was taken at Halloween. Just a couple of weeks before the accident. I framed it because it was the last picture of the kids together,' Mark explains sadly.

I nod as if I have heard Mark say that one hundred times before. There's no shock or need for it to sink in. I'm revisiting a horrible memory, and although it hurts, it's liberating to finally be on the same page as my husband. But some of the facts don't quite fit, and I feel bubbles rip through my tummy. I don't know how much more my mind will allow me to take in.

I take the crumpled article from my pocket and pass it to Mark. My eyes silently plead for the explanation that I may struggle to believe.

He doesn't have to read the print. He seems to know the words by heart.

'It is true, Laura,' he whispers. 'That's what you want to ask, isn't it? Well, the answer is, yes. Yes, you lost more than anyone should ever have to.'

'Are you sure?' I cry.

Mark is beyond words. His head just slowly moves up and down.

I cover my ears with my hands. 'I don't believe you,' I shout standing up and catching a handful of delicate porcelain ornaments from the shelves and flinging them against the opposite wall.

Mark reaches into his wallet and pulls out another photo.

'What the hell?' I ask taking the image before he drops it.

I study the picture. It's definitely the same picture I examined in detail in New York. The tears are in the same jagged places and the same murky sticky tape repairs them, but the image has changed. It's now an exact replica of the framed picture.

'You only see what you want to see,' Mark says.

'No.' I shook my head roughly. 'I don't want to see this.' I caught both pictures and threw them on the ground. They landed face up teasing me.

'I know you don't, but you need to,' Mark snaps back equally as sharply.

He slowly lowers himself to the ground. He leans unsteadily on his hunkers and runs his finger across the faces in the picture. He doesn't check to see if I'm watching. I want to ignore his dramatic posture, but my eyes follow his pointing finger.

'This is Nicole and Lorcan. You, obviously! There I am standing behind you, and that's our baby in your belly. Look.'

He picks the pictures up, dusts them off, and holds them forcefully in my face. He has a strange, frightening expression moulding his face into one I don't recognise. He needs to explain. If I deny him this opportunity, then he looks as though he might implode.

The doorbell rings and startles us. Mark catches my hand. I pull back but his grip tightens. 'You're hurting me,' I shout, but he doesn't let go.

He isn't letting me out of his sight. If I'm afraid of what I might do, so I can only imagine how freaked out he is. I close my eyes as the door opens. I know who to expect, but I'm not ready. I will never be ready.

Nicole waits in the open doorway. Nigel stands beside her. Both wait to be invited in.

'Thanks for calling.' Nigel smiles, reaching forward to kiss my cheek.

'You came?' I say trying to sound monotonic. I didn't want my feelings revealed in my voice.

'Of course,' he replies. 'Once I knew you really had your memory back, I got the next flight. I've waited so long. I have so many questions only you can answer.'

Nicole looks fragile, and I'm almost concerned for her. She wants desperately to hear what I have to say, but she looks as confused as I am.

'Can I see them?' I ask.

'Of course,' Nigel says. He hands me his keys and I hold them beside Nicole's bag. The key rings are a perfectly flawed match. Both Nigel and Nicole smile as they stand side-by-side, holding hands.

'I know you hate me,' I say turning to Nicole. 'I don't blame you; it's all my fault.'

Nicole doesn't speak.

'No one hates you,' Nigel assures. 'It was an accident. You didn't kill him, no one did. Stop hating yourself.'

I sigh heavily. Nigel's kind words don't ease my guilt.

'I may not have put a gun to his head, but I am responsible for his death. I'm a murderer.'

Nicole lunges forward without warning and hugs me so tight I think my head will swell from the pressure. 'Don't say that. Please don't. You are a good person, Laura.'

'Will she be okay,' Nigel says placing his hand firmly on Mark's shoulder.

Mark shrugs.

I race towards the kitchen and beckon for the others to follow me. I put the kettle on, fling the milk and sugar onto the table, and root in the cupboards for a packet of biscuits. Mark looks at the spread on the table. It's six thirty am. No one is either hungry or thirsty. My need to busy myself is embarrassingly obvious, but Mark is smiling at me. He nibbles on a chocolate digestive and scoops some heaped spoons of sugar into his tea. Nigel and Nicole copy his action, but no one speaks.

The silence continues until everyone is, if possible, even more uncomfortable. I can't take it any longer. Every scrambled thought I have spills from my lips in no sensible order, but no one interrupts or questions my stutters. Instead, they hang on each word of my ramblings, trying to piece together as much of a story as they can.

'Ava text me to say Lorcan was so excited about our trip to the park and she would meet me by big willow tree near the pond. It was late and I was rushing. I looked back at the big shiny red kite that I had bought earlier. It had Mickey Mouse on the front, and I couldn't wait to see Lorcan's face light up when I showed him. You know how much he loves…loved,' I corrected myself, 'Mickey Mouse.'

Nicole smiles and nods. The makeup on her cheeks is almost all washed away by her tears.

'I remember the sun shining on the traffic lights. I couldn't see what colour they were. There was no traffic, and I was in such a hurry that I just decided to go for it.'

I look at Mark, Nicole, and Nigel. I want one of them to scream at me. Shout how much they hate me. Something, anything. They don't move. They barely looked away long enough to blink.

'I didn't see her. I swear. It was the sun; it was shining in my eyes. And Ava's car was grey and blended in with the road. I tried to stop. I really did. I slammed hard on the brakes, but the car just kept moving. I was going too fast. Just too fucking fast. It's all my fault.'

I do a lot of apologising, sometimes even to myself, for all the pain that I've caused. I repeat myself often, and finally too exhausted to speak any longer, I cry. Loud, heartbroken sobs fill the air. But it isn't just the sound of my tears. Nicole sobs softly into a damp tissue. Mark coughs roughly in a bid to confine his pain. Nigel's reaction is different. He sits still, his face blank and free from all emotion. But his eyes glisten, and delicate, subtle tears stream down his rosy cheeks with every blink. He doesn't raise his hand to wipe them or accept the tissue that Nicole offers. He's a statue. I soon realise he can't move. He's trapped inside his own harsh exterior with bitter pain attacking the unseen inside. Nicole leans forward and offers Nigel her hand. He grabs on tight. It's a small gesture, but enough to help Nigel finally release some of his hurt as he begins to cry.

'Does this mean you two are getting back together?' I ask inappropriately.

Nicole quickly loosens her grip and lets Nigel's hand fall by his side.

'Don't look so shocked. Did you think I wouldn't remember that you're married to my big, strong brother-in-law here.' I playfully pinch Nigel's biceps and hope that they will laugh.

Nigel giggles sheepishly, but Nicole is still very serious.

'It's not that easy, Laura. I wish it was,' she says.

My cheeks tinge. 'I'm sorry; I shouldn't have said anything.'

'It's okay,' Nicole says.

'Stop forgiving me,' I shout as frustration reaches a high inside me. 'I've made your life a living hell. I can't imagine how hard it must be for you to lose all you have. I thank God every day for my kids. Without them, I would never have been able to get through this.'

Nigel leaps from his chair. Temper flashes in his face like a vicious famished beast on the attack. He pushes his hand beneath the corner of the table and flips it over completely before grabbing his chair that has fallen behind him and smashes it repeatedly against the ground.

'I thought you remembered,' he shouts. 'I thought you fucking remembered.'

He's scaring me. Mark and Nicole seem concerned, but they aren't frightened. They knew Nigel better than I did; maybe they've seen him fly into a furious rage before.

'I do remember,' I stutter, standing up, pleading silently with Mark to rescue me, but he doesn't. He remains seated with his head dropped into his hands.

'No, you fucking don't,' Nigel shouts even louder than before.

'Nigel, please don't,' Nicole begs.

I know he's going to hit me. He's so angry he might even kill me. I can't even fight back, I don't deserve to. If he's insane, then it's because I've driven him to it.

'Now is not the time,' Nicole adds.

'It's never the right time. It will never be the right time. You all tiptoe around the truth as if it's some kind of dirt under the rug. I can't take it anymore.' There's a strange desperation in Nigel's voice, and suddenly, he scares me for a completely different reason. He knows something I don't. There are still aspects of this nightmare that they are hiding from me; facts that I'm hiding from myself.

'Let's make now the time,' I suggest shakily.

'Sit down,' Nigel orders.

I do as he asks.

'You really want to hear this? Because believe me, I really want to tell you.'

My head shakes up and down so fast it's hard to tell if I'm nodding or shivering.

'Okay,' Nigel says as all the anger melts from his face. He rests both his hands on the table beside me and leans the weight of his body into his arms.

'Our son, Lorcan, was five when he died.'

'Your son?' I stutter.

'Shut the fuck up and let me speak,' Nigel commands.

I don't argue.

'And there's not a day that goes by that I don't miss him. I'll never get to watch him grow up. I know it's not your fault, but I hate you for taking him from me.'

'Your son,' I say again; I haven't heard anything after he said the word son.

'What? Did you think he was yours?' Nigel snaps sarcastically.

I stand silent and still.

'Oh Christ, you did,' Nicole says stepping forward with her hand over her mouth. 'You really thought he was your child, didn't you?'

I still don't reply. They are twisting everything, and I don't know what to think.

'I got pregnant just a couple of years after we finished college, Laura. Don't you remember? You were the first person I told.' Nicole speaks softly now, almost whispering. 'You've known Lorcan since before he was born.'

I don't move. I don't even blink. I won't let them see that they're getting to me. They're messing with my head. It's so easy for them. Entertaining even.

'But you let the news slip to my brother here,' Nigel points at Mark as if I don't know who my own husband is. It was infuriating. 'And, as they say, my life was never the same again.'

'Of course, I remember,' I snap, frustrated. I'm not lying to humour them. I really do remember a little boy hugging me tightly and telling me I'm the best aunt in the whole-wide world. I remember his bright eyes just like his mother's and his charming personality like his father.

342

'You smell nice,' he'd tell me every day. I haven't changed my perfume in five years because I never wanted to stop hearing those sweet words. I longed to hear him say them now. I miss him terribly, how could I ever have forgotten. Guilt and heartbreak choke me. I can barely breathe. Nigel and Nicole's eyes burn into me.

'Of course, I fucking remember.' My hands moved to my head and I rub hard.

'You know Lorcan is our son.' Nigel points at Nicole. 'Our son.'

'Yes,' I bark.

'Because no one could ever forget their own child, Laura, could they? No one could forget their own.'

'That's enough,' Mark says angrily. Those are the first words Mark has spoken in hours. 'She doesn't need to hear this.'

'Yes, I do.' I appreciate Mark trying to protect me, but it's too late. 'Please, Nigel...go on.'

Nigel coughs and clears his throat. 'Nicole and I loved him so much. He was our whole world. When he died, we realised that he was the only thing we had in common. I lost my wife three months after I lost my son. By the time I worked up the balls to beg her to take me back, she had fallen for someone else. She's happy and I'm not going to mess it up for her.'

Nigel looks at Mark as he spoke. I don't miss the innuendo.

'I'm sorry,' I say, disappointed by how pathetic the words sounded. I wish there was a better way to express my genuine regret.

Nigel shrugs. 'I thought about wrapping myself up in a little bubble of lies like you, but I'm not as convincing as you are,' he

343

says, temper draining from his words and sadness takes its place.

'Nigel, she has apologised. There's nothing more she can do. She's not a liar,' Mark says.

'Not a liar?' Nigel mimicked. 'She's going around telling everyone how much she loves two kids who don't exist. That's a fucking lie in my book!'

I scream, and I don't stop. Not even when Mark covers my mouth and whispers, 'Shh,' over and over again in my ear. Suddenly, all the jigsaw pieces slammed together in my mind. I could see the bigger picture, and it was a masterpiece of deceit.

It's a seriously elaborate scam. I had to give them credit. For a while, they almost had me convinced I was going crazy. They've certainly done their homework. They knew what to suggest and how to suggest it. I'm the stupid fool who believed them.

I may be naïve and have fallen for a lot of their crap, but how did they ever think they would convince me to forget my kids? No amount of drugs in the world could wipe the memory of their precious faces from my mind. If I wasn't so terrified of their next move, I'd laugh in their faces at their foolish attempt.

'Where are my kids?' I shout even though my voice is muffled as it tries to pass through Mark's fingers. I was suddenly horribly aware of their safety. 'I want to see them now.'

'There are no kids.' Mark can hardly speak he's crying so hard.

'You can cut out the acting now. I've figured out your crappy plan. It won't work.'

'There are *no* kids, Laura,' Mark repeats as if I will accept it a second time around.

'You can have your slut,' I scream and point at Nicole who weeps irritatingly. 'But you can't have my kids. GIVE ME BACK MY BABIES.'

'We lost our baby, Laura. The doctors did everything they could, but they couldn't stop the bleeding; the seat belt had just caused too much damage. They had to perform an emergency hysterectomy. We can't ever have children.' Mark stops abruptly. It's almost as if he knows that just by saying it out loud, he's hammering a stake through my heart.

I race to the windowsill looking for my phone. Mark catches me by my waist and pulls me back. I drop the phone. I yelp loudly as I dive on the ground to retrieve it, clasping it so tightly my knuckles whiten.

'What are you doing?' Mark asks twitching.

His nervous approach gives me a sense of comfort. I guess the pressure is too much for him. I hope he'll crumble and their plan will unravel.

'Using the phone, what do you think?' I bark.

'Who are you calling?'

'Ava,' I snap, although I quickly make a mental note to be more polite. I stare at the three angry faces glaring at me and the full gravity of my vulnerability was reinforced.

'Laura, stop this nonsense. Ava is dead, for God's sake. She died in the crash. You are the only one who survived. It's a miracle that you weren't hurt.'

'Weren't hurt?' I snort. 'I had to learn to walk again, you prick. I spent weeks in the hospital. Don't you think that hurt?'

'You weren't hurt in the crash, Laura. The only thing that was hurt was your mind. Anything that happened to you, you did to yourself. You're ill. Please let me help you. I just want to help you.' Mark reaches his hand out to me, but I slap it away. I covered my ears with my hands and sing, 'La, la, la, la, la,' at the top of my lungs.

Mark grabs my hands and pulls them close to him. He shakes me roughly until I stop.

'If you want to call someone, call Adam. He'll tell you that she's gone.'

'I'm sure with your skill you could have easily twisted Adam into your sick little web. He already hates me; it wouldn't take much to convince him to help you.'

'He doesn't hate you.' Mark softens. 'He's just looking for someone to blame.'

'Yeah, right,' I snap. 'Adam is a womaniser and a scumbag. If he's lost Ava, then it's because he deserved it.'

'Don't say that, Laura. No one deserves that. He lost just as much as you have. All the drinking and women are his way of coping. He idolised Ava and his son.'

'Bullshit,' I bellow, clenching my back teeth together so hard my jaw ached. 'She hasn't even had the baby yet. I want to speak to her. She is the only one I trust.'

'AVA IS DEAD!' Mark roars – his cheeks as red as two ripe cherries and tiny bloodshot threads creep into his eyes.

I decide he's losing the battle to convince me, and it's infuriating him.

Suddenly, a horrible realisation hits me like the slap of a wet tea towel in the face. Mark sounded incredibly convincing when he said Ava was dead. They wouldn't actually hurt Ava, would they? None of this is her fault. *Christ.*

'This isn't working, man,' Nigel says as he offers me a chair at the table.

I gratefully accept. Although I turn it at a right angle before I sit. I wouldn't dare turn my back on any of the three.

'We can't keep this up,' Nigel adds staring at Mark and willing him to agree.

'He's right,' Nicole agrees. 'It's not working, Mark. Surely you must know that by now.'

A tiny smirk creeps out from the fearful frown cemented on my face. They're finally accepting that they've lost. Unless they want another corpse on their hands, they have to give me back my children. If they don't, then I will go to the police. I have evidence now; they will have to investigate this time. I pat my jeans pocket where the fabricated newspaper article is stuffed.

The three of them huddle together like haggard, old witches around a cauldron. They seem to speak in a code and I don't understand. Their strange choice of phrase and waving hand gestures confuse me. I decipher only a minuscule amount of information from their chanting. However, I do notice Nigel and Nicole praise Mark often for his diligence and effort. Clearly, my husband is the ringleader. Nicole is a mere accomplice. That realisation hurts like a blunt blade pirouetting inside my chest.

'You can stall all you want to, but you'll never get rid of me without my children. I won't stop screaming until I see them. You'll have to kill me first.' I will myself to shut up and stop encouraging them. *How stupid could I be?*

I stare blankly at Nigel wondering where he fits into the sordid romance. He's a spare part like me only he's too docile to see it. I decide to educate him.

'You poor, stupid fool,' I say pointing my shaking finger so close to his face I can feel his breath on my hand. 'You're next. If they pulled this crap to get rid of me, then they're not going to wait long before they want you gone, too.' A sadistic 'Ha!' sprays from my lips at the end of the profound sentence.

Nigel simply rolls his eyes. *Asshole.*

'I want my kids *now*. Now…now…now!' I scream.

Mark says something about the noise upsetting the neighbours. *Good.* At least then someone will come around to investigate and their plan will be ruined. His attempts to silence me only inspire me to shout louder.

'Okay,' Nigel says dragging Mark away from me. 'We'll go and get the kids, but you need to be as good as your word and calm down.'

I scowl. 'Fine.'

'Nicole will wait with you,' he adds sternly, clearly unprepared to hear an argument from either of us.

Nicole's disapproval of Nigel's master plan is written all over her face, but she doesn't protest. She simply slides to the ground, tucks her knees against her chest, and rests her head on top. The front door slams, and Nicole and I are alone. After twenty or so long minutes of staring at the top of her scalp, I give up and sit in silence beside her on the floor. Time ticks by in slow motion.

'It's true,' Nicole stutters breaking the stillness of the room. I ignore her.

'You didn't go to New York to live the American dream. You were running away from the Irish nightmare.'

I shut my eyes and try to block out the sound of her voice.

'When you ran away from the hospital, no one knew where you were. Mark was beside himself with worry.'

'I'm sure he had you to look after him,' I growl.

'Your doctor warned that you may have been a danger to yourself. Then Nigel got a phone call from that hotel we all worked in our last summer in college. They said you had turned up there looking for him.'

'He lives in the hotel. I saw the penthouse. What are you talking about?'

I don't want to give Nicole the satisfaction of asking questions, but I'm curious where she's taking her outlandish tale.

'He's renting a nice two-bed in Queens, Laura. It's not the fucking Plaza.'

I crawl to the far side of the room and curl up in a small ball. I can't bear to be near her. I can't listen to any more lies. Nicole is as good a player as the guys; I can see that now. Mark obviously has her well trained.

Nigel and Mark are gone at least a couple of hours, and as soon as Nicole hears the front door creak open, she leaps from the floor and races into the hall where she flings her arms around Mark's neck and kisses his cheek.

I scramble to my feet in her shadow and race towards the door with my arms stretched wide. I can't contain the euphoric excitement I feel at seeing my babies again. But somewhere along the way, I feel like my heart has fallen out the sole of my shoe and been trampled into the ground.

There's no sign of the kids. Instead, Dr. Hammond stands on the open porch. He's wearing the same cold and unforgiving glare that I've learned to hate.

'I think you should come with me,' Dr. Hammond calmly suggests reaching his hand out for me to hold.

I smack it away with all my strength almost knocking him over.

'Where are the kids?' I ask as I watch Nigel reach out to the doctor to help him regain his balance.

'What kids?' Dr. Hammond asks.

'My kids,' I screech. I don't know if his question is genuine and he doesn't know my children are missing, or if he's playing the same sick game as the others.

Dr. Hammond shakes his head solemnly. 'Your baby girl died in the car crash. You don't have any other children.'

I can't bring myself to look at the man as he speaks. I wonder how much Mark had to pay him to get him to play along. Maybe he isn't even a real doctor.

'You bastard,' I scream as Mark locks the car and walks towards the house. 'You tricked me. You evil, evil bastard.'

Mark repeats the same two words over and over. 'I'm sorry.'

It was too late for apologies. I despise him. He's destroyed me, and I can never forgive him. I look at the four faces surrounding me. I'm trapped. Mark has won.

I turn and race towards the back door, my feet slipping on the tiles as I gather speed. I'm just about to grip the handle of the door when I felt Mark's firm arm around my waist pulling me back.

'You need help,' he whispers softly into my ear. 'Please let us help you.'

I thrash wildly against him, but I'm exhausted and no match for his strength.

'I hate you,' I shout at Nigel who doesn't dare look me in the eye. 'Ava and I trusted you and you betrayed us.'

Mark's arms are so tight around me they crush my ribs. My feet no longer touch the ground.

'This way,' Mark says as he carries me outside to where an ambulance waits with flashing blue lights and no siren.

'I love you,' Mark whispers as he kisses my cheek. His lips feel like acid against my skin. I hate him, but I wouldn't create a scene. It would argue against me. A hysterical woman – sleep deprived and emotional – is the textbook picture of neurotic. I won't give them the satisfaction. Instead, I'm composed and I surrender willingly. I know my only choice is to go with the doctor. I'm afraid of what they might do if I don't, but it isn't the end. I will run away. I have before, and I can again. I will bide my time and I will leave, and this time they will never find the kids or me. *Who will be laughing then?*

Epilogue

I like the new curtains I bought earlier that day in town. They sit just right as they hang proudly over the sitting room bay window. I have nearly fallen off the chair twice as I fiddle with the eyelets and pole trying to make sure both sides are even. The kids think my struggle is hilarious.

I beg the children to respect the delicate soft satin material, but I know my pleas fall on deaf ears. My beautiful cream with lavender weave curtains will probably be a foggy grey with chocolate-handprint weave by the end of the week, but I honestly don't mind. Yes, I like pretty things in my home, but the prettiest things I have are looking up at me through three pairs of beautiful big blue eyes.

'I promise I'll get a tissue for my nose next time, Aunt Laura,' Lorcan says, remembering my mini meltdown about a previous runny nose incident with the old curtains.

'Thank you, sweetheart.' I smile tossing my nephew's hair affectionately.

'Me, too,' Bobby agrees not really understanding what he's signing himself up for.

Katie is already christening the bottom of one side of the curtains with the contents of her upside-down bottle, and I know that means they get her seal of approval.

I glance at my watch. I'll have to wait until later to wipe the milky stain out. I need to get ready. Ava and Adam will be here soon. Our dinner reservation is in a little over an hour; I don't want everyone moaning at me for delaying them as usual.

I lift Katie into her playpen and press play on whatever DVD is in the machine, and wait as Bobby and Lorcan crawl up on the sofa.

'Watch your cousin for me, okay?' I request of Lorcan.

'Okay, sure.' He smiles, only giving me half his attention. The movie has started, and I'm clearly a nuisance.

That is one of the reasons I love our apartment in New York more than I ever cared for our house in Ireland. Even if the kids decide to come investigate my whereabouts, there are no stairs for them to tumble down in the large open-plan design.

Soon there are three evenly spaced knocks on the front door, and I curse Ava for being so early.

***

Mark

I watch Laura with a subtle smile. It's refreshing to see her in such high spirits.

'Does she know we're out here?' I ask.

'No,' Dr. Hammond says shaking his head. 'Laura only sees what she wants to see.'

'But she's so lonely in that empty white room,' I say dryly.

'On the contrary, she has lots of company,' Dr. Hammond corrects. 'Like I said, she sees what she wants to see. She wants to experience happy marital bliss with a wonderful young family, so that's what her mind has created for her.'

I watch Laura kiss the air and guess it's the face of her imaginary husband.

'Is that me?' I choke. 'Does she see me?'

'The real you out here peering through this glass? No. But the you she loves in her heart? Yes. She sees you every day,' Dr. Hammond explains.

'Will she ever come home again,' I ask. The words catch in my throat and make me cough.

'Post-Traumatic Stress Disorder affects different people in different ways,' Dr. Hammond says.

'I know. And I understand all that. I've read so much about it on the internet that I can't see straight anymore. But I can't find an article with a definite answer.'

'That's because there isn't one. The mind is a powerful and delicate thing, Mark. Laura can see and hear Ava as clear as she can hear and see you and me.'

'And the meds? Will they start working soon?'

'We hope so, Mark, but what you have to understand is, even when Laura realises the gravity of her loss, she still may not be able to accept it. We've been at this point before. As soon as Laura remembers and as soon as she feels the pain of her loss, her mind resets and we're back to this charade.'

'But she thinks Lorcan is her son, and Bobby, too.'

'Actually, this time she has accepted that Lorcan is her nephew.'

'So that's progress, then,' I beam almost euphoric, but my excitement quickly fades as Dr. Hammond shakes his head.

'It's just a minor change, Mark. It's not unusual to reset with a new twist on the same story every time. It keeps it fresh and makes it more difficult for her head to sieve through clues and find the truth. And, it makes it more difficult for us to help her, I'm afraid.'

'Can't we just tell her the truth? Letting her figure it out on her own doesn't work…maybe if I explain everything. Tell her we could adopt or something. Tell her no one blames her…maybe then she'll be okay.'

'But Laura blames herself, Mark. She can't cope with the guilt. Nicole trusted Laura to pick her son up from school and Laura failed. If Laura hadn't gone to the hairdressers, if she hadn't been running late, if Ava had mentioned she was running late too…It's all hypothetical, but Laura can't get past it. Laura couldn't have known the devastating chain of events that would unfold that day, but she feels as responsible as if she put a gun to all their heads and pulled the trigger. Laura lost her best friend and her little boy. Her nephew. And when she woke in the hospital, her unborn baby had been taken from her body along with her womb. The mind is a fragile thing, Mark. And Laura's just isn't strong enough to cope with her loss.'

I know from Dr. Hammond's delicate choice of words and soft tones that reassuring concerned loved ones is a large part of his job, but I find it difficult to take any comfort.

Dr. Hammond walks to the desk at the end of the poky room giving me a chance to look around. The daunting room reminds me of the observation area used in detective movies where the victim peers through the one-sided glass at the row of prospective criminals on the other side. Laura isn't guilty of any crime, and I feel decidedly uncomfortable spying on her.

Dr. Hammond types an odd combination of numbers and letters into a lonely laptop on the desk.

'This is how we make sure Laura is comfortable,' he explains.

I nod.

'There is a command for everything,' Dr. Hammond explains. 'I control the lights, the door, even the temperature inside the room with this little computer.'

Dr. Hammond adjusts the audio control and soon Laura's voice fills the entire room. I wilt as I listen fondly to Laura's chattering. Her voice is just as beautiful as I remember but hearing it intensifies the pain. I wonder if such extreme security is necessary, but deep down I don't want to know so I decide not to enquire. Besides, the last time I questioned their methods and suggested we try alternative options to jog her memory, Laura arrived on my brother's doorstep in New York. Allowing Laura to play out her fantasy in the real world failed. My wife died in that crash…her body is still here but her soul is gone.

'Today is a good day,' Dr. Hammond says. 'Laura's just back from shopping and is about to head out with friends. I think you may have just arrived home from work.'

Dr. Hammond speaks about Laura's actions as if she's a puppet on a string. *He must see freaks like Laura every day*, I think. But Laura will never be a freak to me. She will always be my wife, and I will always love her with all my heart.

I listen to Laura have a happy one-sided conversation about the events of the day as she applies imaginary blusher to her cheeks with an imaginary brush.

I jump. Laura looks straight at me. She's smiling. I smile back and reach out to her, but I bang my hand against the heavy glass. My heart sinks as I realise she thinks she's looking in a mirror as she puts the finishing touches on her makeup.

I run my hand against the glass and try to remember the soft feel of her face against my fingers.

'Is she happy?' I ask, reluctant to hear the answer.

'It's not real, Mark. Her happiness is not real.'

'That's not what I asked you. I want to know if my wife is happy or not.'

Dr. Hammond points towards Laura's bright smile. 'I think you can see for yourself. She thinks she is happy. Yes.'

'I lost Laura the day our baby daughter died. It's taken a whole year to face that. If this is the only way she can be happy, then I am going to have to accept it and learn to be happy for her. But I miss her like hell. I miss my family so much. I wish I could jump into her imaginary world with her. Do you have a pill for that?'

'You're not the first person to ask me that,' Dr. Hammond assures. 'Unfortunately, I doubt you will be the last.'

'Will you be okay?' Dr. Hammond asks.

'Don't worry,' I say sternly. 'I can afford the best care for her, for as long as it takes. Laura has a great health insurance policy.'

'I meant will *you* be okay?' Dr. Hammond repeats this time exaggerating long vowel sounds. He stands slightly slouched and with his arms crossed over his chest. He's asking more as a friend now than as a professional. Dr. Hammond has grown attached to Laura, and I'm grateful that she's getting the best possible care. I smile as I reluctantly pull my hand away from the glass of Laura's confinement. I can finally allow myself to walk away. I haven't failed her; nothing has, not even the power of her own mind, trapping her. If anything, her mind has saved her. It's released her from the pain that's too much, too hard.

'Yeah, I think I'll be okay…'

Nicole and Nigel knock on the door and walk, holding hands, towards me. Nigel kisses his wife lovingly and nods. Nicole places her hands gently on my shoulders and turns me away from the glass. 'Come on,' she whispers. 'You can come back again next week.'

I hug her gently, taking care not to press on her growing bump. She wipes the last few tears from my eyes and slowly leads me towards the door. I stop in the doorway and blow Laura back a tear-soaked kiss.

Laura doesn't see, of course. How could she? She's in a different world. A happy, wonderful world with beautiful children, a loving husband, and great friends. Her life is perfect.

The End

The idea for this book came about when my son was four years old and he almost died. It was the most terrifying and horrific time of my life and afterwards I couldn't help but think what if...

Acknowledgements

As always there is a list as long as my arm of people to thank for the part they played in this book. Jenny at editing4indies. You really are a star, I'm so sorry this book made you cry (but that's a good thing, right?!)

Najla at Najlaquamberdesigns.com your amazing covers rock my world and you truly are a pleasure to work with.

Natalie and Caroline, my writing heroes. As always, cheers ☺

My lovely beta readers, Kath, Kathrin and Nicola. Your help is so very much appreciated.

My husband, thank you for giving me a family I adore. Being our children's mother is, and always will be, my greatest achievement. I love you.

And finally, and so importantly, thank *you* for reading. I hope you enjoyed the time you spent in Laura's head.

Janelle xx

Printed in Great Britain
by Amazon.co.uk, Ltd.,
Marston Gate.